"They asked me the other day my definition of the perfect lover. And I had it for them, too. A man who can make love to you until four o'clock in the morning—and then turn into a pizza."

—CHARLES PIERCE, "male actress," June 21, 1971

April 20, 1977 The Nevada State Senate (meeting just twenty miles from the nearest legalized brothel) votes to retain the state's sodomy laws.

"As to Anita's fear that she'll be assassinated? The only people who might shoot Anita Bryant are music lovers."

—GORE VIDAL, summer, 1978

September 21, 1982 The Oklahoma Supreme Court awards custody of two eleven-year-old boys to their divorced gay father on the grounds that homosexuality is in itself not grounds for ruling a person unfit for parenthood.

July 15, 1983 San Francisco's legendary Hothouse baths—devoted to the most outré forms of sexual expression—closes its doors in the wake of growing concerns over the spread of AIDS.

"I know how it feels to be a woman because I *am* a woman. And I won't be classified as just a man."

—Rock legend PETE TOWNSEND, publicly acknowledging his bisexuality in the fall of 1990

LEIGH W. RUTLEDGE is the author of the bestselling *Gay Book of Lists*, as well as *Unnatural Quotations* and *The Gay Fireside Companion*. His articles and short stories have regularly appeared in the gay press since the late 1970s. He lives in Colorado.

LEIGH W. RUTLEDGE

THE GAY DECADES

FROM STONEWALL TO
THE PRESENT: THE PEOPLE
AND EVENTS THAT
SHAPED GAY LIVES

A PLUME BOOK

PLUME

Published by the Penguin Group
Penguin Books USA Inc., 375 Hudson Street, New York, New York 10014, U.S.A.
Penguin Books Ltd, 27 Wrights Lane, London W8 5TZ, England
Penguin Books Australia Ltd, Ringwood, Victoria, Australia
Penguin Books Canada Ltd, 10 Alcorn Avenue, Toronto, Ontario, Canada M4V 3B2
Penguin Books (N.Z.) Ltd, 182–190 Wairau Road, Auckland 10, New Zealand

Penguin Books Ltd, Registered Offices:
Harmondsworth, Middlesex, England

First published by Plume, an imprint of New American Library,
a division of Penguin Books USA Inc.

First Printing, June, 1992
1 3 5 7 9 10 8 6 4 2

Photographs from Hairspray *and* Torch Song Trilogy *courtesy of New Line Cinema.*

Ⓟ REGISTERED TRADEMARK—MARCA REGISTRADA

Library of Congress Cataloging-in-Publication Data
Rutledge, Leigh W.
The gay decades : from Stonewall to the present : the people and
events that shaped gay lives / Leigh W. Rutledge.
p.   cm.
ISBN 0-452-26810-9
1. Gay liberation movement—United States—History.   2. Gays—
United States—History.   3. Gay men—United States—History.
I. Title.
HQ76.8.U5R88   1992
305.9'0664—dc20   *91-40495*
OCLC 24699006   *CIP*

Printed in the United States of America
Set in Janson & Gill Sans

Designed by Steven N. Stathakis

BOOKS ARE AVAILABLE AT QUANTITY DISCOUNTS WHEN USED TO PROMOTE PRODUCTS OR SERVICES. FOR INFORMATION PLEASE WRITE TO PREMIUM MARKETING DIVISION, PENGUIN BOOKS USA INC., 375 HUDSON STREET, NEW YORK, NEW YORK 10014.

To John Wilcox, Rich Donley,
and the Air Force test pilot who gave me his flight
jacket one starry winter night when I was 22

ACKNOWLEDGMENTS

For their help in providing me with information and assistance, I would like to thank the Academy of Motion Picture Arts and Sciences Library, Sasha Alyson, Peter Borland, Michel Cinq-Mars at the NAMES Project Foundation, Robert Clark, Gavin Dillard, the Federation of Parents and Friends of Lesbians and Gays, Penny Green, Jacky Griffith, the Institute of Contemporary Art in Philadelphia, Steve Johnson at Close-Up Productions, Jim Kepner, Stephanie Laidman, the Legislative Reference Bureau of Wisconsin, Deacon Maccubbin, John McKay, Liz Mozden at New Line Cinema, Tom Pendleton, the reference department of the Pueblo Memorial Library (proving time and again that what a smaller library lacks in volumes, it can make up for in the intelligence and generosity of its staff), Waldemar Rompca, John Rowberry, Edward Rutledge, Libby Rutledge, S.A.G.E. (Senior Action in a Gay Environment), Chris Schick, Charlotte Simmons, Adele Starr, Steve Schwadron at the office of Massachusetts Congressman Gerry Studds, Mark Thompson, Peter Urbanek, attorney Maura Wogan, and Debbie Woolhite at the *Donahue* show.

A very special thanks to Richard Donley, John Preston, Matt Sartwell, and Sam Staggs.

F O R E W O R D

On the night that the Stonewall riots occurred in 1969, I was celebrating my thirteenth birthday three thousand miles away in an upper-middle-class community just south of San Francisco. So cocooned was I (along with most everyone else who lived there) that news of the event, or of the fledgling gay liberation movement that followed, never reached me, never penetrated to the affluent, "terribly nice" town I lived in. Indeed, my only exposure to homosexuality, or to "gayness" at all, was through books like Havelock Ellis's *Studies in the Psychology of Sex* and Gore Vidal's *Myra Breckinridge*, and the only reason I had even that much exposure was because my parents owned the local bookstore. It was about the same time—what with the increasing urgency of my hormones, and the fact I snuck into a showing of *Midnight Cowboy* (using a fake driver's license)—that my emotional energy became increasingly focused on the realization that I was, just as kids had been yelling at me for years, a "faggot" and a "queer." The gay movement and I, as it turned out, evolved and started growing up at roughly the same time . . .

The last twenty-plus years have, in many significant ways, been the Gay Decades, obviously not only for me, but for the nation (in fact, for the world) as a whole. Not only have the legal advances and guarantees for gay men and lesbians been far greater than in the previous two thousand years, but the "gay sensibility" (a creature, I confess, for which I have no ringing definition) has never been more radically visible in movies, fashion, popular music, commercial advertising, drama, pornography, and culture in general. The effect has been dramatic. The vast majority of Americans now know that Rock Hudson, Malcolm Forbes, and Tennessee Williams were gay, and what's more, a large number of them can even contemplate it without a shiver of horror. Boy George and others like him may have passed from the scene, but their impact has been indelible: by the mid-Eighties, hoards of young people were affecting (or at least talking about) the "androgynous look," and by 1990 an MTV poll showed that over 90 percent of the nation's teenagers could care less whether their favorite musicians were gay, straight, or bisexual. The political battles are still perilous and infuriating, but whereas in 1969 only one state had repealed its sodomy laws, today more than two dozen have. Ironically, many straight Americans have won the right to do what they want to in bed largely through the efforts of enraged and tenacious homosexual activists.

There have been subtler effects as well, from the assimilation (for better or worse) of disco in the Seventies to the unbridled passion for athletic shoes today (did you know it all started on Fire Island in the mid-Seventies?). Every time I turn on the television and see half-naked men (or teenage boys in tight jeans) selling everything from tacos to facial tissue I think how far we've come.

I also think of the hypocrisy. The blinding and at times overwhelming hypocrisy. What, for example, is one to make of an Olivia Newton-John, who professes support for gay rights (and appears in the gay-overtone-laden video for "Physical"), but then personally nixes the involvement of her husband, Matt Lattanzi, in a film version of *The Front Runner* because it wouldn't be "good for his image"? A housewife may wear a dress designed by Perry Ellis, swoon over her favorite soap-opera idol (who, as it happens, is a closeted homosexual), listen to Johnny Mathis, laugh at a sitcom written by a gay writer, praise a conservative Republican politician speaking out on the evening news (unbeknownst to her, he has a fondness for young male prostitutes)—and then go out that night to vociferously protest and condemn the "perverts" demanding rights in her city. (For one of the most howling examples of this mentality, see the entry for **October 26, 1981**.) I know personally several people who, in a burst of liberal exuberance, will comment on how gifted homosexuals are, but they wouldn't sit down at the same dinner table with someone who has AIDS. And tell them that their daughter's fifth-grade teacher is a lesbian, and they quickly grow threatened and uneasy . . .

This, then, is the biography of those decades: part reference book, part social chronometer, a popular history and a nostalgic guided tour, a serious book to be read for pleasure, an informative book that is meant to provide entertainment. Obviously, it is not all-inclusive, but reflects my own curiosities and prejudices, the things that made the most indelible impressions as my friends and I were growing up, "coming out," and maturing, as well as the events that seem to have been watersheds in the growth and increasing visibility of the gay community and gay culture.

A few words of caution. First, it seems necessary to point out in advance that although there is a great deal of material on lesbians and lesbianism here, the overwhelming focus is on gay men, and a true *Lesbian Decades*—with its essential, intertwining themes of feminism, abortion rights, and institutionalized misogyny—must, by necessity, encompass a separate volume written by someone else more qualified.

Second, in a minority of instances, some of the dates listed in this chronology may be subject to debate. Sometimes not even the participants directly involved in a particular event could agree on which day it occurred. Also, it's not uncommon to find *The New York Times*, *The World Almanac*, and several other reference works all contradicting one another on a single, seemingly indisputable fact.

Finally, this book includes a great deal of material not only on gay men and lesbians, but on pop icons, politicians, and other figures who, for one reason or another, have captured the imagination of gay people or had an impact on their lives. The mere inclusion of anyone in these pages cannot therefore be construed as an indication of anyone's bedroom habits or preference in sexual partners.

In the end, despite whatever entertainment and laughter one may draw from it, this book is as much a cautionary tale as it is a history lesson condensed from the past two decades. For while it's easy to scoff at the Jimmy Swaggarts and the Dan Quayles of the world, one should never forget the words of the prominent gay activist who, contemplating an upcoming Supreme Court decision on Georgia's sodomy laws in the mid-1980s, exuberantly predicted to the media, "It's going to be hard for the Supreme Court to find no right of privacy in one's own bedroom." The moral of course is, Never take anything—especially one's individual liberties—for granted.

—LEIGH W. RUTLEDGE

"Homosexuals could be a very potent economic and political force—*if united*. The time has come for new leadership to rise from the wreckage of the past. Here and there are signs of a new movement—dedicated to achieving a place in the sun for all homosexuals."

—*Homosexual rights activist* DICK MICHAELS
June 1, 1969

1969

June 22 Judy Garland—recovering from a recent series of career fiascoes (including one concert at the London Palladium during which she angrily pushed daughter Liza off the stage for stealing the show)—dies from an "accidental" overdose of sleeping pills at her apartment in London. When police first discover the body, it is in the bathroom, fully dressed on the toilet, with the head flopped forward.

Five days later, on the afternoon of June 27, the singer is laid to rest at Ferncliff Mausoleum in Westchester, New York.

June 27 Shortly after midnight, nine plainclothes police detectives enter the Stonewall Inn at 53 Christopher Street in Greenwich Village intending to close the bar for selling liquor without a license. As the bartender, doorman, and three transvestites are arrested and led away, an unexpectedly angry crowd—soon swelling to nearly four hundred—gathers outside and begins throwing coins, beer bottles, and bricks. The arresting officers retreat and try to hole up inside the bar, but the mob—chanting "Pigs!" and "Faggot cops!"—smashes down the door. "We'll shoot the first motherfucker that comes through!" responds one panic-stricken detective, drawing his gun. One of the protesters tries to set the bar on fire—with the police inside—using lighter fluid and matches. Another protester is grabbed at random by the detectives and beaten half a dozen times on the head. Meanwhile, the barrage of bottles, cans, and rocks continues; one group even uproots a parking meter and hurls it toward the officers. The crowd finally begins to disperse with the arrival of police reinforcements. The entire riot has lasted barely forty-five minutes. A brief report of the confrontation—"4 POLICEMEN HURT IN 'VILLAGE' RAID"—appears on page 33 of *The New York Times* two days later.

June 28 Speculating on the whys and wherefores of the previous night's melee at the Stonewall Inn, several observers suggest that Judy Garland's recent death and burial contributed to a sense of gay frustration and outrage. "Judy's death inspired those Stonewall queens," one writer eventually concludes. Others note that there was a full moon. Meanwhile, different people come up with different versions of exactly *who* started the riot: some claim it was a drag queen, others say it was a lesbian, and still others insist it was a straight Puerto Rican boy who threw the first rock and urged gays to "get in there and get those cops!"

———

A second consecutive night of rioting begins in Greenwich Village when a crowd once again gathers outside the Stonewall Inn to protest the previous night's raid. Police tactical units pour into the area to rout angry protesters, who are starting fires, throwing bottles, and shouting slogans of "Legalize gay bars!" "Gay is good!" and "We are the Stonewall girls/We wear our hair in curls/We have no underwear/We show our pubic hair!" The battle between police and protesters lasts nearly two hours. At one point, a group of gay men forms a chorus line and begins doing a can-can routine down the street—until police armed with billy clubs charge and disperse them. Three people are arrested in the night's skirmishes.

June 29 HOMO NEST RAIDED
QUEEN BEES ARE STINGING MAD
—New York *Daily News*

July 2 GAY POWER COMES TO SHERIDAN SQUARE
FULL MOON OVER THE STONEWALL
—Front-page headline in *The Village Voice*

"They've lost that wounded look that fags all had ten years ago . . ."
—Poet ALLEN GINSBERG, *commenting on how different the gay men looked on Christopher Street just after the Stonewall riots, 1969*

Police are summoned for the third time in less than a week, to quell a hostile crowd of nearly five hundred protesters chanting gay pride slogans and marching down Christopher Street. According to one eyewitness, the police, armed with nightsticks, seem bent on massive retaliation: "At one point, Seventh Avenue . . . looked like a battlefield in Vietnam. Young people, many of them queens, were lying on the sidewalk, bleeding from the head, face, mouth, and even the eyes. Others were nursing bruised and often bleeding arms, legs, backs, and necks."

July 9 The first "Gay Power" meeting—an amalgam of street people, socialists, would-be revolutionaries, and members of the Mattachine Society—is held in Greenwich Village. One participant later complains, "Everybody was on a fantastic ego trip, losing sight of the fact that there were *people* involved in this thing."

July 13 *The New York Times* notes that filming is under way for the movie version of Mart Crowley's play *The Boys in the Band*, which is scheduled for release next March. "Is the country ready for *Boys?*" muses reporter Katie Kelly. "Will they stand in line in Omaha? Face it: these are not the all-American boys who made America great. This is not the stuff of which football captains and fraternity boys are made."

July 16　At a second "Gay Power" meeting—this one held at a local Episcopal church—one crowd-member calls for a massive gay protest in front of St. Patrick's Cathedral: "The Catholics have put us down long enough!" Another urges a gay boycott of Bloomingdale's: "They'd be out of business in two weeks!" There is talk of more riots, and of homosexuals arming themselves with guns for an all-out confrontation with the police. "That's the only language that the pigs understand!" cries one protester.

August 13　After a twenty-six-year absence from the screen, Mae West is signed to star as superagent Leticia Van Allen in the forthcoming film version of Gore Vidal's controversial novel *Myra Breckinridge*. Asked if she has any qualms about appearing in such a potentially shocking property, West enthusiastically replies, "Not when the script and the production setup are right, as I feel this one is." She further states that the film's thirty-year-old director, Michael Sarne—whose only previous, notable screen credit was the critically panned *Joanna*—seems like "a very bright young man."

August 17　Presuming it to be a hotbed of homosexuality and illicit sex, Atlanta police raid a local art theater showing Andy Warhol's *Lonesome Cowboys*, and promptly begin taking flash photographs of the astonished audience. Police later try to justify the raid by claiming that the photographs will provide a useful reference file for future vice-squad investigations. One audience member—a well-known local Unitarian minister—promptly files a $500,000 invasion-of-privacy suit against the officers.

August 19　Benning Wentworth, the gay thirty-five-year-old employee of a Defense Department subcontractor, begins a second round of appeals to keep the federal government from revoking his security clearance. In 1966, the government moved to suspend

Rex Harrison and Richard Burton in Staircase. *"Oddly enough, I cared about this film," Burton confided to his diary.*

Wentworth's clearance after an eighteen-year-old male claimed to have had sex with him. Wentworth's counsel tells the press, "We consider the very existence of this case to be part of the government's improper, unethical, and immoral effort to enter into the field of private morality, and to force conformity to a particular sexual code."

August 20   Just three weeks after the abysmal exploitation comedy *The Gay Deceivers* opened in New York (to disparaging reviews and mediocre box office), *Staircase*—"a sad gay story," starring Richard Burton and Rex Harrison as two fussy middle-aged lovers miserable with each other—has its world premiere. Sneak preview cards from Los Angeles have already informed the producers that they have a major flop on their hands, a disaster that provokes one critic to call it "a waddling tale, spattered with ugliness."

"Oddly enough, I cared about this film," notes a plaintive Richard Burton in his private diary, after being informed the film is an unqualified bomb. Burton received a guaranteed salary of

$1.25 million for his role in the movie, regardless of the film's performance at the box office.

August 27 Erica Mann, daughter of novelist Thomas Mann and wife of gay poet W. H. Auden, dies at her home in Zurich. In 1935, Auden was asked by a mutual friend—Christopher Isherwood—if he would marry Mann to help her secure a British passport so she could flee Nazi Germany. Auden's one-word tele-grammed reply—"Delighted"—set into motion what was later called "one of the most agreeable unconsummated marriages be-tween two consenting adults." The relationship between the two developed into a deep, abiding friendship, and although they pur-sued separate lives (and separate sex partners), they remained mar-ried until her death.

September 1 West Germany repeals its laws prohibiting homo-sexual acts between consenting adults. The repeal only applies to male homosexuality, since lesbianism has never been officially pro-scribed by West German law.

Gore Vidal fires the latest salvo in his continuing feud with con-servative columnist William F. Buckley, Jr. In a vitriolic essay for *Esquire* magazine, Vidal denounces Buckley as a "morbid, twisted" man, preoccupied by sex, whose political views mirror "the found-ers of the Third Reich who regarded blacks as inferiors, undeclared war as legitimate foreign policy, and Jews as sympathetic to inter-national Communism." This most recent volley comes after Buck-ley, also in the pages of *Esquire*, blasted Vidal as an "evangelist for bisexuality" whose "essays proclaim the normalcy of his affliction and his art the desirability of it."

The feud—stoked by lawsuits each man has filed against the other—began the previous November when, as television com-mentators for the 1968 Democratic Convention in Chicago, they got into an on-air shouting match in which Vidal described Buckley as a "Neo-crypto-Nazi" and Buckley called Vidal a "queer."

"Not since George Sanders divorced Zsa Zsa Gabor," notes

Time magazine, "has so much talent been wasted on such a nasty spat."

September 3 The American Sociological Association issues a public declaration endorsing the rights of homosexuals and other sexual minorities.

September 15 *Gay Power*—billing itself as "New York's First Homosexual Newspaper"—publishes its premiere issue.

September 25 Half a dozen club-wielding youths attack and beat to death a gay man walking in Wimbledon Common, a popular gay cruising area in London. A self-acknowledged young "fag-basher" later tells the *Sunday Times*, "When you're hitting a queer . . . there's nothing to be scared of . . . 'cause you know they won't go to the law."

October 5 John Osborne's *A Patriot for Me*—a play about the downfall of Colonel Alfred Redl, a homosexual and a spy in Hapsburg Germany—opens on Broadway, to mixed reviews. "One of the problems was that no leading actor wanted to play a queer," Osborne observes about the difficulties in casting the lead role. "It was turned down by several people. Their wives didn't want them to play that sort of part. . . . Even the queer actors wouldn't take the risk." Maximilian Schell eventually accepted the part.

October 6 The Metropolitan Community Church—founded in Los Angeles by the Rev. Troy Perry, who ran a small ad in *The Advocate* inviting gay people to come and worship together—celebrates its first anniversary.

October 7 ". . . deplorable . . . a source of corruption in society . . . abnormal, aberrant . . . deviant, sick, pathological . . . abnormal . . . reprehensible . . . despised . . . perversion . . . distortion . . . abnormality . . . sickness . . . perversion . . . irregular . . . abnormal . . . degeneracy . . . sick . . . perversion . . . sin . . .

pathological, deviant . . . a perversion and a vice . . . evil . . . an offense to public decency . . . abnormality . . . abnormality . . . incurable sickness . . . perversion . . ."
—*Excerpts describing homosexuality, from essayist Will Herberg's article "The Case for Heterosexuality" in* National Review *magazine. "I do not want to heap abuse upon the homosexual," says Herberg at the beginning of his essay, "or to reproach him for his aberrancy. But . . ."*

October 20 The National Institute of Mental Health issues a twenty-page report recommending that the United States follow the lead of Great Britain and other countries that have repealed laws forbidding private homosexual acts between consenting adults. The study—chaired by Dr. Evelyn Hooker of the University of California at Los Angeles—also suggests that the federal government reevaluate its current antihomosexual employment practices.
    Both the President and Congress ignore the recommendations.

October 25 *The Advocate* (which started publication out of Los Angeles in 1967) complains that gay bathhouses across the country are promoting "sex on the assembly line."

October 31 *Time* magazine runs a seven-page feature story on "The Homosexual: Newly Visible, Newly Understood," and offers its readers a kind of "mini" field guide to what it calls the various "homosexual types":

THE BLATANT HOMOSEXUAL: "This is the eunuch-like caricature of femininity that most people associate with homosexuality. . . . He may be the catty hairdresser or the lisping, limp-wristed interior decorator. His lesbian counterpart is the 'butch.' "

THE SECRET LIFER: "Their wrists are rigid, their *s*'s well-formed; they prefer subdued clothes and close-cropped-hair. . . . They fake enjoyment when their boss throws a stag party with nude movies."

THE DESPERATE: "Members of this group are likely to haunt public toilets ('tearooms') or Turkish baths. They may be pathologically driven to sex."

THE ADJUSTED: "They lead relatively conventional lives. . . . Often they try to settle down with a regular lover, and although these liaisons are generally short-lived among men, some develop into so-called 'gay marriages.' "

THE BISEXUAL: "Men and women who have a definite preference for their own sex but engage in occasional activity with the opposite sex and enjoy it."

THE SITUATIONAL-EXPERIMENTAL: "He is a man who engages in homosexual acts without any deep homosexual motivation. . . . In prisons and occasionally the armed forces, men frequently turn to homosexual contacts in order to reassert their masculinity and recapture a feeling of dominance."

After *The San Francisco Examiner* runs an article referring to gay men as "semi-males" and "drag darlings," members of the Gay Liberation Front organize a peaceful march in front of the newspaper's offices. The demonstration turns violent after less than an hour when one of the paper's employees, hanging out a second-story window, heaves a bag of printer's ink onto the protesters below. When demonstrators try to use the ink to scrawl slogans— "Fuck the *Examiner*" and "Gay Is Good"—on the building's windows, police move in to make arrests, and a riot ensues. One protester has his front teeth literally kicked out by the officers; another, a lesbian, is charged with obstructing traffic for falling down in the street while police are beating her. A photographer is arrested for taking pictures; a transvestite knocks one policeman in the head with a placard and then flees. The arrests trigger a second protest march to San Francisco City Hall, where three more demonstrators—shouting "Power to the people!"—are handcuffed and taken into custody.

November 2 A nationwide poll of 27,000 U.S. doctors finds that 67 percent are in favor of legalizing homosexual acts between consenting adults.

November 8 The Rolling Stones cap off the decade with a one-month tour of the U.S., beginning at the Los Angeles Forum and ending three weeks later with a sold-out concert at Madison Square Garden. "Jagger has become the unisex symbol of an age steeped in sex," observes one writer. "He has risen above the hetero-homo categories, this new man who prances and purrs, who cakewalks and postures . . . turning on both boys and girls."

Meanwhile, the group's most recent album—*Through the Past, Darkly (Big Hits Vol. 2)*—is quickly working its way up the nation's Top 40.

"I am not a hippie. All hippies are fags."
—Self-styled revolutionary and "yippie" leader ABBIE HOFFMAN, 1969

November 15 More than a quarter million Vietnam peace protesters march on Washington, D.C., to demand an end to the war in Southeast Asia. Included in the crowd is a contingent of gay activists carrying the Gay Liberation Front banner. When demonstrators arrive at the Justice Department, they are met with tear gas and billy clubs. Says Martha Mitchell, wife of Attorney General John Mitchell, "It looked like the Russian Revolution!" Similar demonstrations are held across the country, including in San Francisco and New York City. One gay antiwar protester later explains, "I dig beautiful Oriental men. Asking me to shoot at them is the same thing as asking heterosexual soldiers to shoot at beautiful young girls that they would like to fuck!"

November 23   Now showing at the Park-Miller Movie Theater in Manhattan: "ALL MALE FILM FESTIVAL IN COLOR! 1ST N.Y. SHOWING! *WHIP'S MEN* plus *TATTOO FUN, BASKET BOYS, GARY & JOHN, FRUSTRATED.* MIDNITE SHOW EVERY FRI. & SAT. NITE. Adm. $5."

December 1   *After Dark*—"The National Magazine of Entertainment"—publishes profiles this month on the New York City Opera, actress Lee Grant, the movie *Z*, and the Stratford-on-Avon Shakespeare Festival—and in the process also manages to get in seven photographs of totally nude men, two photographs of men in their underwear, thirteen photos of men with their shirts off, one photo of a male circus performer in his G-string, and eight more photographs of men in very tight jeans. But of course, it is *not* a gay magazine.

In the nation's bookstores this month: the misnamed *Everything You Always Wanted to Know About Sex, But Were Afraid to Ask* by Dr. David Reuben, a California psychiatrist. America, badly in need of some kind of manual to help it get through the burgeoning sexual revolution, turns en masse to Reuben's titillating and clownishly reassuring descriptions of frigidity, aphrodisiacs, masturbation, and sexual perversion. However, in a twenty-eight-page section titled "Male Homosexuality," Reuben boldly asserts, among other things, that homosexuals can be "cured" if only they want to be badly enough, that gay men "thrive on danger" ("mutilation, castration, and death" are "all part of the homosexual game"), that a significant number of gay men like to secretly wear "carefully molded female genitalia of pliable rubber" under their pants, that all homosexuals are promiscuous, that homosexuals have a bizarre fascination with food ("Some of the fattest people are homosexuals"), that there are no happy "marriages" between two gay men ("Live together? Yes. Happily? Hardly"), and that men who have undergone sex-change operations are "actually castrated and mutilated female imper-sonators."

The book eventually sells more than eight million copies.

ALL MY MEN WEAR ENGLISH LEATHER—
OR THEY WEAR NOTHING AT ALL . . .
—*Suggestive ad fare, using bare-chested men as sex objects, from the makers of English Leather cologne*

December 2   *Look* magazine runs a one-page essay on "The New Homosexuality." On the page facing the article is an ad for *Family Circle* magazine, with the headline, "FRUITCAKES, COOKIES, FABULOUS LOUNGEWEAR, AND MORE!"

December 13   Police enter New York City's Continental Baths and arrest three patrons and three employees, charging the former with committing lewd and lascivious acts, and the latter with criminal mischief. The raid is only the first of several aimed at the Continental in the upcoming weeks.

December 17   Falsetto camp singer Tiny Tim (famous for his stringy hair and his ukulele rendition of "Tiptoe Through the Tulips" on *Rowan and Martin's Laugh-In*) marries his girlfriend, Miss Vicki, on national television, on Johnny Carson's *Tonight Show*. The question on most viewers' minds is, But isn't he *gay?* (The two later have a child—a daughter named Tulip—but eventually divorce.)

December 18   Luchino Visconti's *The Damned*—a sprawling, near-operatic account of the rise of Nazi Germany, as seen through the eyes of a Krupp-like family of German industrialists—has its American premiere in New York City. The film—dripping with depravity and full of homosexual episodes—is advertised with an ominous photo of star Helmut Berger in Marlene Dietrich drag, with the caption, "HE WAS SOON TO BECOME THE MOST POWERFUL MAN IN NAZI GERMANY." Critics, for the most part, are not kind:

"intense and murky . . . a failure"
—ARTHUR SCHLESINGER, JR., *Vogue*

"ponderously perverse . . . I have rarely seen a picture I enjoyed less"

—PAULINE KAEL, *The New Yorker*

"morose . . . sodden with greed, perversion, hatred, and treachery . . . The best thing about the picture is the sets."

—ROBERT HATCH, *The Nation*

"The lavender crowd is already ooh-ing and aah-ing over all those blond young Nazis. The sadomasochists will flip over the machine-gunning of Roehm's Bavarian love-nest."

—WILLIAM A. RUSHER, *National Review*

"Visconti plainly knows the homosexual milieu, yet falsifies it for the sake of sensationalistic effects."

—JOHN SIMON, *New York*

"unbridled bravado . . . bilious . . . it overpowers and finally overwhelms with its own unabashed sensationalism."

—*Time*

December 28 Gay activists announce a plan to take over California's Alpine County—a tiny resort community (population 430) ten miles south of Lake Tahoe—and turn it into a gay "mecca," the first all-gay city in the world, complete with gay housing, a gay civil service, and the world's first museum of gay arts, sciences, and history. Under a recent revision in California law, new residents of the county would have to wait only ninety days before being eligible to vote and recall the county's current officials and then replace them all with a gay slate of local administrators and politicians. Says activist Don Kilhefner, "We are simply following the advice of President Nixon and Spiro Agnew to work within the electoral process."

Although nothing ever comes of the plan, local indignation is summed up by a recently installed sign in one of the county's taverns: "HOMO HUNTING LICENSES SOLD HERE."

December 31 The Cockettes—a transvestite acting troupe soon to define the "gender-fuck" look of the Seventies in such loosely structured camp productions as *Tinsel Tarts in a Hot Coma, Les Ghouls,* and *Les Cockettes de Paris*—premiere their act in San Francisco. A year later, they dedicate their debut performance in New York City to one of their most ardent admirers, author Truman Capote.

In New York theaters this New Year's Eve: Sal Mineo's production of *Fortune and Men's Eyes* (controversial for its onstage depiction of male rape); the nudie musical revue *Oh! Calcutta!*; David Gaard's sentimental play about gay relationships, *And Puppy Dog Tails*; and, of course, *The Boys in the Band*, now entering its second year onstage.

January 10 Doctors in Frankfurt announce they've had considerable success treating "disturbed homosexuals" with an operation that involves disintegrating parts of the brain with a powerful electric shock. One U.S. scientific journal reports that side effects from the operation are "gratifyingly small." Among the "negligible" side effects: amnesia, total loss of libido, and potentially dangerous hormone imbalances in the body. But—the doctors note—"the patient is able to stay out of trouble after his operation and functions better in society."

February 22 Twenty-nine-year-old singer and former Miss America contender Anita Bryant is honored by the Freedoms Foundation for her part in organizing last year's "Rally for Decency" at Miami's Orange Bowl. The rally—whose themes were "We Believe in God," "We Love Our Families," and "Down With Obscenity" —drew over thirty thousand participants, and was prompted by a local concert at which rock star Jim Morrison unzipped his leather pants and performed simulated acts of masturbation and oral sex onstage. Another rally participant, entertainer Jackie Gleason, declares, "I believe this kind of movement will snowball across the United States and perhaps the world."

March 4 Liberace announces he is coming out with his own personal line of men's fashions, the "Mr. Showmanship" collection. "Things that I dared to wear twelve years ago are now in shop windows everywhere," says the entertainer, known for his glitzy and improbable costumes. "I guess I was just another person who was too far ahead of his time." The fashion line—which will feature heavily brocaded suits cut from velvet, Oriental fabrics, and other unexpected material ("I recently went into a shop in Italy and had them make me a suit out of the draperies that were in the window!" says an exuberant Liberace)—is aimed, in particular, at upwardly mobile young executives.

March 8 New York City police stage an early-morning raid on a Greenwich Village gay bar, the Snake Pit, for liquor violations, and arrest more than 150 of the bar's patrons. Later, at the police station, a nervous Argentinean national, Diego Vinales, tries to escape being booked by leaping from the precinct's second-story window; he winds up instead impaling himself on the fourteen-inch spikes of a wrought-iron fence surrounding the station. Astonishingly, he survives, although firemen are forced to cut out a section of the fence, with Vinales still skewered on it, in order to move him to the hospital. The raid prompts one journalist to observe, "It is no crime to be *in* a place that is serving liquor illegally; the only crime is to run such a place. There were no grounds for hauling the customers away." Although charges against the other arrested customers are eventually dropped, Diego Vinales is rebooked for "resisting arrest," and officers are stationed outside his hospital room to make certain he doesn't attempt another escape.

March 17 *The Boys in the Band*—the movie—opens in New York City, directed by thirty-year-old William Friedkin, whose big-screen directorial debut was Sonny and Cher's *Good Times* three

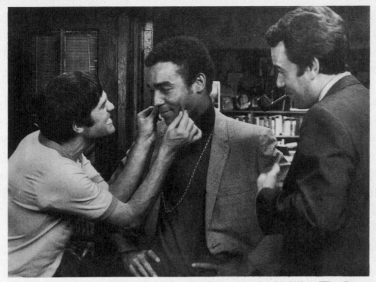

ABOVE: *Cliff Gorman, Reuben Greene, and Laurence Luckinbill in* The Boys in the Band. **BELOW:** *The original, controversial publicity campaign for the movie* The Boys in the Band. *Several major daily newspapers—including* The Los Angeles Times *and* The New York Daily News—*rejected the ad as too provocative.*

years earlier. "I hope there are happy homosexuals," asserts Fried-kin, defending the film's anachronistic portrayal of gay men as morbid, self-destructive creatures. "There just don't happen to be any in my film."

March 20   Rising young rock star David Bowie (born David Jones in London in 1947, but forced to change his name to avoid confusion with Davy Jones of the Monkees) marries a nineteen-year-old Amer-ican, Mary Angela Barnet. Several years later, Bowie tells *Playboy* magazine, "Angela and I knew each other because we were both going out with the same man." The bride eventually acknowledges that she, too, has been a practicing bisexual.

"Life is improving for gay people—no doubt about it. It's the young people today who are responsible for the change—they have made people more tolerant. The kids feel that being gay is your bag; you're not hurting anybody."
—*Thirty-two-year-old gay San Franciscan, 1970*

April 1   *The Advocate* estimates there are approximately 6,817,000 gay men and lesbians living in the United States.

April 7   *Midnight Cowboy* wins the Academy Award as Best Pic-ture, thereby becoming the first X-rated film (as well as the first film to feature an onscreen sexual encounter between two men) to do so. The film's director, John Schlesinger—himself gay—also wins an Oscar, as Best Director.

April 13   In the first of a series of public "zaps" by New York City gay activists, an appearance by Mayor John Lindsay at the Metropolitan Museum of Art is interrupted by angry protesters shouting "Gay Power!" and demanding his support for an end to job and housing discrimination against gay men and lesbians. Six days later, Lindsay's appearance on a local television program is similarly disrupted. The "zaps" culminate in a meeting between gay activists and the mayor's office to discuss the gay community's political grievances.

May 4   Joe Orton's final play, *What the Butler Saw*, has its American premiere at the McAlpin Rooftop Theater in New York City.

May 9   A Phoenix, Arizona, teacher—Mrs. Ingrid Montano— resigns after being condemned by community leaders for having invited a homosexual to come and speak to one of her high school sociology classes. Although Mrs. Montano has the support of her principal (he issues a statement insisting it's better that seniors learn about homosexuality in school rather "than in the alleys or on restroom walls"), she submits her letter of resignation, declaring, "I refuse to compromise on certain issues, and if compromising is part of teaching, forget it. I believe in speaking out honestly. I refuse to be hypocritical."

May 21   Bella Abzug—running for the 19th District congressional seat in New York City—addresses a meeting of the Gay Activists Alliance, becoming one of the first major U.S. politicians to openly court the gay vote. Gay columnist Arthur Bell later notes that Mrs. Abzug looked "for all the world like Dolly Levi . . . and it might as well have been Dolly night at Harmonica Gardens. Bella met with a standing ovation. She deserved it."

May 29   Future gay porn star Glenn Swann celebrates his eleventh birthday. Meanwhile, an impubic Jeff Stryker is looking forward to turning six soon.

May 31   Gordon Merrick's *The Lord Won't Mind*—a glossy, romantic gay love story, described by one critic as "escape fiction for the Gay and Gray set"—begins a sixteen-week run on *The New York Times* best-seller list. Merrick follows up his success with a stream of similar novels—*One for the Gods, Forth Into Light*, et al.— which become increasingly famous more for their fleshy, suggestive covers than for the quality of the material inside.

June 1   A report in this month's *Sexology* magazine concludes that gay men have larger penises than heterosexual men: 3.3 inches versus an average of 3 inches in length limp, and 1.08 inches in width versus a norm of 1 inch.

June 12   In what is described as "the first marriage in the nation designed to legally bind two persons of the same sex," two lesbians—Neva Joy Heckman and Judith Ann Belew—are married by the Rev. Troy Perry in a small ceremony in Los Angeles.

Later, a reporter asks Richard Nixon's press secretary, Ron Ziegler, what the President thinks of same-sex marriages and the rise of gay liberation. "He hasn't been for it, he's not for it, and he won't be for it," responds Ziegler.

> "Somebody was asking me. Said he thought Richard Nixon was obviously homosexual. I said: 'Why do you think that?' He said: 'You know, that funny, uncoordinated way he moves.' I said: 'Yeah, like Nureyev.'"
>
> —GORE VIDAL

June 17   Esteemed British novelist E. M. Forster—famous for such novels as *Howard's End*, *A Passage to India*, and *A Room with a View*—dies at the age of ninety-one in Coventry, England.

June 24   Raquel Welch and Mae West are nearly trampled to death by two thousand overzealous fans at the New York City premiere of *Myra Breckinridge*. At one point, fans break through the barricades and storm Miss West, who is nervously hurried into the theater by police. The film itself opens to some of the most derisive reviews ever heaped on a major motion picture. "As bad as any movie ever made," writes one critic. "A nightmare . . . a horrifying movie," says another. Words like "repulsive," "obscene," and "disgusting" figure prominently in other critics' assessments of the picture. Undaunted, director Michael Sarne promises to continue making more such "revolutionary" films—but, blessedly, no studio ever gives him the opportunity to direct again.

June 28   A Gay Pride parade up New York's Sixth Avenue draws an estimated ten thousand gay men and lesbians to celebrate the first anniversary of the Stonewall riots. "It serves notice on every politician in the state and nation," says one participant, "that homosexuals are not going to hide anymore." Marchers chant slogans of "Two, four, six, eight! Gay is just as good as straight!" and "Out of the closets! Into the streets!" One woman carries a sign reading "Homosexuality Is Not a Four-Letter Word," while another holds aloft a placard reading "Hi, Mom!" A dachshund trotting with its owner has a sign tied to its back: "Me Too!" The parade culminates in a "gay-in" at Central Park, where couples leisurely hold hands, kiss, and smoke pot.

July 2   The Lutheran Church calls for legislation prohibiting discrimination against gay people and for an end to all laws prohibiting homosexual acts between consenting adults.

July 5   In the nation's bookstores this month: *The Love That Dared Not Speak Its Name*—a sympathetic and informative history of homosexuality in Britain—by former member of the British Parliament H. Montgomery Hyde. A noted legal scholar, Hyde has been instrumental in paving the way for British legal reforms regarding private homosexual conduct.

July 6   Track and field star George Frenn makes the cover of this week's *Sports Illustrated*. Several years later, Frenn—holder of the all-time record in the fifty-six-pound hammer throw—publicly acknowledges his homosexuality and becomes a key participant in the first Gay Games.

July 11   *The New Yorker* takes notice of the city's recent Gay Pride parade with a thousand-word "Talk of the Town" item.

July 13 "No! It is the inability to love at all which I consider an emotional illness."
—DEAR ABBY'S *reply to a reader's query, "In your opinion, is homosexuality a disease?" in the morning newspapers*

July 25 The Vatican reaffirms its condemnation of homosexual unions as a moral aberration "that cannot be approved by human conscience, much less Christian conscience."

August 3 *Newsweek* reports on the dramatic shift of American males away from barbershops and crew cuts to salons that feature hairstyling, tinting, and permanents, as well as facials and manicures—all the things that, according to the magazine, "a few years ago would have sent [men] fleeing in a panic of threatened masculinity. Personal hair styling for men, once the cachet of a sophisticated few, is now rapidly spreading into the heartland of Middle America."

Says one hairstylist for men, who recently set up shop in Chicago, "All the local barbers called me 'queer' when I first started here. Then they found out how much I was making and they decided to become 'queer' too."

August 10 In a speech to the American Bar Association, Rita Hauser, the U.S. representative to the United Nations Human Rights Commission, endorses homosexual marriages as a way of controlling global overpopulation. Mrs. Hauser—a lawyer, a Republican, and the wife of the vice-president of GTE—says that laws against same-sex marriages are based on antiquated notions that reproduction is the primary purpose of marriage.

August 17 "I personally sometimes think that the world would be a great deal better if every homosexual individual and organization took an ad in the public press and published the names and addresses of every homosexual they know, identifying them as homosexuals; then maybe they'd come the fuck out of their closets and feel forced to fight for their lifestyle."
—*Gay activist* CRAIG SCHOONMAKER, *an early advocate of "outing"*

August 21   Black Panther leader Huey Newton publicly expresses his solidarity with the Gay Power movement and proclaims that homosexuals "might be the most oppressed people in the society." This immediately puts him at odds with certain other black leaders, most notably Eldridge Cleaver, whose contempt for gay men and lesbians is well documented. In his bestselling book *Soul On Ice*, Cleaver wrote, "Homosexuality is a sickness, just as are baby-rape or wanting to become head of General Motors."

August 24   *The New York Times* runs a front-page story, "HOMO-SEXUALS IN REVOLT," on the growing gay liberation movement.

August 25   *Look* magazine runs a lengthy photo-feature on ten-year-old showbiz wunderkind Michael Jackson, who, as lead singer of the Jackson Five, has brought his family fame and fortune with such hits as "The Love You Save," "A-B-C," and "I Want You Back." "I guess I always knew Michael was an unusual child," says Jackson's mother in the article—though it's unclear whether she's referring to his formidable talent or the occasionally idiosyncratic behavior he exhibits even as a little boy.

In later years, with puberty seeming to elude young Michael, spokesmen for the family vehemently deny rumors that the singer has been given female hormone treatments in order to retain the high-pitched (and lucrative) purity of his voice.

August 27   Elton John, the bespectacled British singer best known for his low-key, romantic single "Your Song," makes his U.S. debut, performing—with almost manic energy—before a large, enthusiastic crowd at the Troubadour in Los Angeles. So successful is this first show (and so impressive are the reviews he garners on the road, as he makes his way performing in concerts across the United States) that by the time he reaches New York City—to appear before a sold-out house at the Fillmore East—he has become an instant superstar.

September 1 Now showing at a drive-in theater near you: Russ Meyer's in-name-only sequel *Beyond the Valley of the Dolls*. "I *am* Super Woman!" declares the demented, transvestite "hero," just before decapitating the beautiful Lance Rock in the final reel. The film—written by future megacritic Roger Ebert and featuring, among other homophobic episodes, the "they-had-it-coming" slaying of two lesbian lovers (one of whom is forced to fellate a gun barrel before having her brains blown out)—goes on to become a major cult item, and is eventually voted by some critics one of the ten best U.S. films of the decade.

"At *The Killing of Sister George* people sat through eighty minutes of boredom to see one very erotic scene at the end," Meyer tells the press. "In my films they don't have to wait."

Harper's magazine publishes "The Struggle for Sexual Identity," in which the author, Joseph Epstein, calls homosexuality "an affront to our rationality, living evidence of our despair of ever finding a sensible, an explainable, design to the world." Adds Epstein, "There is much my four sons can do in their lives that might cause me to anguish, that might outrage me, that might make me ashamed of them and of myself as their father. But nothing they could ever do would make me sadder than if any of them were to become homosexual."

The article—coyly illustrated with a photo of a muscular male torso in an ill-fitting red blouse—prompts a sit-in at the magazine's editorial offices by the Gay Activists Alliance.

September 5 The Colombian government "decriminalizes" homosexual behavior, changing it from a felony to a simple misdemeanor. The maximum penalty is now "only" three years in prison.

September 6 After 1,002 New York performances, *The Boys in the Band* closes on Broadway.

September 12 "Lola"—a song about transvestism and sexual ambiguity ("I'm glad I'm a man and so is Lola . . .") by the British

Actor Edward Everett Horton, perhaps best remembered for his trademark line, "Oh dear, oh dear!"

rock group the Kinks—moves into the *Billboard* Top 40, where it will stay for twelve weeks, peaking at No. 9.

September 23 Actor Paul Burke portrays a brilliant medical researcher forced to acknowledge his homosexuality in the CBS series *Medical Center*. "Unlike so many shows which have dealt with this subject," notes *The Advocate*, "the protagonist . . . did not become a travesty of a human being." The show's scriptwriters, however, still felt compelled to have homosexuality referred to (with much hand-wringing and sorrow) as a "condition."

September 29 Actor Edward Everett Horton—who made a career playing gay characters in the movies, long before Hollywood ever allowed overtly gay characters on the screen—dies at the age of eighty-three in Encino, California. For years, Horton—who was himself gay—lived with his mother on a large southern California estate he had christened "Belly Acres."

September 30 "We watch the activities of the most disruptive gay militants with fascination. We try in vain to detect some rationale in their tactics and philosophy. . . . But it becomes more and more apparent that the so-called gay militants are not so much pro-gay as they are anti-establishment, anti-capitalist, anti-society. They lash out in all directions, destroying everything in sight—gay or straight."
—Advocate *editorial signaling the newspaper's move back to a more comfortably middle-of-the-road political viewpoint, and reflecting growing discontent in the gay community with the increasingly reactionary, and often unfocused, tactics of gay militants*

California state liquor authorities close down the four-year-old Folsom Street leather bar Fe-Be's in San Francisco after reports that patrons are openly having sex in the establishment. "The place was notorious for its Sunday afternoons," one of the bar's regulars says later, "which were pure, unadulterated sex orgies. The whole back of the bar was transformed into a massive grope-a-torium where *anything* happened." Fe-Be's reopens in 1971 and becomes famous for, among other things, its two-foot-high plaster promotional statues—"The Fe-Be's Man"—showing Michelangelo's David in leather pants, vest, and cap.

October I The Presidential Commission on Pornography releases its final report, which—to the consternation of conservative lawmakers hoping for a blanket condemnation of the new sexual openness—recommends instead the repeal of most state, local, and federal laws barring the sale and exhibition of sexual materials to consenting adults. The report also concludes there is no connection between pornography and crime, or between pornography and "sexual deviance." President Nixon denounces the commission as "morally bankrupt" and vows to ignore its recommendations, while evangelist Billy Graham publicly blasts the report as "diabolical." Meanwhile, one dissenting member of the commission, conservative Charles Keating (later to find infamy as a key figure in the savings and loan scandal of the 1980s), writes, "For a Presidential commission to have labored for two years at the expense to the taxpayers

Andy Warhol's Trash: *Counter-culture moves into the mainstream.*

of almost $2,000,000 and arrive at the conclusion that pornography is harmless must strike the average American as the epitome of Government gone berserk."

October 3 Singer Janis Joplin—who once told an interviewer, "I'd've fucked anything, taken anything . . . and I did. I'd take it, suck it, lick it, smoke it, shoot it, drop it, fall in love with it . . ."—dies of a drug overdose after mainlining a shot of unusually pure heroin at the Landmark Hotel in Hollywood. She is twenty-seven.

Just two months earlier, Joplin bought and dedicated a head-stone for the unmarked grave of another bisexual blues singer, Bessie Smith.

October 5 Andy Warhol's *Trash*, starring Joe Dallesandro as an impossibly alluring but impotent heroin addict, opens in New York City. The film—a cross between the grainy porn films of the Sixties and the B-movie campiness of 1950s Hollywood—becomes famous in some quarters primarily for the repetitive baring of what one critic calls Dallesandro's "utterly amazing buns."

> "If you watch carefully you'll see that my best performing comes when I have my clothes off. When I'm dressed I really don't give very good performances. . . . Next time you see a film where I'm naked, watch my face and you'll see what I mean."
> —JOE DALLESANDRO

October 28   Feminist Kate Millett—author of *Sexual Politics* and widely regarded as the national spokeswoman for the women's liberation movement—publicly acknowledges her lesbianism at a New York meeting of the Daughters of Bilitis. In response, the mainstream press suddenly acts as if it has all along been somehow duped by the women's movement—"We all knew they were a bunch of man-hating dykes," seems to be the general reaction—and *Time* magazine in particular uses the revelation to try to discredit both Millett and feminism in general.

November 3   Bella Abzug defeats Republican opponent Barry Farber, by a margin of nine thousand votes, and is elected U.S. Congresswoman from Manhattan's 19th District.

November 11   In a front-page story, *The New York Times* announces the forthcoming publication of a major new novel by E. M. Forster, titled *Maurice*, which has been withheld from publication for fifty-five years (at Forster's request) because of its homosexual theme.

November 20   "I tell you, I never thought I'd see my name in *The New York Times*, right beside Sophia Loren's and God's!" —*Transvestite actress* HOLLY WOODLAWN (*real name: Harold Danhaki*), *basking in all the attention she's receiving as a result of kind reviews for her performance in* Trash

November 21   New York City Councilman Robert Postel charges that the local Spofford Juvenile Detention Center for boys is a nest of brutality, sexual violence, and rape, often involving very young boys, and that in the past several weeks four teenage boys have tried to commit suicide to escape sexual assault there. The center's director, Wallace Nottage, responds by publicly doubting the sincerity of the boys who tried to kill themselves: he calls their suicide attempts "gestures."

Besides trying to hang themselves with bedsheets, some of the boys have made "gestures" with shoelaces and pajama strings knotted into nooses.

November 25   Japanese author Yukio Mishima—obsessed with violence, Japanese nationalism, and homoerotic sadomasochism— infiltrates the Japanese military headquarters in Tokyo, delivers an emotional diatribe about the corruption of modern Japan, and then commits suicide by disemboweling himself in a particularly gruesome act of *seppuku*, which involves carving open his abdomen with a dagger. He is assisted in the ritual by a handsome twenty-five-year-old man (referred to by friends as Mishima's "fiancé"), who immediately decapitates Mishima's corpse and then kills himself as well.

Just hours before his death, Mishima submitted the final pages of his last novel, *The Sea of Fertility*, to his publisher.

November 27   Two gay activists appear on *The Dick Cavett Show* to help explain to the nation what gay liberation is all about.

December 7   Lesbian painter Romaine Brooks, estranged lover of Natalie Clifford Barney, dies in Nice at the age of ninety-six.

December 12   Struggling young pianist and songwriter Barry Manilow takes a job performing—for $125 a night—at New York's increasingly trendy Continental Baths.

December 17   Nine leaders of the women's liberation movement—including Gloria Steinem and Susan Brownmiller—

hold a press conference in New York City to express their "solidarity with the struggle of homosexuals to attain their liberation in a sexist society."

December 20　"The sex thing in pro football is strange. One year the word was out around the league that homosexuality was fairly open in one NFL locker room. One veteran of that team told me that those players who were 'in on the program' would stay after practice until all the straights had left, and then do their thing. According to this player, about fifteen of his teammates were involved."

—DAVE MEGGYESY, *in his newly released book on football*, Out of Their League

December 27　Now showing at Manhattan's Park-Miller Movie Theater: *BOYS IN CHAINS*, plus special added attraction, *Gypsy Boys!*

1971

January 7 The Kremlin announces that the KGB will no longer harass, arrest, or imprison young Soviet males with long hair. However, parents and teachers are still urged to exert whatever social pressure is necessary (including ridiculing long-haired individuals by name in the press) to keep the "tasteless" practice from becoming a nationwide trend.

In its final report to President Nixon, the National Commission on Reform of Federal Criminal Laws urges, among other things, the abolition of all U.S. laws prohibiting homosexual acts between consenting adults.

January 17 U.S. novelist Merle Miller "comes out" in a seven-page essay, "What It Means to Be a Homosexual," in *The New York Times Magazine*. "Without indulging in sensationalism or special pleading," notes *Publishers Weekly*, "but making it clear that he was writing from his own experience, he bridged the gap between the 'straights' and the 'gays' in a way that few recent writers on the subject have done."

"I don't see any great rush of people lining up to declare themselves as homosexuals," Miller says later. "Who is to say they should do so? I think, however, it is rather important. For one thing, you cannot demand your rights, civil or otherwise, if you are unwilling to say what you are."

Miller eventually receives more than two thousand letters in response to the piece, the majority of them overwhelmingly supportive.

January 26 *Look* magazine includes a gay couple—Jack Baker and Mike McConnell of Minnesota—as part of this week's cover story on "The American Family."

January 27 David Bowie arrives in the United States for his first American visit. However, because of a mix-up over work permits, he is prevented from performing live. Still, his habit of wearing dresses in Los Angeles and Texas earns him an enormous amount of free publicity. Later, he makes headlines when he tells one music industry publication, "I'm gay and always have been, even when I was David Jones." So overwhelming is the amount of attention this disclosure receives that the singer begins to openly worry he'll be assassinated on stage, and he hires a phalanx of bodyguards to protect him.

February 1 Frederick Combs, who originated the role of Donald in both the stage and screen versions of *The Boys in the Band*, tells *After Dark* he is currently unemployed and has had to take a part-time job refinishing furniture in Beverly Hills to make ends meet. "You go to all the Hollywood agents," says Combs, "and they say, '*Boys in the Band?* No one knows it in the Midwest.' "

February 10 New York psychiatrist Lawrence Hatterer—author of the recently published *Changing Homosexuality in the Male*—publicly blames the "homosexualization" of America on the $1-billion-a-year "hardcore homosexual pornography industry," and suggests that the stimulating nature of such films may push otherwise "normal" males "over the line" into sexual deviance.

Adds Hatterer, on a publicity tour for his book, "This society is no more going to institutionalize homosexuality than we're going to institutionalize Al Capone."

February 28 MORE HOMOSEXUALS AIDED TO BECOME HETEROSEXUAL
—*Front-page* New York Times *story reflecting a growing line of thought that as gay liberation is increasingly taken for granted on the political scene, attention is now turning to the notion that perhaps "they" can all be persuaded to change*

March 14 More than two thousand protesters march on the steps of the New York state capitol in Albany demanding an end to laws that discriminate against gay men and lesbians.

March 18 Idaho decriminalizes homosexual acts between consenting adults. However, before the law can take effect, the state legislature—under increasing pressure from conservative and religious groups—reverses itself and votes to make them a felony again.

March 24 In defiance of the U.S. Immigration and Naturalization Service, a federal judge grants U.S. citizenship to a twenty-four-year-old acknowledged gay man from Cuba and rules that an applicant's homosexuality cannot, in itself, bar a person from becoming a citizen. "We accept the principle," says the judge (whose political naïveté will be underlined in the years to come), "that the naturalization laws are concerned with public, not private, morality."

April 1 The French leftist newspaper *Tout*, edited by Jean-Paul Sartre, calls for complete sexual liberation in France, including the right of individuals to be freely and openly homosexual. Police begin massive seizures of the publication on the grounds it is "an outrage to public morals."

April 4 Four "reformed" homosexuals go on *The David Susskind Show* to tout their conversions to heterosexuality and praise the therapy of sometime poet and literary critic Eli Siegel, whose doctrine of "Aesthetic Realism" teaches that homosexuality is the result of a distorted philosophical view of the world. Aesthetic Realists—who never use the word "homosexuality" but instead call it "H" ("How long have you been H?" "Is she H?" "Do you think there's a relationship between how your mother treated you and H?")—number less than twenty, despite the fact that Siegel has been plying his theories in the academic world since 1945.

May 1 John Wayne complains to *Playboy* magazine that there are too many "perverted" movies being made, and singles out *Midnight Cowboy*, which he sarcastically refers to as a "*wonderful* love story about two fags."

May 6 The Gay Activists Alliance "Firehouse"—a combination gay community center and social club, meant as an alternative to New York's bars and baths (many of which are still operated by organized crime)—opens in SoHo.

May 9 Andy Warhol's play *Pork* opens at the La Mama Experimental Theater in New York City. Among the cast is an extremely talented, inordinately overweight sixteen-year-old drag queen named Harvey Fierstein.

May 15 The Rolling Stones album *Sticky Fingers*—featuring a cover photo of a man's blue-jeaned crotch with an actual working zipper incorporated into the cardboard (and then when you open the zipper, a second photo of a man's bulging white briefs underneath)—enters the nation's Top 40, where it stays for twenty-six weeks, four of them in the No. 1 slot.

Some record stores refuse to sell the album to anyone under eighteen.

May 17 New York City Mayor Lindsay throws his political support behind a gay rights bill being considered by the New York City Council.

May 26 Mexican labor contractor Juan Corona is arrested and charged with the murders of twenty-five itinerant farm workers in California. The dead workers—many of whom are never identified—have been found in shallow graves in orchards and along the banks of a nearby river, some of them buried with their shirts pulled over their heads, some with their pants yanked down, and others, reportedly, with their genitals mutilated. Although Corona's lawyer eventually tries to blame the murders on deranged homosexuals (and attempts to prove in court that Corona himself couldn't have committed them because he is "hopelessly heterosexual"), the overwhelming weight of evidence—a "death ledger" that Corona has kept of the killings, his bank receipts found in some of the graves, a host of bloodied weapons and knives found hidden in his house—suggests that Corona is himself the guilty party after all, and he is convicted of all twenty-five slayings and sentenced to twenty-five consecutive life terms in prison.

May 27 Luchino Visconti's *Death in Venice*—based on the classic novella by Thomas Mann—wins the Grand Prix at the Cannes Film Festival.

June 21 Self-described "male actress" Charles Pierce—doing drag impersonations of everyone from Jeanette MacDonald to Eleanor Roosevelt—begins a week-long nightclub stint in San Francisco that draws rave reviews and instantly becomes the hottest ticket in town. "*Hi* there," Pierce greets his audiences every night, waving an oversized peacock fan in their direction. "Sorry I'm late tonight, but you just can't *imagine* how I have to be squeezed into this costume. Actually, these aren't my tits, you know; they're my balls."

"To call Charles Pierce a female impersonator," observes critic Clive Barnes, "is a little like comparing a Rolls-Royce with a Toyota. . . . He is a fantastically funny and outrageous man. . . . He might even give transvestism a good name, and have perfectly normal sailors riffling through their mother's closets."

THE WIT AND WISDOM OF CHARLES PIERCE

"Sex is like bridge: if you don't have a good partner, you better have a good hand."

"What happens if you cross Billie Jean King and Bo Derek? You get a DC-10."

"Marie Antoinette, dainty queen of France. . . . Surely not the only queen of history that lost her head over a basket."

"Patti Page—you remember her. . . . That doggie in the window was just her reflection."

"How the hell do you have sex with Shelley Winters? Roll her in flour, look for a wet spot."

"They asked me the other day my definition of the perfect lover. And I had it for them, too. A man who can make love to you until four o'clock in the morning—and then turn into a pizza."

July 1 The *International Times*—a London-based underground newspaper—unsuccessfully appeals its recent conviction on charges of indecency for having run, in addition to its regular personals ads, a monthly column of classifieds exclusively for male homosexuals. In upholding the conviction, the judges rule that, whatever the legality of homosexual acts themselves, public encouragement of such behavior must remain a crime.

An article by an outraged University of California professor in *The Humanist* profiles some of the psychiatric abuses at the state's Atascadero State Hospital, a facility near Santa Barbara where "sex offenders and cultural deviants" (including a large number of convicted homosexuals) are incarcerated. In particular, he describes the brutal use of aversion therapy to "cure" homosexuals: a patient is shown pornographic pictures of nude men, and every time he achieves an erection a powerful jolt of electricity is run through his penis until he is no longer able to become sexually aroused. Although some doctors claim the conditioning is purely psychological, there is increasing evidence that the patients' penile tissue is actually being burned and destroyed by the electricity, to the point that an erection is physiologically impossible. Concludes the professor, "I don't know what patients and staff are like when they are not in the institution, but judging from their behavior there, I would feel a great deal more secure about the world if the patients went home at night and the staff stayed locked up."

Other abuses reported at the facility:

■ attempts to "cure" homosexuality through the forced injection of panic-inducing drugs that bring the patient to the brink of death
■ the forced injection of Prolixin, a personality-altering drug that induces psychoses, extreme physical pain, and substantial brain damage
■ experiments with extreme and exotic forms of lobotomy to "cure" homosexuality

Says one of Atascadero's research chiefs, of his patients, "These men have no rights. If we can learn something by using them, then that is a small compensation for the trouble they have caused society."

Among the "troublemakers" incarcerated at Atascadero are men arrested for "lewd and lascivious conduct," including one man convicted of having kissed his boyfriend in public, and so-called "compulsive masturbators," including a young man whose landlady accidentally saw him masturbating in the bathroom and called the police; he was arrested and convicted on charges of public lewdness.

July 10   The Austrian Parliament decriminalizes homosexual acts between consenting adults.

August 29   Nathan Leopold—who rose to infamy in the 1920s when he and "close friend" Richard Loeb attempted to commit the perfect murder by brutally slaying a fourteen-year-old boy, Bobby Franks—dies at the age of sixty-six in Puerto Rico. Paroled in 1958, Leopold spent his final years in San Juan, where he worked as a $10-a-month assistant in a missionary hospital.

September 21   John Schlesinger's new film *Sunday, Bloody Sunday*—starring Peter Finch and Glenda Jackson as two lonely people (one a middle-aged gay doctor, the other a cynical divorcée) sharing the same young male lover—opens to rave reviews in New York City. Critics in particular praise the sensitive, matter-of-fact screenplay by Penelope Gilliatt (who goes on to win a New York Film Critics Award for her work, but is by-passed for an Oscar in favor of Paddy Chayevsky's screenplay for *The Hospital*), as well as the performances by Finch and Jackson. Amid the generally glowing media attention, there are reports that one of Peter Finch's real-life ex-lovers, singer Shirley Bassey, ran from the theater physically ill after viewing the film's mouth-to-mouth, passionate kiss between Finch and actor Murray Head.

Bassey later acknowledges, "I saw it, and, oh, I couldn't bear it. . . . When he kissed that boy, it *destroyed* me. It spoiled the whole film for me. . . . This new permissiveness in films—I think it's ridiculous and frightening."

October 1   Connecticut becomes only the second state in the U.S. (after Illinois, in 1961) to abolish its laws prohibiting homosexual acts between consenting adults.

October 4   W.W. Norton publishes E. M. Forster's *Maurice*, written in 1913 but dedicated by Forster "to a happier year." The book—about a young man coming to terms with his homosexuality in Edwardian England—provokes an avalanche of lukewarm and strangely mystified reviews, often written by critics with a coying and disingenuous sense of regret. What *could* poor Forster have been thinking? seems to be the general reaction. The happy ending in particular incenses several critics:

"a fairy tale . . . flawed and failed . . . an infantile book."
                    —CYNTHIA OZICK, *Commentary*

"his palest work . . . the ending is very faint."
                    —WALTER CLEMONS, *Newsweek*

"The entire book is a wish-fulfillment fantasy."
                    —VIVIAN MERCIER, *The Nation*

"inert and self-indulgent."
        —FRANK KERMODE, in a review archly titled, "A Queer Business," in *The Atlantic*

"The distance between the Edwardian love that dared not speak its name and the rhetoric of the Gay Liberation Front is simply too great. . . . *Maurice* is dispensable to almost everyone."
                    —CHRISTOPHER PORTERFIELD, *Time*

For many gay men—less interested in politics than in a humane and positive reflection of their lives—the book remains a moving and still-relevant portrait of growing up gay in a staunchly heterosexual environment. Meanwhile, *The New Yorker* notes that the really melancholy thing about *Maurice* is simply "that there will never again be an autumn book list with a new novel by that late and most eminent Fellow of King's College, Cambridge."

October 9 The Navy reveals that, whereas in 1964 it discharged 42 men for drug use and 1,586 for homosexuality, last year it discharged 5,672 for drug use and 479 for homosexuality. Officials attribute the lopsided change to disgruntled sailors now preferring to claim drug use, rather than homosexuality, as an excuse for getting out of the military.

October 12 The New York City Department of Consumer Affairs recommends repealing a law that has for years technically prohibited homosexuals from being employed in—or even frequenting—the city's bars, cabarets, and dance halls. "Homosexuals have a right to congregate in places of public accommodation," says one city spokesman. "They have a right to a drink."

October 25 Homophobic author Philip Wylie dies, at the age of sixty-nine, in Miami. Wylie wrote *Generation of Vipers* and *Sons and Daughters of Mom*, in which he assailed American morals and coined the term "momism" to decry what he claimed was the emotional tyranny of women over American men. The ultraconservative Wylie was particularly incensed by the hippie movement of the 1960s, and frequently railed against "girl-haired boys."

November 1 The offices of London's Olympia Press are raided by representatives of Scotland Yard who seize, among other things, copies of the recently published *Homosexual Handbook* by Angelo d'Arcangelo. Although actual charges are never brought against Olympia, police continue to raid the publisher's office several times over the next few months, and harass and threaten the publisher's printer, distributor, and production agent.

November 17 Sex researchers in St. Louis claim to have discovered that heterosexual men have as much as 40 percent more testosterone in their blood than homosexuals do.

December 10 Nixon Supreme Court nominee William H. Rehnquist—who, according to sworn testimony, actively "harassed" and "discouraged" blacks from voting in Phoenix elections, and who opposed a Phoenix civil rights ordinance on the grounds that property rights are more important than the rights of black people to go into whichever drugstore they please—is confirmed by the U.S. Senate, 68 to 26.

Once seated on the court, he quickly reveals himself to be as hostile to the rights of gay people as he has apparently been to the civil liberties of everyone else.

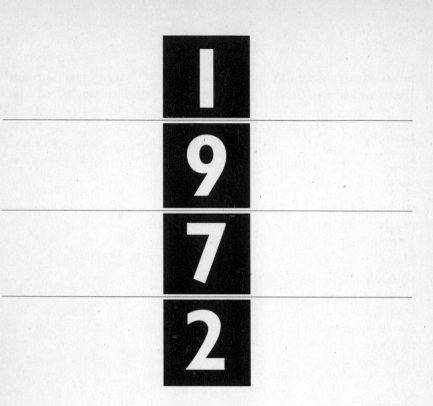

1972

January 1 "To tell you the truth, I think every man should be fucked up the arse as a prelude to fucking women, so that he'll know what it's like to be the receiver. Otherwise, he'll forever go about thinking that he's doling out joy unlimited to every woman he fucks."
—*Feminist* GERMAINE GREER, *who also expresses the belief that "lesbianism will probably be the only way to persuade men that they've got to offer [women] a different deal"*

A recent study, published in *Science* magazine this month, suggests that male homosexuality may be determined in the womb as a result of certain kinds of chemical or hormonal stress endured by the pregnant mother.

January 9 Internationally renowned dancer Ted Shawn—who consistently blamed his late-blooming homosexuality on the numerous extramarital affairs of his famous wife, dancer Ruth St. Denis—dies at the age of eighty in Orlando, Florida.

January 19 *Variety* reviews Wakefield Poole's groundbreaking gay porno film *Boys in the Sand*, with the soon-to-be-legendary line, "There are no more closets." The handsomely produced film— about a group of men cruising for quick sex on Fire Island—be- comes the most successful porn producton of its kind, grossing nearly $6,000 in its first *hour* at the 55th Street Playhouse in New York City, and turns its star—twenty-eight-year-old, clean-cut, blue-eyed Casey Donovan—into an instant gay celebrity, the stan- dard for gay porn actors in the years to come. With its fluid cam- erawork and sensual music, the film represents a major departure from the cheap and shoddy gay porn films of the past, in which entire sequences were sometimes out of focus and cum shots were frequently accompanied on the soundtrack by "Climb Ev'ry Moun- tain" and "June Is Busting Out All Over."

January 20 In the nation's bookstores this month: *Kathleen and Frank: The Autobiography of a Family*, in which English-born Amer- ican author Christopher Isherwood publicly discusses his parents, his childhood, and, for the first time, his homosexuality. "The idea of declaring your homosexuality in print seems so wonderfully simple," he says later. "I can't imagine what all the fuss is about. . . . I don't know why people have doubts about coming out."

January 27 The New York City Council vetoes a proposed gay rights ordinance that would have prohibited discrimination against gay men and lesbians in employment, housing, and public accommodations.

February 2 Lesbian voluptuary Natalie Clifford Barney, as fa- mous for her numerous lesbian affairs and romances as for her poetry and weekly artistic salons, dies in Paris at the age of ninety- five. Her funeral, like her salons, is held on a Friday.

Ad for the Continental Baths: "Lil-lian Roth, everybody, sings there now."

"I'm going to make Attila the Hun look like a faggot."
—*Former Philadelphia police commissioner* FRANK RIZZO, *inaugurated as the city's mayor in early 1972*

February 13   The film *Cabaret*—based on the hit stage musical, and on Christopher Isherwood's autobiographical novel *Goodbye to Berlin*—has its world premiere in New York City, with all of the film's major stars (including Michael York, Liza Minnelli, Joel Grey, and Marisa Berenson) in attendance. Notable for its brilliantly staged musical numbers, its perfect casting, and its deeply penetrating air of decadence (despite the fact that it contains no nudity or onscreen sex), the film goes on to become a smash hit at the box office and wins eight Oscars at next year's Academy Awards. (It loses Best Picture, however, to *The Godfather*.) For many young gay men just coming out of high school in the post-Stonewall years, York's portrayal of an attractive and sympathetic bisexual represents one of the first big-screen validations of their sexual longings.

February 20 "In a city where nightclubs are shutting down faster than a row of standing dominos can tumble, there are three thousand people waiting to get into the Continental Baths to see the freaky Miss M."
—*Critic* REX REED *on the astonishing success of twenty-six-year-old singer Bette Midler, whose venue at the Continental Baths has catapulted her to national attention, including a guest shot on* The Tonight Show. *"My career took off when I sang at the Continental Baths in New York," Midler says later. "Those tubs became the showplace of the nation. I made 'em respectable. Lillian Roth, everybody, sings there now." So respectable do the Baths in fact become that, a little more than a year later, noted operatic soprano Eléanor Stéber holds what is described as a "black towel" concert there.*

March 4 The California Department of Motor Vehicles reports that while an overwhelming majority of the sixty-five thousand personalized license plates in the state have presented no censorship problems for state officials, a few messages—including HOMO, GAYLIB, EAT ME, and LOVE69—have been banned.

March 7 East Lansing, Michigan, becomes the first city in the U.S. to ban discrimination in city hiring on the basis of sexual orientation.

March 15 Former senator Eugene McCarthy, campaigning once again for the Democratic nomination for President, promises that, if elected, he will work to abolish all legal discrimination against gay people. He loses the nomination four months later to ill-fated candidate George McGovern, who has also vowed to support gay rights and who later takes the considerably risky political step of allowing two nationally televised speeches in support of gay rights on the same night he accepts the presidential nomination at the Democratic National Convention.

March 22   The Equal Rights Amendment, banning discrimination on the basis of sex, passes the U.S. Senate. Detractors immediately claim it will destroy the nuclear family, give broad civil rights to homosexuals, and even mandate "unisex" rest rooms in public places. Still, by year's end, twenty-two of the necessary thirty-eight states have ratified it.

April 3   The U.S. Supreme Court effectively upholds a lower court ruling giving state governments the right to refuse employment to gay men and lesbians. The court had refused to review the case of an openly gay man turned down for a job at a Minnesota university library because of his homosexuality.

The decision draws the approval of at least one major newspaper, the New York *Daily News*, which remarks (in an editorial, "ANY OLD JOBS FOR HOMOS?"): "Fairies, nances, swishes, fags, lezzes—call 'em what you please—should of course be permitted to earn honest livings in nonsensitive jobs. But government, from federal on down, should have full freedom to bar them from jobs in which their peculiarities would make them security or other risks." The paper never suggests how a man working in a college library might pose a security, or any other kind of, "risk."

April 10   The Missouri Supreme Court upholds the lower-court conviction of a gay man sentenced to ten years in prison for violating the state's sodomy laws.

April 27   Testifying before Congress on behalf of the FBI's annual $336 million budget, director J. Edgar Hoover assures the House Appropriations Committee that there are no gay activists in the Bureau. "We don't allow any types of activists in the FBI, gay or otherwise," says Hoover. "I ask not for average personnel but for those above average in character, education, and personal appearance."

May 2   J. Edgar Hoover dies of a heart attack at the age of seventy-seven. The main provision of his will—leaving the bulk of his $551,000 estate to his close companion of more than forty years,

Clyde Tolson—renews longtime speculation over his sexuality: Were they lovers? Was Hoover gay? Straight? Asexual? Hoover and Tolson were so inseparable, and so much alike in their thinking, that Washington insiders often referred to them as "the Unipersonality."

"I was in love once when I was young," Hoover remarked before his death, dispelling questions about his private life, "but then I became attached to the Bureau."

Later revelations indicate that Hoover was so incensed by rumors he might be homosexual that he often sent out field agents to harass and intimidate anyone known to suggest he was gay. Among those harassed were a beauty salon owner in Washington, D.C., (one of her clients, it turned out, worked in the FBI's records division) and a woman in Cleveland, Ohio, who repeated rumors about Hoover's sexuality to members of her bridge club.

May 23   Delaware becomes the sixth state to repeal its sodomy statutes. Oregon, Hawaii, and Colorado have also recently abolished their sodomy laws.

June 19   The first officially proclaimed "Gay Pride Week"—decreed by the city council several weeks earlier—gets under way in Ann Arbor, Michigan.

June 25   William Johnson becomes the first openly gay man to be ordained a minister by a major denomination, the United Church of Christ.

Peace activist Dr. Benjamin Spock joins this year's Gay Pride march in New York City. Commenting on the demonstration, *The New York Times* notes that, "Several fathers, apparently thinking a parade was coming, hoisted their children onto their shoulders, only to go ashen-faced as the marchers passed."

Meanwhile, playwright Tennessee Williams tells one magazine, "I think that these gay liberationist demonstrations are pathetic. When you see some drag queens going around in Cadillac convertibles blowing kisses, they make it worse. Unfortunately, homosexuals are trained by society to make a travesty of themselves."

June 27 *Gay News*—England's first national gay newspaper— makes its debut.

July 14 "We don't need gay liberation. We have always been liberated out here in The Grove."
                    —*Fire Island resident, quoted in* The New York Times

August 22 On a suffocatingly hot Tuesday afternoon, twenty-seven-year-old John Wojtowicz and an eighteen-year-old friend, Sal Naturale, enter a branch of the Chase Manhattan Bank in Brooklyn intending to rob it, so that Wojtowicz, who is living on welfare, can get money for his gay lover's sex-change operation. Unfortunately, the robbery goes awry and, with the arrival of the police, Wojtowicz suddenly finds himself saddled with nine hostages he doesn't want. The resulting media circus—lasting some fourteen hours—draws thousands of curiosity-seekers eager for some relief from the stultifying monotony of the heat. Inside the bank, the atmosphere of tension and fear slowly turns to one of almost frenetic giddiness as the hostages realize that their captors, far from being vicious criminals, are generally mild-mannered and inept. "We cried, we laughed and joked. We took it as it came," says one hostage later. "We never really thought we'd be harmed," says another, "because the gunmen treated us so nicely." A third later describes the mood as having been more "like a party" than a bank robbery. At one point, Wojtowicz calls and orders pizzas for everybody, and tips the delivery boy $2,000. Later, Wojtowicz's mother, gay lover, and friends (as well as a psychiatrist) are brought forward to try to talk him into giving himself up. He refuses.

The standoff finally ends when, on their way to the airport to a jet they think will fly them to freedom, the two would-be armed robbers are overpowered by the police and Naturale is shot to death.

The entire episode later forms the basis for the 1975 movie *Dog Day Afternoon*, which Wojtowicz—serving a twenty-year term

Actor Tony Randall. A day at the ball-game, a night at the porn theater . . .

in prison for armed bank robbery—dismisses as "a piece of garbage."

August 25 *Life* magazine runs a feature on the first all-male beauty pageant in the U.S., the Mr. Adonis Contest, held in Florida. The winner, twenty-four-year-old Robert Le Clair, is described as "36–30–32."

September 1 On the heels of one recent controversy in which he bitterly complained to *Opera News* about the "hordes of homosexuals who come to the opera and scream and *squeal* over these broken-down sopranos," Tony Randall now tells *After Dark* that he recently went to an all-male porn theater with some friends in Los Angeles. "Just terrible," says the actor. "Just disgusting. Guys sucking each other's cocks. There's nothing to watch in that. It confirms something I've always suspected about homosexuality— they don't like it. These guys never got aroused." In the same interview, Randall—who has made a career playing nervous, servile, and somewhat-less-than-exactly-virile characters—asserts, "There is no such thing as homosexuality—it's just something invented by a bunch of fags."

September 4   U.S. swimmer and dental student Mark Spitz is elevated to international male heartthrob status when he wins a record seven gold medals at the summer Olympics in Munich. His newfound celebrity spawns a best-selling poster that shows him in skimpy swim trunks with all seven medals gleaming around his neck.

September 13   *The Paul Lynde Show*—in which the gay actor is sorely miscast as a suburban family man with zany kids and wacky in-laws—debuts on ABC. It lasts one season.

September 15   In the nation's bookstores this month: John Francis Hunter's *The Gay Insider USA*, a combination national bar guide, gay liberation pep talk, and gay community resource almanac. "A must for today's aware gay on the go," says *David* magazine.

September 17   The TV series *M*A*S*H* premieres on CBS and within a year has introduced television's first on-going transvestite (but still unequivocally heterosexual) character, Corporal Klinger, who dresses in outlandish female ensembles in a futile attempt to get himself discharged from the military.

September 28   David Bowie performs to a sold-out crowd at New York City's Carnegie Hall. For many of the singer's screaming fourteen-year-old fans, the highlight of the evening comes when Bowie—dubbed "The King of Camp Rock"—simulates an act of fellatio on lead guitarist Mick Ronson.

Meanwhile, with the release of *The Rise and Fall of Ziggy Stardust and the Spiders from Mars*, Bowie has his first hit album in England. The album cover shows the orange-haired singer in a skintight, turquoise jumpsuit open to his navel.

Melody Maker magazine later votes *Ziggy Stardust* the most influential album of the decade.

October 8 Nearly a hundred gay demonstrators disrupt the sixth annual convention of the Association for the Advancement of Behavioral Therapy in New York City to protest the continued use of aversion therapy to "treat" homosexuality. "Aversion therapy is Clockwork Orange!" shouts one outraged protester. Other demonstrators condemn it as "torture" and "a cruel joke on gay people."

"They're picketing the wrong people," complains one behavioral therapist. "The therapists here have no moral quarrel with homosexuality. All we want to do is offer assistance for homosexuals to lead a more comfortable, spontaneous, and creative life."

October 11 Convicted twenty-two-year-old would-be assassin Arthur H. Bremer—who tried to gun down Alabama Governor George Wallace in a Maryland parking lot six months earlier—complains to prison authorities that he's recently been the target of repeated homosexual advances from his fellow inmates.

"One of the nicest—whatever you want to call it—loves of my life was a woman."

—Folk singer JOAN BAEZ, *acknowledging in a 1972 interview with a Berkeley newspaper that she once had a lesbian affair*

October 30 Elton John gives a command performance for the Queen of England at the Royal Variety Show in London.

November 1 *That Certain Summer*—a much-publicized if generally inoffensive made-for-TV movie about a fourteen-year-old boy who learns the truth about his divorced father's homosexuality—airs on ABC. Despite mostly favorable reviews in the media (liberal critics call it "dignified," "sensitive," "intelligent"), it still draws the ire of some viewers, who demand to know why such "filth" is being broadcast into their homes. Meanwhile, there are reports that anxious ABC producers doctored the script at the last minute to avoid controversy. In the original ending, the boy—angry and confused—refuses to say goodbye to his father, but then later regrets it and muses remorsefully, "I should've said goodbye to him . . ." In the more downbeat version actually aired, the boy displays no such regret, and the final shot is of the father—tearful and shamefaced—wondering whether he'll ever hear from his son again.

November 7 Jesse Helms—a fifty-one-year-old former Sunday-School teacher from Raleigh, North Carolina—is elected to his first term in the U.S. Senate.

December 1 *Boys in the Sand* star Casey Donovan makes the cover of *After Dark* magazine. Earlier, the magazine featured an interview with Donovan, including full-page pictures of the porn celebrity cavorting nude on a trapeze. But of course, it *still* isn't a gay magazine.

January 15 *An American Family* premieres on PBS. The twelve-episode documentary examines seven months in the lives of a so-called average American family: the Louds of Santa Barbara, California. As the series progresses, however, viewers begin to realize they're getting more than they may have bargained for: an uncomfortable look at the emotional turmoil underlying much of suburban America in the Seventies. By episode nine, Mrs. Loud has told her husband she wants a divorce. Even before that, viewers have witnessed the "coming out" of one of the Louds' five children, eighteen-year-old Lance, who cheerfully characterizes himself to the press as "Homo of the Year."

An aficionado of blue lipstick and leather, Lance goes on to become the lead singer in a short-lived rock band, The Mumps, while his mother acknowledges in an interview, "Homosexuality certainly isn't anything I would choose for a child of mine."

The New York Department of Motor Vehicles bans certain offensive three-letter combinations—including FAG and DYK—from
appearing on either standard or personalized license plates.

January 27   Two gay men—the latest victims in a series of grisly
murders of homosexuals in New York City—are found stabbed to
death (and their pet poodle drowned in a bathroom sink) in an
apartment in Brooklyn. In recent weeks, police have also found a
twenty-nine-year-old gay man dead of multiple stab wounds in his
Greenwich Village apartment; two other gay men, also stabbed to
death, in an apartment on Varick Street; and the partly decomposed
bodies of two more young men, one a college student, floating in
the Hudson River. Several of the victims were said to be devotees
of the city's leather bars.
    The pattern of murders bears a disturbing resemblance to the
1970 Gerald Walker novel *Cruising*, in which a killer ritualistically
butchers men he has picked up in gay S&M bars.

January 28   After years of negotiation, a Vietnam peace agreement
is finally signed in Paris by representatives of the United States
and North and South Vietnam. U.S. Secretary of State Henry
Kissinger later confesses of the principal North Vietnamese
negotiator: "I thought that Le Duc Tho had discovered some
hidden physical attraction for me. He couldn't keep his hands
off me."

February 4   French actress Maria Schneider, currently enjoying
a windfall of media attention from her steamy performance in *Last
Tango in Paris*, acknowledges to *The New York Times* that she is
bisexual. "I've had quite a few lovers for my age," admits the
twenty-year-old. "More men than women. Probably fifty men and
twenty women. . . . Women I love more for beauty than for sex.
Men I love for grace and intelligence."

March 4   Two weeks after the National Organization for Women
passed a resolution establishing the fight for lesbian rights as a "top

priority," feminist Betty Friedan publicly accuses "man-hating" lesbians of trying to take over the organization.

March 7 The stabbed and sexually mutilated body of a ten-year-old boy, Luis Ortiz, is discovered in an apartment building stairwell on New York City's West Side. Although police have no leads in the case, the gruesome killing is repeatedly referred to in the press as "a homosexual murder."

March 11 *The New York Times* reports on the growth of international travel tours aimed exclusively at the gay market.

March 26 The inimitable Noel Coward, seventy-three, dies in Jamaica.

March 31 Lou Reed's "Walk on the Wild Side"—a backhanded tribute to Joe Dallesandro and other members of Andy Warhol's inner circle—enters the nation's Top 40, where it stays for eight weeks, peaking at No. 16.

April 18 The Minnesota State House of Representatives votes 69 to 46 to *retain* the state's sodomy laws.

May 1 In the wake of *Cosmopolitan* magazine's recent success running a nude centerfold of actor Burt Reynolds, a new magazine for straight women—*Playgirl*—makes its debut on the nation's magazine racks. The magazine's initial printing—six hundred thousand copies—sells out in less than a month, and at its peak the magazine garners a monthly circulation of almost two million readers. The publishers later deny—rather hopelessly—that the readership is composed of any significant number of gay men.

"I'm buying it for my girlfriend," suddenly becomes a commonly heard pretext at magazine stands and checkout counters across the country.

May 6 Mary Renault's *The Persian Boy*—second in her trilogy of historical novels about Alexander the Great—ends a twenty-three-week run on *The New York Times* best-seller list. Regarded by many as Renault's finest work, the book portrays Alexander and his military campaigns as seen through the eyes of his young male lover, a Persian castrato, Bagoas. Renault—herself a lesbian—has written a large number of historical novels dealing with male homosexuality, including *The Last of the Wine* and *Fire from Heaven*, as well as the lesbian-themed *The Middle Mist*. Gore Vidal calls her Alexander novels "one of this century's most unexpectedly original works of art."

Six hundred gay men and lesbians form a human chain, hand in hand, across the George Washington Bridge in New York City, to protest for gay rights.

May 19   An officially sanctioned gay student dance at Princeton University draws three hundred participants.

May 21   Charles Ludlam wins an Obie Award—one of *The Village Voice*'s tributes to distinguished Off Broadway and Off Off Broadway theater—for his drag performance in the title role of *Camille*, a camp reworking of the Dumas novel by Ludlam's Ridiculous Theatrical Company. Says *The New York Times* of Ludlam's performance: "This is no facile female impersonation. . . . Carefully he skirts camp, varying his pose from a tremulous fragility to a Tallulah assertiveness. . . . Once again, poor Camille dies, but this time we laugh."

   Camille goes on to become the cornerstone of Ludlam's repertoire, a series of increasingly hilarious parodies, including *The Mystery of Irma Vep* and *Der Ring Gott Farblonjet*, the latter an epic send-up of Wagnerian opera. "I don't want to be laughed with," says Ludlam. "I want to be laughed *at*."

June 9   Bette Midler's "Boogie Woogie Bugle Boy" enters the *Billboard* Top 40, where it stays for eleven weeks.

June 10   *The New York Times* reports on the sudden soaring popularity of the drug methaqualone ("Quaaludes"), especially among

college students, the disco set, and those who insist it has aphro-
disiac qualities. "Quaalude is the real glamour drug of the year,"
says one narcotics expert. According to its fans, the drug induces
a dreamy, sensuous feeling of relaxation; others report that it merely
puts them to sleep.

June 11   Haworth Press announces plans to publish the *Journal of
Homosexuality*, an academic quarterly devoted to scholarly research
on the subject. The first issue—featuring articles on gender identity, transsexualism, and public attitudes toward homosexuality, as
well as a review of the 1815 *Africaine* courts-martial, in which four
British seamen were hanged for "buggery"—premieres a year later,
in the fall of 1974.

June 14   *The Rocky Horror Picture Show* (originally titled "They
Came from Denton High"), a campy stage musical spoof of trashy
horror films, opens at London's experimental Theatre Upstairs,
where it becomes such a hit that it soon has to be moved to a theater
with a seating capacity eight times larger.

June 23   In the wake of a recent Supreme Court decision giving
individual communities the power to prosecute creators and dis-
tributors of material offensive to local standards—even when the
rest of the country may not find the material offensive at all—law
enforcement officials in New Jersey stage a massive weekend raid
confiscating six allegedly obscene movies, including Andy Warhol's
Flesh and *Lonesome Cowboys*, from local theaters. "We don't feel these
types of films are proper," says a local official.
　　One film producer labels the court's decision—which could
force publishers, writers, filmmakers, songwriters, and others to
fight legal battles in individual communities all over the country—
"totally insane."

July 3   David Bowie announces he is retiring.

July 5   Shelley Winters plays a lesbian mobster, "Mommy," in the
blaxploitation crime drama *Cleopatra Jones*.

July 6 Infuriated and disgusted by "all those young punks who have been beating up" gay men in San Francisco (and equally angered by police indifference to such attacks), a gay Pentecostal Evangelist, the Rev. Ray Broshears, founds the so-called Lavender Panthers, a group of street vigilantes who patrol the city's gay meeting areas to ward off potential attacks from "fag-bashers." Shortly after their founding, the Panthers also begin holding classes in self-defense skills for gay men. "Middle America has always had a little tinge of homophobia," Broshears tells *Time* magazine. "But I've had it up to here. All this queer-bashing has simply got to stop."

August 8 The American Bar Association passes a resolution urging the repeal of state laws prohibiting homosexual acts between consenting adults. The association refrains, however, from going so far as to urge civil rights protection for gay men and lesbians.

August 9 New York City Police Commissioner Donald Cawley issues a citywide directive admonishing police officers about using "derogatory" expressions when addressing or referring to homosexuals. He urges them instead to begin using the terms *gay* and *homosexual* whenever possible.

August 27 "I, for one, have become a big fan of homosexuals. I've become a fag moll really. There's nothing more fun than fags."

—*Model turned actress* MARISA BERENSON

September 8 The normally sedate Miss America pageant becomes a focal point for national controversy when one of the contestants—twenty-two-year-old opera singer Michelle Annette Cote (Miss New Hampshire)—is quoted in the press as having voiced her support for both women's and gay liberation. Her remarks so infuriate one of her official sponsors, conservative New Hampshire publisher William Loeb, that he runs a front-page editorial denouncing her in *The Manchester Union Leader* and withdraws his financial support. (The crown, as it turns out, goes to Miss Colorado.)

The controversy follows last year's dispute, when Miss Vermont publicly voiced her approval of premarital sex and said she vehemently opposed Richard Nixon's policies in Southeast Asia.

September 18 Businessmen on New York's West 44th Street complain about a movie theater—right next to Sardi's restaurant —that has recently started showing X-rated gay porn films. "There's a certain class, a certain atmosphere, a certain quality to our street," says the owner of Sardi's. "We want to maintain our distinctive atmosphere." Broadway producer Alexander Cohen is more direct: "We will drive the vermin away," he tells reporters.

September 20 In what has been hyped for months as The Battle of the Sexes, Wimbledon champion Billie Jean King crushes self-confessed "male chauvinist" Bobby Riggs 6–4, 6–3, 6–3 at the Houston Astrodome. The match arose from Riggs's public assertions that female athletes lack the strength and endurance of men and that no female tennis player could beat him. The game—which results in lucrative payoffs for both players—winds up being more spectacle than sporting event: King arrives at courtside on an ornate gold litter carried by five muscular men in togas, while Riggs makes his entrance in a golden rickshaw pulled by six big-breasted women nicknamed "Bobby's Bosom Buddies."

Commenting on the frenzied, circus-like atmosphere surrounding the game, *The New York Times* notes that, "Perhaps the calmest person in the house throughout the match was a twenty-five-year-old pale, willowy blonde, a former hairdresser from Beverly Hills, Calif. She sat on the sidelines in a flowered halter dress next to Billie Jean, when the player rested. She was Marilyn Barnett, Mrs. King's secretary, who earlier in the day had said that she had 'good vibrations' [about the match]."

September 28 Gay poet W. H. Auden dies, at the age of sixty-six, in Vienna.

October 1   *In Touch*, a Los Angeles-based gay "slick" magazine featuring "tasteful" black-and-white centerfolds of nude men (but no erections allowed), makes its debut on the nation's magazine racks.

Hoping to cash in on the burgeoning "beefcake" craze in America, *Penthouse* magazine unveils its own soft-core magazine for straight women, *Viva*. Although *Viva* tries hard to outclass its competition—thicker paper, more artistic photography, fewer "How Your Horoscope Can Affect Your Love Life" articles—the magazine is crippled by its late entry in the market and eventually folds, leaving *Playgirl* to dominate the field.

October 2   Former New York City health administrator Dr. Howard J. Brown publicly acknowledges his homosexuality. "I know of homosexual priests, clergymen, dentists, politicians," says Brown. "When I served in Mayor Lindsay's cabinet . . . there were other homosexual Commissioners known to me. . . . You get to a point where you want to leave a legacy—in a sense this can help free the generation that comes after us from the dreadful agony of secrecy, the constant need to hide."

A short time later, Brown announces the formation of a new gay civil rights group, the National Gay Task Force, of which he will be a director.

"Gay liberation has become a nine-to-five job—there's no other way to do it."
—RONALD GOLD, *communications director of the newly formed National Gay Task Force, 1973*

November 5   The U.S. Supreme Court upholds the constitutionality of Florida's sodomy laws.

Republican Party henchman Donald Segretti is sentenced to six months in prison for having circulated, as part of the Nixon re-election campaign, bogus letters (written on Edmund Muskie's stationery) that accused Democratic presidential candidate Henry "Scoop" Jackson of having twice been arrested for committing homosexual acts.

December 10   Australian novelist Patrick White, sixty-one, is awarded this year's Nobel Prize for Literature. "I see myself not so much a homosexual," says White, who is gay, "as a mind possessed by the spirit of man or woman according to actual situations or the characters I become in my writing. Ambivalence has given me insights into human nature, denied, I believe, to those who are unequivocally male."

December 11   Having first gained access to the studio by posing as a broadcast journalism student, gay activist Mark Allan Segal interrupts a live broadcast of the *CBS Evening News with Walter Cronkite* and holds up a sign, "Gays Protest CBS Prejudice," for the cameras. He begins to read a statement demanding more balanced coverage of gay men and lesbians before four technicians wrestle him to the ground and drag him away. Segal, who has previously interrupted broadcasts on other networks, says he was outraged at a host of recent biased and pejorative stories about homosexuals on CBS.

Ironically, several years later, he reveals that Walter Cronkite was in sympathy with his aims. "We've been good friends ever since," says Segal. "He's a wonderful, understanding man."

December 15   Declaring that "by itself, homosexuality does not meet the criteria for being a psychiatric disorder," the governing board of the American Psychiatric Association votes to recommend that homosexuality no longer be classified as a mental illness. Instead, only people who are dysfunctionally distressed by their homosexuality will be classified as having a "sexual orientation disturbance."

Four months later, the APA's full membership votes to approve the recommendation, 58 percent to 42 percent.

December 20 For the second time in two years, the New York City Council rejects a proposed gay rights ordinance for the city.

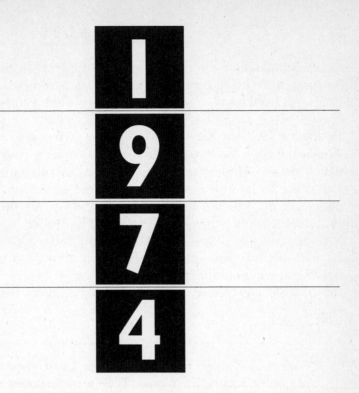

January 7 An eighteen-year-old Arkansas youth sentenced to die in the electric chair for his part in the murder of a farmer who he said had made homosexual advances to him is given a reduced sentence of nine years in prison with the possibility of parole after only two and a half years. "You are young and life is not over for you if you make a contribution," says the presiding judge, who found the original sentence too extreme. "Good luck."

January 15 *After Dark* publisher Jean Gordon issues new editorial guidelines prohibiting the use of the word "gay" in any advertising copy submitted to the magazine.

January 23 Two Denver men are arrested by undercover vice officers and charged with "lewd fondling in public" after one gives the other a quick kiss on the cheek while exiting the dance floor of a local gay bar. Later, a jury takes only ten minutes to find the couple not guilty. "Someone should be brought to task for this case," complains one of the jurors to the press. "I think the defendants were being harassed by the police. I don't believe a gay bar is that public a place, and even if they were kissing—so what?"

February 19　*The Pat Collins Show*—an A.M. program on New York's WCBS-TV—broadcasts live this morning from the Continental Baths. "How would you—or I—cope with a man who preferred the baths to us?" Collins breathlessly asks her viewers. In one segment, she sits by the Continental's pool and interviews proprietor Steve Ostrow—who says he'd like to see bathhouses for heterosexuals one day—while nude young men, apparently indifferent to the cameras, go splashing by. Collins also interviews a towel-clad gay grandfather for the show.

　　WCBS-TV receives only one complaint about the program.

> "When I used to go to the baths when I first came out, the baths were a cathedral to me. They were precious environments. I used to have dreams about living at the baths. I thought I'd love to stay there for a week, a month, to never come out of the place."
>
> —ANDREW HOLLERAN

March 2　Elton John's "Bennie and the Jets" begins a sixteen-week run in the nation's Top 40, where it crests at No. 1.

March 18　Sex Week—an officially sanctioned activity of the University of Alabama in Tuscaloosa—gets under way with a standing-room-only lecture by a male-to-female transsexual. Other activities for the week include a showing of Russ Meyer's X-rated *Harry, Cherry and Raquel*, lectures by porn star Linda Lovelace and *Screw* magazine publisher Al Goldstein, and the performance of a student play about homosexuality, *Boys Will Be Girls, Girls Will Be Boys*. "It's an opportunity for students to expose themselves to extremes of sexuality," says one of the student organizers of the week. Local criticism of the event is minimal.

March 21   Transvestite actor Candy Darling dies of cancer and pneumonia at the age of twenty-six.

April 2   Having inexplicably fascinated the nation for roughly six months, the fad of "streaking" reaches its apogee when gay photographer and former advertising executive Robert Opel, thirty-eight, plunges naked across the stage during a live broadcast of the Academy Awards ceremony in Los Angeles. Opel's "streak," almost certainly the most widely witnessed stunt of its kind, occurs during the most popular part of the telecast, the announcement of the award for Best Picture, thus guaranteeing him an estimated audience of more than one billion television viewers worldwide.

April 15   In the nation's bookstores this month: Patricia Nell Warren's *The Front Runner*, the moving (though some would say soap-operatic) story of coach Harlan Brown and his love affair with the beautiful but doomed Olympic track contender Billy Sive. Warren's book—which is seen by many as *the* breakthrough novel about gay love—prompts one reviewer to write, "It still seems jarring that a woman could have gotten so deeply, so sharply, so movingly into the gay male psyche." To which Warren (an editor at *Reader's Digest* and a long-distance runner herself) responds: "Is it such a big deal for a woman to write about gay men? I don't honestly think so. These reactions, to me, are simply proof that gay men have been made to feel so alienated from society that they are convinced no one can understand them. Yet from my point of view, there's nothing they experience that falls outside the realm of the human and the understandable."

Although the novel seems increasingly dated with each passing year after its publication, it eventually sells more than three hundred thousand copies. Warren's subsequent efforts—*The Fancy Dancer* and *The Beauty Queen* (the latter a *roman à clef* about an Anita Bryant-like antigay crusader)—do not fare nearly as well with critics or the book-buying public.

Also in the nation's bookstores: Rita Mae Brown's *Rubyfruit Jungle*, the rollicking confessions of lesbian Molly Bolt, described by *Ms.* magazine as "a female Huck Finn." Originally published by a small feminist press in Vermont, the book proves so popular that Bantam buys the rights and brings out a mass-market paperback edition, which becomes a best-seller.

April 18 Conservative columnist William Safire endorses gay rights legislation. "When we fail to give [homosexual men and women] the equal protection of the law," says Safire (who counts among his closest friends gay attorney Roy Cohn), "then it is the law that is 'queer.'" Safire acknowledges, however, that he still believes homosexuality is abnormal and immoral.

May 1 Studio One opens in Hollywood. The labyrinthine establishment, one of the biggest of its kind (it has four bars, a dinner theater, a jewelry concession, and a game room), quickly establishes itself as L.A.'s premier gay nightclub, the disco to end all discos, drawing such celebrity regulars as Richard Chamberlain, Bette Midler, Elton John, and Charles Nelson Reilly, and featuring a seemingly endless dance floor that is packed on weekends with shirtless boys bumping and sweating (and snorting amyl nitrite) to the likes of George McCrae's "Rock Your Baby" and Van McCoy's disco anthem, "The Hustle." It also achieves minor renown as perhaps the only gay bar in the world in which Nancy Reagan has ever been photographed, when she attends a celebrity tribute there to film director Joshua Logan.

Less than a week after a military coup overthrew the forty-two-year dictatorship of Premier Antonio de Oliveira Salazar and his followers, gay activists march for the first time in Portugal, demanding an end to the country's sodomy laws and a repeal of all other statutes that discriminate against gay men and lesbians.

May 13 Mary Quant Cosmetics announces it is now actively marketing makeup (including eyeshadow, mascara, and lipstick) for men. "Let's face it," says the president of the company, "plenty of men are already wearing makeup. . . . They might as well buy ours."

May 14 The first federal gay civil rights bill, extending antidiscrimination protection to gay men and lesbians under the 1964 Civil Rights Act, is introduced in Congress. Among the bill's initial sponsors are New York Congresswoman Bella Abzug and Congressman Edward Koch.

May 23 In the heated atmosphere following the defeat of yet another gay rights ordinance by the New York City Council, *Village Voice* columnist Arthur Bell kicks conservative councilman Matthew Troy (who opposed the bill) in the shin. Troy retaliates by slapping Bell in the face.

 The bill's defeat sparks a sit-in at St. Patrick's Cathedral.

May 24 *The New York Times* reports that Soviet film director Sergei Paradzhanov—whose most famous work is the 1964 film *Shadows of Forgotten Ancestors*—has been sentenced to six years in a labor camp after being convicted in Kiev on charges of having committed homosexual acts.

 The vehemently conservative (and usually anti-Soviet) U.S. publisher William Loeb publicly expresses his approval of the action in an editorial in *The Manchester Union Leader*. "This is one of the reasons why the Soviet Union is presently stronger than the United States," argues Loeb. "The Soviets understand that permissiveness in regards to homosexuality has always resulted in the downfall of a nation."

May 27 In light of recent public revelations by Mick Jagger, Joan Baez, Maria Schneider, and others, *Time* and *Newsweek* each do articles, within two weeks of one another, on "Bisexual Chic."

June 1 Insiders at *Playgirl* magazine grudgingly acknowledge that nearly 20 percent of the magazine's readership is male—although circulation audits show the figure is probably closer to 40 percent.

The first Lambda Rising Bookstore, c. 1976. PHOTO COURTESY DEACON MACCUBBIN

June 5   A poll in *The Advocate* finds that 60 percent of its readers think that park queens and men who cruise public bathrooms are "a disgrace and discredit to gays" and are holding back progress toward gay civil rights.

> "Most guys are better cocksuckers than women. Nine out of ten blowjobs in a porno theater are superior, 'cause the guys are really into it."
>
> —Screw *magazine publisher (and avowed heterosexual)*
> AL GOLDSTEIN, *1974*

June 8   The Lambda Rising Bookstore opens its doors in Washington, D.C., with a stock of three hundred titles and average sales of about $25 a day. By 1987, it has opened a second store, established a thriving mail-order business, offers more than twenty thousand titles, and has annual sales of $1.5 million. "We really didn't expect it to make any money," says owner Deacon Maccubbin in retrospect.

June 16 A fistfight breaks out at a Philadelphia playhouse when ten gay activists interrupt a lecture by Dr. David Reuben and denounce him as "a criminal" for his views on male homosexuality. One policeman and a protester are injured in the melee.

June 30 The fifth-annual Christopher Street Liberation Day Parade in New York City draws the largest crowd ever: an estimated forty-three thousand people, compared to nineteen thousand the previous year.

July 6 At the annual Polk Street Fair in San Francisco, a gay man is arrested for "assaulting a police officer with a tambourine."

July 11 After a local TV news show runs an exposé on nude sunbathing at Venice Beach, the Los Angeles City Council votes 12 to 1 to institute a total ban on public nudity in the city. "I've never received more concern on any one issue than this one," says one councilman, who has been deluged with mail urging him to vote in favor of the ban. "When an issue like murder comes up, I get two cards."

July 31 The Centers for Disease Control estimate that gay or bisexual men account for as much as one-third of the syphilis cases in the U.S.

September 27 Seven major advertisers—including Bayer Aspirin, Listerine, Gallo Wine, and Ralston Purina—yank their ads from a forthcoming episode of *Marcus Welby, M.D.*, "The Outrage," which deals with a fourteen-year-old boy who is raped by his male science teacher. The boycott comes in response to lobbying by gay activists, who condemned the show for fostering "a false and negative stereotype of homosexuals" as child molesters.

October 1 "Taboo? You don't know the half of it. For years we've been trying to break down the ridiculous puritan ethic that's kept this piece of apparel on the last page of catalogs and in the classified section of commercial publications, and what happens every time? We submit an ad to a magazine like *Sports Illustrated*, everybody's outraged, and, wham!, back come the letters and memos calling us irresponsible businessmen, sensationalists, perverts, you name it. All just over a completely respectable ad for an athletic supporter."
—JOHN O'NEILL, *advertising manager for Bike Athletic Products, manufacturers of one of the nation's most popular jockstraps*

October 15 The Gay Activists Alliance "Firehouse" is destroyed by arson.

October 18 Benjamin Britten's opera *Death in Venice* has its U.S. premiere at the Metropolitan Opera, with Britten's lover, tenor Peter Pears, in the lead role. "Honestly, you are the greatest artist that ever was," says Britten, in a letter to Pears just before the debut. "What have I done to deserve such an artist and man to write for?" Responds Pears: "I am here as your mouthpiece and I live in your music. . . . I love you."

October 30 Principal shooting begins on a film version of *The Rocky Horror Picture Show*, with Tim Curry slated to play Dr. Frank-N-Furter ("a sweet transvestite from transsexual Transylvania"), and costarring Susan Sarandon and Barry Bostwick.

October 31 The Cycle Sluts—a group of fourteen men sporting lingerie, heavy makeup, and beehive hairdos, while maintaining their beards, mustaches, hairy chests, and leather jackets—premiere their act in Los Angeles. The group is only the latest to take advantage of the rising popularity in "gender-fuck."

November 5 Elaine Noble is elected to the Massachusetts state legislature, becoming the first openly lesbian state representative in U.S. history.

First openly lesbian state representative in U.S. history, Elaine Noble, elected November 5, 1974. THE PRIDE INSTITUTE

November 18 *The New Yorker* publishes its first gay-themed short story, "Minor Heroism," by Southern writer Allan Gurganus.

December 1 With the publication of Charles Gaines and George Butler's *Pumping Iron*—a photo-book devoted to the careers and rivalries of international bodybuilders (chief among them Austrian title-holder Arnold Schwarzenegger)—and the release of a movie of the same name three years later, bodybuilding starts on the road to respectability again, advancing within a few short years to the status of a nationwide craze. Eventually, weightlifting sets and home bodybuilding gyms become as much an inventory staple of stores like Sears and Montgomery Ward as toolboxes and television sets, with new muscle-building gadgets (some of them almost science-fictional in design, and often with suggestive names like "Butt Attack" and "The Butt Buster") appearing on the market every month. For many people, a trip to the local magazine stand becomes a flashback to the Fifties, with such titles as *Muscle Mania* and *Men's Health* replacing the *Demi-Gods* and *Physique Pictorials* of yesteryear.

Schwarzenegger himself—hulking, conservative, barely articulate, and with a face strangely suggestive of an android—goes on to epitomize the obsessions of an entire beefcake-crazed decade, as he eventually becomes one of the major international movie stars of the 1980s.

December 4 Two Baptist ministers in New Milford, Connecticut, threaten to file suit against city officials after the local school board makes Home Economics a required course for sixth-grade boys. "By having a young boy cook or sew, wearing aprons, we're pushing a boy into homosexuality," complains one of the ministers. "It's contrary to what the home and the Bible have stood for."

"My son doesn't want the course," says the other minister, "and I don't want him to be a sissy."

December 7 Gloria Gaynor's "Never Can Say Goodbye" begins a ten-week stay in the *Billboard* Top 40.

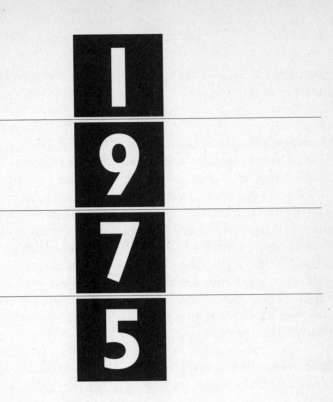

January 4 The Internal Revenue Service rejects a joint tax return filed by two Minneapolis gay lovers.

January 7 Before the county attorney can discover what's happened and file an injunction against them, two gay men in Phoenix, Arizona, legally obtain a marriage license and are wed in a ceremony at the local Church of Christian Fellowship. The wedding causes an uproar, which turns violent after local newspapers repeatedly —and rather pointedly—publish the men's address: the two are subjected to daily protest demonstrations outside their living-room window and are finally forced to move after a man wielding a butcher knife breaks into their apartment and threatens to kill them. A Superior Court judge, citing the Bible, later voids the marriage.

January 10 The Chicago Board of Education approves a plan that for the first time would allow the city's public school teachers to answer students' questions about homosexuality.

January 15   Wakefield Poole's *Moving!*—"Featuring the steel ball-bearing scene you have heard so much about!!"—opens in Los Angeles.

January 20   Terrence McNally's comedy *The Ritz* opens in New York City. Originally titled *The Tubs*, the play was first performed at the Yale University Repertory Theater during the 1973–1974 season. At the time, it was about a closeted gay garbageman tracked down to a bathhouse by his distraught relatives, including his anxious wife and his virulently homophobic brother-in-law. However, before the New York opening, McNally altered the plot and changed the main character into a *heterosexual* businessman who hides in a gay bathhouse to escape his murderous, Mafioso brother-in-law. The new version garners generally positive reviews. "I laughed a lot, and who should ask for anything more?" writes Clive Barnes, in *The New York Times*.

Cast member Rita Moreno goes on to win a Tony Award for her memorable performance as Googie Gomez, a less-than-accomplished entertainer hoping to get her big break singing at the baths.

January 24   *Hot l Baltimore*, a controversial new ABC sitcom produced by television innovator Norman Lear and loosely based on Lanford Wilson's hit play, debuts on Friday nights. The plot—about a once-posh, now-seedy hotel full of generally sympathetic eccentrics—includes a South American prostitute, a latent lesbian, and two gay male characters, middle-aged lovers Gordon and George.

It lasts only five months.

January 29

QUICK FINANCIAL AID NEEDED FOR Gay male for college & new clothes. Would be willing to do anything reasonable to earn it. All proceeds would be greatly appreciated.

AMPUTEE WANTED, PHILA. PA AREA Leg above knee, white, for brotherly love. Eastern U.S.

CUM ON YOUR CARPET? Spill a drink, etc.? Call Sam or Wayne for professional rug & upholstery cleaning. Insured, bonded. Bank Americard accepted.
NO TRACE CARPET CLEANERS

Mgmt., PR or similar job wanted by hung male. Have BA, refs & res. Need $800 + /mo.

PLEASE HELP ME GET FACE SURGERY I need plastic surgery very badly. I'm 23 years old and was good-looking until car accident. Need funds badly to pay for this three-part surgery. Just can't live like this. My last ad brought in $50. Nose surgery alone is $950 plus hospital. I beg for your help and letters. All letters will be answered. God bless all my brothers. Mail to . . .
—*Selection of personal ads from the current* Advocate

January 31 The American Association for the Advancement of Science passes a resolution deploring discrimination in "any form" against gay men and lesbians, and notes that "homosexuals, transvestites, transsexuals . . . may be valued members of their professions, capable of making great contributions to the progress of science and to the national welfare. . . . Discrimination constitutes a loss to science and an injustice to these individuals."

February 1 In the nation's bookstores this month: composer Ned Rorem's *The Final Diary*. A follow-up to his previous, critically acclaimed Paris and New York diaries, Rorem's latest volume of self-revelation is just as full of penetrating insights on culture, music, and high society, and just as candid about homosexuality as its predecessors—perhaps *too* candid, as some reviewers begin to complain about his enumeration of orgasms and an entry in which Rorem, sitting alone in New York City on a Saturday night, moans, "Everybody's fucking but me." The book, as it turns out, is mis-

American composer Ned Rorem: extravagantly talented, gay—and sometimes very frustrated. JACK MITCHELL

named, since Rorem publishes yet another volume three years later, *An Absolute Gift: A New Diary*, and another volume after that, *Nantucket Diaries*, in 1988.

February 12   A Los Angeles entertainment columnist reports that director Ken Russell is collaborating with Elton John on a rock-opera film version of Shakespeare's *Hamlet*, with David Bowie set to play Ophelia.

Nothing comes of the venture.

———

"Oh, honey, I'd be so happy if you turned nelly. Queers are just better. I'd be so proud if you was a fag and had a nice beautician boyfriend. I'd never have to worry. I worry you'll work in an office, have children, celebrate wedding anniversaries. The world of a heterosexual is a sick and boring life!"

—*"Aunt Ida" imploring her nephew "Gator" to give up his heterosexuality in the new film* Female Trouble *from Baltimore auteur John Waters, whose previous effort,* Pink Flamingos, *has become an unexpected underground classic. "For those with a predilection for cruel comedies," says one critic, of* Female Trouble, *"this is must-viewing with some of the sickest one-liners in underground film history."*

March 11 The Madison, Wisconsin, city council votes unanimously to extend civil rights protection to gay men and lesbians.

March 26 After the local district attorney's office rules there are no county laws preventing two people of the same sex from getting married, a county clerk in Boulder, Colorado, issues a marriage license to two gay men. Over the next month, she issues five more licenses to same-sex couples. "I don't profess to be knowledgeable about homosexuality or even understand it," says the clerk, Clela Rorex. "But it's not my business why people get married. No minority should be discriminated against."

Rorex herself soon becomes the object of national attention and begins receiving death threats and harassing phone calls, including one from a caller who screams, "I hope you suffer, because God doesn't like this!" One disgruntled cowboy tries to protest the gay marriages by applying for a license to wed his favorite horse, an eight-year-old mare; Rorex rejects the application on the grounds that the horse is underage.

April 1 *Mandate*—the gay "Magazine of Entertainment and Eros"—makes its debut. Although the magazine initially bears more than a passing resemblance to its closeted cousin *After Dark*, it features explicit male nudes and entertainment features with an openly gay slant—all put together under the watchful eye of editor John Devere (whose real name is John Dever, but who has added an extra "e" to his name somewhere along the line), a former professor of comparative literature. At its peak, *Mandate* has a circulation of about 110,000.

April 3 New Mexico becomes the tenth state to repeal its sodomy laws.

April 12 The Arizona State House of Representatives votes 37 to 3 to pass an "emergency measure" specifically banning same-sex marriages.

Two weeks later, the Colorado Attorney General also rules that gay and lesbian marriages are illegal and orders Clela Rorex to stop issuing licenses to same-sex couples who apply for them.

April 30 Now showing at a porn theater near you: Fred Halsted's *Sextool*, a kaleidoscopic and often surreal porn-fest of fist-fucking, S&M, raunchy fellatio, nipple-piercing, male rape, bondage, and hustler sex, all presented in a fast-paced, quick-edit style that defies the tradition of most previous (visually lethargic) gay porn films. Says one magazine, "The film could single-handedly reverse the annual spring slump in raincoat sales." *Variety* dubs Halsted "the Ken Russell of S&M homoerotica."

A short time later, Halsted issues a press statement announcing his marriage to the film's young costar, Joey Yale. "In our opinion," says the press release, "we are entering into the status of HALSTED CO-PERSONS. I am Fred Halsted. Joseph Yale will be Joseph Halsted. He is not my wife and I am not his husband, but we will both be HALSTED CO-PERSONS."

May 1 Recently published reports confirm that Paul Newman is running into serious financial difficulties with his plan to direct and star in a film version of *The Front Runner*. Meanwhile, there is intense speculation over who will play the role of Billy Sive—if and when the film is ever made—with everyone from Richard Thomas to Robert Redford mentioned in the press as a possibility.

Newman eventually lets his option on the book drop. It is briefly picked up by producer-director Frank Perry (*The Swimmer*, *Diary of a Mad Housewife*), who also eventually abandons plans to film the book.

May 12 California repeals its 103-year-old sodomy laws.

Former governor Ronald Reagan tells *Christianity Today* he would have vetoed the repeal if he had still been in office. "I have always believed that the body of man-made law must be founded

upon the higher natural law," says Reagan. "You can make im-
morality legal but you cannot make it moral."

"We're having trouble enough convincing our men that they
should accept women as equals. Can you imagine what it would
do to morale if we gave them a queer as their partner?"
—*Spokesman for the Los Angeles Police Department, calling for a reinstatement
of California's sodomy laws, 1975*

May 15 Operators of "The Liberace Tour"—a recently begun
ninety-minute tour of Liberace's thirty-room Hollywood mansion,
including a peek at the star's basement and closets, as well as a
fifteen-minute film in which he shares some of his fondest recol-
lections and favorite moments—report that initial business is
"brisk."

May 19 Gay porn phenomenon "Jack Wrangler" is born when a
sometimes struggling twenty-eight-year-old actor, Jack Stillman,
steps onstage between porn films at the Paris Theater in Los Angeles
and performs a live striptease in Western drag. The son of an
established show business family (his father was one of the producers of *Bonanza*), Stillman takes the *nom de porn* "Wrangler" from
the famous brand of cowboy jeans. "I wanted *big* responses from
people," he says later. "I didn't want people to just like me—I
wanted them to *lust* after me!" It is, many commentators note, a
triumph of style over substance: Wrangler has neither the typically
hunky body of a gay porn idol (in fact, one critic calls him
"scrawny") nor the baby-faced, barely-out-of-their-teens looks usually required of such performers. Still, he stars in his first gay porn
film—*Ranch Dudes*, a fifteen-minute "loop" featuring him masturbating in a corral—a short time after his Paris Theater debut, and
goes on to become a ubiquitous presence throughout the Seventies
in gay magazines, films, newspapers, and advertising.

May 21 *A Chorus Line*—conceived, directed, and choreographed by Michael Bennett—opens at the Public Theater in New York City. It is an immediate hit, and goes on to become the longest-running Broadway show in history, with 6,137 performances by August 1990.

May 23 "As you no doubt expected, I am declining your invitation to participate in the celebration of 'GAY PRIDE WEEK.' While I support your organization's constitutional right to express your feelings on the subject of homosexuality, I am obviously not in sympathy with your views on the subject. I would much rather celebrate 'GAY CONVERSION WEEK,' which I will gladly sponsor when the medical practitioners in this country find a way to convert gays to heterosexuals. Very truly yours . . ."
—*Letter from L.A.'s notoriously homophobic police chief*, ED DAVIS, *to organizers of Hollywood's Gay Pride Week*

June 1 *Drummer*, the first gay "slick" devoted to S&M erotica and the interests of the gay leather community, makes its debut. The premiere issue—forty pages long, and edited by a straight woman, Jeanne Barney—features articles on prison life and various gay biker clubs, as well as an excerpt from the novella *My Brother, My Slave*.

June 4 Accu-Jac II, the latest advance in home masturbation technology, is unveiled by JacMasters of Los Angeles. Unlike the company's two previous, popular Accu-Jacs, this most recent model "will *fornicate* you *as well as* masturbate you, and has a speed control, depth control, suction and stroke length control!" Price for all this mechanical bliss: $550.

June 7 Due to the ambiguous wording in a recently passed rape penalties bill, state legislators in New Hampshire inadvertently repeal the state's laws against homosexual acts, and don't even realize they have done so until local gay publications start boasting about it. "Gays throughout the nation may well win their freedom through the fault and stupidity of straights," writes one commentator. "It would appear that nearly everyone involved was asleep at the switch," laments the ultraconservative *Manchester Union Leader*, in its call for new, even tougher antisodomy laws.

The repeal is allowed to stand.

June 18   Melina Mercouri and Alexis Smith portray lesbian lovers in the new film *Once Is Not Enough*, based on Jacqueline Susann's best-selling novel.

June 19   The American Medical Association passes a resolution urging the repeal of all state laws prohibiting homosexual acts between consenting adults.

July 1   *Blueboy* magazine—"The National Magazine About Men"—makes its first appearance on magazine stands across the country, and quickly establishes itself at the forefront of a growing pack of increasingly explicit gay magazines combining nudes and erotic fiction with articles on dating, politics, and gay culture. The magazine's publisher is Donald Embinder, a former advertising representative for *After Dark*.

July 3   The U.S. Civil Service Commission rules that homosexual applicants will no longer be automatically disqualified from federal employment, but will now be considered on a case-by-case basis.

July 15   Santa Cruz County becomes the first county in the United States to prohibit job discrimination against gay people.

July 23   Evangelist Billy Graham publicly endorses ordaining male homosexuals as ministers, though he hedges on the question of whether women should enjoy the same right.

August 13   With more than thirteen hundred discos from coast to coast (many of them having opened in the last year), and dance hits such as Shirley and Company's "Shame, Shame, Shame" firmly entrenched in the nation's Top 40, *The Advocate* declares 1975 "The Year of the Disco."

August 15   In the nation's bookstores this month: *Consenting Adult* by Laura Hobson, the groundbreaking mainstream novel about a young gay man's coming out as seen through the eyes of his trying-to-be-understanding mother. Although the book is instantly attacked by some gay activists (who complain that it never deals rigorously enough with the issues of homophobia and gay liberation), it eventually becomes a staple in the coming-out process for thousands of young gay men, who buy it for their parents either as a prelude or an adjunct to the Big Revelation.

August 27   "At a time when the straight world shows signs of drifting towards androgyny, the gay world seems to be moving towards strict sexual identity. . . . Gay men are discovering their manhood."
—Human Behavior *magazine, on the growing gay male obsessions with leather, button-fly Levi's, flannel shirts, mustaches, beer, and weightlifting*

September 8   *Time* magazine features gay Air Force sergeant Leonard Matlovich—who is in the midst of a legal battle to be reinstated in the armed forces—on this week's cover, with the bold headline: " 'I AM A HOMOSEXUAL': The Gay Drive for Acceptance." The article thrusts Matlovich into the limelight (later NBC will make a made-for-TV movie about him), and he becomes an instant gay media hero, eventually running (albeit, unsuccessfully) for political office in San Francisco.

September 11   The New York City Council once again defeats a gay rights ordinance.

September 29   An episode of *All in the Family* features Archie Bunker using mouth-to-mouth resuscitation to save the life of a woman—only to learn that "she" is actually a "he" in drag.

October 1   In the nation's bookstores this month: *Bless This Food: The Anita Bryant Family Cookbook*. "Anita Bryant, famous singer, wife, mother and Christian, shares the joys of her own family togetherness and faith in this wondrous personal compendium of spiritual wisdom, down-to-earth everyday experiences and heavenly recipes. Much more than a cookbook, this is the story of a family devoted to Christ."

Also in bookstores: C. A. Tripp's *The Homosexual Matrix*, a study of the biological, social, and political implications of homosexuality, concluding with the observation that sexual diversity enriches both the individual and the broader needs of society, and that trying to eliminate homosexuality from society would be comparable to reaching "into some giant computer nobody understands and . . . yanking out transistors." One critic applauds it as "the second great contemporary landmark [after the Kinsey reports] in the study of homosexuality."

October 8 "I was fighting for gay rights before it became fashionable. Way back in the '20s, in New York, I got a hold of the police and started explaining to them that gay boys are females in male bodies. That's the yogi philosophy—take it or leave it. The police were really rough on homosexuals then. I said, 'Now look fellas, when you're hitting one of them, just remember, you're hitting a woman.' That straightened them out. They stopped beating up the gay boys."
—MAE WEST, *conveniently forgetting that "back in the '20s" she also referred to homosexuality as a "cancer" and to homosexuals themselves as "perverts," and once acknowledged she put gay characters in her plays to warn the public about homosexuality's "effects upon the children recruited to it in their innocence."*

October 16 Deputy Mayor of Los Angeles Maurice Weiner is arrested during a vice-squad raid on a gay porn theater in Hollywood. He later resigns from office after being convicted of having groped an undercover police officer at the theater.

October 17 *The San Francisco Examiner* reports that kidnapped newspaper heiress Patty Hearst—abducted on February 5, 1974, and only recently captured by the FBI—apparently participated in lesbian and group sex acts during her sojourn with the Symbionese Liberation Army.

October 23   Elton John becomes the first performer to play L.A.'s Dodger Stadium since the Beatles were there in 1966. He makes his appearance in a heavily sequined, skintight, red-white-and-blue Dodgers uniform.

October 25   Silver Convention's dance single "Fly, Robin, Fly" begins a thirteen-week climb up the nation's Top 40, where it will crest for three weeks at No. 1. A week later, the semi-raunchy dance single "That's the Way (I Like It)"—by K.C. & The Sunshine Band—also begins a thirteen-week run in the *Billboard* Top 40.

November 1   In the nation's bookstores this month: Tennessee Williams's *Memoirs*, in which America's foremost playwright tells all, including:

■ the details of his fourteen-year, often agonizing love affair with Frankie Merlo
■ the two times he was raped in his life, once by a young beach boy and once by a Mexican ("I had a very attractive ass and people kept wanting to *fuck* me that way")
■ the details of his tumultuous relationship with his mother (the model for Amanda Wingfield in *The Glass Menagerie*), and the nightmare of his sister Rose's insanity and subsequent lobotomy
■ how he used to cruise Times Square during World War II and pick up GI's and take them back to the local "Y" for sex

Although *The New York Times Book Review* calls it "a raw display of private life," several other critics suggest that while the homosexuality of America's greatest playwright has been common knowledge for years, it is somehow unseemly for him to talk about it in public.

November 2   After a private dinner at which he emphatically complains to friends about the growing epidemic of violence in the city, Italian film director Pier Paolo Pasolini drives to the outskirts of Rome, where he picks up a seventeen-year-old boy who—after an argument over money—first bludgeons the director with a nail-studded two-by-four, then runs over him several times with a car. The boy is charged and later convicted of murder.

November 3 *The Wall Street Journal* runs a front-page article on the growing influence and success of *The Advocate*.

December 1 In an essay titled "Are Lesbians 'Gay'?" feminist Jill Johnston questions how much gay men and lesbians really have in common and concludes, "Considering the centrality of lesbianism to the Women's Movement it should now seem absurd to persist in associating lesbian women with the male homosexual movement. Lesbians are feminists, not homosexuals."

December 9 *The Washington Star* begins a controversial series on homosexuality in American sports. Among the revelations: "Some of the biggest names in football, including at least three starting quarterbacks in the National Football League, are homosexual or bisexual."

The series so inspires former Washington Redskins linebacker Dave Kopay that, after reading the first installment, he immediately agrees to "come out" in an interview with the series' author, Lynn Rosellini. Two days later, Kopay's public revelation of homosexuality is on every major wire service in the country.

Reader response is overwhelmingly negative. Says University of Maryland basketball coach Lefty Driesell, "It is beyond my comprehension that a responsible sports editor could stoop to such trash when there are so many good things to write about in sports. What about the kids who read this stuff?" And from Mike McCormack, head coach of the Philadelphia Eagles: "My reaction was one of sickness. I don't know first-hand of any homosexuality and I don't know where it would fit in."

Kopay later collaborates on a book about his life, *The Dave Kopay Story*, which—everyone's much-voiced disgust aside—becomes an immediate best-seller.

December 11 In an election increasingly seen as a mandate for the future course of the city, liberal Democrat George Moscone is elected Mayor of San Francisco, beating his opponent—arch-conservative John Barbagelata—by a much smaller margin than expected, a mere 4,315 votes.

December 26   "I plan to appeal the decision. I am secure in the belief that I am a good mother, despite the verdict of ten Dallasites who are uptight about homosexuality."
—MARY JO RISHER, *after a jury in Dallas takes custody of her nine-year-old son away from her because she is a lesbian. Risher subsequently loses her appeal and is ordered to pay her ex-husband $22 a week in child support.*

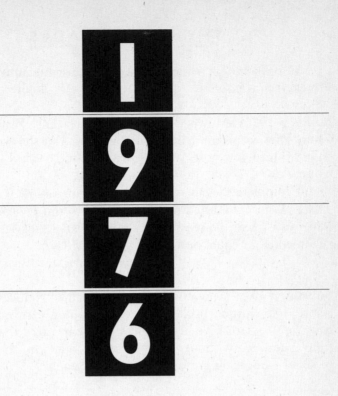

January 15 In its newly released "Declaration on Certain Questions Concerning Sexual Ethics," the Vatican:

- calls homosexuality "a serious depravity" that "can in no case be approved of"
- reviles masturbation as "a grave moral disorder" that violates New Testament teachings and signals a rejection of God
- condemns premarital sex and the growing sexual openness of society in general
- warns priests and bishops that, "It will especially be necessary to bring the faithful to understand that the church holds these principles not as old and inviolable superstitions, nor out of some Manichaean prejudice, as is often alleged, but rather because she knows with certainty that they are in complete harmony with the divine order of creation and with the spirit of Christ."

The document spurs anti-Catholic demonstrations in both Florence and Turin.

January 19 Hollywood fashion designer Earl Blackwell names Elton John to his annual list of the "Ten Worst-Dressed Women in the World."

"I am completely against arbitrary discrimination. I am and have always been committed to the civil rights and civil liberties of all Americans. I see no reason why homosexual Americans should be excluded from equal protection under the law."

—HUBERT HUMPHREY, *endorsing gay rights*

February 10 Cartoonist Garry Trudeau introduces a gay character, Andy Lippincott ("sensitive, brilliant, aware"), to his *Doonesbury* comic strip. Five newspapers refuse to carry the sequence of strips dealing with Andy's "coming out" to a romantically inclined—but soon crestfallen—Joanie Caucus.

February 12 Actor Sal Mineo, thirty-seven, is stabbed to death outside his West Hollywood apartment. Despite widespread rumors that he was the victim of "rough trade," his killer turns out to be a twenty-one-year-old drifter who apparently murdered the actor for the "fun" of it.

February 16 *Time* magazine reports that far-right, homophobic evangelist Billy James Hargis—author of the Christian best-seller *Is the School House the Proper Place to Teach Raw Sex?*—has become embroiled in a growing scandal, in which he reportedly had sexual relations with at least four male students at his ultraconservative American Christian College in Tulsa, Oklahoma. Stopping just short of suggesting that the Devil made him do it, Hargis—who is married and has four children—blames his behavior on malfunctioning "genes and chromosomes."

February 21 A Detroit jury awards more than $200,000 in damages to a man who contends he was "turned into" a homosexual by a 1975 automobile accident in which his car was rear-ended by another vehicle.

March 2   Proclaiming that "the people of Anchorage should not be forced to associate with sexual deviates," Anchorage, Alaska, mayor George Sullivan vetoes a municipal civil rights ordinance that would have extended protection in housing and employment to gay people.

"Homosexuality is so much in fashion it no longer makes news. Like a large number of men, I, too, have had homosexual experiences and I am not ashamed."

—MARLON BRANDO, *in a French magazine interview*

March 5   Campaigning for reelection in Peoria, Illinois, President Gerald Ford tells an audience of more than eight thousand university students that gay civil rights is "a new and serious problem" for which he has no "pat" answers. He adds, however, that, "I always try to be an understanding person as far as people are concerned who are different from myself."

March 7   Pier 48—an abandoned building on the Hudson River that has served for years as a favorite meeting place for gay men seeking quick, anonymous sex—is obliterated by fire.

March 12   At a campaign stop in Los Angeles, Georgia governor and Democratic presidential candidate Jimmy Carter tells an audience that, if elected, he would be willing to issue an executive order banning discrimination against gay people in housing, employment, immigration, and the military.

March 17   Italian film director Luchino Visconti dies at the age of sixty-nine.

March 25　William Carter Spann—a self-confessed heroin junkie and bisexual hustler who also happens to be Jimmy Carter's nephew—begins a three-year prison term for having robbed several San Francisco gay businesses, including the Mint and the Grubstake, at gunpoint. "I hate gay bars," Spann later tells interviewer Randy Shilts. "That's why I robbed them. People paying ninety cents a beer for friendship. It's good they caught me, because once I robbed all the gay bars, I was going to rob every pawnshop, every bail bondsman. All the people who were preying off society." In the same interview, Spann acknowledges having once managed a "puppy farm"—a stable of fourteen- to seventeen-year-old male hustlers—in Los Angeles.

March 29　By a vote of 6 to 3, the U.S. Supreme Court upholds the constitutionality of Virginia's sodomy laws.

April 1　"The great love team of the late Sixties and early Seventies is not some modern parody of Garbo and Gilbert, Gable and Lombard, or Rogers and Astaire. It is Robert Redford and Paul Newman."
—DAMON WEST, *commenting on the pairing of Redford and Newman in two of the most popular films of the last ten years,* Butch Cassidy and the Sundance Kid *and* The Sting

April 2　The owner of a New Jersey dinner theater cancels an upcoming production of *The Boys in the Band* after learning that the play is about homosexuality. "The Clam Broth House is a family restaurant," says manager Arthur Pilez, "and I do not feel that this kind of play is the type of entertainment we want."

April 3　"Go on and have your own rally. Our people want hard work. We don't want gay work. We don't want gay jobs. You have your gay jobs. You just do your own thing and stay away."
—*Presidential candidate Senator* HENRY "SCOOP" JACKSON (*D-Washington*), *responding to gay hecklers at a campaign rally in Queens, New York*

April 4   Pope Paul VI takes the unprecedented step of publicly denying recent press accusations that he is, despite his antigay utterances, a practicing homosexual himself. "Pray for our humble person," the Pope tells an audience of about twenty thousand people, from his balcony overlooking St. Peter's Square, "who has been made the target of scorn and horrible and slanderous insinuations by a certain press lacking dutiful regard for honesty and truth." Most recently, the accusations have surfaced in the Italian magazine *Tempo*, in an article by gay author Roger Peyrefitte.

April 7   Civil rights crusader and U.S. Congresswoman Barbara Jordan (D-Texas) infuriates her gay supporters when she publicly refuses to cosponsor federal gay rights legislation. "That's the very thing I can't do," Jordan tells one newspaper. "I do not feel that politically I can do that." She says she is afraid she will lose voters' support if she becomes associated with the gay cause.

   Earlier, on a radio talk show, Jordan became angry over comparisons between gay liberation and the black civil rights struggle of the Sixties. "There is no way," she said indignantly, "that I can equate discrimination on the basis of sexual preference with discrimination on the basis of skin color."

Rock star Ted Nugent acknowledges to *The Advocate* that although he remembers very vividly "getting it on" with other guys when he was ten or eleven ("I was a gay bandito"), the thought of homosexuality now "nauseates" him utterly.

April 10   More than one hundred Los Angeles police officers—armed with guns and aided by two tactical helicopters circling overhead—stage a massive raid on a gay charity "slave" auction being held at the Mark IV Baths by the city's leather community to aid the local gay and lesbian community center. Forty of the auction's participants—including, paradoxically, some of the would-be "slaves"—are arrested on charges of violating the state's "involuntary servitude" law. Later, in the face of mounting adverse publicity—including angry denunciations from U.S. Senator Alan Cranston and L.A. Mayor Tom Bradley—the district attorney's office drops charges against thirty-six of the participants, but books four of the auction's organizers on charges of "pandering" (i.e., acting as pimps).

Final estimated cost of the raid, in taxpayer dollars: $17,800.

April 17 The Lavender World's Fair—the first all-gay world's fair, featuring a "Spectacular Grandstand Concert," "Special Lesbian Guest Stars," "The World's Largest Outdoor Disco"—is scheduled to get under way at the Los Angeles County Fairgrounds. Unfortunately, the event never completely materializes ("It was just a bunch of booths selling porno equipment," says one observer), and a near-riot occurs when several thousand people, having paid $7 a ticket, show up for a concert by the Pointer Sisters, only to be told that they will not appear.

April 18 Michael Bennett's *A Chorus Line* sweeps the Tony Awards, winning nine in all, including one for Best Musical and one for Best Direction.

April 21 Carol Burnett tells an in-flight magazine, "Gay liberation . . . just may be the answer to an overpopulated world."

May 1 *Christopher Street* magazine makes its debut. The premiere issue—with contributions from Paul Goodman, Edmund White, Rita Mae Brown, and Elaine Noble—features a cover drawing of an abandoned closet.

Says publisher Charles Ortleb, of the publication's highbrow tone, "No one will ever masturbate over this magazine."

Banned from a theater near you: Roger Earl's *Born to Raise Hell*, a gritty S&M action film featuring fist-fucking, water sports, bondage, and genital torture. Advertised with such come-ons as "Not for the squeamish!" and "Banned in L.A.!," it soon acquires a legendary status among gay porn aficionados, and transforms one of its stars—cheerfully sadistic topman Val Martin—into a gay cult celebrity.

Author Armistead Maupin. "Straights can learn a lot from us gay people," he once said. "We teach straight people so many things about sexuality. Like, perhaps, not to take it quite so seriously . . . not to kill each other over it." TERRY ANDERSON

May 3 *A Chorus Line* wins the Pulitzer Prize for drama.

Also winning a Pulitzer this year: Ned Rorem, for his composition *Air Music.*

May 10 Embroiled in one of the worst British sex scandals in recent decades, Liberal Party leader Jeremy Thorpe is forced to resign from office following months of newspaper stories about his alleged homosexual involvement with a former male model, Norman Scott. Three years later, Thorpe (who adamantly denies he is a homosexual) is tried—and acquitted—on charges of having conspired to murder Scott in order to silence him about the affair.

May 14 Montreal police begin a systematic series of raids aimed at harassing and closing down local gay bars and bathhouses. The raids are part of an attempt to "clean up" the city before the opening of the summer Olympics in August.

Club Baths decides to permanently close its Montreal facility as a result of the raids.

May 21 Jimmy Carter announces that, if elected, he will support and sign a federal civil rights bill outlawing discrimination against gay men and lesbians.

May 24 Armistead Maupin's daily serial, "Tales of the City," makes its debut in *The San Francisco Chronicle*.

June 1 IS GAY LIB DEAD?
—*Question posed on the cover of this month's* Vector *magazine. (The answer, from a variety of gay activists, is a resounding "No.")*

June 10 West Virginia becomes the sixteenth state to repeal its sodomy statutes. Two weeks later, Iowa becomes the seventeenth.

June 11 Benjamin Britten is knighted by Queen Elizabeth. A year later, his lover, Peter Pears, is knighted also.

June 23 The FBI confirms that it has been keeping domestic surveillance files on *The Advocate*.

June 24 G. Harold Carswell—nominated to the U.S. Supreme Court by Richard Nixon in 1970, but later rejected by the Senate because of his views on racial segregation—is arrested for attempting to commit "an unnatural and lascivious act" with an undercover vice officer in Tallahassee, Florida. He later pleads no contest to a reduced charge and is fined $100. One newspaper calls his arrest "the latest in an endless stream of ironies left over from the Nixon era."

July 4 Foreskin aficionado Bud Berkeley founds the Uncircumcised Society of America ("U.S.A." for short) in San Francisco, and eventually brings out an entire book—titled, of course, *Foreskin*—on the joys and history of uncircumcised penises.

July 13 *Blueboy* publisher Donald Embinder predicts that the magazine's circulation may eventually top one million.

July 19   Writing in *New West* magazine, a former Los Angeles vice cop acknowledges that L.A. police officers routinely beat up gay men, and adds that, "The L.A.P.D. has always maniacally prosecuted vice and victimless crimes far beyond what they have to do."

July 28   San Francisco health authorities warn there has been a sudden, widespread outbreak of gastrointestinal diseases—including shigellosis and amebic dysentery—among members of the city's gay community. They warn that, in terms of contracting the infections, "rimming" is an especially risky practice.

August 1   A recent UCLA study finds no evidence to support the supposition that a lesbian mother's sexual orientation has any influence one way or another on the general mental health or sexual orientation of her children.

———————

Despite incontrovertible evidence that he actually had sex and achieved orgasm with his victim, a twenty-year-old Massachusetts man, Kristin Asmussen, is charged with manslaughter, not first-degree murder, and sentenced to only eighteen years in prison after he pleads self-defense in the brutal stabbing murder of an older gay man. Asmussen claims he was only fending off the sexual advances of forty-three-year-old Reginald Rockwell when he whipped out a knife and stabbed Rockwell to death. The comparatively lenient sentence comes despite the fact that traces of Asmussen's semen were found all over the car seat near Rockwell's body. Justifying the outcome of the case, one of Asmussen's defense attorneys points out that Rockwell was, after all, "a homosexual who was visiting his problems upon the general public."

August 2   Despite the fact that "wet T-shirt" contests for women are all the rage throughout the city, a Minneapolis bar, Duff's, is denied a renewal of its liquor license after it sponsors a "wet Jockey shorts" contest for men.

August 27   Transsexual tennis star Renee Richards (formerly Dr. Richard Raskind, a New York ophthalmologist) is barred from playing in the women's division of the U.S. Open tennis championships on the grounds that she is still biologically a man. She is ordered to undergo a chromosome test.

"I pride myself on being without question Yale's first (and oldest) woman graduate."

—RENEE RICHARDS

September 1   *Blueboy* magazine publishes a special theme issue, "S&M 1976." Far from examining anything even remotely connected to the leather community, the issue features a photo layout of a man emasculating himself in a blood-splattered bathtub, as well as other photo features emphasizing razor blades, bloodied skulls, and burning matches inserted in a man's urethra. The issue creates a mild uproar in the gay community and draws criticism from both *The Advocate* and *Drummer* magazine. (*Drummer* calls it "*Blueboy*'s boo-boo.") It also outrages a number of the magazine's regular readers, some of whom threaten to cancel their subscriptions in disgust. Shortly afterward, Adrienne Scott "resigns" as the magazine's editor-in-chief. Later, *Blueboy* tries to hawk excess copies of the tasteless issue, with full-page ads that read, "BANNED IN CANADA AND BELGIUM! NOW A COLLECTOR'S ITEM! LIMITED TIME OFFER!"

September 2   The Centers for Disease Control report the worldwide outbreak of a new strain of penicillin-resistant gonorrhea.

September 11   A California appeals court upholds the lewd-conduct convictions of two gay men in their twenties, who were arrested by police for "kissing in public," in a parked car at a freeway rest stop. The two men are ordered to register with the state as sex offenders.

September 12   The Rev. Malcolm Boyd, best known for his 1960s best-seller *Are You Running With Me, Jesus?*, "comes out" in an interview in *The Chicago Sun-Times*.

"After I publicly announced that I am gay," Boyd later recounts in his book *Gay Priest*, "I was plunged into controversy far deeper than I could ever have imagined. The sheer fury of much 'Christian' reaction took my breath away. A letter-writer to a religious publication pensively ruminated that it would have been nice if a recent national church convention had 'ordered a public burning' of 'the collected works of Malcolm Boyd.' Is the burning of books, as the Nazis did, in accordance with 'Christian' ethical responsibility?"

September 20   *Executive Suite*—a new prime-time soap opera about corporate intrigue, sex, and money—premieres on Monday nights on CBS. One subplot of the byzantine series deals with a latent lesbian and her equally latent homosexual husband.

Campaigning for reelection throughout the Midwest, President Ford tells gay activists he wasn't aware that homosexuality is used as a basis for denying foreign immigrants residence in the U.S. "I was not familiar with that as a hindrance to a person coming into the United States," says Ford. "I think that is a matter that ought to be looked at and I will have my people do so."

There is no evidence he ever does.

September 30   *The Nancy Walker Show*, featuring a gay character—Nancy's secretary and roommate, Terry, played by Ken Olfson—premieres on ABC. It lasts three months.

October 1   Porn star Marc Stevens introduces a new line of stoneware pipes and other "collectibles" cast from molds of his illustrious ten-and-a-half-inch endowment.

October 7   "There's nothing wrong with going to bed with some-body of your own sex. I think everybody's bisexual to a certain degree. I don't think it's just me. I just think people should be very free with sex. They should draw the line at goats."
—ELTON JOHN, *publicly acknowledging his bisexuality for the first time, in an interview in* Rolling Stone

October 20   Ads for "Gay Weekend"—a board game in which players try to accumulate as many "tricks" as possible and collect game pieces that, when finally assembled, form various desirable men—appear in *The Advocate*.

November 2   Jimmy Carter is elected President of the United States by a margin of 50 percent to 48 percent over his Republican opponent, Gerald Ford. "I'll never tell you a lie," Carter pledges to the nation.
      In California, virulently conservative Republican Robert K. Dornan, a former TV producer and talk-show host, is elected to his first term in the U.S. House of Representatives.

November 3   *The Advocate* reports that author Mary Renault has received over one thousand photographs from young actors wanting to play the role of Bagoas, if and when *The Persian Boy* is ever finally made into a film.

November 6   Patrick Dennis, author of *Auntie Mame*, dies at the age of fifty-five in New York City.

November 8   *Newsweek* features a cover story on "Disco Mania." Meanwhile, the nation's No. 1 song is Rick Dees's "Disco Duck."

November 10   Recent legal trends to the contrary, divorced les-bian mother Lynn Ransom of Oakland, California, is granted cus-tody of her two small children by an Alameda Superior Court judge.

December 1   Florida authorities finally release a fifty-five-year-old man from a state mental hospital, twenty-six years after he was incarcerated there for having had sex with another man. The man, Willard Eugene Allen, was institutionalized in 1950, when he was twenty-nine, after police arrested him for committing a homosexual act. Although the specific "lewdness" statute under which Allen was charged was eventually taken off the books, Allen's case was forgotten, and recommendations by his doctors that he be released were ignored for nearly two decades.

December 4   Benjamin Britten dies at the age of sixty-three.

December 15   San Francisco proctologist Gerald Feigan reports having recently seen an unprecedented upsurge in the number of men needing to have bizarre objects—including flashlights, pop bottles, light bulbs, chocolate bars, and various fruits and vegetables—removed from their rectums.

January 10 The Episcopal Church of New York ordains an openly lesbian woman, Ellen Marie Barrett, as a minister.

January 12 *The Advocate* reveals that the CIA has been collecting information on some three hundred thousand people who have been arrested in the U.S. for committing homosexual acts. The CIA's exact interest in these people is never fully explained.

January 18 Despite some highly publicized opposition from Florida orange juice spokeswoman and former beauty queen Anita Bryant, Miami becomes the first major Southern city in the U.S. to pass a gay rights ordinance, prohibiting housing and employment discrimination against gay men and lesbians. Bryant—a devout born-again Christian, best known for her role as a national spokeswoman for the Florida citrus industry and for her homey concerts at various state fairs and conventions across the country—denounces the new law and immediately vows to galvanize the nation's

Christians to challenge it. "If homosexuality were normal," she likes to say, "God would have created Adam and Bruce." Few of the country's gay activists take her seriously.

January 29   Thelma Houston's "Don't Leave Me This Way" begins a seventeen-week run in the nation's Top 40, peaking for one week in the top position.

January 31   The Washington, D.C., Human Rights Commission fines a local gay bar, the Grand Central, $6,450 for persistent and repeated discrimination against blacks and women. One former Grand Central employee testifies that the bar's management openly pursued a policy of racial discrimination, especially on weekends, to keep the bar from becoming "too black." Blacks, he said, were charged, among other things, a $3 cover charge (whites were not), or were denied entry altogether. On at least one occasion, bartenders were instructed to charge "nigger" patrons an extra dollar for a glass of water.
    The case—and others like it, from San Francisco to Atlanta—brings to the forefront growing concern and anger over many gay bars' policies of discrimination against other minorities.

February 7   The State Department lifts its sweeping ban on the employment of gay people and announces that it will henceforth consider gay applicants on a case-by-case basis.

February 8   In a historic first, White House aide Midge Constanza meets with officers of the National Gay Task Force to discuss what the Carter administration can do to further the cause of gay rights. Six weeks later, a second meeting—this time with two dozen gay rights advocates—is held.

February 11   CBS's *Executive Suite* goes off the air, a scant five months after its premiere.

February 23   After a TV producer cancels plans to develop a weekly television series around her, Anita Bryant complains to the press that she is being "blacklisted" in Hollywood because of her crusade against homosexuals. "The blacklisting of Anita Bryant has begun," she tells reporters, though how one can be blacklisted from a town where one has not exactly been a fixture isn't explained.

Responds gay activist Bob Kunst, "She wants to cause gays to lose their jobs and she complains because she lost a job. The lady is a hypocrite."

March 1 *Playgirl*'s "March Discovery" is Jimmy Sexton. The magazine neglects to mention that Sexton is a former model for the Athletic Model Guild and has starred in two gay porn films, "Voluptuous Scouts" and "Jimmy's Toy Soldier."

Blueboy Forum, which bills itself as the nation's first gay-oriented television show, debuts on New York cable.

March 14 *The New York Times* criticizes what it calls "Miami homosexualdom" for trying to organize a boycott against Anita Bryant and the Florida citrus industry. Ms. Bryant, the paper asserts, has every right to act on her strongly held convictions—implying somehow that homosexuals don't.

March 15 *Three's Company* premieres on ABC. Introducing a new breed of comedy to American television—"jiggle comedy," one critic calls it (or "the tits and ass show," according to another)—the sitcom revolves around three Southern California roommates: two amply proportioned young women (who often dress as skimpily as possible) and one unemployed guy who likes to pretend he's gay for the sake of appearances. The virtually plotless show—which consists almost entirely of sexual innuendo and double entendres—stays in the Nielsen Top Ten for the next six years, although its constant spicy interplay (albeit, more bark than bite) draws the ire of several religious groups.

March 17 Two years after having repealed its state sodomy laws, the Arkansas state legislature votes to repeal the repeal, and reinstates criminal penalties for homosexual acts between consenting adults. The state's Democratic governor, David Pryor, signs the new bill into law without comment.

March 20 "Homosexuality is nothing new. Cultures throughout history have dealt with homosexuals almost universally with disdain, abhorrence, disgust—even death. . . . The recruitment of our children is absolutely necessary for the survival and growth of homosexuality. Since homosexuals cannot reproduce, they *must* recruit, *must* freshen their ranks. And who better qualifies as a likely recruit than a teenage boy or girl who is surging with sexual awareness."
—Full-page ad taken out in *The Miami Herald* by Anita Bryant, who, having organized her supporters under an umbrella organization called "Save Our Children," claims to have more than six times the necessary signatures to put Miami's new gay rights ordinance to a test in a referendum election June 7. Meanwhile, the Arkansas State House of Representatives *unanimously* passes a special resolution commending Bryant for her antigay crusade. Says the Arkansas lawmaker who introduces the resolution, "When you go against God's law, you have no human rights."

March 27 "For an organized group who feel they have a grievance that they are not treated fairly, for them to have a right to put that grievance before high officials and say 'We want redress,' that to me is what the essence of America is all about. What I feel about gay rights or any other group doesn't have a thing in the world to do with it."
—*White House Press Secretary* JODY POWELL *on* Face the Nation, *defending the Carter administration against charges that it panders to gay activists*

April 1 Not content to leave well enough alone with its notorious "S&M 1976" issue just a year earlier, *Blueboy* now publishes an "Odd Sex" theme issue, which features, among other things, an army officer wearing black lace panties under his trousers and a man in a jockstrap making love to a female mannequin. This and other recent anomalies—centerfold models with lilies coming out of their anuses, and some models posed with exotic-looking transvestites—leave some readers scratching their heads and wondering: Who exactly is the magazine trying to turn on with these images?

April 16   A New York judge rules that transsexual tennis player Renee Richards is eligible to play in the women's division of the U.S. Open tennis championships and does not have to undergo a chromosome test.

April 20   The Nevada State Senate—meeting a scant twenty miles from the nearest legalized brothel and just across the street from the nearest casino—votes to *retain* criminal penalties (one to six years in prison) for homosexual acts between consenting adults, and, under a new amendment, prohibits the parole of anyone convicted of such acts unless it can be shown they will not be "a menace to the health, safety, and morals of others."

April 25   *Village Voice* critic Andrew Sarris hails Woody Allen's latest film, *Annie Hall*, as "a return to good old-fashioned heterosexual romance" on the nation's movie screens.

After former "Ronald McDonald" Bob Brandon publicly announces he is gay, the McDonald's Corporation seeks an injunction forbidding him from ever dressing as the corporate clown again, or from stating or implying that "Ronald McDonald" is also a homosexual.

April 26   Studio 54 opens in New York City and immediately establishes itself as the nation's foremost disco, a haven of drugs, lewd dancing, beautiful boys, conspicuous consumption, and celebrities (among the regulars are Truman Capote, Halston, Liza Minnelli, Andy Warhol, and Roy Cohn), all served up with such an urgent air of exclusivity that dozens of nobodies line up every night hoping against hope to be let in to what is, after all, essentially a big empty building with loud music and flashing lights. So deeply ingrained does the nightclub become in the nation's consciousness that all visitors to New York—farmers, insurance salesmen, housewives from Dubuque—find themselves being breathlessly asked upon their return home, "Did you go to Studio 54?"

> "We like some guys with guys because it makes the dance floor hot, you know? There are certain people who come that we know are good. But I'll tell you something—I wouldn't let my best friend in if he looked like an East Side singles guy."
>
> —*Studio 54 co-owner* STEVE RUBELL

April 29   Remarking that he would not want "a known homosexual teaching *my* children," Florida governor Reubin Askew urges Miami voters to repeal their controversial new gay rights ordinance.

May 1   With one *Blueboy* centerfold layout to his credit and another coming up in *Drummer* magazine—plus standing-room-only appearances in live shows from Los Angeles to Washington, D.C.—a 23-year-old, dark, mustached model known only as "Roger" becomes the current nine days' wonder of gay pornography.

National Lampoon publishes a special gay parody issue, and illustrates it with a cover drawing of King Kong—with heavy makeup and hoop earrings—ogling a tiny and very reluctant Jeff Bridges, star of the 1976 remake of *King Kong*.

In the nation's bookstores this month: Roger Austen's *Playing the Game: The Homosexual Novel in America*, a literate and at times wryly funny history of the gay novel from the nineteenth century to the 1960s.

May 4   A company in Beverly Hills markets a personalized beach towel—the "Beach Cruiser"—for gay men. Each towel is monogrammed with the buyer's name and phone number in huge black letters.

May 15 *60 Minutes* broadcasts a segment on child pornography, which, after a cursory mention of adult males with an erotic interest in little girls, focuses on adult homosexuals who "prey" on small boys.

May 16 With the Dade County vote only weeks away, NBC broadcasts *Alexander: The Other Side of Dawn*, a made-for-TV movie about an innocent and confused country boy who comes to Hollywood, is exploited by rapacious homosexuals, gets arrested for prostitution, is exploited by a rapacious homosexual football player, gets arrested for drug possession, and finally finds happiness moving to Mendocino County with the girl of his dreams.

May 23 In the midst of a growing national frenzy over child pornography, congressional hearings begin on proposed legislation that would make it a felony to photograph or film anyone under the age of sixteen in the nude. Although the law—which eventually passes—is intended to stem what is being touted as "the uncontrollable surge" in child sexual abuse, it winds up occasionally leaving some parents in the very messy position of having to prove that their personal photos of infant children bathing or romping diaper-less are meant for the family photo album and not for circulation by ruthless pornographers.

Nebraska governor James Exon vetoes legislation that would have repealed the state's sodomy laws. A week later, the Nebraska legislature overrides his veto.

May 25 An early-morning fire at New York City's famous Everard Baths leaves nine men dead and seven others critically injured. "I was walking my dog when I smelled smoke and heard screams," says one eyewitness. "I ran around the corner and men were hanging naked from the second story ledge, falling to the pavement. Men were everywhere . . . running in all directions in towels and shorts. The smoke was black. Just then the first fire truck pulled up. It was a catastrophe."

Fire officials later blame the blaze on a smoldering mattress in one of the baths' cubicles, and on the absence of a working sprinkler system in the building.

The San Francisco school board votes 7 to 0 to include materials on homosexuality and gay lifestyles in the sex education curriculum of the city's public schools.

May 27 Wyoming repeals its laws against homosexual acts between consenting adults.

May 30 In an essay applauding the efforts of Anita Bryant in Florida, columnist George Will condemns gay rights ordinances as "part of the moral disarmament of society," and predicts that if the current trend continues, homosexual marriages will soon flourish across the United States and gay people *will even be allowed to adopt children.*

June 1 A DAY WITHOUT HUMAN RIGHTS IS LIKE A DAY WITHOUT SUNSHINE
                                      —*Popular gay T-shirt in Miami*

June 4 John Cheever's *Falconer*—whose central character, Farragut, finds spiritual redemption through a homosexual affair with a young prison inmate—moves to the top of the *New York Times* best-seller list. It eventually becomes the best-selling American novel of the year.

June 6 Jerry Falwell—a still virtually unknown evangelist hosting television's *Old Time Gospel Hour* in Lynchburg, Virginia—decries the gay rights ordinance in Miami and tells *Newsweek* magazine, "So-called gay folks just as soon kill you as look at you."

"The gay community is entitled to all the legal protection that other unpopular minorities enjoy. . . . There is no reason to believe that the fair treatment of gays will in any way impair the essential family

unit. Besides, legal rights should not depend on majority approval of individual lifestyles."
—*American Civil Liberties Union chairman* NORMAN DORSEN

"We're not afraid. We've put on the armor of God."
—*Anita Bryant's husband,* BOB GREEN, *expressing optimism about to-morrow's gay rights referendum*

June 7   Voters in Dade County, Florida, repeal their controversial gay rights ordinance by a margin of more than 2 to 1. The defeat stuns many observers, some of whom still have not taken Anita Bryant seriously.

June 8   In response to yesterday's defeat in Dade County, a spontaneous gay rights march in New York City draws between five thousand and ten thousand demonstrators. Similar marches are held throughout the country. Declares one activist in Indianapolis, "We expect violence."

Meanwhile, the Crown and Anchor Motel—one of the largest motels in Provincetown, Massachusetts—announces it has permanently removed orange juice from its menu. A short time later, Hollywood composer Paul Williams and his wife take out a full-page ad in *Variety* to announce they will no longer serve screwdrivers (or any other drink made with orange juice) at their home.

Florida governor Reubin Askew signs into law a bill outlawing same-sex marriages and prohibiting homosexuals from adopting children.

June 17   Vice-President Walter Mondale angrily storms from a Democratic fund-raising rally in San Francisco after a demonstrator interrupts his speech, demanding, "When are you going to speak out on gay rights?"

June 26   Police in Barcelona break up a Gay Pride march by firing rubber bullets into the crowd of four thousand demonstrators. Dozens of the marchers are seriously injured.

In the United States, this year's Gay Pride parades draw the largest number of participants ever: more than three hundred thousand in San Francisco and nearly seventy-five thousand in New York City.

June 29 Hoping to dispel rumors that it has donated money to Anita Bryant and other antigay crusaders—and hoping to defuse a growing gay boycott of its product—the Coors Beer Company takes out full-page ads in *The Advocate* to declare that "members of the Coors family *have not* contributed either financially or in any other manner to any antigay rights campaigns or organizations."

The ads neglect to mention that patriarch Joseph Coors is a right-wing extremist, founder of both the ultraconservative Heritage Foundation and the group "Colorado Businessmen for Christ."

July 1 *The New York Times* announces it will no longer accept display advertisements for X-rated pornographic films.

"While many church people are duped by their brainwashed, pink-panty preachers into believing that we should merely pray for the homosexuals, we find that we must endorse and support the law of God which calls for the death penalty to the faggot slime. . . . It is true that they will have to die, the whole filthy bunch of them. The sooner the better!"
—*Editorial (under the headline "GAS GAYS") in* The Torch, *a white supremacist newspaper. In the same issue, a Miami housewife is quoted as saying: "The Bible I believe says to stone them. Of course they did not have electric chairs in those days, nor did they have gas chambers. I am not really fussy about the method only the results, a clean decent environment for my children."*

July 4 The editor and publishers of London's *Gay News* are put on trial for having recently published a poem—"The Love That Dares To Speak Its Name," by noted scholar-translator James Kirkup—in which a Roman centurion removes the body of Christ from the cross and performs an act of fellatio on it. The paper is charged under a little-known—and little used—blasphemous libel law, which makes it a crime to ridicule or impugn Jesus Christ or any part of the Holy Scriptures. During the trial, the prosecution repeatedly links all homosexual acts to child molestation while portraying the *Gay News* as a biweekly manifesto for pedophilia. After Judge King-Hamilton disallows any defense of the poem (or the newspaper) on literary or theological grounds, a guilty verdict becomes a foregone conclusion, and *Gay News* editor Denis Lemon becomes the planet's only living convicted blasphemer.

July 7   Rod Stewart's "The Killing of Georgie"—about a small-town gay teenager who comes to New York and is soon murdered by "fag-bashers"—enters the Billboard Top 40, where it peaks at No. 30.

July 8   *Diversions and Delights*—a one-man play starring Vincent Price as Oscar Wilde—has its world premiere in San Francisco. Nine months later, it moves to Broadway.

July 17   Mormon Church president Spencer W. Kimball blames the continuing drought in the western United States on society's growing toleration of homosexuality.

July 27   "Through Anita Bryant, the gay movement has been 'born again' in greater numbers and with greater determination than ever before. The success of her hysterical 'Save Our Children' campaign in Dade County resurrected a slumbering activism and converted apathy to anger and action."
—The Advocate, *on the recent resurgence of gay political activism in the wake of the Dade County gay rights defeat. The defeat has reportedly resulted in an upsurge in the membership rosters of various gay rights organizations.* "Anita Bryant," *says* The Nation, *in an editorial endorsing federal gay civil rights legislation,* "is the best thing ever to happen to American homosexuals."

August 1 Bette Midler declines an offer to debate Anita Bryant on the issue of gay rights in the pages of *Rolling Stone* magazine.

The U.S. Navy announces it will abandon its recent fashion experiment, in which sailors wore coat-and-shirt uniforms, and return to the traditional white caps, jumpers, and snug-fitting bell-bottom trousers.

August 8 Reflecting the recent success of Jonathan Katz's *Gay American History* and other gay-themed titles from mainstream publishers, *Publishers Weekly* runs a special feature on the sudden boom in gay publishing. "The gay market is affluent and has good readers," says one bookseller. "They will not hesitate to spend money on items they want." Both *The Village Voice* and *The New York Times Book Review* also carry articles this month on the deluge of gay titles suddenly being released by the big publishing houses.

August 10 A company in Coconut Grove, Florida, markets an Anita Bryant dartboard for $9.95.

August 12 Meeting in Rhode Island, the Fraternal Order of Police passes a resolution opposing the hiring of gay or lesbian police officers. Several weeks later in Los Angeles, the International Association of Chiefs of Police follows suit.

August 20 The second annual National Gay Rodeo gets under way in Reno, Nevada. Though a distinct improvement over the first one (which was attended by only about 125 people), it still draws only a few hundred spectators and suffers from severe disorganization and an overriding air of campiness, giving no clue that in two or three years it will become one of the major annual gay events in the western United States.

Syndicated columnist Mike Royko names Anita Bryant to a list of "The Ten Most Obnoxious Americans," and asks, "If God dislikes gays so much, how come he picked Michelangelo, a known homosexual, to paint the Sistine Chapel while assigning Anita to go on TV and push orange juice?"

August 24   "You have to tread such a fucking narrow line to be a queer these days, that I kind of pine for the old days when you were just an ordinary homosexual getting along and making it and having fun too, all the way. You didn't have to believe in liberation as the only path to heaven—your attention was more, like, centered at the crotch, and you could enjoy it without making speeches about it."

—*Author* SAMUEL STEWARD *(a.k.a. "Phil Andros")*

September 3   With one hit single, "Love to Love You, Baby," behind her, and another, "I Feel Love," in *Billboard*'s Top 40 for thirteen weeks, singer Donna Summer becomes the undisputed Queen of Disco, a position she reaches largely due to her gay fans, who dance away much of their weekends to her sexually provocative (if generally mindless) music.

September 7   Christine Jorgensen sues United Artists for trying to market a 1970 movie about her life, *The Christine Jorgensen Story*, as a "campy B movie." The film, Ms. Jorgensen indignantly asserts in her suit, is not a "B movie"—it is "a classic."

September 13   *Soap* premieres on ABC, with an unknown thirty-year-old comic, Billy Crystal, cast as the on-going gay character Jodie, and former world champion pole vaulter Bob Seagren as his bisexual football-player lover.

September 16   Operatic virtuoso Maria Callas, fifty-three, dies in Paris, after a long seclusion following a critically reviled series of comeback concerts. Her sudden death sets off a wave of grief among her very large contingent of gay fans. So intense is her hold over some gay admirers that, several years later, Terrence McNally will write an entire play, *The Lisbon Traviata*, the centerpiece of which is a lengthy, obsessive discussion between two gay men about the virtues of Callas's singing.

September 18 A highly promoted four-and-a-half-hour gay rights benefit at the Hollywood Bowl—the "Star Spangled Night for Rights"—turns ugly when comedian Richard Pryor takes to the stage and criticizes the event for concentrating solely on the rights of gay men and lesbians. As the audience reacts to him with catcalls and boos, Pryor turns increasingly hostile, with such angry rebuffs as "Motherfuck women's rights!" and "When the niggers was burning down Watts, you motherfuckers were doing what you wanted to do on Hollywood Boulevard and didn't give a shit about it." "Kiss my happy rich black ass!" Pryor finally yells, leaving the stage. The evening ends with a gala fireworks display set to a performance of "God Bless America" by the Hollywood Festival Orchestra.

September 22 In the nation's bookstores this month: *The Naked Civil Servant*, the autobiography of English homosexual Quentin Crisp, best known for—being a homosexual. Although the book was originally published in England in 1968—to decidedly mixed reviews (*The Observer* called it "entertaining"; *The Times Literary Supplement* called it "intolerably arch and jaunty")—it wasn't until 1976, when PBS aired a British-made film of Crisp's life (starring John Hurt), that he suddenly became a cult figure in the United States, and Holt, Rinehart and Winston decided to publish the book. Crisp's glib wit and unique perspective on life soon make him a much sought-after celebrity and, like Oscar Wilde before him, he eventually launches a one-man show, *An Evening with Quentin Crisp*, crisscrossing the U.S. delivering witticisms on style, homosexuality, housekeeping, and marriage.

October 1 Pier Paolo Pasolini's controversial final film, *Salo, 120 Days of Sodom*, makes its U.S. debut at the New York Film Festival. Although the film (with its graphic depictions of sodomy, torture, excrement-eating, and mutilation) is advertised as some kind of highbrow existential treatise ("An agonized scream of total despair!" says one ad), many critics find it repulsive and irredeemable—a "bitter, empty end" to Pasolini's career, as one writer calls it. In Italy, copies of the film are seized by government censors before it can even be shown. (After several appeals—including a petition signed by writer Alberto Moravia and poet Eugenio Montale—it is finally released.) At its San Francisco premiere, the film is greeted by equal measures of booing and cheers.

October 7   *The Advocate* celebrates its tenth anniversary with a party at the National Press Club in Washington, D.C.

October 14   At a press conference in Des Moines, Anita Bryant is hit in the face with a cherry cream pie by gay activist Thom Higgins. The singer does not press charges.

October 18   Citizens United to Protect Our Children announces it has failed to come up with the necessary twenty-five thousand signatures to force a recall election of Portland, Oregon, mayor Neil Goldschmidt. The group wanted to recall Goldschmidt for declaring a "Portland Gay Pride Day" last June.

October 20   A distraught gay man in Grand Island, Nebraska, commandeers a Frontiers Airline jet with thirty-two passengers aboard and demands $3 million in cash as well as the release of his male lover from a jail in Atlanta. The incident, repeatedly referred to in the press as a "gay hijacking" (apparently, as *The Advocate* points out, to distinguish it from all those "heterosexual hijackings"), ends with the man releasing the hostages and shooting himself to death.

October 24   Eight men are killed and six others injured in a fire at a gay porn theater in Washington, D.C. According to witnesses, the theater's only emergency exit was padlocked and there were no fire sprinklers in the building. Among the dead are an Army major, a former church pastor, and an aide to Congressman Butler Derrick.

November 2   SAGE—Senior Action in a Gay Environment—is founded in New York City. Among the group's stated goals:

■ "to increase the visibility of gay and lesbian seniors and help improve the image of all seniors in the media"
■ "to outreach and locate gay and lesbian seniors who are homebound and isolated"
■ "to create educational and recreational activities for all gay and lesbian seniors"

In other words, to keep older people who are gay and lesbian—with all their wisdom, experience, and *joie de vivre*—from being forgotten, isolated, and disregarded by an increasingly ageist society that perversely idolizes a pretty young face (no matter how vacuous) as the be-all and end-all of success and importance.

November 6   Phil Donahue, tagged by one writer as "the television celebrity who has done the most good for the gay movement in the United States," celebrates the tenth anniversary of his trendsetting talk show.

November 8   Forty-seven-year-old camera store owner Harvey Milk—having run unsuccessfully for public office three times before—becomes the first openly gay person elected to the San Francisco Board of Supervisors, defeating seventeen other contenders (including five other gay candidates) for the seat. Milk is elected supervisor from the newly created 5th District, encompassing the heart of the city, including the Castro area.
His election sets off a huge celebration, described by one reporter as resembling "New Year's Eve on Market Street." "The feeling there was just one of total joy," says Milk's campaign manager, Anne Kronenberg. "And it was more than just a candidate winning. It was the fact that all of these lesbians and gay men throughout San Francisco who had felt they'd had no voice before, now had someone who represented them."
Also elected to the San Francisco Board of Supervisors: former policeman Dan White, who ran with the slogan, "Crime is number one with me!"
"I think of the fourteen-year-old boy or girl in Des Moines," Milk said shortly before election day, "who realizes his or her own

homosexuality. The parents throw them around. Schoolmates taunt them. The state calls them criminals. They may end up being alcoholic closet cases—but one day, they're going to open up a paper and see that an openly gay person was elected to the San Francisco Board. That's going to give them hope."

Bachelor candidate Ed Koch, having survived the first of several campaigns in which speculation over his sexual orientation was an issue, is elected Mayor of New York City.

November 12   Former *Jeopardy* host Art Fleming plays a bisexual cop in a gay-themed episode—"Death in a Different Place"—of the police-buddy series *Starsky and Hutch*. In the same episode, Charles Pierce plays a female impersonator in a gay nightclub.

November 28   By a vote of 5 to 1, the Aspen, Colorado, city council passes a gay rights ordinance that forbids discrimination against gay men and lesbians in employment, housing, public accommodations, and public services. Despite such progressive legislation, the famed ski resort—an odd (and to some repellent) mixture of fur-swathed celebrities, white-shoed wanna-bes, and Rocky Mountain rednecks—continues to see a number of homophobic incidents, including the case of a popular local bar that physically ousts several visiting gay couples after they try to take to the dance floor together.

November 30   Gay playwright Terence Rattigan—perhaps best known for his drama *Separate Tables*, which was later sanitized of all homosexual elements for a 1958 film starring Burt Lancaster, David Niven, and Rita Hayworth—dies in Bermuda at the age of sixty-six.

December 7   "Well, we finally made it to network television, the big time. We're living proof that the moral fiber on which this country lives has died."
—BETTE MIDLER, *during her first network television special, on NBC*

December 11 The Castro Steam Baths—the third San Francisco gay bathhouse in less than a year to be victimized by arson—goes up in flames. One man is killed.

December 15 The provincial government of Quebec adds gay men and lesbians to the list of groups whose civil rights are legally protected under the province's Charter of Human Rights.

December 16 *Saturday Night Fever*—starring John Travolta as a Brooklyn boy who just wants to dance all night—opens at movie theaters across the country. Although some critics interpret the film as officially ushering in a nationwide age of disco, it in fact comes as the disco phenomenon has already peaked and is about to decline. Still, it becomes one of the top box-office hits of the year (and sets off a brief fashion craze for three-piece white suits), and the album—featuring the Bee Gees doing songs like "Staying Alive" and "Night Fever"—eventually becomes the biggest-selling soundtrack of all time. Travolta later wins the Best Actor of the Year award from the National Film Board.

December 26 *People* magazine names Anita Bryant one of "The 25 Most Intriguing People of 1977."

December 30 Toronto police raid the offices of Canada's foremost gay newspaper, *The Body Politic*, and seize twelve cartons of financial records, manuscripts, and subscription lists. Three of the newspaper's staff are charged with "using the mails to distribute immoral, indecent, and scurrilous material." The raid was ostensibly prompted by a recent article in which the newspaper examined the man-boy love controversy.

Six years and more than $100,000 in legal fees later, the newspaper is acquitted.

In the nation's bookstores: *The Joy of Gay Sex* by Dr. Charles Silverstein and Edmund White, and *The Joy of Lesbian Sex* by Dr. Emily Sisley and Bertha Harris. The B. Dalton bookstore chain soon announces it will not display the books on its open shelves, but will sell them "to adult customers by request only."

December 31 Manufacturers report that sales of amyl nitrite have topped the four-million-bottle mark this year, up from only nine hundred thousand in 1973.

January 1 *Good Housekeeping* readers name Anita Bryant "The Most Admired Woman in America."

January 9 Sir John Gielgud, Jean-Paul Sartre, Simone de Beauvoir, and twenty-six other international celebrities take out a full-page ad in *Time* magazine to protest the recent series of political backlashes against gay people in the United States. "We are alarmed," reads the ad, "by the campaign of Anita Bryant . . . and the fact that many politicians in America, who do not personally believe in discrimination against homosexuals, lack the courage to stand up to this bigotry. . . . President Carter's human rights policy can gain credibility only if the rights of homosexuals in the United States of America are bound inseparably to human rights for all people."

January 15 With the Dade County gay rights defeat barely six months old, national attention now turns to California, where arch-conservative state senator John Briggs and his followers are circulating petitions for a state ballot proposition—the so-called "Briggs Initiative"—that would bar gay people, or "anyone advocating a homosexual lifestyle," from teaching in the public schools.

Given the high rate of child molestation among heterosexuals (90 percent or more of the national total), another state senator, Democrat Alan Robbins, asks Briggs to expand his efforts to include a ban on *heterosexual* teachers in the state as well.

"That's something I'd rather not answer. . . . I know that there are homosexuals who teach children and the children don't suffer. But this is a subject I don't particularly want to involve myself in. I've got enough problems without taking on another."
—PRESIDENT CARTER, *answering the question, "Would you be upset if you knew Amy was being taught by a homosexual?"*

January 23 New York City mayor Ed Koch issues Executive Order 50, which forbids discrimination against gay men and lesbians in municipal government, including by those groups or agencies that do business with or receive funds from the city. The order—challenged by the Salvation Army and the Roman Catholic Archdiocese of New York, among others—is eventually struck down in the courts.

January 26 *The Oklahoma Times* reports the recent formation of two "teen" chapters of the Ku Klux Klan, comprised mostly of fifteen- and sixteen-year-old boys whose primary activity—attacking and assaulting gay men in public parks and outside gay bars—is being actively encouraged by their parents.

February 1 Popular gay artist Tom of Finland—a former advertising illustrator whose erotic drawings of exaggeratedly muscled and well-endowed men first appeared in *Physique Pictorial* in the late

1950s—has his first U.S. exhibit, at Robert Opel's Fey Way Gallery in San Francisco.

February 7   The Oklahoma State House of Representatives passes a so-called "Teacher Fitness" statute, which allows local school boards to fire homosexual teachers or *any* teacher "advocating . . . encouraging or promoting public or private homosexual activities"—even, theoretically, if that means the teacher has merely joined an organization (such as the ACLU or the National Gay Task Force) that is publicly working for an end to discrimination against gay people.

The bill's sponsor, State Representative John Monks, assures his supporters that the bill "covers both queers and lesbians."

The National Gay Task Force later files suit to challenge the law's constitutionality.

February 15   "My cock plunged faster and faster in and out of the quivering, clutching asshole. The small room was filled with the sexy scent of sweat and male musk. Perspiration poured from us to splatter on the concrete floor, and we kept fucking. Suddenly, my body went stiff. Snapping my head back, I let out a deep groan. My belly slapped against his muscular ass cheeks. I poured flaming lava into my victim's gut. 'Oh, shit, I'm cummmmmmmming! Fuck, shit, ohhhhhhhh!' "
—*Standard fare from* Blueboy's *new companion jack-off magazine,* Numbers

March 1   Gay author and literary agent Paul Scott—who wrote *The Jewel in the Crown* (later made into a PBS series), and whose clients at one time included John Fowles, Arthur C. Clarke, and Muriel Spark—dies at the age of fifty-seven.

March 20   The San Francisco Board of Supervisors passes what is described as "the most stringent gay rights law in the country." Only one of the eleven supervisors—Dan White—votes against the ordinance.

March 26 Currently showing at Manhattan's Eastside Cinema: the acclaimed documentary *Word Is Out*, interviews with twenty-six gay men and lesbians (aged twenty to seventy) who talk about their lives, their loves, and coming out. Critic Janet Maslin calls it "graceful, funny, and often very moving. . . . Even filmgoers who imagine they'd rather sit through root canal work than find out what it's like to be homosexual may wind up unexpectedly captivated by the film's friendly, even-handed approach to a potentially divisive subject."

In Canada, the film is given an X rating by the Canadian Censorship Board, which objects to its subject matter. The X rating is usually reserved for films with extreme sex, violence, or obscene language.

April 1 "They are the most boring group imaginable. They're so fucking pontifical. I just got a press release from them claiming to speak for all gay people. They're really hilarious: they always speak in the third person plural, 'We, as gay people . . .' I don't trust anyone who comes across like that."
—*Columnist* ARTHUR BELL, *deriding the National Gay Task Force*

April 25 Following the recent gay rights defeat in Dade County, Florida, voters in St. Paul, Minnesota, vote to repeal their four-year-old gay rights ordinance by a margin of 2 to 1.

May 1 Robert La Tourneaux, who originated the role of "Cowboy" in both the stage and screen versions of *The Boys in the Band*, does a nude cover and photo layout for *Mandate* magazine.

May 2 "I could never be gay. I'm a lousy dancer and dresser."
—PHIL DONAHUE, *in an interview in* TV Guide

May 9 By a margin of 5 to 1, voters in Wichita, Kansas, repeal a recently enacted city ordinance that would have prohibited job and housing discrimination against gay men and lesbians. Less than two weeks later, Eugene, Oregon, becomes the fourth U.S. community in less than a year to repeal a gay rights law.

May 15 In the nation's bookstores this month: *Chrome*, a gay science-fiction novel by former Hollywood heartthrob (and now openly gay novelist) George Nader. *Publishers Weekly* calls it "the first homosexual robot love story" and notes, "The main focus is on the several graphic love scenes. . . . There is also quite a lot about massage technique." The book is dedicated to Nader's lover of many years, Mark Miller.

    Also in bookstores: Malcolm Boyd's *Take Off the Masks*, the first book in which he openly discusses his homosexuality. It is the only one of his twenty books not reviewed by *The New York Times*.

May 17 *Thank God It's Friday*—a kind of bargain-basement *Saturday Night Fever*, with Donna Summer as an aspiring disco diva crooning "Last Dance," and assorted other young performers (including Jeff Goldblum and Debra Winger) as glamour-hungry patrons at a glitzy L.A. disco—premieres in Los Angeles. One critic calls it "a must-see for morons."

May 25 More than fifteen thousand gay men and lesbians attend a special "Gay Night" at Disneyland to benefit the Los Angeles Gay Community Services Center. It is the largest private party the amusement park has ever had.

May 30 Commenting on the recent proliferation of good-looking men in national advertisements, Burt Reynolds tells Barbara Walters in a nationally televised interview, "You ever see these guys? I mean I could be bisexual for one of those guys. Those guys are gorgeous." The remarks set off a wave of speculation—lasting well through the next decade—about Reynolds's true sexual orientation.

June 1   In an interview in *Playboy* magazine, the now internationally famous Anita Bryant:

■ insists that homosexuality inevitably leads to sadomasochism, drug abuse, and suicide
■ claims that homosexuals are called *fruits* because they eat "the forbidden fruit of the tree of life" (i.e., semen)
■ reveals that if the gay rights ordinance had passed in Dade County there was "a group of prostitutes who were going to initiate similar legislation permitting whores to stand up in front of kids in the classroom and then ply their trade"
■ objects to people using the terms *queer* or *faggot*, but says that *homo* isn't really all "that bad"
■ acknowledges she's never read the Bible cover to cover
■ advocates homosexual behavior being classified as a felony punishable by at least twenty years in prison, even for young first-time "offenders"
■ says that all Jews and Muslims are "going to hell" because they haven't embraced Jesus Christ as their personal savior
■ asserts that no matter what happens in her marriage, divorce isn't "in my vocabulary"

The *Annals of International Medicine* reports that an intestinal parasite—*Giardia lamblia*—previously restricted to parts of the Soviet Union and the Colorado Rocky Mountains, is showing up with alarming frequency in gay men across the United States.

Asses—a 180-page, oversized coffee-table book compiled by Tom Houston and devoted to loving photographs of all kinds of bare buttocks (especially those of muscular young males)—appears in bookstores across the country.

June 7   The Briggs Initiative qualifies for the November ballot in California, where it will be listed as Proposition 6.

ALL THE WORLD LOVES A STAR

"Oh, Squeaky Fromme, where are you when we need you?"
—JOHN WATERS, *asked his opinion of Anita Bryant*

"I was crazy about her—the sweetest little singer—and thought she should have won Miss America that year she didn't. But now I feel absolute disgust for her."
—*President Carter's mother,* MISS LILLIAN

"As to Anita's fear that she'll be assassinated? The only people who might shoot Anita Bryant are music lovers."
—GORE VIDAL

June 11 The first annual New York City Police vs. Gay All-Stars softball game ends with a police victory, 12–4, over the gay team. Sixth Precinct Police Captain Aron Rosenthal says he hopes the game has helped "us all see beyond the labels and stereotypes that reduce human beings to one-dimensional characters." Nine years earlier, the Sixth Precinct was notorious for its harassment and abuse of gay people, and for its arbitrary raids on numerous gay bars, including, one night in June 1969, the Stonewall Inn.

"I find that the book deals rationally and unsensationally with the sexual practices of a substantial segment of the male population. However repugnant the concept of anal sex may be to the heterosexual observer, it is, I find, the central act of homosexual practice. To write about homosexual practices without dealing with anal intercourse would be equivalent to writing a history of music and omitting Mozart."
—*Canadian judge D. C. J.* HAWKINS, *ruling in 1978 that* The Joy of Gay Sex *is not obscene and that Canadian customs acted improperly when it confiscated shipments of the book to Glad Day Bookshop in Toronto*

June 14   The U.S. Patent and Trademark Office rejects an application by *Gaysweek* magazine to register its name, claiming that it is "immoral."

June 25   Spurred on by the recent spate of gay rights defeats across the country and by the new threat from Proposition 6, this year's Gay Freedom Day Parade in San Francisco draws an estimated three hundred fifty thousand marchers. The parade culminates in a rally at City Hall, where Harvey Milk tells the marchers, "I want to recruit you. I want to recruit you for the fight to preserve your democracy from the John Briggs and the Anita Bryants who are trying to constitutionalize bigotry. We are not going to allow that to happen. We are not going to sit back in silence as three hundred thousand of our gay brothers and sisters did in Nazi Germany. We are not going to allow our rights to be taken away and then march with bowed heads into the gas chambers. On this anniversary of Stonewall, I ask my gay sisters and brothers to make the commitment to fight. For themselves. For their freedom. For their country."

July 1   "I've never had a gay experience in my life."
—PERRY KING, *feeling compelled to assert his heterosexuality in an interview for the new film* A Different Story, *in which King convincingly plays a gay man who falls in love with and marries a lesbian*

In a *Ladies' Home Journal* poll, junior and senior high school students name Adolf Hitler and Anita Bryant as the two people who have "done the most damage in the world."

July 3   Actor James Daly, whose homosexuality has been an open secret in Hollywood for years, dies at the age of sixty in Marina del Rey, California. His live-in lover—male model Randal Jones—files a million-dollar "palimony" suit against the estate after being evicted from Daly's condominium by the actor's daughters.

The Village People. Clockwise from top: Victor Willis (Motorcycle Man), Alexander Briley (Sailor), Glenn Hughes (Leatherman), Felipe Rose (Indian), David Hodo (Construction Worker), and Randy Jones (Cowboy).

July 15 The largest gay rights march in Australian history ends with fourteen of the more than two thousand demonstrators being arrested on charges of offensive behavior and resisting arrest.

July 27 New Jersey repeals its sodomy laws.

July 29 The Village People's disco single "Macho Man" begins a six-week run in the nation's Top 40. It will eventually go gold.

The group—formed in 1977 by openly gay record producer Jacques Morali (who says he first came up with the idea while watching men dance at a disco in Greenwich Village)—consists of six masculine archetypes: the leatherman, the cop, the soldier, the construction worker, the cowboy, and the Indian. They draw the unlikely approbation of *The New York Times*, which calls them "amusing" and "blissfully free of any sort of musical pretension or significance." The *Times* also notes that their widespread success "attests to the continuing permeation of homosexual ideas into the mainstream."

August 20 John Briggs's efforts to have gay teachers purged from the California school system is dealt a severe blow when former governor Ronald Reagan publicly announces his opposition to Proposition 6. "I don't approve of teaching so-called gay lifestyles in our schools," says Reagan, "but there is already adequate legal machinery to deal with such problems, if and when they arise." Reagan aides privately acknowledge that it was "a close call" for Reagan whether to oppose or support the controversial proposal.

Meanwhile, a *Los Angeles Times* poll shows that state voters are sharply divided over the initiative, with only 49 percent saying they would vote against it if the election were held today.

September 1 In the nation's bookstores this month: Andrew Holleran's *Dancer From the Dance*, an elegiac, sometimes bitter novel about the shallowness of much of gay life in the Seventies. The haunting prose style and vivid re-creation of certain familiar mainstays of big-city gay life—discos, drug use, fickleness in cruising and love—lead some readers to misinterpret the book, rather obstinately, as a nostalgic celebration of a chaotic epoch. Says Holleran later, "I was depressed by New York gay life and all the things I wasn't getting from it, and when people thought I had glamorized the circuit, I was shocked, because I had wanted to criticize it."

Harvey Rosenberg—the New York entrepreneur who successfully brought out "Balls: The Candy to Give You Courage"—markets "Gay Bob," an anatomically correct $14.95 doll dressed in tight blue jeans, flannel shirt, and boots. The doll comes packaged in its own miniature closet.

A gay Colorado Springs soldier who had requested immediate discharge from the armed forces (but was denied it unless he produced the names of men he had had sex with) forces the military's hand by showing up for lunch one afternoon at the base mess hall dressed in full drag, including low-cut dress, wig, earrings, makeup, and sunbonnet. Although one outraged colonel denounces the stunt as an attack "against the ideals of manlihood," the soldier is granted an immediate discharge.

"I hated to reinforce the stereotype," says former staff sergeant Bill Douglas. "Obviously, most gay soldiers aren't effeminate at all and female impersonators are less than 1 percent of male homosexuals—but it was the only way I could get to the brass."

October 1   An article in *The American Journal of Psychiatry* suggests that sniffing amyl nitrate may be a contributing factor in certain kinds of cancer.

November 1   "Of the 2,639,857 faggots in the New York City area, 2,639,857 think primarily with their cocks."
—*Author* LARRY KRAMER, *best known for his screenplay for the Ken Russell movie* Women in Love, *in his controversial new novel* Faggots, *which one gay magazine calls "a revolting piece of work"*

November 7   Janet Flanner—who for almost fifty years wrote *The New Yorker*'s "Letter from Paris," and who was part of both Natalie Barney's and Gertrude Stein's circles—dies at the age of eighty-six in New York City.

———————————

To the relief of gay people nationwide—who have been desperate for some kind of political victory after the seemingly endless string of defeats over the past seventeen months—Proposition 6 is soundly defeated in California by an unexpectedly wide margin of 59 percent to 41 percent. "GAY HAPPY DAYS ARE HERE AGAIN!" proclaims *The San Francisco Chronicle* in a banner headline.

In Seattle, voters buck a nationwide trend and *retain* their city's gay rights ordinance, by a margin of 63 percent to 37 percent.

Meanwhile, voters in California's ultraconservative 39th District (encompassing most of Orange County) elect lawyer William E. Dannemeyer to his first term in the U.S. House of Representatives.

———————————

"Every gay person *must* come out. As difficult as it is, you must tell your immediate family, you must tell your relatives, you must tell your friends if indeed they are your friends, you must tell your neighbors, you must tell the people you work with, you must tell

the people at the stores you shop in. And once they realize that we are indeed their children, that we are indeed everywhere—every myth, every lie, every innuendo will be destroyed once and for all. And once, once you do, you will feel so much better."
—HARVEY MILK, *in a speech following the defeat of Proposition 6*

November 11 The Village People's single "Y.M.C.A." debuts on *Billboard*'s Top 40, eventually reaching the No. 2 slot (and going platinum) during its twenty-week run on the nation's dance charts. The actual Y.M.C.A. briefly considers filing suit against the singing group.

———————

Claiming that he can't make ends meet on a supervisor's paltry salary, Dan White angrily resigns from the San Francisco Board of City Supervisors. A few days later, he begins an unsuccessful campaign to retract his resignation.

November 15 Famed anthropologist Margaret Mead, who once noted that "Extreme heterosexuality is a perversion" and who was herself bisexual, dies in New York City at the age of seventy-six.

November 26 ABC airs *A Question of Love*, a made-for-TV movie starring Gena Rowlands and Jane Alexander as lesbian lovers involved in a bitter custody battle for one of the women's children. Although the most explicit physical contact between the two is a scene of one brushing the other's hair, the program is interrupted at regular intervals by an on-air announcement warning, "Due to subject matter, parental discretion is advised."

November 27 Informed that San Francisco mayor George Moscone is about to announce a replacement for him on the city's Board of Supervisors, Dan White straps a snub-nosed .38 pistol to his shoulder, tosses ten extra cartridges into his pocket, and then has a friend drive him to City Hall, where he sneaks in through a side window to avoid the metal detectors. A few minutes later, he pumps two bullets into Mayor Moscone's chest, and then two more (just to make certain he's dead) into the mayor's skull. White then reloads his gun, crosses City Hall, and uses five bullets to assassinate gay city supervisor Harvey Milk.

White's attorneys later claim that he reloaded his gun not because he had any specific intention of shooting Milk, but rather because, as a former policeman, he just instinctively felt uncomfortable carrying around an unloaded weapon.

San Franciscans react to the double assassination with a massive candlelight march down Market Street. An observer calls it "one of the most eloquent responses of a community to violence."

November 28 THE CITY WEEPS
—San Francisco Examiner *headline*

December 1 In his new book *Disco*, pop culture junkie Albert Goldman—later to write a critically reviled biography of John Lennon—asks the burning question of the decade, "Is Disco God?" Meanwhile, *Time* magazine reports it has counted twenty-two simulated orgasms in the Donna Summer song "Love to Love You, Baby."

December 2 Harvey Milk's friends scatter his ashes over the Pacific Ocean. Ten days later, Dan White enters a plea of not guilty. Bail is set at $1 million.

December 11 On a brutally cold winter night, Chicago suburbanite John Wayne Gacy sodomizes, tortures, and then strangles to death a fifteen-year-old boy, Robert Piest. He dumps the boy's carcass in the Des Plaines River. A short time later, police show up at Gacy's door to question him about Piest's disappearance. To the officers' astonishment, Gacy begins nervously babbling about a seven-year career of murder, torture, rape, and kidnapping. His confessions result in the discovery of twenty-six more corpses, some of them never identified, beneath his house.

December 22 The seemingly surefire movie team of Lily Tomlin and John Travolta, in the much-anticipated Christmas release *Mo-*

ment by Moment, backfires when the film, an insufferable romantic melodrama about a Malibu housewife and her "kept boy," draws venomous reviews and flops at the box office. "The number of people who like it could convene in a Pinto," notes one critic. The fiasco was directed by Tomlin's longtime colleague Jane Wagner.

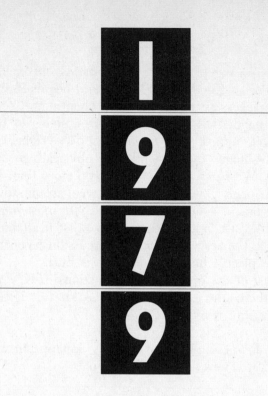

January 8 Acting San Francisco mayor Dianne Feinstein names forty-year-old gay auditor Harry Britt to fill Harvey Milk's seat on the San Francisco Board of Supervisors.

January 20 Gloria Gaynor's "I Will Survive" begins a seventeen-week climb up *Billboard*'s Top 40, where it will finally peak at No. 1.

January 25 An astrologer commissioned by *The Advocate* to chart a horoscope for the gay rights movement in 1979 predicts:

- It "will be a complicated year, as varied and heterogeneous as a rich bouillabaisse."
- "There will be increased confusion ahead."
- "1979 will be a fiery year."
- "Change is coming."

February 1   A gang of teenage boys stands outside Tennessee Williams's home in Key West, Florida, and begins throwing beer cans and firecrackers at the house while chanting, "Come on out, faggot!" The incident is just the latest in a string of bizarre homophobic attacks aimed at the openly gay playwright. Less than a week earlier, Williams and a friend were physically assaulted after leaving a Key West gay bar, and shortly before that, Williams's gardener—an openly gay man who often went around town crying, "I am a sick woman!"—was shot to death. "In most small towns," says one Key West resident, "they realize that if a famous person is hurt there, there are worldwide repercussions: your town gets known as the place where so and so was hurt. . . . Tennessee Williams is one of the great tourist attractions in Key West. You would think the country or city would see that he is comfortable here, safe here, can work here."

February 6   Tennessee Williams's dog is kidnapped from the playwright's backyard, never to be seen again.

February 17   "You Make Me Feel (Mighty Real)," from openly gay singer Sylvester, moves into the Top 40, where it will stay for thirty-six weeks, peaking at No. 3. It is Sylvester's second Top 40 hit.

February 22   Studio 54 throws a gala fifty-second birthday party for closeted gay attorney and former McCarthyite Roy Cohn, once deemed "the most vicious person in America." The event draws several hundred of the city's most glittering luminaries—including Donald Trump and Barbara Walters, as well as leaders of both the Republican and Democratic parties, and most of the city's elected officials—and features a two-foot-high birthday cake that is a replica of Cohn's head.

March 1   "From the interesting confusion of De Niro, Hoffman, and Pacino, we swing to the fairly opaque, sometimes sullen ultrabutch glamour of, say, Nick Nolte or Stallone, men whose style

ABOVE: *Playwright Tennessee Williams. "Everybody knew I was a gay playwright. Many, many years ago* Time *was the first publication to spell it out, that I was homosexual. I didn't give a damn."* GEORGE DANIELL **BELOW:** *Openly gay disco star Sylvester: The beat of a different drummer . . .* JEFF KA

of being men touches on the adolescent, the high school quarterback."
—NATHAN FAIN, *on the growing dominance of jock "beefcake" in the nation's movie theaters*

March 8   *The New York Times* runs a front-page photograph of six men being executed by firing squad in Iran for allegedly having committed crimes of "homosexual rape." Since the Ayatollah Khomeini's rise to power just four weeks earlier, there have been growing reports of gay men—as well as Jews, Baha'is, "blasphemers," "heretics," former members of the Iranian aristocracy, and others—being blackmailed, imprisoned, tortured, dismembered, hanged, and/or shot. By the time Khomeini gets around to celebrating the first anniversary of his Islamic revolution, the body count is reportedly in the thousands.

March 31   "In the Navy"—a song the U.S. Navy briefly considers using as a recruitment theme, until the full implications of the lyrics are explained—begins a thirteen-week run in the nation's Top 40.

"I've heard it on the radio, it's great," says one Navy spokesman before learning of the song's gay subtext. "The words are very positive, they talk about adventure and technology. My kids love it."

It is the Village People's last hit single in the U.S.

April 2   Having proclaimed "Disco Mania!" in a cover story two years earlier, *Newsweek* now features disco diva and gay cultural icon Donna Summer on its cover with the headline "DISCO TAKES OVER!"

April 6   Reviewing a current exhibit of pictures by thirty-two-year-old photographer Robert Mapplethorpe, a critic for *The New York Times* remarks that Mapplethorpe's work "gives one the creeps."

April 9   Maggie Smith wins a Best Supporting Actress Oscar for her portrayal of the angst-ridden wife of gay antique dealer Michael Caine in *California Suite*.

April 23   "The first time I saw men wearing Adidas running shoes as part of casual wear was in the homosexual community on Fire Island several years ago. Now it has become a fashion staple in the straight world."
—*A top male fashion model quoted in* Time *as part of a discussion on the strong influence of the "gay aesthetic" in mainstream American fashion and pop culture*

April 25   Jury selection begins in the murder trial of Dan White in San Francisco. Among those finally selected to sit in judgment of the former cop and city supervisor: an employee of the U.S. Army, a woman married to a cook in the county jail, and a retired cop who, it is learned later, is a friend of Dan White's uncle.

Meanwhile, published reports indicate that the city's policemen and firefighters have contributed more than $100,000 to White's defense fund.

April 28   Donna Summer's "Hot Stuff"—a rhythm-drenched paean to sexual urgency—begins a seventeen-week climb up the *Billboard* Top 40, where it eventually peaks at No. 1. Two months later, Summer's ode to prostitution, "Bad Girls," enjoys a similar success.

May 1   *Drummer* magazine begins running "Mr. Benson," an S&M fiction serial by one Jack Prescott that proves so popular—with its portrayal of what many see as *the* definitive topman—that it spawns, among other things, an entire line of T-shirts ("Looking for Mr. Benson," "Mr. Benson?" "Mr. Benson") that begin appearing in gay neighborhoods across the country. The series, as it turns out, is actually the work of well-known gay author John Preston, who eventually lays claim to the story and brings it out as a novel.

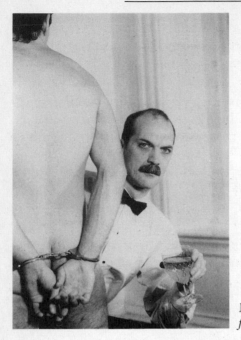

Mr. Benson *author John Preston and friend*. DIANE ELZE

In the nation's bookstores this month: *Homosexuality in Perspective*, the long-awaited inquiry into the sex lives of gay men and lesbians by the nation's most famous sex therapists, William Masters and Virginia Johnson. Among the duo's findings:

■ Committed homosexual lovers (those who have been together at least one year) communicate better than do heterosexual partners and have a more relaxed and solicitous understanding of their lovers' specific sexual needs and how to fulfill them.
■ Compared to heterosexual partners, lesbian couples devote an "extraordinary" amount of time to lovemaking.
■ Heterosexual fantasies are relatively common among gay men and lesbians.
■ Homosexuals, generally, are more adept in their lovemaking technique than heterosexuals.
■ In regard to sex in general, there are no significant physiological differences between homosexuals and heterosexuals.

The book quickly comes under fire, however, for Masters and Johnson's assertion that they have developed a course of therapy —with a 65 percent success rate—for those gays who genuinely wish to "convert" to heterosexuality.

May 16 "Good people—fine people from fine backgrounds—just don't kill people in cold blood."
—*Dan White's defense attorney, trying to convince jurors that White isn't really a killer at heart*

May 20 San Franciscan David Kloss wins the first annual Mr. International Leather title, in Chicago.

May 21 Dan White is found guilty on two counts of voluntary manslaughter, *not* first-degree murder, in the shooting deaths of George Moscone and Harvey Milk. The verdict—precipitated in part by White's claim that a steady diet of junk food diminished his capacity to act rationally on the day of the killings— unleashes a wave of rage and disbelief in the gay community, culminating in a massive riot—the White Night riot—at City Hall. By the time the violence is over, gay demonstrators— chanting "We want justice!" and "He got away with murder!"— have burned a dozen police cars; more than 160 people, including 50 policemen, have been injured. Damage in and around City Hall is estimated at $1 million. Proclaims one of the protesters, "Society is going to have to deal with us not as nice little fairies who have hairdressing salons, but as people capable of violence."

Meanwhile, in response to the verdict, a group of the city's policemen throw a celebration party at a downtown hotel. Says one of the cops, "We're celebrating. We were at City Hall the day [the murders] happened and we were smiling then. And we were there again tonight and we're still smiling."

White is later sentenced to seven years and eight months in prison, with the possibility of parole after only five years. "Sara

Jane Moore got life for *missing* Gerald Ford!" notes one indignant observer.

June 1   "A streetwise kid who figures he can make a lot of money by packaging his slick portraits and S&M photographs as art . . . blatantly tailored to appeal to interior decorators with vulgar taste . . . silly and tacky . . . contrived, offensive . . . nauseated me . . . I was appalled . . . These images were not born of passion, but of boredom and cynicism . . . stagy . . . insidious . . . shocking . . . malignant . . ."
—*Excerpts from an attack on the photography of Robert Mapplethorpe, not by Jesse Helms or Anita Bryant, but by* Christopher Street *magazine*

"The Bible says that just before Jesus comes to take all good Christians to heaven, there will be times when men will have unnatural affections towards other men."
—*A Christian activist, sharing her belief that Armageddon is just around the corner*

The Moral Majority is formed. The organization—composed of conservative, evangelical Christian activists, and based in the appropriately named community of Lynchburg, Virginia—has as its stated goals an opposition to gay rights, abortion, feminism, pornography, Communism, and the SALT II treaty. "Jesus was not a pacifist," says founder Jerry Falwell, defending the new militancy of his followers. "He was not a sissy."

June 19   "I'm not trying to get into new avenues. I'm just trying to deal with this one matter before me. I assume some people will be critical, but look at it this way: The man doesn't beat his son, and when you look at all the cases of child abuse you get from so-called straights, you grasp for words."
—*A state judge, awarding permanent legal custody of a thirteen-year-old boy to an openly gay minister in Catskill, New York. The minister had adopted the boy twelve months earlier, but had to fight for custody of him after he publicly acknowledged his live-in relationship with another man.*

July 1 The new Susan B. Anthony dollar—a small, octagonal coin meant to eventually replace the dollar bill—is unveiled by the U.S. Mint. The new currency proves so unpopular with the American public (for one thing, it is almost indistinguishable from a quarter) that mint officials are forced to curtail its production by the mid-1980s. Still, it is the first time an American woman—let alone one widely reputed to have been a lesbian—is featured on a U.S. coin.

July 7 Martina Navratilova and Billie Jean King win the women's doubles championship at Wimbledon.

July 12 With a crowd of several thousand spectators chanting "Disco sucks! Disco sucks!" Chicago disc-jockey Steve Dahl holds an antidisco rally in the city's Comiskey Baseball Park, burning hundreds of disco albums in center field.

July 25 Hundreds of irate demonstrators show up on Manhattan's Lower East Side to protest location shooting for William Friedkin's new film, *Cruising*, which deals with a series of grisly mutilation murders within the city's gay leather community. As gay extras (recruited by Friedkin for verisimilitude) relax between shots, demonstrators shout "Judas! Sell your brothers for thirty pieces of silver!" One man is arrested in the protests. "There will be killings," predicts gay journalist Arthur Bell. "The film will increase the hostility towards gays and give people ideas on how to act out that hostility."

Earlier in the day, the National Gay Task Force issued a statement calling the film "a gross distortion of the lives of gay men . . . portraying them as violent and sex-obsessed," and asked Mayor Koch to withdraw Friedkin's permit for shooting the film on the streets of New York. Koch declined.

Meanwhile, the film's producer, Jerry Weintraub, defends the movie by telling one reporter, "This is not out of Billy Friedkin's head or my head. We are depicting what is really there"—apparently forgetting that the movie is, after all, based on a novel, and one written in 1970 at that.

"I could never have *bought* this publicity," says an exuberant Friedkin.

September 1   Researchers at Columbia University conclude that homosexuality is not determined by hormones or other physiological factors, but is rather the result of upbringing and psychological influences.

———————————

"I don't think homosexuality is a life-filling subject. It's not a subject I would choose for my films. I don't think homosexuality is even an evening-filling subject."
—*Gay German film director* RAINER WERNER FASSBINDER, *whose critically acclaimed films include* The Bitter Tears of Petra von Kant *and* The Marriage of Maria Braun, *but only one of whose major films,* Fox and His Friends, *deals to any significant degree with homosexual characters*

September 17   Stephen M. Lachs becomes the first openly gay judge in the country when he is appointed to the Superior Court of Los Angeles by California governor Jerry Brown.

September 18   William Friedkin assures *The New York Times* that, as part of his research for the film *Cruising*, he sometimes disguised himself in leather and snuck into some of the city's gay leather bars.

September 19   "The first time I walked down the stairs to show my mom my transvestite outfit, she was a little upset. . . . It's fun to see people freak out at something that's not that weird."
—*An Arizona teenager, one of growing legions of devotees of the film* The Rocky Horror Picture Show, *which opened, flopped, and then found new life as an audience-participation experience on the midnight movie circuit*

> "With all the cross-dressing and everything else, I think it has an incredible exuberance to it that holds up. I think it's like a club that you can go into and it doesn't matter what you look like or who you are or what sex you are or what you want to be. . . . I think it's great, because it says, 'Don't dream it, be it.' "
>
> —SUSAN SARANDON, *on the unexpected longevity of* The Rocky Horror Picture Show

October 1 Pioneering lesbian film director Dorothy Arzner (*Christopher Strong, Craig's Wife, The Bride Wore Red*) dies at the age of eighty-two in La Quinta, California. Arzner had been in retirement since 1943.

October 14 The first national Gay and Lesbian Civil Rights March on Washington draws over one hundred thousand participants, becoming the climax of the decade-long gay liberation movement. "It was such a feeling of power," says one participant later, "like the storming of the Bastille." The old decade seems to be ending on a triumphant note for gay politics. Unfortunately, the national news media barely take notice.

October 21 *The New York Times* reports that eighteen boxes of recently unsealed correspondence between former First Lady Eleanor Roosevelt and American journalist Lorena Hickok will be the subject of a forthcoming book by Doris Faber. The letters—3,360 in all—had been largely ignored by researchers until recently, and raise the heretofore unimaginable possibility that Roosevelt may have had a lesbian affair with Hickok:

> "Hick darling . . . I couldn't say *je t'aime et je t'adore* as I longed to do, but always remember I am saying it, that I go to sleep thinking of you."

"Hick dearest . . . You have grown so much to be a part of my life that it is empty without you."

"Hick darling . . . I ache to hold you close."

"Oh, dear one, it is all the little things, tones in your voice, the feel of your hair, gestures, these are the things I think about and long for."

Unbeknownst to the public, Hickok lived in the White House with the Roosevelts for four years, shortly after FDR took office.

November 5 Interviewed by a reporter from *The San Francisco Examiner*, producer Allan Carr grows increasingly hostile when asked whether a forthcoming film biography of the Village People, *Can't Stop the Music*, will have the seemingly inevitable gay overtones. "It won't and it isn't," snaps Carr. "You don't spend $13 million to make a minority movie." Later, one of the group's members, Randy Jones ("Cowboy"), tells *The Advocate* he isn't worried about losing gay fans over the film (which will costar Valerie Perrine, Steve Guttenberg, and Olympic champion Bruce Jenner): "Look, we're making a big-budgeted movie, and movie money is conservative money—do you realize thirteen-year-old girls buy more of our records than anyone else?"

November 13 The San Francisco Police Department swears in its first openly gay police officers. Within a year, one out of every seven new recruits for the department is either gay or lesbian.

November 16 Martin Sherman's *Bent* begins previews at the New Apollo Theater in New York. An emotionally devastating drama about Nazi persecution of homosexuals, with Richard Gere and David Dukes as two men who become lovers in a concentration camp, the play draws rave reviews on Broadway and is later named one of the ten best plays of the year by *The New York Times*.

December 6 Satcom III—an RCA communications satellite devoted to transmitting religious broadcasts across the North American continent twenty-four hours a day—is launched into space.

By some estimates, there are now more than fourteen hundred radio and television stations in the United States specializing in Christian broadcasting. And the number is growing.

December 16   Accomplished prankster Barry Bremen—a thirty-two-year-old married insurance salesman who has previously masqueraded as a Kansas City Kings basketball player and a member of the New York Yankees—dons a blond wig, falsies, and a custom-made Dallas Cowboy Cheerleaders uniform and tries to sneak into the cheerleading squad in the middle of a Dallas–Washington Redskins game. He gets out one cheer—"Go, Dallas!"—before security men tackle and handcuff him. Unlike previous teams, who have been largely amused by his impostures, the Dallas management publicly blasts him as a "pervert," slaps him with a hefty lawsuit for trespassing and creating a nuisance, and tries to have him banned for life from Dallas Cowboys games.

1980

January 10 The Sisters of Perpetual Indulgence, a group of gay male "nuns"—part camp, part street theater, part social satire— "on a mission of holy hilarity," forms in San Francisco. Among the order's first "novitiates": Sister Missionary Position, Sister Homo Fellatio, and Sister Mary O'Stop. "We're tapping into a very old and venerable tradition within the gay male community," says Sister Missionary Position. "The drag queen as nun—it's one of the classic 'types.'" One of the sisters, Boom-Boom, eventually runs, unsuccessfully, for public office in San Francisco, and the group as a whole—with its public parodies of organized religion and its openly explicit "wars" against venereal disease, AIDS, and homophobia—draws the frequent ire of Jerry Falwell, who often uses them as an example of the "degeneracy" of the gay community.

Similar "sisterhoods" eventually start up in Canada, Australia, and England.

January 18 Having been sentenced to three and a half years in prison for income tax evasion, Studio 54 owners Steve Rubell and Ian Shrager are reported to be looking for someone to buy the now-fading, financially troubled discotheque.

Noted gay photographer and costume designer Cecil Beaton—who won Academy Awards for his costumes for *Gigi* and *My Fair Lady*—dies in England at the age of seventy-six.

January 21 President Carter—unaware that any religious pandering he attempts will soon be overshadowed by a Republican candidate whose propensity for such pandering will become legendary—takes time to remind a meeting of the National Religious Broadcasters that he is, just in case they've forgotten, a born-again Christian.

January 22 Having recently taken on William Friedkin's *Cruising*, the National Gay Task Force now holds a press conference to denounce another United Artists film, *Windows*, starring Elizabeth Ashley as a deranged lesbian who will stop at nothing—including psychological torture and rape—to "win" the affections of a recently divorced female neighbor. The film is doubly shocking to many since it represents the directorial debut of the otherwise extraordinarily gifted black cinematographer Gordon Willis, who, it is pointed out, should've known better.

February 1 Paul Schrader's disco-saturated morality play, *American Gigolo* (with Richard Gere as a high-priced Beverly Hills hustler who doesn't "do fags"), opens nationwide and immediately sets a new standard for male nudity in films when Gere bares not only his buttocks but his genitals, in a drawn-out scene during which he plaintively stares out a window while having an identity crisis.
    Despite its inherent homophobia, the entire film—with chic clothes, great-looking sets, and lots of flesh (all smothered in a pulsating disco soundtrack that one observer calls "music to turn tricks by")—seems somehow, rather perversely, rooted in the gay

aesthetic. "At the time," Schrader says later of the film, "we were at the apex of the gay movement in all its manifestations, especially in the arts. . . . The influence was everywhere—in our fashion, in disco, in the drug scene. It affected that film's aesthetic, too. All my friends at the time were gay."

February 4 Donna Summer shocks millions of her fans when she tells *People* magazine that she has recently become a born-again Christian and that God created disco music "so that I could be successful." Although some of her gay admirers could conceivably overlook this, they can't overlook it when, a few years later, she reportedly describes AIDS as having "been sent by God to punish homosexuals."

February 11 "It's perfectly all right with me. Some of the most gifted people I've ever met or read about are homosexual. How can you knock it?"

—LUCILLE BALL, *asked her opinion of gay rights*

February 15 William Friedkin's *Cruising* opens at movie theaters across the country—and is immediately blasted by gay and straight film critics alike, not only for its odious message (which seems to be that homosexuality is some kind of communicable disease that drives men to murder) but for what one critic calls its "hopelessly fouled up . . . narrative loopholes [and] unconvincing plot twists."

Friedkin (apparently oblivious to what the commotion is really all about) tells one magazine defensively, "It's funny that members of the gay community will go to see an out-and-out gay porno film that shows the same thing as *Cruising* depicts, but when that setting is presented by a major studio, members of the same community are terrified"—leading some commentators to note that most gay porn films don't show vivisection and murder as a postcoital inevitability in gay life.

Meanwhile, amid all the generally derisive reviews, *Cosmopolitan* hails the movie as "a film of stunning impact."

March 1 "I don't believe in the gay movement. . . . I think they should stay to themselves, just climb back into the cupboards. . . . I don't believe they are gay at all, they are very unhappy."
—*Australian-born media mogul* RUPERT MURDOCH, *soon to have control not only of Twentieth Century Fox and the Fox Broadcasting Network, but* TV Guide, The New York Post, The Chicago Sun-Times, *and a host of other influential publications and television stations*

March 6 Novelist Marguerite Yourcenar, author of *Memoirs of Hadrian*, becomes the first woman to be elected to the prestigious Académie Française since its founding 350 years ago by Cardinal Richelieu. Moans one dissenter, "A woman, as a woman, simply has no place in the Académie. . . . The Académie has survived over 300 years without women, and it could survive another 300 without them." Meanwhile, amid speculation about her forty-year live-in relationship with another woman, Yourcenar tells the press, somewhat contemptuously, "Because I lived with a woman for forty years, people assume I'm a lesbian."

March 12 After deliberating for less than two hours, a Chicago jury finds John Wayne Gacy guilty of thirty-three murders and sentences him to die in the electric chair.

March 21 "This so-called born-again Christian President is not acting very born-again. God's judgment is going to fall on America as on other societies that allowed homosexuality to become a protected way of life."
—*Fundamentalist Christian* BOB JONES, *president of Bob Jones University, condemning President Carter's perceived "leniency" on the issue of homosexuality. In the same remarks, Jones adds that it is impossible for a homosexual ever to be a Christian.*

March 24 In an article titled "The Gay World's Leather Fringe: Do Homosexual Males Consciously Seek Danger?" *Time* magazine (sounding eerily reminiscent of *both* Dr. David Reuben and William Friedkin) insists that gruesome homicides, dismembered corpses, and mutilated genitals are all commonplace hazards among the gay community's leather set—and then adds that any disclaimers to the contrary are simply "unconvincing." No statistical evidence for the claims is offered, although the movie *Cruising* is cited five times as proof of their validity.

March 27 *Anita Bryant's Spectacular: My Little Corner of the World*—an hour-long religious special meant to bring the nation back to "decency, morality and wholesome family life"—appears on television. Joining in tonight's crusade: Pat Boone, Efrem Zimbalist Jr., and General William Westmoreland. Later, the Pentagon comes under heavy criticism for having given Bryant the use of special facilities at West Point, and the use of the West Point Glee Club, free of charge for the telecast. "The arrangement," says *The New York Times*, "raises serious questions relating to the traditional separation of church and state."

Meanwhile, several other celebrities—including Art Linkletter, Jack LaLanne, and Lawrence Welk—have taken up Bryant's call to help halt the spread of the nation's gay rights movement.

April 1 *High Society* magazine runs a photo layout of a black male model—"Chocolate Thunder"—with an alleged nineteen-inch endowment, and offers "$1,000 an inch" to any man who can surpass that length.

April 15 In the nation's bookstores this month: Gay Talese's *Thy Neighbor's Wife*, an examination of sexual mores and experimentation in the United States. Despite a cover blurb announcing, "This is a book about America and about sex. It is about the men and women who shaped our sexual revolution. It is about the men and women who have lived it and are living it right now," there is no mention at all of male homosexuality in the book and the only references to lesbianism are in a standard heterosexual male context of, "Wow, I'd love to fuck two chicks at the same time." Says Talese, "This is not a book that deals with homosexuality or feminism or midget wrestlers."

It is an immediate best-seller.

> "I'm not really involved in any gay issues at the moment. My own anxieties have subsided with the times."
>
> —Playwright MART CROWLEY *(author of* The Boys in the Band*),*
> *working in 1980 as producer of the hit TV series* Hart to Hart

April 21　Illinois Congressman John Anderson—running for the Republican presidential nomination, but soon to break away as an independent candidate—publicly announces his support for federal gay rights legislation. "If freedom under our constitution is to have a real meaning," says Anderson, "this legislation is a natural extension of one's individual rights."

April 23　The first wave of the so-called "Mariel boatlift" brings a flotilla of ragtag boats and other craft bearing hundreds of refugees from Cuba to the United States. By the time it's all over, a total of 101,476 Cubans—among them several thousand homosexuals—have arrived in this country.

　　Several months later, there are published reports that a large number of the gay Cubans have not yet found sponsors and have been forced to continue living in hastily constructed refugee camps, where conditions are said to be "deplorable."

April 26　CBS broadcasts an hour-long documentary—*Gay Power, Gay Politics*—that purports to be about the emergence of gay political clout in San Francisco, but instead focuses obsessively on the more outré (and photogenic) aspects of gay sexuality—including sadomasochism, transvestism, and public sex in the city's parks—while making those acts seem like the focus of the entire gay rights movement. In one long segment, a sadomasochistic "consultant" describes the use, one by one, of various leather toys, and then explains why a police nightstick makes such a handy dildo. In another, leering close-ups track the arrival of drag queens at the city's Beaux Arts Ball, while a voice-over narration compares modern-day San Francisco to the decadence of 1930s Berlin. "The camera never got above the crotch level," one gay activist later complains.

The program outrages the San Francisco Board of Supervisors, which sends an angry letter of protest to CBS. Later, reacting to a complaint from the National Gay Task Force, the National News Council rules that CBS did indeed unfairly "exaggerate political concessions to gays and make those concessions appear as threats to public morals and decency. . . . Justification cannot be found for the degree of attention given to sadomasochism or the treatment of the Beaux Arts Ball and the Halloween sequences." The network is also faulted for doctoring the show's soundtrack in such a way as to bolster its conclusions.

Maureen Reagan, daughter of presidential candidate Ronald Reagan, addresses a fund-raising dinner for a gay GOP group in Los Angeles and tells the audience that despite her father's opposition to gay rights *and* his public remarks calling homosexuality "unnatural" *and* his growing political alliance with various leaders of the religious Right (including Jerry Falwell and Phyllis Schlafly), "he is a man who believes in fair play."

April 29 The Rev. Pat Robertson—quickly gaining increased national exposure on his burgeoning Christian Broadcasting Network—leads two hundred thousand evangelical Christians in a "Washington for Jesus" rally in the nation's capital. Says Robertson, in a speech to the demonstrators, "There is one ruler over the affairs of man—God Almighty. The Congress and the President are secondary to us."

Also speaking at the rally is the Rev. Jim Bakker (of television's popular *PTL Club*), who tells the crowd, "America has one last chance. God, help us to put the Bible back in our schools and our public life."

April 30 *Young, Gay and Proud*—the first gay-themed title from the Boston-based publisher Alyson Publications—arrives in bookstores. The publishing house—founded by gay activist Sasha Alyson—goes on to become the country's principal gay small press, giving many prominent gay writers, such as Michael Nava, their start, and Alyson himself—through his political activism and his outspoken opinions on controversial subjects (including unsafe sex, which he later bans from any novels he publishes)—emerges as one of the most influential figures in gay literature in the Eighties.

May 1 "My feeling is it's probably the safest park in the city now. If you scream, you know 15 guys will pop out of the bushes to help you . . ."
—*Longtime San Francisco resident* ISABEL WADE, *commenting in* The San Francisco Examiner *on gay cruising and public sex in the city's Buena Vista Park. In the same article, a San Francisco policeman reveals that gay men are usually not arrested for having sex in the park, so long as "they do it within the privacy of their own bush."*

May 19 The first Gay American Arts Festival gets under way in New York City.

May 22 Anita Bryant—having claimed just two years ago that the word wasn't even in her vocabulary—files for divorce from her husband of twenty years, Bob Green. "Right now," her mother tells the press, "she's off of men, and I don't blame her."

The marriage is officially dissolved four months later.

May 30 Having successfully sued his high school for the right to do so, Rhode Island teenager Aaron Fricke takes a male date, Paul Guilbert, to the senior prom.

June 1 "HOW TO BLOW YOURSELF: Yoga instructor has developed 4 basic exercises for self-love; these simple daytime exercises can make nights alone more fun. For instructions send name and address with $2.00 to . . ."
—*Classified ad in* Christopher Street

June 3 Three local gay rights measures in California—in Davis, San Jose, and Santa Clara County—all go down to defeat in referendum elections.

June 20 *Can't Stop the Music*—the sanitized film "biography" of the Village People—opens nationwide to a drubbing by critics and audiences alike. *The Advocate* calls it "thunderingly bad," while *The New York Times* dismisses it as "mostly dead air . . . no spontaneity, no variety." The anticipated hoards of adoring teenage girls stay away, and, having offended gay audiences even before its release, the film quickly disappears, memorable to some only for the occasional fleshiness of such numbers as the "Y.M.C.A." locker room–swimming pool sequence.

June 21 With a recent influx of straights threatening to take over the once predominantly gay resort Cherry Grove on Fire Island, local gays begin wearing T-shirts that read "STRAIGHTS OUT OF CHERRY GROVE" and "STRAIGHTS GO HOME." They also begin the practice—disconcerting to many heterosexuals—of loudly rating straight men and women on a scale of 1 to 10.

June 24 The Democratic Party adopts a gay rights plank for its 1980 party platform.

July 1 In the wake of Calvin Klein's success selling men's designer jeans with model Robert Ianucci shirtless on billboards and in magazines, a "beefcake wave" hits Madison Avenue, with everyone from Jordache Jeans to ADS Speakers hawking products with naked, or half-naked, men. Eminence Underwear advertises its product with a full-page ad showing a handsome cowboy—clad only in his hat and his briefs, with a long lasso dangling from one hand—with the ad copy, "WHAT FAMOUS COWBOY HORSES AROUND IN FRENCH BRIEFS?" Jockey International hires Baltimore Orioles pitcher Jim Palmer to pose in various briefs to hawk its new line of "European-styled" (i.e., very tight-fitting) Elance underwear. (The national ad campaign results in Palmer being mobbed by hundreds of women, including one shouting "Grab his underwear!" during an appearance at a Chicago shopping mall.) Paco Rabanne Cologne begins what is perhaps the most provocative campaign, with magazine ads showing a half-naked man on the phone in a bed full of tousled sheets, having a pointedly erotic conversation with his previous night's lover:

"Hello? What time did you leave?"
"I took your bottle of Paco Rabanne cologne."
"What on earth are you going to do with it . . .?"
"I'm going to take some and rub it on my body when I go to bed tonight. And then I'm going to remember every little thing about you . . . and last night."
"Do you know what your voice is doing to me?"

July 7 "The first all-singing, all-dancing horror film . . . chilling . . . a celebration of greed, narcissism, unbridled ambition and the triumph of mediocrity. . . . If this is the movie musical event of the '80s, we've got nine grim years ahead."
— Newsweek's DAVID ANSEN, *on* Can't Stop the Music

July 21 Thirty-two-year-old Italian Enso Francone, in Moscow for the summer Olympics, chains himself to a fence in Red Square to protest Soviet persecution of homosexuals. With Western journalists looking on, a group of KGB officers moves in and drags Francone away, though not before also surrounding and beating an NBC cameraman.

August 7 "When I was in drag on television, there were murmurings around—'Is Milton gay?' What if I was? Whose fucking business is it? I'm for it. I voted for gay rights. When the gays marched on Washington, they had the goddamned right to do it."
— MILTON BERLE

August 9 Eight San Franciscans begin offering public shares in the Atlas Savings and Loan Co.—the first openly gay-run savings and loan association in the country—which intends to open its first office, in the heart of the city's Castro district, in November. "I don't wear dresses. I don't wear makeup and I don't hang out in bars," says one of the founders, John Schmidt. "The impression I want to leave with people is that not all gays are that way. Gay people pay taxes, support charities and hold good jobs. They are also good business."

August 14   The name of black gay activist Mel Boozer is placed in nomination for Vice-President of the United States at the Democratic National Convention in New York City. "Would you ask me how I dare to compare the civil rights struggle with the struggle for lesbian and gay rights?" asks Boozer, in a passionate address to the convention. "I can compare them and I do compare them, because I know what it means to be called a 'nigger' and I know what it means to be called a 'faggot,' and I understand the differences in the marrow of my bones. And I can sum up that difference in one word: *none*. Bigotry is bigotry. Discrimination is discrimination. It hurts just as much. It dishonors our way of life just as much. And it betrays a common lack of understanding, fairness, and compassion just as much."

As expected, Carter and Mondale are renominated as the party's candidates.

September 1   Gay porn idol Johnny Harden appears as *Playgirl* magazine's "Man of the Month," under the *nom de heterosexual* Jean Carrier.

After a San Francisco columnist suggests that gay men wear stuffed bears instead of colored handkerchiefs in their back pockets to indicate their various sexual specialties, gift shops in the city experience a run on hundreds of tiny teddy bears that begin appearing as part of "the gay look" not only all over the Castro district, but eventually nationwide, even in nude model layouts and in advertisements in national gay magazines.

The fad reaches its apex when one San Francisco company begins marketing "Leather Teddy," a small stuffed bear complete with real black leather chaps, vest, and cap, for $125.

In the nation's bookstores this month: *Christianity, Social Tolerance, and Homosexuality*, John Boswell's comprehensive—and

Errol Flynn in Virginia City *(1940). Apparently, it was all right to bring up the statutory rape charges, but* bisexuality . . . *Truman Capote, among others, claimed to have had a fling with him.*

iconoclastic—study of homosexuality in medieval Europe. The book—which attempts to clarify the origins of modern Christian hostility toward homosexuality, while challenging the long-held presumption that that hostility was inherent in the Christian faith from the beginning—is instantly acclaimed in both the gay and the mainstream press.

September 9   The Leonard Matlovich case reaches its conclusion when a federal judge orders the Air Force to reinstate Matlovich with full back pay. To avoid reenlisting him, however, the Air Force offers him a financial settlement of $160,000, which—having fought his case in court now for more than five years—he accepts.

September 15   *Christopher Street* magazine reveals it has 8,451 subscribers, with a total paid circulation of about 22,000.

September 20   The Saint—a cavernous, members-only gay disco featuring nearly 2,000 revolving lights, a massive centerpiece planetarium projector, a 76-foot-high dome over the dance floor, and a sprawling balcony area meant for intimate sexual encounters—opens in New York City. Within a few short weeks, nearly 3,000 men have paid $250 to join, and an inexhaustible waiting list has been established.

"I'm scared to death of what's emerging in the gay middle class. I was at the Saint in costume the other night and I was petrified. I felt like Jezebel when she came into the room with a scarlet dress. No one wanted to go near me. Everyone was so afraid to be different. I call it a gay middle-class vacuum. This conformity is a dangerous thing."

—*Gay entertainer "HIBISCUS" (George Harris), founder of the Cockettes*

September 30 The daughters of late actor Errol Flynn file suit in a Canadian court to "clear" their father's name, after a biography—*Errol Flynn: The Untold Story* by Charles Higham—claims the movie star was a Nazi spy and an avidly practicing bisexual. The two daughters are reported to be particularly upset by the book's contention that Flynn had sex with both Tyrone Power and Howard Hughes. However, because U.S. law holds that the dead cannot be libeled (and therefore damages cannot be collected in their name), the two women are forced to file their suit in a foreign country.

October 3 Conservative activist Representative Robert Bauman (R-Maryland)—a staunch supporter of the Moral Majority, and one of the founding members of the American Conservative Union—is arrested in Washington, D.C., for soliciting sex from a sixteen-year-old boy. "I have been plagued by two afflictions," he tells reporters at a press conference, "alcoholism and homosexual tendencies. But I do not consider myself a homosexual."

Soon afterward, reelection billboards bearing Bauman's face

and the slogan "For All the People" are vandalized with spray paint to read "*Blows* All the People."

The voters do not return him to Congress.

October 22 Senator Thomas Eagleton (D-Missouri) appears in federal court to deny accusations by his niece that he is a homosexual. "It's absolutely and totally false," says Eagleton, whose niece is on trial for having tried to blackmail him. Despite his denial, the niece persists in her claim that the Senator "is bisexual, if not totally gay," and claims that he once had a torrid weekend romance with another well-known U.S. senator in Key West.

In 1972, Eagleton had been dropped as George McGovern's running mate, ostensibly because he had once undergone shock treatments for depression.

October 30 *The Advocate* reports on the recent gay tourist boom in the Russian River area in northern California, revealing that cabins which sold for only $12,000 four years ago are now priced upwards of $100,000. Says one longtime resident of the area, "When I see a lodge being improved I always know it's gay if they put up a six-foot fence."

November 1 Robert Kronemeyer's new book, *Overcoming Homosexuality*, recommends, among other things, a strict vegetarian diet to "cure" gay men and lesbians of their sexual orientations.

November 4 Oklahoman Don Nickles (or as Ronald Reagan once inadvertently called him at a campaign rally, "Don Rickles") is elected to his first term in the U.S. Senate. A staunchly conservative Republican, Nickles soon makes a name for himself as a Bible-thumping homophobe whose voting record on gay issues is every bit as conservative as Jesse Helms's.

In Massachusetts, former state legislator Barney Frank—a faithful advocate of gay and lesbian rights—is elected to his first term in the U.S. House of Representatives.

Nationally, Jimmy Carter is defeated 51 percent to 41 percent (with nearly 7 percent of the vote going to independent candidate John Anderson) by former actor Ronald Reagan, whose conservative coattails apparently account for the ousting of such staunch Senate liberals as George McGovern, Birch Bayh, and Frank Church. Democrats also lose thirty-three seats in the House of Representatives.

November 9　　Two San Francisco gay men are brutally attacked and beaten by a gang of twenty young Hispanics near the city's Dolores Park. The two men suffer stab wounds, broken bones, and severe lacerations.

November 15　　In the nation's bookstores this month: *Buns* by Christie Jenkins, a ninety-six-page photographic paean to men's buttocks, soon to be followed by *Cheeks* (more male buttocks, this time from the editors of *Playgirl*), *Zippers* (devoted to men's flies), and *Body Parts* (a sexual potpourri of men's legs, buttocks, chests, arms, crotches, and feet).

November 19　　Two gay men are killed and six others wounded when a thirty-eight-year-old former transit cop opens fire on a New York gay bar, the Ramrod, with a submachine gun. The assailant, Ronald Crumpley (who says he was acting on orders from God), is later found not guilty by reason of insanity. Throughout his trial, he repeatedly referred to gay people as "agents of the devil."

November 22　　Mae West dies in Los Angeles at the age of eighty-eight. Contrary to rumors that have been circulating for years, she is *not*, after her death, revealed to have been a man masquerading all those years as a woman.

November 24　　Presidential offspring and Joffrey Ballet dancer Ron Reagan—so widely rumored to be gay that his father seemed compelled to issue denials from the campaign trail—marries girlfriend Doria Palmieri in New York City.

November 27 *Bosom Buddies*—starring Tom Hanks and Peter Scolari as two oversexed New York boys who dress in drag to live at the all-girl Susan B. Anthony Hotel—premieres on ABC.

December 1 "I have a lot of man in me."
—*Singer* GRACE JONES, *featured nude this month in erotic poses with another woman in* Hustler *magazine*

Unaware that they are about to plug into one of the most potent gay male trends of the new decade, *Drummer* magazine publishes a new feature, *Drummer Daddies: In Search of Older Men*, that results in a deluge of reader mail (including photos, personal experiences, and fantasies), all surrounding the search by many gay men for an older, authoritarian daddy figure and lover. So potent is the new trend—which seems, blessedly, to bely the old myth that gay life ends at thirty—that *Drummer* eventually publishes entire special editions devoted to the phenomenon. The "daddy craze" also eventually gives rise to a new gay publication, *Daddy: The Magazine*, as well as a "Dial-A-Daddy" phone jack-off service.

The *American Journal of Psychiatry* publishes an article citing religious conversion as a cure for homosexuality.

Anita Bryant tells *The Ladies' Home Journal* she no longer feels as militantly as she once did about gay rights. "The answers don't seem so simple now," acknowledges the singer, who also admits to having been unfaithful to her ex-husband. "I'm more inclined to say live and let live."

December 5 *The New York Native*—a weekly newspaper started by publisher Charles Ortleb to help support his financially ailing *Christopher Street*—makes its debut.

December 10 Claiming that his trial judge made a technical error during sentencing, Dan White asks for—and is denied—a sixteen-month reduction in his prison sentence.

December 14   The film *La Cage aux Folles* ends a record-breaking nineteen-month run at the 68th Street Playhouse in New York City. "I don't know of any movie that has run at one theater in the United States for nineteen months," says a spokesman for the Motion Picture Association of America. "It probably is a record." The theater's owner, Meyer Ackerman, reports it was common for people to come back and see the film as many as four or five times.

A zany farce about two gay lovers running a nightclub that specializes in transvestite revues, the movie goes on to become the highest-grossing foreign film of all time, a distinction it holds until the release of *The Gods Must Be Crazy* four years later.

December 18   The New York State Court of Appeals abolishes the state's sodomy laws.

December 20   According to recently released statistics, at least one person a day is physically assaulted in New York City for being gay.

1981

January 1 Continuing its tradition of using good-looking gay centerfold models and then writing copy that makes them out as all-American jocks in search of the perfect "foxy lady," *Playgirl* chooses gay porn star J.W. King—appearing under his real name, James Waldrop—as its "Man of the Month."

January 12 *Dynasty* premieres on ABC. The convoluted story line—about a Denver oil baron and his materialistic, bickering family, all of whose members, according to one critic, are "either filthy rich and disgusting, or not-so-rich and disgusting"—includes a subplot about the tycoon's homosexual son, Steven (played by Al Corey). In fact, the opening season cliff-hanger finds the family patriarch on trial for having murdered Steven's male lover. Although the series eventually moves to number one in the ratings—and inspires an entire line of *Dynasty* clothes, *Dynasty* perfumes, *Dynasty* jewelry, and even *Dynasty* fine china (while reviving the sinking career of one slightly overbearing British screen siren)—it barely finishes nineteenth in its premiere season, well behind *Dallas*, *The Dukes of Hazzard*, and *The Love Boat*.

January 19   President Carter serves his last full day in office. Contrary to expectations raised during his 1976 campaign, he has never issued an executive order banning discrimination against gay people in housing, employment, or the military.

January 20   Capping off a four-day, $11 million celebration in the nation's capital—the most expensive roster of inaugural parties in American history—sixty-nine-year-old former B-movie actor Ronald Reagan is inaugurated as the fortieth President of the United States, ushering in a new national wave of social conservatism. Even before taking office, Reagan has begun filling his administration with neoconservative activists, many of whom are outspokenly antigay. The Moral Majority's chief Washington lobbyist, Robert Billings, is appointed to a high post in the Department of Education, while Faith Ryan Whittlesey, a born-again Christian who has publicly expressed her disgust for the gay community, is appointed head of the White House liaison office. Edwin Meese—a vitriolic conservative who barely seems to believe in civil rights for blacks and Hispanics, let alone gay men and lesbians—is named chief White House counselor, with Cabinet rank.

Nancy Reagan tells *The Washington Post* that her husband's election signals the country's "return to a higher sense of morality." "It kind of filters down from the top somehow," she adds.

January 23   American composer Samuel Barber, who twice won the Pulitzer Prize for music and who was for many years the lover of noted operatic composer Gian Carlo Menotti, dies in his Manhattan apartment after a long illness. He was seventy.

February 1   An article in *High Fidelity* magazine suggests that Russian composer Peter Ilyich Tchaikovsky did not die of cholera as has been widely assumed for more than eighty years, but in fact committed suicide to avoid an impending scandal over his passionate interest in the nephew of a prominent Russian duke.

February 4 U.S. Congressman Jon Hinson (R-Mississippi)—having been arrested five years earlier on similar charges at the Iwo Jima Memorial—is arrested for performing an act of "oral sodomy" with a twenty-eight-year-old man in the rest room of a House of Representatives office building.

"That men's room had practically been a whorehouse," says one unnamed source, "and half the administrative aides on the Hill had been working it. It was outrageous for Hinson to do that right on the Hill."

Hinson pleads no contest and is given a thirty-day suspended sentence.

February 5 Armed with crowbars and sledgehammers, police in Toronto stage a massive (and highly destructive) raid on four local gay bathhouses, and arrest 305 men, the largest civilian mass arrest in Canadian history and the largest mass arrest of gay men in North America. One arrestee tells the press that during the raids, cops answered the bathhouse phones and cheerfully told callers, "Yeah, it's a busy night, come on down."

The raids prompt a riot by more than three thousand angry demonstrators the following night. "It was our Stonewall," says one participant.

February 10 Shortly after eight o'clock in the evening, a heavy fire races through the upper floors of the Las Vegas Hilton Hotel, killing eight people, injuring 198, and causing over $10 million in damages. Police later arrest a busboy—twenty-three-year-old Philip Bruce Cline—who claims he accidentally started the fire with a marijuana cigarette while having sex on the eighth floor with a hotel guest named "Joe." Cline is later convicted of murder and arson and, despite the prosecution's request for the death penalty, he is sentenced to eight consecutive terms of life imprisonment without the possibility of parole.

_____

The Moral Majority announces it will launch a $3 million media campaign—including billboards, TV commercials, and newspaper ads—against homosexuality and gay rights in San Francisco. "I agree with capital punishment," says a spokesman for the group, "and I believe homosexuality is one of those [acts] that could be coupled with murder and other sins." The city, he adds, has become "the Sodom and Gomorrah of the United States and the armpit of this perverted movement."

February 19   *The New York Times* reports that attorney Roy Cohn has gained unprecedented access to the Reagan administration and may soon have a hand in selecting federal judges and U.S. prosecutors. The article notes that, shortly after the election, members of the Reagan inner circle threw a lavish party for Cohn, ostensibly in recognition of his fund-raising efforts in New York City.

   Asked if he has any ethical qualms about appearing before a judge he may have helped to appoint, Cohn tells the newspaper he's certain any judge would "bend over backwards to let you know you're not getting a break."

March 4   A twenty-year-old Kansas City truck driver, David Groves, is found guilty of murder in the June 1980 shooting death of a gay man. Groves had told police "it was an honor" to kill a homosexual.

March 28   Donna Summer's "Who Do You Think You're Foolin' " enters the *Billboard* charts at No. 40, where it hangs on for two weeks before disappearing from sight.

March 31   "Women's liberation and gay liberation [are] part of the same thing: a weakening of the moral standards of this nation. It is appalling to see parades in San Francisco and elsewhere proclaiming 'gay pride' and all that. What in the world do they have to be proud of?"

—NANCY REAGAN, *quoted in* The Globe

April 1   *Ebony* magazine runs a feature article asking the question, "Is Homosexuality a Threat to the Black Family?"—and, happily, concludes it is not. Moreover, the article—written by a black psychologist—seeks to dispel the myth that whites somehow "introduced" homosexuality into the black community to weaken and destroy it.

April 12   Four gay men are beaten—one to death—when six North Carolinians wielding logs and shouting "We're going to beat some faggots!" lay siege to a gay sunbathing area along the Little River near Durham.

April 21   Two gay men are arrested when a policeman spots them giving each other a brief good-bye kiss at the Fort Lauderdale airport. They are later convicted of creating a public nuisance and given probation.

April 28   Former Beverly Hills hairdresser Marilyn Barnett files a multimillion-dollar "palimony" suit against tennis pro Billie Jean King, claiming the two had a lesbian relationship for seven years and that she is therefore entitled to the tennis star's Malibu beach house as well as half of King's earnings from the period when they were together. Although King at first dismisses Barnett's claims as "untrue and unfounded," she later holds a press conference to acknowledge the relationship. But, she adds, she is not a lesbian. ("I hate being called a homosexual," she tells *People* magazine, "because I don't feel that way. It really upsets me.") Meanwhile, King's husband, Larry, publicly takes the blame for the affair, suggesting that his repeated long business trips away from home may have forced Billie Jean to look for love and affection somewhere else.

Despite a renewed national debate over homosexuality in sports (How many are there? What are they doing there? Should "they" be role models for "our" children?), commentators are for the most part sympathetic:

"The sex lives of individual athletes are strictly their own business."

—*Sports Illustrated*

"Billie Jean managed to turn a tawdry legal blackmail attempt by an ex-girlfriend into a personal portrait in courage."

—PETE AXTHELM, *Newsweek*

"Anyone who drops her now should be ashamed. I think if you turn your back on someone, you lose some points. Someone up there is a scorekeeper."
—*New York advertising agent* JERRY DELLA FEMINA, *on reports that would-be sponsors (including Avon) are reconsidering using Billie Jean for product endorsements*

"For some people, homosexuality pushes a button of profound hostility and terror. . . . I'm sure that Billie Jean's reluctance to be open about this time of her life came from a profound understanding of that core of bigotry."
—*Syndicated columnist* ELLEN GOODMAN

May I   A new report in the *Annals of Emergency Medicine* shows that inhaling "poppers" can lead to certain forms of anemia in some individuals.

May 5   After customs officials at New York's JFK Airport find a gay love letter in his luggage, British traveler Phillip Fotheringham is denied entry into the United States and forced to return home on the next flight back to London.

> "When you run a business, you don't go around asking people what their sexual preference is. I am not concerned with sexual preference."
> —ANITA BRYANT, *on the occasion of her recently having opened a women's clothing boutique in Alabama*

May 6   PBS begins airing the much-publicized four-part television drama *The Search for Alexander the Great*, which, despite its attempts to deal with the complexities of the Macedonian conqueror's personality, never really touches on his homosexuality at all. (Hephaestion is briefly noted to have been Alexander's "best friend.") Says San Francisco columnist Terence O'Flaherty, "To recount the life of Alexander the Great without dwelling on his homosexuality is like telling the story of Mother Cabrini without mentioning her Catholicism."

May 14   The Reagan administration cancels a White House subscription to *The Advocate*. During the Carter presidency, *The Advocate* arrived regularly every two weeks at the Oval Office. Quips the newspaper, "Maybe Nancy dislikes the pink section," in reference to the insert featuring personal ads and "adult" products.

May 15   In the midst of Lesbian/Gay Awareness Week at the University of Florida, a fraternity-circulated petition asserting that "Homosexuals need bullets—not acceptance" draws the signatures of almost fifty people. "We don't have anything else to do," says one of the petition's organizers. "We're just out here having a good time. I don't believe in queers."

May 16   More than twenty people marching in a gay rights demonstration in Helsinki, Finland, are arrested by the police and charged with "encouraging lewd behavior."

May 21   "It's parents who get uptight, not children. Children will gravitate to people if they know you've got a good heart, if you're kind and good. Adults have this fear and transfer it to children. They assume if someone is a homosexual, they're bad. I don't think it makes any difference."

—BILLIE JEAN KING

May 28 "It seems important to keep ideas separate from personalities, at least until both can be appreciated in their own rights. . . . I'm trying to say that assessing my book on the basis of what one can second-guess about my personality does not seem the most productive first-line approach. . . . I would rather people responded to my ideas than to me."
—*Historian and author* JOHN BOSWELL, *dodging—with some grace— what everyone seems to want to know, "But are* you *gay?" as if it had some relevance one way or the other to his research*

May 30 "You won't find too many homosexual murderers on television these days. But you won't find too many gay doctors or lawyers, either. A lot of people have said, 'To hell with the whole issue.' "
—*TV producer* DAVID GERBER *(who came under heavy fire in 1974 for an episode of* Police Woman *in which three lesbians were portrayed as murdering residents of a nursing home for their money), on the growing resentment in Hollywood over gay groups trying to prescribe how gay men and lesbians should be depicted on television*

June 1 With the publication of the anthology *Meat* (and its arrival at No. 1 on the national gay best-seller list), thousands of gay readers are suddenly introduced to *The Manhattan Review of Unnatural Acts* (from which the anthology is drawn), a small New York City-based magazine that *The Village Voice* once labeled "the roughest, raunchiest, most explicitly sexual gay publication." Although the anthology, with its kinky headlines and no-nonsense jack-off prose style, is intensely erotic, and sometimes startlingly funny—"Youths Remove Jockey Shorts, Sit on Coach's Face," "Closet Queen Cop Gets His," "20-Year-Old Gets His Head Under Guardsman's Kilt"—the similarity in many of the stories' details, and the repetition of certain key phrases, lead some readers to speculate whether these "true experiences" are true at all, or whether most of them have been written by the magazine's founder, Boyd MacDonald. The book's success spawns an entire series of equally successful sequels, including *Cum*, *Flesh*, and *Sex*.

June 3   A Maryland court upholds a state law making oral sex—between homosexuals *or* heterosexuals—a crime. The court's written decision quotes heavily from Deuteronomy, Leviticus, and Exodus.

June 11   "Bodybuilding is rapidly becoming *the* pastime of gay America, with big biceps now as sure an indication of homosexuality as limp wrists once were. Especially on the West Coast, hordes of gay hunks and aspiring hunks can be seen walking around town with their gym bags—now a *de rigueur* piece of gay equipment—either going to or coming from their daily workout. . . . I have a friend who is so ashamed of his physique that he bought a set of weights at Sears to use at home so he could build up his body enough to go to a gym."

—LENNY GITECK, *on the gay muscle-building craze*

June 15   Procter and Gamble chairman Owen Butler announces that his corporation is withdrawing its commercials from fifty network television programs that feature too much sex, violence, or profanity. The announcement comes in response to complaints from the Coalition for Better Television (a Moral Majority-type group headed by the Rev. Donald Wildmon, who is also president of the National Federation for Decency), which is trying to organize national boycotts of TV shows that do not support or adequately portray "traditional family values." Says Butler, "We think the coalition is expressing some very important and broadly held views. . . . I can assure you we are listening very carefully to what they say."

June 17   Senator Roger Jepsen (R-Iowa) introduces the so-called "Family Protection Act" ("to strengthen the American family and to promote the virtues of family life") in Congress. The bill mandates, among other things, that no person who is homosexual, or who even intimates that homosexuality is an acceptable lifestyle, can receive federal funds under such programs as Social Security, welfare, veterans' benefits, or student assistance. It also requires that all textbook materials used in public schools reinforce the traditional "role of men and women," with no ambiguities in societal sex roles or sexual relationships. Although the bill disappears and reappears several times in Congress over the next few years, it is never passed.

Jepsen later loses his 1984 bid for reelection, after revelations about his membership in a private "health" spa that turned out to be a house of prostitution.

June 18   The so-called McDonald Amendment—prohibiting Legal Services Corporation from assisting in "any case which seeks to promote, defend or protect homosexuality" (in other words, prohibiting the LSC from taking on any gay discrimination cases, including the custody battles of lesbian mothers)—is passed by the U.S. House of Representatives, 281 to 124. The measure was introduced by ardently homophobic congressman Larry McDonald, a conservative Democrat from Georgia.

June 24   People for the American Way—a group recently formed by television producer Norman Lear to combat the growing "climate of fear and repression" fostered by "moral majoritarians"—announces it will begin airing a series of television commercials, starring Carol Burnett, Goldie Hawn, and others, emphasizing the importance of social diversity and political pluralism in America.

June 25   "I was in San Francisco last year for Gay Pride XI, and the parade struck me as very different from those I had seen before. It didn't seem to be a mass outpouring of anger and determination. There weren't hordes of unaffiliated but impassioned marchers. In fact, there was hardly anyone in the parade who wasn't in some witty costume, on a horse or float or bike, or part of a clearly defined group ('Gays Against Brunch'). The real crowds weren't in the street but at the curb, laughing and cheering. They were, I

thought, the same mobs who might have turned out for St. Patrick's Day or the Chinese New Year."
—*Essayist* RICHARD HALL, *on the change in tone over the past ten years of Gay Pride marches*

June 29 Two fifteen-year-old Indiana boys stab to death a thirty-seven-year-old gay man in a parking lot in Burnham, Illinois. They are later caught and charged with murder and armed robbery.

June 30 Florida governor Bob Graham signs into law the so-called "Trask Amendment," which prohibits the appropriation of any state funds to universities that grant recognition to gay student groups. The amendment is later struck down as unconstitutional by the Florida Supreme Court.

July 1 "Who are we to knock it if someone is gay? I think every man or woman has the right to choose how to live his or her own life. . . . There is such an injustice involved in Billie Jean's situation. She is the one whose personality, intelligence and charisma made women's tennis what it is today. . . . Her enthusiasm and her courage, I would hate to see her lose any of that because that would be an even bigger injustice than the invasion of her privacy."
—CHRIS EVERT LLOYD, *defending Billie Jean King in* Tennis World *magazine*

July 3 *The New York Times* reports the outbreak of a rare form of cancer, Kaposi's sarcoma, among forty-one previously healthy gay men. Dr. Alvin Friedman-Kien of New York University Medical Center says that at least nine of the men have "severe defects in their immunological systems."

July 6 A federal judge rules that a Houston ordinance prohibiting men from cross-dressing is unconstitutional.

July 9 Republican Senator Barry Goldwater—looking increasingly moderate these days, compared to such up-and-coming conservative spokesmen as Jesse Helms and Jerry Falwell—publicly expresses his irritation with the rancorous intolerance of the New Right, and tells reporters he thinks that "every good Christian ought to kick Falwell right in the ass!"

July 13 "One executive told me I couldn't be a hit singer because I didn't have any element of submission in my voice."
—*Lesbian singer* HOLLY NEAR, *profiled in* People *magazine*

July 20 Despite having privately acknowledged her bisexuality to officials from the Immigration and Naturalization Service, Czechoslovakian-born tennis champion Martina Navratilova is finally granted U.S. citizenship, six years after she defected.

Nine days later, she is officially "outed" in the New York *Daily News* by reporter Steve Goldstein.

"It was really a joke, if you think about it," says Navratilova in 1985, in her autobiography, *Martina*, "people drooling over little tidbits about whether I'm this or that. . . . I never thought there was anything strange about being gay. Even when I thought about it, I never panicked and thought, Oh, I'm strange, I'm weird, what do I do now?"

> "I'd like to see somebody at the top whom the younger players can look up to. It is very sad for children to be exposed to it. . . . Because of the lesbian influence, there are now some players who don't even go to the tournament changing rooms."
> —*Born-again Christian and former Wimbledon champion* MARGARET COURT, *on lesbianism in professional tennis*

July 21 George Hamilton plays the twin roles of Don Diego Vega and his look-alike gay brother Bunny Wigglesworth in the new farce *Zorro, the Gay Blade*. It is roundly panned by the critics.

July 26 Poet and translator Dr. Jeanette Howard Foster—author of the groundbreaking 1956 bibliography *Sex-Variant Women in Lit-*

erature (which she originally had to publish with a vanity press, since no other publisher would handle it)—dies in Arkansas.

August 1   MTV makes its premiere on the nation's cable systems. Within months, the network's astonishing rise in popularity makes videos a sudden necessity in the music industry, and many of the clips themselves become little more than miniature "soft-core" porn films, selling scantily clad teenage girls, male beefcake, violence, lots of sex, and so much phallic imagery that the network itself eventually begins airing a series of commercials spoofing its own obsessions with fire hoses, big guitars, and other priapic symbols. Just as "talking" films wrecked the careers of several fine actors whose voices weren't clear or resonant enough, so rock video now threatens to leave behind many would-be singers and musicians who aren't particularly photogenic or whose asses don't look cute in tight jeans.

August 2   Thirteen years after her teenage son left a goodbye note on the dining-room table—"Dear Mother and Dad, I have left home because I'm a homosexual"—Los Angeles mother Adele Starr, along with some two dozen other concerned parents from around the country, founds Parents and Friends of Lesbians and Gays, a national support group for parents of homosexual children. "The law said my son was a criminal," says Starr, who is elected the group's first president. "The church said he was a sinner, and the medical profession said he was sick. Books implied that I caused it all. . . . What those of us with gay children have learned is that there's nothing wrong with our kids, but there's a lot of problems in the community out there."

The organization eventually gives rise to almost two hundred chapters nationwide, with more than seven hundred thousand copies of its pamphlet, *About Our Children*, in circulation.

August 15   In the nation's bookstores this month: *The Celluloid Closet*, Vito Russo's groundbreaking exploration of how homosexuality has been portrayed in the movies, from silent films to the present. Says Russo, in a subsequent edition of the book, "The history of the portrayal of lesbians and gay men in mainstream cinema is politically indefensible and aesthetically revolting. . . . Gay visibility has never really been an issue in the movies. It's *how* they have been visible that has remained offensive for almost a century."

August 26   Roger Baldwin, one of the founding members of the American Civil Liberties Union, dies in New Jersey at the age of ninety-seven. Though heterosexual, Baldwin was one of the earliest political crusaders in the fight to abolish state sodomy laws and other discriminatory laws against homosexuals in the U.S.

———————

Mary Morgan, the first openly lesbian judge in the U.S., is appointed to the San Francisco Municipal Court by California governor Jerry Brown.

August 28   The Centers for Disease Control reveal that cases of Kaposi's sarcoma, as well as a rare parasitical form of pneumonia —pneumocystis—are inexplicably increasing across the country. More than 90 percent of the cases have been diagnosed in gay men. One researcher speculates the diseases may be linked to the men's "sexual lifestyle, drug use, or some other environmental cause."

September 1   "The last of my films that my parents saw was *Mondo Trasho* in 1968. . . . They left the theater in tears and told me I was going to die in a mental institution, go insane or commit suicide."
—*Gay film director* JOHN WATERS, *now enjoying increasing mainstream success with his latest film*, Polyester, *starring Tab Hunter and Divine*

———————

The International Football Federation suggests that the sight of soccer players "jumping on top of each other, kissing and embracing"—and, of course, patting each other's rear ends—after scoring a goal or winning a match is offensive and should be banned.

September 13   A gay tourist from Seattle is stabbed to death when he and a friend are the victims of an unprovoked attack while walking down Polk Street in San Francisco. According to police, thirty-one-year-old Nicholas Ritus was stabbed more than twenty times after a group of men pulled up alongside him in a Pontiac and asked, with seeming innocence, "Are you dudes gay?" The survivor of the attack, thirty-four-year-old Barry Mabus, later recalls, "We were walking down the street, laughing. We were saying San Francisco isn't such a scary place after all."

Three men are later arrested in connection with the murder.

September 18 *Mommie Dearest*, starring Faye Dunaway as a demented and not-quite-so-motherly Joan Crawford, opens at movie theaters across the country, making the lines "No more wire hangers!" and "Don't fuck with me, fellas—this ain't my first time at the rodeo!" instant camp classics, especially among gay men. Within months, midnight showings of the film (in the tradition of *The Rocky Horror Picture Show*) are springing up around the country: audience members often show up dressed as Crawford and arm themselves with scrub brushes, cans of tile cleaner, pruning shears, and, of course, wire hangers. Several years later, Dunaway acknowledges that her performance in the film was high camp, and confides to an interviewer that her decision to play the role was probably a major career mistake.

September 21 Conservative Arizona judge Sandra Day O'Connor—nominated to fill the Supreme Court vacancy left by departing moderate Potter Stewart—is confirmed by the U.S. Senate, 99 to 0.

October 1 The U.S. House of Representatives rejects a bill to decriminalize homosexual acts between consenting adults in the District of Columbia.

With competition among gay magazines growing fiercer every month, Donald Embinder sells the now financially ailing *Blueboy* and leaves his position as the magazine's publisher. Due to confusion (or just plain greed) during the transition, some of the magazine's current writers are left with uncollectible invoices and are never paid for their work. Meanwhile, the magazine begins a quick succession of different editors (five in eighteen months), and the magazine's quality—already iffy when Embinder sold it—begins a quick tailspin that reaches its nadir when model photographs are occasionally published upside down and the printing becomes so cheap that entire layouts are indecipherable because of ink splotches and bleeding colors. Still, the name *Blueboy* is enough to keep the magazine limping along for several more years.

October 2 *Taxi Zum Klo* (literally, "Taxi to the Toilet")—Frank Ripploh's cheerfully explicit (and largely autobiographical) film about a gay German schoolteacher pursuing casual sex at almost any cost—is shown as part of the New York Film Festival. *The Village Voice* calls it "the first masterpiece about the mainstream of male gay life as it has developed since Stonewall." *The New York Times*, in a generally positive review, notes that the "most unnecessary line of dialogue any recent film has had to offer" comes when Ripploh—putting on his leather regalia and swallowing a tablet of LSD—tells his lover, "Don't wait up for me. I'll be late tonight." Ripploh made the film, which goes on to win numerous awards, for under $40,000.

October 11 San Francisco's Bulldog Baths—which bills itself as the largest gay bathhouse in the United States—celebrates its third anniversary with a "Biggest Cock in S.F." contest.

When a twenty-one-year-old, heavily made-up, androgynous black singer named Prince, clad only in his bikini underwear, opens for the Rolling Stones at a concert in Los Angeles, he is booed off the stage with screams of "Faggot!" and "Fucking queer!" and several members of the audience begin throwing cans and other trash at him. One magazine dubs him "Little Richard, before God and after Max Factor," while another observer describes the singer as looking "as if he just fell into a vat of pubic hair."

October 24 The first National Conference on Lesbian and Gay Aging is held in California. "There are many advantages in being old," says one participant, "but I can't think of one."

October 26 Diet guru Richard Simmons makes the cover of *People* magazine—just as his syndicated television show is being canceled by some local stations because, in the words of one irate station manager, "No one can stand looking at that faggot." Despite the local defections, however, Simmons's fitness program still draws nearly four million viewers a day, and his popularity is neatly summed up by one housewife quoted in *People*: "I used to watch Donahue, but I turned him off because he had so many programs about these gays. . . . I do exercises with Richard now, and he makes me feel younger."

October 28 *Love, Sidney*—a situation comedy starring Tony Randall as a lonely, middle-aged gay man living with an unwed mother and her young daughter—premieres on NBC. Although the original made-for-TV movie on which the series was based dealt (albeit, subtly) with Sidney's homosexuality, the actual series never mentions it, and—in the face of growing criticism from Christian media watchers like Jerry Falwell and Donald Wildmon—everyone associated with the series goes out of his way to deny that Sidney is, ever was, or ever will be gay. The denials continue even after the series is canceled in 1983.

"It really wasn't about a homosexual character," affirms one NBC spokesman. "It was about an unusual family where a single man lived with a woman."

"There was no actual reference to his homosexuality except on the pilot," acknowledges an NBC publicist.

"He was not gay," star Tony Randall tells *The Advocate*.

November 1 Internationally renowned photographic model Tula—an extraordinarily beautiful woman who has appeared in print ads for bras, Smirnoff Vodka, and numerous other products—graces the cover of this month's *Creative Photography* magazine. The cover coincides with her appearance as one of "James Bond's girls" in the new film, *For Your Eyes Only*. A short time later, however, a British tabloid reveals that she is really Barry Cossey, a Norfolk boy who had a sex-change operation in 1974. Although the revelation inevitably cuts into Tula's modeling work, she parlays her newfound notoriety into two extraordinary books about her life and, later, a provocative eight-photo nude layout in *Playboy* magazine.

In the nation's bookstores this month: *Bette: The Life of Bette Davis*, in which author Charles Higham—having previously asserted that Errol Flynn was both a Nazi spy and a bisexual—now claims that Joan Crawford "for years nourished a secret desire" for Bette Davis. Writes Higham, "No lovesick male tried harder in those happy, half-forgotten days to seduce a beautiful woman than Crawford did in her pursuit of Davis." According to Higham, Crawford routinely sent Davis love letters, expensive perfume, and long-stemmed roses in an effort to "woo" her.

November 15   The Census Bureau reveals that only 59.8 percent of American households can now be classified as "traditional" (i.e., comprised of at least one heterosexual, married couple). The figure compares with 78.2 percent just after World War II.

November 23   For the tenth time in a decade, the New York City Council refuses to pass a city ordinance prohibiting discrimination against gay men and lesbians.

December 1   *Christopher Street* publishes John Preston's "Goodbye, Sally Gearhart," a bombshell article on the growing political chasm between lesbians and gay men on the issues of pornography, promiscuity, and S&M. "NOW and its sister organizations have simply escalated the 'if onlys,' " writes Preston. "If only gay men wouldn't indulge in promiscuous sex, would give up explorations of sadomasochism, would cease any exploration of intergenerational sex, then we would be okay. . . . It is very clear that the *maleness* of gay men presents an image that many feminists find repulsive."

The article provokes an avalanche of mail, including letters from Sally Gearhart ("Most feminists probably don't give a tiny damn about the sex that gay men have together as long as in their lives they actively oppose the oppression of all women") and novelist Merle Miller ("I have always been alarmed by the feminists who raid [adult] bookstores. They are enemies of the first amendment and of gay men, no matter what they pretend").

December 8 The New York City Gay Men's Chorus becomes the first openly gay musical group to play Carnegie Hall, with a Christmas concert featuring traditional holiday music and the world premiere of *The Chanticleer's Carol*, a piece written especially for the Chorus by composer Conrad Susa.

December 31 A New Year's Eve celebration for two Minneapolis gay men—Rick Hunter and his lover, John Hanson—turns into a nightmare when they are first attacked by a gang of youths screaming "Faggots!" outside a local gay bar, and then subsequently attacked again, this time by the police, who, after arriving on the scene, let the teenagers escape and instead begin beating Hunter and Hanson with their nightsticks. Hunter and Hanson are then arrested for assaulting the youths who attacked them and are charged with disorderly conduct and interfering with police work. The bizarre episode continues when Hunter, requiring medical attention for a series of bloody injuries to his head, is taken by police to the emergency ward of a nearby hospital, where, according to the staff, the officers continue to physically abuse him, in plain view of everyone there, while loudly calling him a "faggot" and a "sissy."

With the help of testimony from several eyewitnesses, both men are eventually acquitted of the charges against them. The officers involved in the brutalization are never disciplined.

With time running out on his administration as governor of California, Jerry Brown makes eighty last-minute appointments to the state judiciary, including openly gay attorney Herb Donaldson to a bench in San Francisco. Donaldson becomes one of only four openly gay judges in the country, all of them appointed by Brown.

1982

January 4 Edmund White, Larry Kramer, and four other men found Gay Men's Health Crisis, Inc., a nonprofit New York-based organization to assist people with AIDS.

January 7 *Dynasty* parties are "in"—so "in" that numerous gay bars begin having *Dynasty* nights, while some gay men plan their entire social schedules around Wednesday-night get-togethers to watch the show. Complains one lesbian of her lover's obsession with the series, "I couldn't even read the newspaper when it was on. She'd complain I was making too much noise crinkling the pages."

January 10 Paul Lynde—who daily brought a taste of the gay sensibility into American homes via his participation on the game show *The Hollywood Squares*—dies of a heart attack in Beverly Hills at the age of fifty-five.

January 15 "Is it true that gay people are sexier than non-gay people?"
—Cosmopolitan *editor* HELEN GURLEY BROWN, *asking one of her typically incisive questions, of National Gay Task Force director Lucia Valeska, on the syndicated* Helen Gurley Brown Show

January 17 Voters in Austin, Texas, reject, by an almost two-to-one margin, a ballot proposal that would have specifically *allowed* housing discrimination on the basis of sexual orientation. The measure was put on the ballot by a group calling itself "Austin Citizens for Decency," who stressed their fear—groundless, to say the least—that Austin might one day "become another San Francisco."

January 27 Testifying at congressional subcommittee hearings on federal gay rights legislation, Connie Marshner of the National Pro-Family Coalition equates homosexuality with child abuse and murder.

"Are you saying child slaughter and homosexuality are the same thing?" asks Rep. Ted Weiss (D-New York).

"I think they're in a very close category," says Marshner.

February 5 The film *Personal Best*—starring Mariel Hemingway and Patrice Donnelly as competing athletes who have a lesbian affair while training for the Olympics—opens in New York City. In an interview in *The New York Times*, director Robert Towne reveals that the film's crew endured personal harassment and even death threats while filming certain key scenes on location in Oregon. Not only were there numerous bomb threats to the set, but, according to Towne, "Somebody pointed a gun at my secretary and said, 'Get out of town.'"

The film itself garners generally rave reviews in the mainstream media, but is received less enthusiastically by gay critics, some of whom complain that the lesbianism is treated like bed-wetting or acne: an "awkward" phase that otherwise "normal" girls go through before finding the perfect man.

February 10   Continuing to exhibit his uncanny ability for finding the least qualified candidate to do a sensitive job, President Reagan nominates Philadelphia radio evangelist Sam Hart to fill a vacancy on the U.S. Civil Rights Commission. From his electronic pulpit in the past, Hart has not only blasted the Equal Rights Amendment and condemned the use of busing to achieve racial integration, but has denounced civil rights protection for gay men and lesbians, explaining that, "Homosexuals can repent like any other sinner, and God by His graces can make them anew and they can become decent, respectable citizens in our society."

"It does not appear," says one senator, "that Reverend Hart is an advocate for civil rights as most people understand the term."

Two weeks later, in the face of mounting opposition—including questions about the authenticity of his tax returns, and uneasiness over the fact he had never even registered to vote until a few months earlier—Hart asks President Reagan to withdraw his nomination. He angrily blames "the homosexuals" for sabotaging it, though in fact everyone from the NAACP to the Philadelphia Conference of Baptist Ministers publicly opposed him.

February 12   Just a week after the premiere of *Personal Best*, *Making Love* opens at movie theaters across the country. Producers time the release of the film to coincide with the Valentine's Day weekend and push the film with a glitzy publicity campaign featuring a suggestive Richard Avedon photograph of the film's stars, Harry Hamlin, Kate Jackson, and Michael Ontkean. However, critics generally ridicule the movie, singling out what is repeatedly described as its "squeaky-clean" depiction of gay men and the homosexual lifestyle—a criticism they for some reason never level when reviewing similar dramas in which all the characters are straight.

"The more radical elements of the gay culture are going to be disappointed by all the films coming out now sponsored by the major studios. A lot of people of that ilk feel they're way beyond where these films take us. But the more intelligent know there has to be a groundbreaking ceremony, which is what this is."
—HARRY HAMLIN

February 20   An article in the British-American medical journal *Lancet* suggests there is evidence to show that inhaling "poppers" damages the immune system.

February 24   Jerry Falwell is hit in the face with two fruit pies by protesters at the annual convention of the Bible Baptist Fellowship. The incident provokes a brief riot when some of Falwell's followers try to attack the protesters.

February 25   Wisconsin becomes the first state in the U.S. to enact a statewide gay rights statute.

March 1   The national gay hardcover best-sellers, according to *Christopher Street* magazine:

1. *The Mayor of Castro Street* by Randy Shilts
2. *Sons of Harvard: Gay Men from the Class of 1967* by Toby Marotta
3. *Anal Pleasure and Health* by Dr. Jack Morin
4. *Gravedigger* by Joseph Hansen
5. *Funeral Games* by Mary Renault

"Sexual preference is established very early, long before the child even knows he or she has genitals. You may supply your sons with footballs and your daughters with dolls, but no one can guarantee that they'll enjoy them."
—*The Kinsey Institute's* ALAN BELL, *shattering one set of sexual stereotypes while inadvertently reinforcing another*

March 2   One gay man is brutally beaten and another castrated during an early-morning attack by "fag-bashers" on New York City's West Street piers.

March 14   "Does Mary Poppins have an orgasm? Does she go to the bathroom? I assure you, she does."
—JULIE ANDREWS, *responding to questions about how she, the perky novitiate of* The Sound of Music *and the saccharine governess of* Mary Poppins, *could first bare her breasts in* S.O.B. *and now play a "homosexual impersonator" in the forthcoming comedy* Victor/Victoria

March 18   Police raid a Washington, D.C., male escort service—"Friendly Models"—and cart away more than a dozen boxes of business records, including the names and addresses of several hundred of the service's clients.

March 19   *Victor/Victoria* opens nationwide to generally rave reviews. Only *Christian Century* (which calls it "mincing" and "tiresome") and Pauline Kael (who finds it hackneyed and misogynistic) seem to object to it. The Blake Edwards farce—based on a 1933 German film, *Viktor und Viktoria*, and featuring Robert Preston as probably the most relaxed and affable homosexual ever scripted into a major studio motion picture—goes on to become a huge box-office hit, and achieves, in some ways, what nearly thirteen years of gay liberation have not: an impression on the general public's consciousness of homosexuals as compassionate and likable people who should be left alone to live and love as they please.

   Robert Preston, meanwhile, is nominated for an Oscar for his performance, and later wins an award of special recognition, as does the film itself, from the Alliance for Gay Artists.

March 21   A major retrospective of Paul Cadmus's paintings opens at the William Benton Museum in Storrs, Connecticut, where, for the first time since the U.S. Navy banned it in the 1930s, his most famous painting, "The Fleet's In," is publicly displayed. The work—a large graphic caricature of lusty sailors flirting with "floosies" in a park—was commissioned during the Depression under the

Actress Sharon Gless. At least in their search for a "more feminine" actress, CBS executives chose one who was supremely talented.

Works Progress Administration, but soon became so notorious, and so infuriated the Navy, it was yanked from the Corcoran Gallery in Washington, D.C., in 1934 and put into storage for forty-seven years.

Later, the current exhibit moves to the Hudson River Museum in Yonkers. "These paintings and drawings take one aback," says one critic, "because of their subject matter: the male nude seen from a distinctly erotic point of view. . . . Had Cadmus chosen a female subject, we would have taken this work easily in stride. Titian's sensual sexual enjoyment of his nude women is something we expect and even approve of. Why, then, shouldn't Cadmus, who has never bothered to conceal his own feelings on the subject, do the same with men? Why indeed, it suddenly occurs to the viewer."

March 25   The first female "buddy" series on TV, *Cagney & Lacey*, premieres on CBS. Originally conceived in 1974—by producer Barney Rosenzweig and feminists Barbara Avedon and Barbara Corday—it was initially rejected by the three major networks before finally becoming a 1981 made-for-TV movie and, eventually, a weekly series with Tyne Daly and Meg Foster cast as two New York detectives battling pimps, killers, chauvinists, rapists, and, occasionally, each other.

Rave reviews for the series aside, CBS executives eventually conclude that the two women are coming across as lesbians to the nation's TV viewers ("We perceived them as dykes," one network executive tells *TV Guide*), and the intensely talented Foster is replaced by a "softer, more feminine" actress, Sharon Gless.

At its peak, the show rises to No. 10 in the overall Nielsen ratings.

April 1   Casey Donovan begins writing an advice column for the new gay magazine *Stallion*.

"We're fine for show during Gay Pride Week when a little color is needed, or for a quick fuck in the dark, when none of their friends are looking, but middle-class whites don't want to pass along any useful job or investment information or include us in their social circles. They don't hire us to work in their bars and businesses, and after a roll in the hay, they just may not speak the next time they see you."
—*Black gay man quoted in an* Advocate *article on racism within the gay community*

April 2   The film version of James Kirkwood's *Some Kind of Hero* opens—with all the homosexual episodes excised.

April 9   An article in the *Journal of the American Medical Association* claims that gay men who take the passive role in anal intercourse may have a twenty-five to fifty times greater risk of anal cancer than heterosexual men.

April 23   British comedian Benny Hill—a lifelong bachelor known for his habit of dressing in women's clothing on his popular weekly television series—tells a U.S. reporter, rather emphatically, "I am not gay."

April 30 "It's terribly fashionable to be homosexual at the moment, isn't it?"
—*Actor* JOHN HURT *(who, fashionability aside, nonetheless makes it clear he isn't, pointing out he's been married for fifteen years), in a publicity interview for the new comedy* Partners, *which opens (and bombs) nationwide today. The film—co-starring Hurt and Ryan O'Neal as two men who pose as gay lovers to solve a murder in Los Angeles—was written by Francis Veber, who also wrote* La Cage aux Folles, *and features, in the words of Vito Russo, "every neanderthal stereotype in the book." Critic Rex Reed calls the film "dumb," "creepy," "stupid," "tasteless," "homophobic," "sleazy," and "superficial."*

May 1 *Scientific American* accepts an ad from the California-based organization Lesbian and Gay Associated Engineers and Scientists, after another magazine, *Science News*, refused to run it.

May 3 "I don't hate homosexuals. Yes, the gays have rights—the same rights as any other American who is suffering from a deep personal problem."
—JERRY FALWELL, *trying a more unctuous approach in his never-ending crusade against homosexuality*

May 11 Voters in Lincoln, Nebraska, go to the polls to decide whether or not to accept a proposed gay rights ordinance for the city. Leading the fight against the initiative is local psychologist Paul Cameron—a former schoolteacher and founder of the antigay Family Research Institute—who has asserted, among other things, that gay and lesbian teachers are forty-three times more likely to molest a child than are heterosexuals. Some of Cameron's other pronouncements:

▪ "Most murderers commit a crime and are punished, but gays are promiscuous and do bad deeds constantly, and as such, are worse than murderers."
▪ "A shocking 40 to 60 percent of all gays show evidence of infection from the AIDS virus."

■ "I haven't met [a homosexual] yet who wasn't a fairly vicious person."

■ "We practice the Christian faith in our family and if my son was gay, it would be one of the most horrible things that could happen. If it had happened, my son would be disowned."

The gay rights ordinance goes down to defeat, 78 percent to 22 percent, and Cameron—soon to be disbarred for unethical conduct from the American Psychological Association and placed under investigation by the American Sociological Association for "falsifying and distorting" scientific studies on homosexuality—launches a new career for himself as an "expert witness," opposing gay rights ordinances from Texas to Maine. He also becomes a paid adviser to Representative William Dannemeyer, as well as a frequent guest on Pat Robertson's *700 Club*.

May 12   Canadian police once again raid the country's largest gay newspaper, *The Body Politic*, this time because of an article the paper ran on fist-fucking.

May 31   *The New Yorker* publishes "Territory," a gay-themed short story by twenty-one-year-old literary wunderkind David Leavitt.

June 1   "*My* tits will never sag! My body will never droop! You can quote that—'Kip Noll will *never* get fat, he will always be the same'. . . . Even when I'm sixty, I'll still weigh and look the same. If I do gain weight, it will be because I *need* a few extra pounds to look good."
—*Gay porn "flavor of the month"* KIP NOLL, *defensive on the subject of aging*

June 10   German film director Rainer Werner Fassbinder, thirty-six, dies of an overdose of cocaine and tranquilizers in Munich.

June 11   With the release of *Grease 2*—the much anticipated sequel to the most successful movie musical of all time—the face, and body, of improbably good-looking Maxwell Caulfield begin showing up on postcards, magazine covers, and posters across the country, and Caulfield himself is hyped as everything from "the next James Dean" (traditionally the kiss of death for any young star) to "the male equivalent of Farrah Fawcett-Majors." Despite the deluge of publicity, Caulfield never quite achieves male heartthrob status with the American public, and both he and the movie have pretty much vanished from sight by the end of the month.

June 18 Lesbian author Djuna Barnes (once described as "the Greta Garbo of gay literature" because of her extreme reclusiveness in later years) dies at the age of ninety in New York. Her best-known books include *Nightwood* and *The Ladies Almanack*, the latter a satire of Natalie Barney and her lovers.

June 22 After years of gossip and speculation about his sexuality, singer Johnny Mathis officially "comes out" in an interview in *Us* magazine. "Homosexuality is a way of life that I've grown accustomed to," he tells the magazine. "What's the big deal about my sexuality? . . . And what does it have to do with the art of making beautiful music?" Mathis has recorded over seventy albums, sixty of which have gone either gold or platinum.

June 27 This year's Mr. International Leather, Luke Daniels, makes a dramatic entrance at the Los Angeles Gay Pride Parade when he appears atop a huge semi with two bound and hooded slaves dangling from either side of the cab and a motorcycle escort of four leathermen in front.

June 30 After a ten-year struggle, the Equal Rights Amendment falls just three states short of the thirty-eight necessary for ratification, and is defeated.

July 1 *Torso* magazine debuts.

––––––––––––––

On the video shelf: *The Boys of San Francisco*, from gay porn *auteur* William Higgins, whose two previous films—*Pacific Coast Highway* and *The Boys of Venice*—have been smash hits with the rapidly growing home-alone-with-your-VCR set. Says director John Waters on the "video revolution" (which, thanks to lower-priced machines and cassettes, is currently undergoing an explosive expansion), "The success of video is directly related to self-abuse."

After Dark, already in serious financial trouble for months, misses both its June and July issues. The magazine—which, in a desperate bid to cash in on the burgeoning gay market, has finally admitted that, well, yes, maybe it *is* a gay magazine after all—plods on awhile longer before finally disappearing from the magazine racks for good; by then, no one notices it's gone.

July 9 'GAY PLAGUE' SHOWING UP
AMONG HAITIAN REFUGEES
—Miami Herald *headline*

July 13 In the wake of a series of CBS reports alleging that a major homosexual ring is operating in the U.S. Congress and that gay sex is being demanded of congressional pages in exchange for favors and promotions, the House votes to begin an investigation into the matter. A year's worth of hearings, however, turn up no evidence to support the network's accusations, and in fact reveal that CBS based its reports solely on hurried interviews with one former page, who later flunked a lie-detector test. The hearings do, however, bring to light a consensual affair Representative Gerry Studds (D-Massachusetts) had with a seventeen-year-old page in 1973 (the page subsequently described the relationship as "one of the more wonderful experiences of my life"), and an affair that Representative Daniel Crane (R-Illinois) had with a seventeen-year-old female page in 1980.

July 16 A federal judge rules that the Immigration and Naturalization Service's policy of excluding foreign gays from entering the United States is unconstitutional and violates guarantees of free speech and free association.

July 17 Queen Elizabeth's personal bodyguard, fifty-year-old Commander Michael Trestrail, is forced to resign after British newspapers reveal he is gay and has been involved in a long-term relationship with a male prostitute. Later, reports surface that Prime Minister Margaret Thatcher wanted to make "gays in the Palace" a public issue, until the Queen summoned her to Buckingham Palace and told her to mind her own business.

July 22 "I don't think there is a 'gay lifestyle.' I think that's superficial crap, all that talk about gay culture. A couple of restaurants on Castro Street and a couple of magazines do not constitute culture. Michelangelo is culture. Virginia Woolf is culture. So let's don't confuse our terms. Wearing earrings is not culture; that's a fad and it passes."

—RITA MAE BROWN

August 3 Twenty-eight-year-old gay Atlantan Michael Hardwick is arrested on sodomy charges after police—trying to serve a warrant for a minor traffic violation—show up at his home and find him in bed performing fellatio on a male companion. "I'm in bed with this guy," says Hardwick later, "and I hear the door to my room open. A little later, I look up, and there's a man standing over us in full police drag. My first thought was, *This can't be happening!*"

Hardwick is thrown into jail for twelve hours after his arrest, and the resulting court case—over the constitutionality of Georgia's sodomy laws—becomes a *cause célèbre* in the gay community, culminating in an appeal of Hardwick's conviction to the Supreme Court in 1986.

August 5 The Philadelphia city council passes a gay rights ordinance, which quietly passes into law after Mayor William Green refuses to either veto it or sign it.

August 17 A federal judge repeals the sodomy laws of Texas, on the grounds that they are unconstitutional. Shortly afterward, conservative state legislators—and even a few who normally aren't so conservative but who want to score some easy points with voters who are becoming increasingly panicked over AIDS—begin a campaign to put new laws on the books, laws that will pass approval with the federal bench. They finally succeed three years later with the passage of a bill that prohibits homosexual sodomy only.

August 26   The first national television special on AIDS—*AIDS: The Mysterious Disease*—appears on PBS.

August 28   The first annual Gay Olympics—later called simply the Gay Games, after a successful lawsuit by the U.S. Olympic Committee—opens at Kezar Stadium in San Francisco. Rita Mae Brown hosts the opening ceremonies, and tells a cheering audience, "We are here today, not to celebrate homosexuality, but to celebrate and affirm individual freedom. . . . The only people who are queer are people who don't love anybody."

September 5   Nationally known nutrition expert Howard Appledorf, who rose to prominence in the 1970s with his vocal defense of junk food, is murdered in his apartment in Gainesville, Florida. When police find the body, it is sprawled on the living-room floor wrapped in a sheepskin rug and surrounded by plates of half-eaten food, leading detectives to speculate that the killers enjoyed dinner while watching Appledorf suffocate. The walls of the apartment are smeared with slogans—"Howard we love you" and "Murder" —written in barbecue sauce.

A short time later, police arrest three young men—two with previous prostitution convictions, and one of them carrying Appledorf's credit cards—and charge them with first-degree murder in connection with the bizarre slaying. One of the youths later acknowledges that he and his friends were high on LSD when they killed Appledorf. He says they smeared slogans on the walls "to make it look like crazy people did it."

September 15   In the nation's bookstores this month: *New York Times* food critic Craig Claiborne's *A Feast for Laughter*, a "memoir with recipes," in which Claiborne not only openly acknowledges his homosexuality for the first time, but further reveals that he once had a sexual relationship with his father.

"There was one reason I was serious about writing this book," says Claiborne. "It was a chance to state my homosexuality. The lack of awareness in this country is incredible and there are so many women across the country who respect my work. I felt that if I could increase their awareness that being gay is not a bad thing, doesn't make you an evil person and that they don't have to be ashamed if their child is gay, or if I could give comfort to one kid because of my coming out and declaring my homosexuality, the book would have been worth writing."

Also in bookstores this month, Edmund White's critically acclaimed novel *A Boy's Own Story*. *The New York Times Book Review* calls it "compelling . . . extraordinary . . . a cross between *Catcher in the Rye* and *De Profundis*."

September 21   The Oklahoma Supreme Court awards custody of two eleven-year-old boys to their divorced gay father and rules that homosexuality is not in itself grounds for ruling a person unfit for parenthood.

September 29   Twelve people are injured and $30,000 in property is destroyed when two dozen police officers raid "Blues," a New York gay bar frequented by blacks, on the alleged grounds that there had been complaints of a disturbance there. According to witnesses, police barged into the bar with guns drawn and yelled, "This is a motherfucking raid—every faggot to the rear!" The officers then proceeded to empty the cash register and destroy bottles of liquor and other property. At one point, an officer fired his gun into the floor and told the crowd, "These are faggot suppositories!" After the raid, twelve of the bar's customers are taken to local hospitals for treatment of injuries. The raid later provokes a protest march by nearly four hundred lesbians and gay men through Times Square. Mayor Koch and other city officials condemn the police action, the cause of which is never fully explained.

Democratic presidential hopeful Walter Mondale publicly expresses his support for an end to discrimination against lesbians and gay men.

September 30 The country's ongoing beefcake craze reaches a new apogee with the arrival of a looming twenty-two-hundred-square-foot billboard in Times Square advertising Calvin Klein briefs. The billboard features Brazilian pole-vaulter-turned-model Tom Hintnaus reclining (with his eyes closed and his hands on his bare thighs) wearing nothing but a dazzling white pair of the new designer underwear. "They look," says one department store executive of the new briefs, "as if they really fit." Meanwhile, dozens of smaller versions of the billboard (at bus and subway stops) are stolen by zealous admirers, and Bloomingdale's reports that it has sold nearly five thousand pairs of Calvin Klein briefs in the first five days since they went on sale.

October 1 Former Los Angeles Dodger Glenn Burke "comes out" in an interview in *Inside Sports*.

October 2 "I've gotten foolish letters, stupid letters. There are sick, sick people out there. Our society is made up of a bunch of sick people."
—*Convicted mass murderer* JOHN WAYNE GACY *(still appealing his death sentence), on the hate mail he receives in prison*

October 5 Police in Norfolk, Virginia, raid a local art theater showing *Taxi Zum Klo* and confiscate copies of the film, which they declare violates the city's antiobscenity statutes. Rather than fight the charges, the theater's management pleads guilty and pays a fine of $500.

October 13 Jerry Falwell and National Gay Task Force director Virginia Apuzzo argue over gay rights on the *Donahue* show.

October 14   Twenty-three-year-old Scott Thorson files a $113-million "palimony" suit against Liberace, claiming that he and the pianist "lived together as man and wife" for more than six years. Thorson—who worked as Liberace's chauffeur and sometimes escorted the entertainer onstage during concerts—later agrees to a $95,000 settlement (as well as a Rolls-Royce and several dogs) from Liberace.

October 15   Madlyn Murray O'Hair addresses the national convention of the Gay Atheists League of America.

In the nation's bookstores: Alyson Publications' reissue of the short-story anthology *$TUD*, by literary gadfly, tattoo artist, and cheerfully lusty man of letters Samuel Steward, writing under the name "Phil Andros." Originally published in 1969 (by a somewhat-less-than-reputable publisher who later had himself committed to an insane asylum to avoid his creditors), the collection now sets into motion what is described as "a renaissance of reputation" for Steward, who is in his seventies.

October 21   A forty-nine-year-old Miami, Florida, high school coach resigns after being charged with committing "an unnatural lascivious act" with another man in the back of a van. The coach, Bob Lewis, calls the act an "isolated incident" and denies he is gay. "What he did is his personal life and nobody else's business," says the mother of one of Lewis's football players. "The players still support him all the way."

October 25   Northern Ireland repeals its sodomy laws.

November 1   *Christopher Street* publishes Andrew Holleran's "Journal of the Plague Year."

November 11   Despite having previously lambasted the Moral Majority as "dangerous" and "malicious," Yale President A. Bartlett Giamatti welcomes Jerry Falwell to the school and, at alumnus

George Bush's urging, has a long private meeting with the Moral Majority leader.

Falwell later assures reporters that he and Giamatti "agree" on most issues.

November 12   "This is a human rights issue you're fighting, make no mistake about it. Keep up the fight."
—Newsweek *Washington bureau chief* MEL ELFIN, *accepting a gay group's award in recognition of the magazine's coverage of gay and lesbian community issues*

November 19   A California judge throws Marilyn Barnett's "palimony" suit against Billie Jean King out of court.

December 1   The top five all-time best-selling gay porn videos, according to a survey conducted by *Torso* magazine:

1. *El Paso Wrecking Co.*
2. *The Idol*
3. *L.A. Tool and Die*
4. *Sex Magic*
5. *The Boys of Venice*

———————

A recent survey by the group Black and White Men Together finds that fewer than 4 percent of the employees at San Francisco's nearly one hundred gay bars are black, Asian, or Hispanic.

December 2   Veteran gay filmmaker Jack Deveau—who founded Hand In Hand Films and produced such gay porn classics as *Left-Handed*, *Drive*, and *Good Hot Stuff*—dies of cancer in New York City.

December 17   Dustin Hoffman becomes America's favorite (heterosexual) transvestite in the film *Tootsie*, which premieres today and goes on to become one of the highest-grossing films of the year.

December 18 The Quebec parliament overwhelmingly approves a measure that gives the domestic partners of gay men and lesbians legal recognition and access to economic benefits previously restricted to heterosexual couples.

A week earlier, Mayor Dianne Feinstein vetoed a similar bill in San Francisco.

December 31 Number of stories on AIDS published in *The New York Times* this year: five. Number of stories the *Times* ran on the Rubik's Cube: nine. On the problems of panda fertility: thirteen. On dog care: forty-eight.

"This has been a bad year for people who like to sleep around."
—*The London* Economist, *on the rapidly expanding AIDS crisis,* 1982

1983

January 3 In a feature-length story on up-and-coming comedian Eddie Murphy, *Newsweek* assures its readers, "With Murphy you don't squirm, you giggle: he's not bad, just naughty." Avoiding completely the issues of Murphy's misogyny and savage homophobia, the magazine goes on to praise him, with a kind of astonished admiration, for being "the cleanest-cut comic around, one who doesn't smoke, drink, or use drugs."

January 13 Two lesbians, Zandra Rolon and Deborah Johnson, are refused service when they try to sit in the romantic dining section—an area of special booths curtained off from one another—in a Los Angeles restaurant. The management offers them another table, but when the two women refuse to move, the maître d' yanks the table out from under them and tells them they can sit there all night if they like, no one will wait on them. He then claims that a city ordinance prohibits the restaurant from seating any gay or lesbian couple in such a section.

Sixteen months later, after being successfully sued by the women, the restaurant holds a "Death of Romance" evening and announces it will dismantle the romantic dining section altogether rather than ever seat a lesbian or gay male couple there. "True romantic dining died on this date," say the restaurant's owners in an ad taken out in *The Los Angeles Times*. Rolon and Johnson's lawyer, Gloria Allred, sees it somewhat differently: she calls the successful lawsuit against the restaurant "the death of bigotry."

January 15   On the video shelf: *Brothers Should Do It*, a pairing of supposed "brothers" Jon King and J.W. King—who are, in fact, not brothers at all, despite the titillating ad copy that suggests, "There'd always been something special between J.W. and his kid brother Jon." Still, the "brothers" gambit proves so popular in gay porn that videophiles are soon bombarded by the sex romps of Ross Henson ("brother" of popular gay model Bill Henson), as well as an endless stream of films pairing Kip Noll with any number of his "brothers," including Marc Noll and Scott Noll, none of whom are his brothers either.

January 20   Howard Cruse's comic strip "Wendel," about the life, loves, and search for respect of gay writer Wendel Trupstock, debuts as a regular feature in *The Advocate*.

January 24   Hollywood director George Cukor—known for such films as *My Fair Lady* (1964), *A Star Is Born* (1954), *The Philadelphia Story* (1940), and *Camille* (1936)—dies at eighty-three in Los Angeles. Shortly before his death, he came closer than he ever had to publicly acknowledging his homosexuality. "I didn't put on any big act," he told *The Advocate*. "You know, a lot of people are so funny. They go out with girls and all that, and that's absolutely ridiculous. I didn't pretend."

February 1   "I don't care what I play. I'll play Polish faggots, midgets, women, anything. Any role."
—ROBERT MITCHUM, *who in the same interview in* Esquire *describes himself as having been "a faggot's dream" in his youth*

February 10   A spokesman for the San Francisco Giants tells a banquet audience that the Giants are planning to set up a special seating section for the team's gay fans. Instead of the grandstand, he says, to considerably less mirth than anticipated, "we're going to call it the 'fruit stand.' "

February 12   *Kissing To Be Clever*—the debut album of the British group Culture Club—begins a thirty-eight-week run in the *Billboard* Top 40. The album spawns three hit singles, including "Do You Really Want to Hurt Me?" and "I'll Tumble 4 Ya."

"In my professional career, I have never encountered a more frustrating and depressing situation. People who you know are likely to die ask what they can do to help themselves, and you are forced to say, more or less, 'I have no idea.' "
—Houston physician DR. PETER MANSELL, *on the lack of adequate treatments for AIDS, 1983*

February 15   Lesbian playwright Jane Chambers, author of *A Late Snow* and *Last Summer at Bluefish Cove*, dies of a brain tumor at the age of forty-five.

February 25   Tennessee Williams dies, at the age of seventy-one, in his suite at the Hotel Elysee in New York City. He reportedly choked to death on a plastic cap while trying to open a "child-proof" pill bottle with his teeth.

March 1   In the nation's bookstores this month: *Odd Girl Out* and four other lesbian "pulp" novels from the 1950s, long out of print, but now reissued by Naiad Press. Once considered titillating trash by straight readers (but indispensable reading to the nation's lesbians), the novels were written by Ann Bannon, who was married at the time of their publication and only separated from her husband and "came out" many years later. "My God," said one of Bannon's grown daughters, discovering that her mother had been secretly writing underground novels all those years, "this is fantastic!" Her other daughter—a born-again Christian—was, according to Bannon, not nearly as pleased over the revelation.

Vanity Fair magazine is resurrected by Condé Nast. Its legions of gay fans are soon referred to in publishing circles as "Vanity fairies."

March 8   Another gay rights bill goes down to defeat in the New York City Council.

March 13   An article on Robert Mapplethorpe in *The New York Times*—"Is Mapplethorpe Only Out to Shock?"—concludes that Mapplethorpe's work is "undeniably distasteful," and adds, "Rather than educate, these pictures titillate; rather than addressing the conventions of pornography, they *are* pornography." The author labels Mapplethorpe's photographs "intentionally distasteful" and "chic narcissistic exhibitionism."

"I want to focus on things the camera has never captured before; that's my obsession as a photographer."
—ROBERT MAPPLETHORPE

March 15   A West Virginia kindergarten teacher, Linda Conway, is forced to resign from her job after parents complain she *looks* like a lesbian. She files a $1 million lawsuit against the school board.

March 19   More than seven hundred gay rights supporters march through downtown Dublin in what is described as the city's first gay rights demonstration. The march is triggered by a recent court ruling giving suspended sentences to five Dublin youths who beat a thirty-one-year-old gay man to death in one of the city's parks. In court, the boys acknowledged brutalizing and physically assaulting some twenty homosexuals over the previous summer.

March 31 "There is more money given today for military bands than for all of the arts projects put together. I hate Reagan and everything he stands for. His ideas about the arts are worse than contemptible—they're tragic. One hundred years from now we're going to be judged exclusively on the culture we leave, not on the countries we destroy through Reagan's regime."

—NED ROREM

April 1 The FBI admits it has kept surveillance files on the National Gay Task Force, the Mattachine Society, the Daughters of Bilitis, the Gay Activists Alliance, the Gay Liberation Front, the Society for Individual Rights, the East Coast Homophile Organization, and One, Inc.

The AIDS Medical Foundation is founded in New York City by forty-one-year-old Robert Mehl. Later, the organization will combine with the National AIDS Research Foundation to become the American Medical Foundation for AIDS Research (AMFAR).

April 4 With half-naked men used to sell everything from beer to toothbrushes (and prime-time television increasingly dominated by shows that feature such beefcake idols as Tom Selleck, Jon-Erik Hexum, and Adrian Zmed), *Time* magazine declares 1983 "The Year of the Hunk."

April 14 Citing financial problems, Great Britain's only national gay newspaper, *Gay News*, ceases publication after eleven years.

April 21 San Francisco is chosen as the site for the 1984 Democratic National Convention. Republicans later use this as ammunition in the presidential campaign, repeatedly referring—with a knowing smile—to "those San Francisco Democrats."

April 29 *Querelle*—Rainer Werner Fassbinder's last film, based on a novel by Jean Genet—opens in New York City. The film—a lurid and surreal mixture of sodomy, decadence, murder, and more sodomy, starring Brad Davis and a grotesquely made-up

Jeanne Moreau—is almost universally panned by critics, one of whom suggests it should have been titled *A Guy in Every Port.*

April 30   More than eighteen thousand people fill Madison Square Garden for what is dubbed "the biggest gay event of all time," a benefit performance of the Ringling Brothers and Barnum and Bailey Circus to raise money for Gay Men's Health Crisis in New York City.

May 1   Chocolate-chip-cookie shops are flourishing along San Francisco's Castro Street.

May 5   Wisconsin becomes the twenty-seventh state to legalize homosexual acts between consenting adults.

May 12   "After we finished the film, I thought it was really important that when I went around the country talking about it, that we'd never do the number of 'Oh, this isn't a movie about homosexuality . . . it's about people.' I heard that a lot after *Personal Best* and *Making Love.* It may be good advertising for a general audience, but if you're not proud of what you do, then why do it in the first place?"
—*Director* JOHN SAYLES, *discussing his recently released, highly acclaimed film* Lianna, *about a married woman coming to grips with her lesbianism*

"The biggest mistake I ever made was telling that *Melody Maker* writer that I was bisexual."
—DAVID BOWIE, *recanting his famous 1972 revelation about his sexuality. Asked why, after all these years, he has suddenly decided to scorn the admission, Bowie explains, "I wanted to be part of society again and not an alien freak." Says one rock commentator, "The former King of Glitter Rock, once the very symbol of rock and roll decadence, has anointed himself the Yuppie King."*

May 17   With congressional hearings on the federal response to AIDS only weeks away, the Reagan administration refuses to allow congressional investigators access to crucial federal documents and files on the disease, and further stipulates that federal AIDS researchers may not speak to congressmen unless at least one high-ranking Reagan staff member is present.

May 19 Two years into the AIDS epidemic, ABC's *20/20* does its first story on the widening medical crisis. A producer at the network acknowledges that the show's executives refused for more than a year to do a story on the disease, but changed their minds when they suddenly heard "reports of infants getting it."

May 25 Ronald Reagan fires three members of the U.S. Civil Rights Commission and names noted lawyer Robert Destro—who once fought to deny gay rights groups tax-exempt status with the IRS—to fill one of the vacancies.

June 1 In the nation's bookstores this month: *The Simply Divine Cut-Out Doll Book*, a book of paper dolls of transvestite star Divine, complete with various eye-catching ensembles, including "Jungle Jezebel," "Miami Bound," and "Space Command," from St. Martin's Press.

June 5 *Torch Song Trilogy*—Harvey Fierstein's poignant, autobiographical four-hour comedy about one gay man's battle for acceptance and respect—wins the Tony Award as Best Play of the 1982–1983 season. Accepting the award in front of a live television audience, one of the play's producers punctuates his thank-you speech by pointedly acknowledging the support of his male lover—a gesture that generates considerable dismay and controversy in the weeks to come.

"I've written a play," says Fierstein, "in which homosexuals don't commit suicide at the end or repent their evil ways. The basic theme is self-respect, the realization that homosexuals can be just as moral as heterosexuals."

June 9 "I'm gay. . . . This is the first time I've talked about it openly. I don't like to talk about my sexual inclinations. People are not special because they like one thing better than another in bed.

. . . It happens that people who have to go through this particular sexual syndrome are forced to refine certain receptive instruments in the mind and soul: they become much more sensitive, more ready to talk and to deal with things of the spirit. They suffer more than the normal person. I think it is not easy to be a gay. I know this. You have to go through a very, very anguishing time."
—*Italian director* FRANCO ZEFFIRELLI, *"coming out" in an* Advocate *interview with writer Edward Guthmann*

June 12   Alice Walker's *The Color Purple* debuts on *The New York Times* best-seller list. Lavishly praised by gay, lesbian, and straight readers alike, the book chronicles the brutalization of a black woman by various men in her life and her ultimate triumph (with the help of a bisexual blues singer) in freeing herself from degradation.

The eventual news that Steven "Raiders of the Lost Ark" Spielberg will direct a movie version leaves many of the book's fans gaping in disbelief and disappointment—a disappointment that is largely justified when the film is released two years later, with all the lesbian elements either deleted or politely glossed over.

June 14   The first gay high school in the country, Philadelphia's Byton High, holds graduation exercises for the class of '83. Size of the graduating class: three males, one female. The school was started in 1982 for gay teens as an alternative to the public school system.

June 16   *The New York Times* publishes its first front-page story on AIDS.

June 19   Jerry Falwell tells a group of his followers in Lynchburg, Virginia, that AIDS is "the judgment of God," and adds, "Have you ever stopped to consider that if God decides to judge a country, there's no medication to stop him?"

June 21   For the first time since Ronald Reagan took office, White House officials agree to meet with representatives of the gay com-

Congressman Gerry Studds. He originally served on President Kennedy's White House staff, and was first elected to Congress in 1972.

munity. The purpose of the gathering is to discuss the administration's response to the AIDS epidemic.

July 11 Not to be outdone by its competition, *Time* magazine runs its own feature-length article on Eddie Murphy, in which the writer, oblivious to gays, women, and people with AIDS, gushes, "More than any other entertainer in recent memory, Eddie Murphy just plain makes people feel good." In the same article, director John Landis calls Murphy's humor "dazzling!"

July 14 In the wake of a House Ethics Committee's recommendation that he be reprimanded for a sexual affair he had ten years ago with a seventeen-year-old congressional page, Representative Gerry Studds publicly acknowledges his homosexuality, becoming the first member of Congress ever to do so.

July 15 The Hothouse—San Francisco's legendary four-story, ten thousand-square-foot baths, devoted to the most outré forms of gay sexual expression, including bondage, discipline, water sports, fist-fucking, and scat—closes its doors in the wake of growing concerns over the spread of AIDS. Meanwhile, the Club Bath chain reports that business at its New York and San Francisco facilities is down by more than 50 percent.

"Before AIDS, going to the baths had an aura almost like smoking. People knew it wasn't too good for them, but it was socially acceptable. Now it has the aura of shooting heroin."
—MARK CHATAWAY *of New York's Gay Men's Health Crisis, Inc.*

"Sexual activity in places like baths or sex clubs should no longer be associated with pleasure—it should be associated with death. We need a new style of educational campaign."
—HARRY BRITT

Sporting a new mini-Rambo body (shaped in part by the film's director, Sylvester Stallone), John Travolta takes to the nation's movie screens with a six-years-in-the-making sequel to *Saturday Night Fever, Staying Alive*. Although the movie embraces many of the current obsessions of mainstream America—perfect musculature, driving career ambition, emotional uplift at any cost (Tony Manero is now a Broadway dancer trying to sweat and pant his way to the top)—the film is so utterly lacking in charm or charisma that it fares miserably with audiences and is lambasted by critics, one of whom predicts that its final production number—"Satan's Alley," a gaudy and raunch-ridden sequence laden with special effects—will become a camp classic.

July 16 *Sweet Dreams (Are Made of This)*—the debut album of the Eurythmics—moves into the Top 40, where it will stay for seventeen weeks. The album's title track becomes a hit single, catapulting the group's gender-bending lead singer, Annie Lennox, to international fame.

July 18   Gay photographer Bill Bader, whose work appeared regularly in such magazines as *Honcho* and *Mandate*, dies from AIDS at the age of thirty-one in Los Angeles. "I'm in a position now where I don't feel I'm going to physically heal myself," he said a week before his death. "To continue to be optimistic would be sheer denial because the writing is on the wall. The cancer is progressing quite rapidly and my health is deteriorating very fast. I'm down twenty-five pounds. . . . There's nothing I regret in my life, nothing I feel has been left undone. I'm proud of how I lived."

July 20   With public approval of Congress near an all-time low, the House votes 420 to 3 not merely to reprimand Gerry Studds but to officially censure him, stripping him of his chairmanship of the Coast Guard and Navigation Subcommittee. "We are here to repair the integrity of the United States House of Representatives," proclaims a sanctimonious Newt Gingrich (R-Georgia). One irate Democrat suggests that the representatives are simply "trying to show how pure they are."

July 26   Mick Jagger turns forty.

August 1   A suburban mother writing in *Redbook* advises other mothers that "carpenters, fishermen, and regular guys" pierce their *left* ears, and that teenage boys should be forewarned *not* to pierce their right ears, or they may be mistaken for homosexuals.

Anita Bryant—still running a dress shop in Selma, Alabama—becomes a national spokeswoman for "Silent Witness" sunglasses, "The Subtle Way to Tell the World You're a Christian." The sunglasses' frames are ornamented with crosses, fish, and other Christian symbols.

August 2   Former conservative lawmaker Robert Bauman—finally acknowledging that, yes, he is gay—testifies before the Amer-

ican Bar Association's panel on homosexuality and urges the ABA
to draft a resolution supporting gay rights.

August 4   After more than a week of angry and outspoken opposition from local fundamentalists, the eighth-annual National
Reno Gay Rodeo opens without incident. Earlier, a group calling
itself the Pro-Family Christian Coalition tried to get the rodeo
banned on the grounds it was really "an orgy" and that homosexuals
were "riddled with disease and full of repugnant practices. We
declare that to be un-American." In response, a hundred local citizens and businesses placed a full-page ad in the Reno newspaper
declaring their support for the rodeo, and even the local Chief of
Police noted that the rodeo traditionally presents far fewer law-
enforcement problems than similar "straight" events. Despite anonymous threats that snipers will be on hand to gun down spectators
and participants, an estimated twenty thousand people show up
for the event's opening ceremonies.

August 5   In the new film *Risky Business*, twenty-one-year-old new-
comer Tom Cruise lip-syncs and dances in his underwear to Bob
Seger's "Old Time Rock & Roll"—and instantly establishes himself
as one of the most bankable young movie actors of the new decade.
He also immediately establishes a huge gay following, which sticks
with him even after he continues to make one brainless formula
picture after another.

A man who in 1981 maced, kidnapped, and imprisoned a nineteen-
year-old woman—all on orders from her parents—in order to
try to "deprogram" her of her alleged lesbianism pleads guilty to
charges of assault.

August 21   The musical stage version of the film *La Cage aux Folles*
opens on Broadway.

August 26 "We believe that the rights of all people must be protected and guaranteed. We believe that the gay and lesbian community must be supported in their civil rights as well as their right for their own sexual preference."

—CORETTA SCOTT KING

September 1 Longtime gay rights opponent Larry McDonald is killed, along with 268 other passengers, when Korean Air Lines Flight 007 is shot down by Soviet fighter pilots after it strays into Soviet air space. Says one political observer, "Do you suppose it was God's judgment on homophobia?"

In the nation's bookstores this month: *The Matt Dillon Quiz Book*, a $2.25 paperback devoted to everything America ever wanted to know about one of the nation's favorite "teencake" idols. The book, notes one critic, "takes trivia into a dimension that's science-fictional." Still, it receives considerable exposure in the gay press.

September 15 "Better than I've ever felt in my life."
—GERRY STUDDS, *asked how he feels now that he's "come out"*

September 17 Vanessa Williams of New York is crowned the country's first black "Miss America"—a title she must relinquish ten months later, when *Penthouse* magazine announces plans to publish a handful of old nude photos of her in erotic poses with another woman. "I am not a lesbian and I am not a slut," Williams tells the press, which nonetheless refers to her in headlines as "Vanessa Undressa" and "Mess America." Meanwhile, *Penthouse* publisher Bob Guccione publicly likens the scandal to Watergate and compares Williams to Richard Nixon.

September 25 New York Philharmonic pianist Paul Jacobs dies of AIDS at the age of fifty-three. Says a close friend, "He did not 'go gentle into that good night'—he was very angry about the disease that is destroying people."

September 27   "AIDS is not the only issue in the nation tonight. Be concerned about AIDS, but also sickle-cell anemia. . . . Be concerned about the human rights of gays, but also Native Americans trapped on reservations, and blacks in ghettos. I would urge you, as I urge black people . . . the bigger you get beyond yourselves, the more you protect yourselves."
    —JESSE JACKSON, *addressing a gay fund-raising dinner in New York*

September 29   Among the men advertising their services in the "MODELS/MASSEURS" personals in this week's *Advocate*: Tim Kramer, J. W. King, Beau Mathews, Todd Baron, Colt's Bruno, Frank Vickers, and Mark Scott.
    In the same issue, number of companies using "AIDS" in their ad copy (to sell everything from "poppers" to T-shirts): thirteen.

October 4   The AFL-CIO votes to support gay rights legislation at the federal, state, and local levels.

October 15   At the outset of his long-awaited first HBO comedy special, *Delirious*, comic Eddie Murphy launches into a vicious tirade against "faggots," and then, after throwing off a string of tasteless jokes about AIDS, segues into a parody of *The Honeymooners* in which the "punch line" has Ralph Kramden begging Norton to fuck him in the ass. "Faggots aren't allowed to look at my ass while I'm onstage," Murphy tells his adoring fans, most of whom are teenage boys. "I'm afraid of gay people. Petrified. I have nightmares about gay people." Although some members of the audience are waving signs "EDDIE MURPHY FOR PRESIDENT," others watching at home suddenly find themselves wildly *un*enthusiastic about the comedian.

"A prenatal hormonal mixup can certainly produce a homosexual child. They often have delicate features, smooth and
nearly hairless faces, and high-pitched voices. They walk like
females and have feminine mannerisms. They love to be around
women, learn to make up their faces while very young, and
can do wonders with their own hair and the hair of others.
They would prefer to be with girls than with boys."
—Syndicated columnist ANN LANDERS *on homosexuality, 1983*

October 31 Popular Falcon model Dick Fisk, twenty-eight, is
killed with his lover in a car accident outside Atlanta.

November 1 In this month's issue of *Hustler* magazine, publisher
Larry Flynt satirizes Jerry Falwell as an incestuous drunk who lost
his virginity to his nymphomaniac mother one night in an outhouse.
Falwell sues.

November 3 Ohio senator John Glenn—running for the Democratic presidential nomination—tells the National Gay Task Force
he does not support federal gay rights legislation. "I will not advocate or promote homosexuality," says Glenn. "Nor would I do
anything as president that could be interpreted as advocacy or
promotion of homosexuality."
    Glenn's later remarks that homosexuals should not be teachers,
soldiers, spies, or Y.M.C.A. directors prompt his New York state
campaign chairman to resign in disgust.

November 5 An unemployed, self-described "musicologist"—
twenty-nine-year-old Marc Christian—moves into Rock Hudson's
mansion on Mulholland Drive, ostensibly to house-sit while Hudson is away in Israel for two months filming *The Ambassador*.

November 11 A thirty-five-year-old gay man in Washington,
D.C., William Hassell, is abducted and forced to strip at knifepoint
by two teenage boys who then repeatedly slash him, kick him,

urinate on him, and threaten to hack off his testicles. Six months later, the two assailants are given probation by a Superior Court judge who says he is "satisfied" by the boys' claims that Hassell made unwanted sexual advances to them. Says *The Washington Post*, in an editorial criticizing the lenient sentence, "There is no question that the assault had the character of torture. The way Judge Nunzio described the crimes, you would think it was nothing more than 'boys will be boys.' "

November 15 *Mandate* magazine rejects an offer to publish some recent pictures by photographer Robert Mapplethorpe because "none of the models have hard-ons."

November 23 A federal judge concludes that the First National Bank of Louisville, Kentucky, did not practice wrongful discrimination—or violate constitutional guarantees of freedom of religion—when it ordered one of its employees to either give up his position in the local chapter of Dignity—a gay Catholic group—or resign from the bank. The employee, branch manager Samuel Dorr, was forced to leave his job in 1981 after he refused to quit the gay organization.

December 13 Mary Renault dies in Cape Town, South Africa, at the age of seventy-eight.

December 16 Mel Brooks's *To Be or Not To Be*, a remake of the 1942 Ernst Lubitsch classic, becomes the first mainstream film not only to acknowledge Nazi persecution of homosexuals but to make it a key plot element. The new film features an openly gay character, dresser Sasha Kinski (James Haake), who is arrested by the Nazis, forced to wear a pink triangle, and threatened with deportation to a concentration camp.

1984

January 6 Having served barely five years for the murders of George Moscone and Harvey Milk, Dan White is paroled from prison. His release prompts protest rallies in both San Francisco and Los Angeles. "Yesterday was the last day Dan White could be assured he'd live through the whole day," says one protester, pointedly eating a Twinkie before several thousand demonstrators in San Francisco. "I don't call for violence, but who knows, maybe one of us someday will be a little depressed, maybe off our diets, and who knows what may happen."

Having been ordered by his parole board to stay away from San Francisco, White settles in Southern California.

January 10 Ten months before the presidential election, *The Advocate* endorses Walter Mondale and urges gay people to get involved in his campaign.

January 11   The staid and often homophobic *Wall Street Journal* deems that staff writers may now use the word "gay" as a synonym for "homosexual" in their articles and headlines.

January 16   This week's *People* magazine reassures its readers that while Cher may be playing a lesbian in the new film *Silkwood*, "She Still Loves Glamour, Glitz, and Guys Who Can Kiss!"

February 14   Acknowledged bisexual Elton John marries a German-born recording technician, Renate Blauer, in Sydney, Australia. Cynics close to the couple privately comment that he has found "a cover, not a lover."

February 15   Writing in the *Journal of the Canadian Medical Association*, physician Peter Sullivan suggests that homosexuality is not a true sexual orientation at all, but rather an "acquired addiction" like alcoholism and drug abuse. Citing the media-reported case of one gay man with AIDS who claimed to have had more than a thousand sexual contacts in a single year, Sullivan boldly asserts that, "Homosexuality shows . . . resemblances to uncontrolled addiction, particularly obsession to the point of reckless disregard for the effect on personal, family, social and work life. . . . Homosexuality is not, as the homosexual community claims, an alternative lifestyle but rather another manifestation of the disease of addiction. It may thus be possible to establish a treatment program for homosexuality similar to the programs presently available for treating chemical addiction." His theory draws fire from a variety of doctors and researchers, who label it "sinister," "pejorative," "ludicrous," "amusing," "incredible," and "tragic."

February 28   Michael Jackson dominates this year's Grammy Awards when he wins a record eight trophies for his album *Thriller*, which goes on to become the best-selling album of all time. The awards ceremony itself—later dubbed "the gay Grammys" by one critic—opens with former disco diva Donna Summer doing a splashy if somewhat sanitized rendition of "She Works Hard for the Money." Other highlights of the evening:

■ Singer Annie Lennox appears in convincing male drag to perform the hit "Sweet Dreams (Are Made of This)."

■ Boy George is named Best New Artist of the Year and tells the audience, via satellite from London, "Thank you, America. You've got good taste, style, and you know a good drag queen when you see one." (Quips Joan Rivers, "You look like Brooke Shields on steroids.")

■ A rousing performance of the musical drag number "I Am What I Am," from the Broadway show *La Cage aux Folles*, rounds out the evening; *The New York Times* later reports that during the song, ceremony host John Denver looked "rather stunned."

March 1 "What television will never give us is a Steven Carrington who lives the way most gays do, particularly young urban gays who have seen Christopher Street."
—*Media critic* RICHARD M. LEVINE, *on the double-edged nature of the success of* Dynasty, *which is currently No. 3 in the Nielsens*

March 6 A casting of George Segal's "Gay Liberation" sculpture—temporarily placed at Stanford University until a decision can be reached whether to install it permanently in San Francisco or Los Angeles—is attacked and damaged by a hammer-wielding vandal. Later it is vandalized a second time, by someone who spray-paints the word "AIDS" on it.

March 13 Claiming "an absence of compelling need" for such legislation, California governor George Deukmejian vetoes a gay rights bill that would have prohibited job discrimination on the basis of sexual orientation.

March 26 The profound differences between the Reagan and Carter presidencies—already glaringly obvious to everyone in the country—are further underlined when President Reagan awards the Presidential Medal of Freedom to country singer Tennessee Ernie Ford. Other recent Reagan awardees: Warren Burger, Whittaker Chambers, Frank Sinatra, Walter Annenberg, and Caspar Weinberger. By contrast, Jimmy Carter had given the Medal to

Tennessee Williams, Margaret Mead, Beverly Sills, Roger Baldwin, and Earl Warren, among others.

April 1 *Mandate* magazine, only nine years old, publishes a special "10th Anniversary Issue!"

April 9 CITY BARS SEX AT BATHS
                              —*The San Francisco Examiner*

April 10 EXPERT WARNS: WORLD OF FUTURE WILL BE RUN BY GAYS!
       HOMOSEXUALS ARE PREPARING TO TAKE OVER CORPORATIONS AND THE GOVT.!
                              —The Sun, *a supermarket tabloid*

April 16 Boy George—a sudden if unlikely pop idol to thousands of the country's teenage boys and girls—makes the cover of this week's *People* magazine. His soaring popularity sets off a national debate over androgyny and increasingly fey rock stars as role models, a debate that reaches its climax several months later when he and Jerry Falwell are paired on *Face the Nation* to argue about homosexuality.

BOY GEORGE SETS THE RECORD STRAIGHT

"I'm neither straight nor gay. I'm just very confused."

"What frightens people most is that I'm not confused about my sexuality."

"I'm not gay and I'm not a transvestite, no matter what anybody thinks. I'm basically very much a man."

"I'm not trying to fool anybody into thinking I'm heterosexual."

"I'm not gay."

"Basically, I'm not all that keen on sex."

"I wish I were Matt Dillon's underwear."

April 23   The gay sexual revolution comes crashing to a halt when Secretary of Health and Human Services Margaret Heckler announces that the "probable" cause of AIDS has been discovered: a transmissible virus that has recently been isolated by U.S. and French researchers. Although the full implications are slow to sink in, the announcement puts an end, at least in theory, to both oral and anal sex without protection, and represents an erotic disaster of sorts for the legions of gay men who cherish swallowing or being infused with their partner's semen. As a result, within months a push begins in the gay community to eroticize "safer sex" (sex without an exchange of body fluids), with "safe sex" jack-off stories, comic books, seminars, pamphlets, porn videos, and more making their debut every month. Still, for many gay men (often constricted from acknowledging it, for fear of being labeled irresponsible), sex will never be the same.

May 1   *Advocate Men* debuts on the nation's magazine stands.

May 11   The United Methodist Church votes to ban the ordination and appointment of avowed homosexuals as ministers.

May 27   Actor Rock Hudson—concerned over a small but persistent growth on the back of his neck—learns from a dermatologist in Beverly Hills that he has Kaposi's sarcoma. A definitive diagnosis of AIDS comes a few days later.

May 29   On the video shelf: *The French Lieutenant's Boys*, starring Philip André and Sergio Canali.

May 30   By a vote of 5 to 4, the U.S. Supreme Court strikes down a New York state law that prohibited loitering in a public place for the purpose of engaging in or soliciting "deviant sexual intercourse."

June 1   American society's growing obsession with the male posterior—in TV commercials, print ads, music videos, and more—reaches its peak when marketing executives decide to put Bruce Springsteen's denim-clad ass (rather than his face) on the cover of his new album *Born in the USA*. Springsteen's rear gets even more prominent exposure in the album's first video, *Dancing in the Dark*, where director Brian de Palma's camerawork rather lovingly dwells on the singer's buttocks squeezed into a pair of very tight gray jeans. Comments *Newsweek* magazine, "Homosexuality always openly celebrated male beauty, and there's little doubt that the general acceptance of a gay subculture has encouraged an outspoken appreciation of masculine sexuality in the mainstream culture."

June 2   Gay columnist Arthur Bell, fifty-one, dies of complications from diabetes.

June 3   Harvey Fierstein wins his third Tony Award, this time for Best Book of a Musical for *La Cage aux Folles*. In open defiance of the Tonys' executive producer—who had begged everyone to "please, *please* avoid last year's embarrassment" (referring to the winner who had thanked his male lover in front of the live television audience)—Fierstein goes ahead and lavishly, pointedly, thanks his male lover. "Before that," he says later, "I couldn't have cared less if I won, since I had two Tonys already; but suddenly the gauntlet was down. I had to win just to prove that we ain't gonna take that kinda shit."

   La Cage aux Folles also wins Tonys for Best Musical, Best Actor in a Musical, Best Score, Best Director of a Musical, and Best Costume Design.

June 14   Ronald Reagan is asked at his twenty-fifth press conference whether he supports federal civil rights legislation prohibiting job discrimination against gay men and lesbians.

   "Well," says the President, after a moment of confusion, "I just have to say I am opposed to discrimination period."

   "But would you support the measure, Mr. President?" asks the reporter.

   "What?" says Reagan.

   "Would you support the measure?"

"I want to see what else they have there," Reagan finally answers uncertainly, before moving on to the next question.

June 29   Nestor Almendros's documentary *Improper Conduct*—a film detailing the savage persecution of homosexuals by the Castro regime in Cuba—opens in limited release in San Francisco, Miami, and Puerto Rico. Almendros—the Academy Award-winning, openly gay cinematographer of such films as *Days of Heaven*, *Sophie's Choice*, and *Chloe in the Afternoon*—codirected the film with documentary filmmaker Orlando Jimenez Leal. Both men are exiles from Cuba, though they acknowledge having originally supported Castro's overthrow of the Batista government.

June 30   The Unitarian Church votes to recognize and approve ceremonies celebrating the union of gay and lesbian couples.

July 1   Annie Lennox denies that her group, the Eurythmics, has any particular gay or lesbian following, and tells one interviewer, "From the people who come to the shows—the people who *really* like you—I don't see it, and I've talked to a lot of people out there."

July 10   "My husband introduced me to swinging. . . . I've found that I enjoy it very much, but for a reason I don't think he expected. I have learned to enjoy sexual encounters with other women. . . . I am not really interested in making it with other men at these parties. The hostess of our favorite club is organizing women-only parties. I am dying to attend, but I am really afraid I will meet a woman who is a lesbian and fall in love with her. . . . I can no longer honestly imagine living with my husband for the rest of my life. How can I tell if I was meant to be a lesbian?"
—*Question to* Advocate *advice columnist* PAT CALIFIA. *Califia's response: "Once you've started to explore your sexuality, you can't go backward without being frustrated and unhappy. . . . Take things one small step at a time. Don't make any sweeping decisions before you have to. I think your first problem is what to wear to this party. Have fun."*

July 11 Boston Mayor Ray Flynn approves a gay rights ordinance that prohibits job and credit discrimination against lesbians and gay men.

July 12 Walter Mondale chooses New York congresswoman Geraldine Ferraro as his running mate, the first woman vice-presidential candidate on a major party ticket.

July 13 Appearing on a San Francisco talk show, an obviously irritated Jerry Falwell offers $5,000 to anyone who can prove he once called the Metropolitan Community Church "vile and Satanic" and its members "brute beasts." Gay activists immediately produce a video tape of the March 11 *Old Time Gospel Hour*, in which Falwell not only said exactly that, but added that there will "be a celebration in heaven" when the MCC is "annihilated." When Falwell refuses to pay the $5,000 as promised, the activists take him to court and successfully sue him for the money.

Brothers—a weekly sitcom about three Philadelphia brothers, one of whom is gay—premieres on the Showtime cable TV network. The series—created and written by veterans of such mainstream shows as *Cheers* and *Taxi*—was rejected three years earlier by NBC. Although the show will quickly establish a loyal gay following, it is the high-flying performance of Philip Charles MacKenzie as the fey and irrepressible "Donald" that keeps it going for several years, even after the scripts have turned a bit mawkish and anemic.

July 14 Prince—having recovered from a rocky career start, when teenage audiences didn't quite know what to make of him—makes the *Billboard* Top 40 with his album *Purple Rain*. It stays there for forty-two weeks, twenty-four of them at No. 1.

*Singer Johnny Mathis: Proof that nice—
and candid—guys don't always finish last.*

"I think Tom Cruise is a total hunk. I like his muscles; I like
real big, beefy, brawny guys. I like someone who can really hurt
me in bed, someone who looks like he could be mean. . . . I've
been gay ever since I was old enough to want sex. It's always
been with men. Ever since I realized I was gay, I've been totally
open about it."

—Rock musician **DAVID DIAMOND** *of the group Berlin, 1984*

July 16 *U.S. News & World Report* reports that gay men and lesbians, with an estimated seventeen million potential voters, now
make up the seventh largest voting bloc in the United States after
women, evangelical Christians, the young, the elderly, blacks, and
union members.

July 19 Gay author Roger Austen, forty-eight, commits suicide
near his home in Seattle. According to friends, Austen had been

depressed over his inability to find a publisher for either his biography of writer Charles Warren Stoddard or his book on the Newport Naval Station scandal of 1919. He had attempted suicide once before, in 1981.

July 20 With the release of the critically acclaimed fantasy *The Never Ending Story* this week, and accolades for *Das Boot* three years earlier, openly gay German film director Wolfgang Petersen becomes one of the hottest directors of the decade—a status he maintains until the release of his next film, *Enemy Mine* (about a hermaphroditic alien and a macho earthling stranded together on an inhospitable planet), which fares poorly with audiences and is excoriated by critics, many of whom seem particularly uncomfortable with the sexual ambiguities and homoerotic undercurrents of the storyline.

July 29 Forty-year-old gay San Franciscan John O'Connell is murdered, and another man injured, when five men, all in their late teens or early twenties, drive into the city from nearby Vallejo looking to "beat up some fags."

July 30 With the opening ceremonies of the Los Angeles Olympics only days away, rumors begin to spread that many of the U.S. team's top athletic contenders are homosexual. Among those most frequently cited: track and field star Carl Lewis (who later issues one emphatic denial after another), gymnast Mitch Gaylord, and diver Greg Louganis. It is later speculated that Lewis—who wins four gold medals at the games—receives few offers to do commercial endorsements because the gossip, true or not, has become so firmly entrenched in the public mind.

August 1 In the nation's bookstores: *Home Before Dark*, a family memoir in which John Cheever's daughter, Susan, reveals that her father (who died of cancer in 1982) struggled against homosexual impulses all his life and only permitted himself an affair with another man a few years before his death.

August 7 "Pity the poor gay and lesbian Marxists in today's world. They are constantly forced to go into contortions to justify the obvious dictatorial piggery of Castro every time evidence of his excesses comes to light."
—VITO RUSSO, *on the "left-wing" backlash against Nestor Almendros's* Improper Conduct, *specifically an attack in* American Film *magazine that claims the film was part of a CIA plot to discredit Castro*

August 13 Jimmy Swaggart, Phyllis Schlafly, James Robison, and Jerry Falwell all testify before the Republican Party platform committee in Dallas, pressing for (and getting) a strongly pro-family, antigay, antiabortion platform. "There were no moderate religious folks who testified," notes one delegate.

August 17 A three-man federal appeals board—including judges Robert Bork and Antonin Scalia—unanimously upholds the expulsion of a gay petty officer from the U.S. Navy and contends that homosexuality is "almost certain to be harmful to morale and discipline" in the armed forces. "Private, consensual homosexual conduct is not constitutionally protected," concludes Bork, in the panel's written decision. He goes on to suggest that homosexuality is particularly pernicious in a military context, since homosexual officers might use their authority to forcibly seduce enlisted men. The twenty-seven-year-old petty officer in question was expelled from the Navy in 1981 despite what even the Navy acknowledged was his "unblemished service record and many citations praising his job performance."

August 19 On the eve of the Republican National Convention in Dallas, President Reagan issues a statement reaffirming his support for "traditional" family values, and adds that his administration "will resist the efforts of some to obtain government endorsement of homosexuality."

August 20 An associate of Prince tells *People* magazine that despite numerous rumors, the singer is not, *absolutely not*, gay. "He's not at all," adds the coworker.

August 22   Jerry Falwell delivers the benediction at the Republican National Convention.

August 25   Author Truman Capote—whose earlier masterpieces have been increasingly overshadowed by his often foolish public behavior and the specter of his unfinished *roman à clef, Answered Prayers*—dies at the home of close friend Joanna Carson in Bel Air, California. He was fifty-nine.

September 4   Gay rights supporter and former Dade County Commissioner Ruth Shack—one of the chief architects of the county's controversial 1977 gay rights ordinance—loses her bid to become mayor of Miami.

A recent National Gay Task Force survey on antigay violence in eight major U.S. cities reveals that an overwhelming majority of gay men and lesbians have been verbally harassed at one time or another for their sexual orientation. In addition, a tenth of the women, and almost a quarter of the men, report having also been hit, kicked, or beaten because of their homosexuality.

September 5   In response to a recent cascade of press stories insinuating that the singer is gay (including one fictitious item claiming that he had an affair with Boy George), Michael Jackson's personal manager holds a much-publicized press conference in West Hollywood to refute widespread rumors that his client is a homosexual. He warns that Jackson will henceforth sue any periodical publishing "new fantasies" about his sex life.

   Says Jackson, in a printed statement distributed to reporters, "NO! I've never taken hormones to maintain my high voice. NO! I've never had my cheekbones altered in any way. NO! I've never had cosmetic surgery on my eyes. YES! One day in the future I plan to get married and have a family. Any statements to the contrary are simply untrue. . . . We all know that kids are very impressionable and therefore susceptible to such stories. I'm certain that some have already been hurt by this terrible slander. In addition to their admiration, I would like to keep their respect." Adds Jackson's publicist, Norman Winter, "If little girls want to grow up and marry Michael, now they know they've got a chance."

"There does not appear to be any precedent," says *The Los Angeles Times*, "for a celebrity going to such lengths to proclaim his or her heterosexuality."

September 24 A New York psychiatrist expresses his belief that AIDS is caused by depression, brought on by an internalization of all the negative messages coming from groups like the Moral Majority.

October 1 In the nation's bookstores this month: *Copland, 1900 Through 1942*, the first volume of American composer Aaron Copland's memoirs. Despite an assertion early on that it is "impossible" to separate "knowledge of an artist's life" from "the enjoyment and understanding of his art," Copland proceeds to do exactly that, in a memoir that makes no mention of his homosexuality, the great loves of his life, or anything else particularly personal, beyond the *angst* and turmoil of composing.

———————

"Most English critics are literally cripples. Some of them have got wooden legs or skin disease, or they're homosexual!"
—*Perennially homophobic playwright* JOHN OSBORNE, *discussing the revival of his play* A Patriot for Me, *which fares no better now with critics than it did nineteen years ago*

———————

In Touch runs a contest offering teencake star Matt Dillon's used T-shirt (from the film *Rumble Fish*) as the sole prize. Says the magazine, "Yes, a shirt that has actually touched Matt's tender flesh, caressed those pretty brown nipples, rubbed those firm young muscles, soaked up that sweet sweat, hugged those slim hips, probably even been in his dressing room when he was nude." Hundreds of readers submit entries (one man alone submits a total of 180), and the prize finally goes to one Robert Lopez of Los Angeles.

October 22   "The press has been trying to get into my pants for years. It's not that I have anything to hide. I just want to do my own thing."
—*Singer* BARRY MANILOW, *deflecting a question from* People *magazine about his sexual orientation*

October 25   Republican candidate Louie Welch, running for mayor of Houston against incumbent Kathy Whitmire, loses nine points in the polls after he unwittingly blurts over an open microphone that the best way to contain the AIDS epidemic is to "shoot the queers." "The bottom fell out within twenty-four hours," says one of Welch's consultants. "It clearly pushed the younger undecided voters into Whitmire's camp."

   Ten days later, Whitmire wins reelection by a margin of 57 percent to 43 percent.

October 26   Arnold Schwarzenegger—the 1980s' answer to Johnny Weissmuller—bares his buttocks in *The Terminator*. He is only the latest in a recent crush of actors—including Jeff Bridges, William Hurt, and Sean Penn—shedding their clothes in front of movie cameras.

October 30   Political consultant Bruce Decker urges gay men and lesbians to reelect Reagan in a guest editorial in *The Advocate*. "Thanks to a strong economy and defense, gays and lesbians enjoy more freedom in our republic than in any other country in the world," writes Decker. "President Reagan has demonstrated a commitment, in spite of pressure from the religious Right, to the belief that social policy should not be dictated from Washington. . . . The President has demonstrated in his actions that he opposes discrimination in all forms. . . . His Administration's careful and caring humanitarian efforts to research matters of immunology that are well on their way to relieving the suffering and sorrow of AIDS victims demonstrate the basic goodness of the man. . . . In his second term as President, Ronald Reagan will be open to us in a meaningful way, not pander to us with actionless rhetoric like his Democratic predecessors."

Responds Virginia Apuzzo, in a counter-editorial urging readers to vote for Mondale, "The Reagan Administration has served notice that all our yesterdays should be restored tomorrow."

"I'd like to write gay children's plays. People don't want to admit there are gay children. Wouldn't it be nice to let a gay child see a play where the prince gets the prince? We need that."
—*Playwright* ROBERT PATRICK, *best known for such highly acclaimed works as* Kennedy's Children *and* T-Shirts

November 1   Independent Hollywood producer Jerry Wheeler, who now holds the option on the book, announces that production will begin in late September on a film version of *The Front Runner*.

November 3   Jack Haber, former editor-in-chief of *Gentlemen's Quarterly*, dies of AIDS at the age of forty-five.

November 6   Four more years: Ronald Reagan is reelected President of the United States, garnering 59 percent of the popular vote to Mondale's 41 percent. In the electoral vote, Mondale carries only Minnesota and the District of Columbia. For many civil rights activists, the burning question suddenly becomes: can the Supreme Court's remaining liberals—three of whom are approaching their eightieth birthdays—hold on long enough, before Reagan has a chance to appoint another conservative justice to the high court?

Meanwhile, in California, West Hollywood becomes the first "gay city" in the United States, after voters there decide to turn the previously unincorporated area into a self-governing municipality and elect a largely gay city council to run it. Population of the new 1.9-square-mile city: 35,000, an estimated 40 percent of whom are gay or lesbian. Twenty-three days later, the newly installed city council approves a sweeping gay rights ordinance.

And in Minnesota, despite a hate campaign that has tried to link homosexuality with child molestation and other social ills,

Karen Clark—an openly lesbian state representative—is elected, 69 percent to 31 percent, to her third term in office.

December 1 In the nation's bookstores this month: Michael Bronski's *Culture Clash: The Making of a Gay Sensibility*, which embraces a number of widely heralded and often controversial theories, including the notion that gay culture's infiltration into the mainstream (via fashions, fads, books, and movies like *La Cage aux Folles*) is ultimately a more powerful political weapon against homophobia than many of the legal battles fought in the last fifteen years. "Just passing a law doesn't change people's feelings," notes Bronski.

"Michael Jackson will have a very limited career because he is stereotyped as what he is and it is not a stereotype which can grow and mature with age. Nobody will want to see a fifty-year-old androgyne with a high-pitched voice with white hair smeared with goop and holding a white glove."
—*One critic's assessment of Michael Jackson's future in the music industry*

December 5 Berkeley, California, becomes the first city in the U.S. to extend spousal benefits to gay city employees and their live-in lovers. To qualify under the new program, applicants must fill out and submit an "Affidavit of Domestic Partnership."

December 8 *Welcome to the Pleasuredome*—the debut album of the British group Frankie Goes to Hollywood (two of whose members are openly gay)—hits the *Billboard* Top 40, where it will stay for fourteen weeks, peaking at No. 33. The album contains the hit single "Relax."

Meanwhile, a video of "Relax"—depicting an orgy at a gay leather bar—is banned by MTV, and the group is forced to shoot a significantly tamer, concert video of the song for airplay.

A Virginia jury rules that while Larry Flynt did *not* libel Jerry Falwell in a 1983 *Hustler* magazine parody portraying the Moral

Majority leader as an incestuous drunk, Flynt should still pay Falwell $200,000 for having caused him "emotional distress."

The Supreme Court later unanimously overturns the award.

December 18   *The Times of Harvey Milk*, directed by Robert Epstein, wins the New York Film Critics' Award for Best Documentary of 1984.

1985

January 1 "EDDIE MURPHY, A NEW KIND OF STAR—YOUNG, HIP, AND *STRAIGHT!*"
—*Cover headline from* Cosmopolitan

"It's the ultimate mind-fuck, in some ways even better than reality. It's what I call wash-and-wear sex. It doesn't require small talk, or putting your trick into a cab afterwards. You get exactly what you want. It's like television; you can turn it on and turn it off, in the privacy of your own home at any hour of the day or night."
—*Los Angeles owner of one of the many, suddenly flourishing gay phone sex companies*

January 8 "I'm neither dreading 1985 nor eagerly looking forward to it. I shall really go on exactly as if it were 1984—but then, I

always go on as if it were 1926, so it doesn't make any difference."

—QUENTIN CRISP

January 15   In the nation's bookstores this month: *The Scott Madsen Poster Book*, described as "the ultimate in male pin-up art." The oversized paperback—devoted to "tasteful" flesh shots of Soloflex poster boy Scott Madsen—becomes an instant best-seller in gay bookstores.

January 19   By a four-to-one margin, Houston voters reject a measure that would have banned discrimination against homosexuals in city hiring.

   Shortly before the election, members of the Ku Klux Klan marched in opposition to the ordinance, urging voters to "TAKE A STAND WITH THE KLAN."

January 28   *People* magazine begins picking an annual "Sexiest Man Alive."

February 1   Joanne Woodward, Yoko Ono, Lily Tomlin, Anaïs Nin, Joyce Carol Oates, Erica Jong, Helen Reddy, and more than a hundred other prominent women sign the *Ms.* magazine "petition for freedom of sexual choice," which condemns "the attempt by government to interfere in the sexual lives of consenting adults, and the failure by government to protect the civil rights of people who suffer such interference from others."

February 4   Laura Hobson's *Consenting Adult* becomes an ABC made-for-TV movie starring Marlo Thomas, Barry Tubb, and Martin Sheen.

   At a press conference for the film, Sheen—a believer in reincarnation—offers the opinion that people are born homosexual because of events and actions in their previous lives.

February 5   Homophobic conservative Patrick Buchanan is named Ronald Reagan's new White House director of communications.

Two and a half weeks later, Edwin Meese is confirmed as U.S. Attorney General.

February 24 "I'm not a homosexual and I don't smoke pot, so what would I say?"
—LILLIAN CARTER, *declining an invitation to appear on* Donahue

February 27 "They are trying to turn every political and legislative issue—from the federal budget to the war in Central America—into a test of faith. They have married their primitive religious and political views to the most ultramodern communications technology. And they have unprecedented access to, and influence over, public officials at the highest levels of government. . . . They believe the Bible mandates *all* their positions—not only on religious issues but on political, social, economic and foreign policy issues as well."
—ANTHONY PODESTA, *president of People for the American Way, on the unprecedented political clout of the Christian Right*

March 1 "Sex on camera ain't always easy! Technical difficulties or no technical difficulties, I've had to work with people where I've had to go into the next room with a dirty magazine to get a hard-on."
—*Gay porn star* "BIG" BILL ELD *revealing one of the little-known occupational hazards of his line of work*

March 2 The FDA licenses the first HIV blood test.

———

Age of Consent, the debut album of the openly gay British pop group Bronski Beat, enters the *Billboard* Top 40, where it will stay for three weeks. The album contains the haunting dance tracks "Smalltown Boy" and "Why," both of which, not surprisingly, become huge hits at gay clubs across the United States.

"Bronski Beat is young, uncertain, and facing numerous challenges. Given their outspokenness and the disastrous record
of topical bands, they'll have a thorny future, contending with
bigotry as well as the immutable expectations of their audience.
They are clearly an original talent, but only time will tell if they
can remain true to their ideals and survive the confines of their
advocacy."

—Rolling Stone, *reviewing* Age of Consent

March 5   On the video shelf: *Biff's Wet Buns*—"The Ultimate in
Spankography"—from Control-T Studios.

March 10   William Hoffman's *As Is*, a play about AIDS, opens at
New York's Circle Repertory Theater. "At one point," says Hoffman, "I put on my bulletin board, 'God will protect me if I write
about this.' I started the play as therapy for myself: What if I come
down with it? How do I behave? It was my attempt to bring myself
back to sanity."

Less than six weeks later, Larry Kramer's *The Normal Heart*,
also about AIDS, opens at the Public Theater.

March 13   Barely a week after a local police officer publicly called
it a "porno palace," Miami's only legitimate gay bookstore—
Lambda Passages—is closed by city officials for "zoning violations."
The store reopens a short time later, after the management removes
all materials that might be construed as pornographic by city
officials.

March 15   A new study in the *Journal of the American Medical
Association* concludes that AIDS is most likely *not* spread by casual
contact.

March 23   In the midst of a multimillion-dollar fund-raising drive
to help his financially ailing Liberty University, Jerry Falwell prom-

ises to give a "solid 14-karat gold ring" to anyone who pledges a "gift" of more than $1,000. People who pledge $200 are offered a tape recording of Falwell reading the Psalms, and those who give $100 get a recording of some of Falwell's speeches.

March 25　"I certainly can't go ahead and award a Rookie Cowgirl of the Year buckle to someone who may be a cowboy."
—*American Rodeo Association president* AL SAMUELS, *on the controversy surrounding Kia Sadeski, this year's Rookie Cowgirl of the Year winner, who, it appears, may actually be Paul Sadeski, a female impersonator and alleged male prostitute from Pine Bush, New York*

———————

The Times of Harvey Milk wins this year's Academy Award for Best Feature-Length Documentary. Accepting the Oscar, producer Richard Schmeichen thanks, among others, his male lover.

March 26　A tie vote (4 to 4) in the U.S. Supreme Court effectively overturns a controversial Oklahoma law that would have banned homosexuals—or those defending or "promoting" a homosexual lifestyle—from teaching in the state's public schools. The four justices who vote to *uphold* the law: William Rehnquist, Sandra Day O'Connor, Byron White, and Warren Burger. The rare tie vote is the result of the absence of Justice Lewis Powell, due to surgery.

March 29　*The Los Angeles Times* comes out in favor of gay rights and urges the U.S. Supreme Court to take a stand on more gay-related issues.

March 30　In a radical departure from the days when he used his position as Los Angeles Chief of Police to malign and harass gay men and lesbians, former homophobe Ed Davis—having already expressed his support for a statewide gay rights bill in California—now publicly blasts antigay politicians in the state as "a bunch of maladjusted jerks" and rejects pressure from an evangelical Christian group that he take a public pledge refusing donations or endorsements from gay political groups. "I close this letter," writes Davis to the ultraconservative American Coalition for Family Val-

ues, "by asking you to take a few minutes to read two short documents with which you may not be familiar—the Declaration of
Independence and the Bill of Rights."

In the 1970s, Davis was regarded as one of the gay movement's
primary political enemies in California, and his later election to the
California state assembly was seen as yet another defeat for the
cause of gay rights. His recent political change of heart, though
welcome, leaves many gay politicos baffled.

April 1 The Harvey Milk School, a city-funded high school for
gay and lesbian teenagers in New York City, begins holding classes
in a Greenwich Village church, with an initial enrollment of twenty
students. The school is comprised mostly of openly gay and lesbian
youths who have been beaten up, threatened, harassed, or repeatedly abused at other schools, often to the point where they had
stopped attending classes altogether. "At least here," observes one
grateful student, "we can be ourselves."

April 13 Gay porn star Val Martin dies of AIDS.

April 14 The first annual Gay Erotic Film Awards is held in Los
Angeles. Named Best Picture of the Year: Arthur Bressan's *Pleasure
Beach*, starring Johnny Dawes. The actual award—a gold statuette
of a nude man holding a star against his chest—is dubbed "The
Harvey," after Harvey Milk.

April 15 "We must conquer AIDS before it affects the heterosexual population."
—*U.S. Secretary of Health and Human Services* MARGARET HECKLER,
*giving a uniquely unreserved glimpse into the Reagan administration's
attitude toward the AIDS epidemic*

April 20 National Democratic Party Chairman Paul Kirk Jr. calls
gay rights a low-priority "fringe issue."

April 21 Fashion celebrity Rudi Gernreich—who designed the
topless bathing suit and the "Thong" (and who, unbeknownst to

many, was one of the early founders of the Mattachine Society)—
dies of cancer at the age of sixty-two. Despite a *New York Times*
obituary claiming that he lived alone and that "there are no sur-
vivors," Gernreich in fact had a lover of thirty-one years, Dr. Oreste
Pucciani.

May 1   Jim Yousling leaves as editor of *In Touch* magazine. Under
Yousling's three-year tenure, the magazine has moved from being
just another gay slick—photos of nude men, erotic fiction, and an
occasional celebrity interview or article on venereal disease—to one
of the only consistently hilarious gay magazines that takes neither
itself nor being gay in general too seriously: a kind of hybrid of
Blueboy, *Tiger Beat*, and *National Lampoon*. Subsequent editors are
never quite able to recapture Yousling's deft feeling for whimsy,
eroticism, and butch camp.

May 10   Visiting St. Michael's Hospice in Herefordshire, England, Princess Alexandra of the British royal family inquires about
the hospital's financial situation. "Are you well endowed?" she asks,
turning with prim dignity to one of the hospital's directors, Dr.
Jeffrey Kramer. After a moment of stunned silence, a lady-in-
waiting quickly ushers the Princess into a nearby rest room, where
they both reportedly collapse with uncontrollable laughter.

May 12   Seven days after President Reagan visits a Nazi war cemetery in Bitburg, West Germany (and tries to justify the visit by
equating Nazi war dead with victims of the Holocaust), a gay group
in Hamburg unveils a granite memorial at the site of the Neuen-
gamme death camp, in memory of the estimated two-hundred-fifty-
thousand gay men who were murdered by Nazis in the concentration camps.

May 13   A nationwide poll of young adults, aged eighteen to
twenty-four, names Eddie Murphy the most admired person in
America. Ronald Reagan is No. 2.

Naiad Press's Barbara Grier (right) with partner Donna McBride. HONEY LEE COTTRELL

May 21 After a U.S. Circuit Court of Appeals rules that Georgia's sodomy laws are unconstitutional, the Georgia State Attorney General vows to appeal the decision to the U.S. Supreme Court. Says one gay activist, confident of victory, "It's going to be hard for the Supreme Court to find no right of privacy in one's own bedroom."

Unhappy with the conclusions reached by previous commissions on the subject, Attorney General Edwin Meese now spends more than half a million dollars for the creation of a new national commission on pornography, and then essentially mandates its conclusions—to find "more effective ways in which . . . pornography could be contained," to "study . . . the problem of pornography," to illuminate "the relationship between exposure to pornographic materials and antisocial behavior"—before a word of testimony is even heard.

May 23 The Massachusetts House of Representatives votes overwhelmingly to prohibit gay people from becoming foster parents.

May 31 Rejecting a grant application from the AIDS Foundation of Houston, the United Way of the Texas Gulf Coast announces it will "not fund AIDS-related projects."

June 1 Naiad Press's publisher, Barbara Grier, comes under heavy fire for having sold excerpts of the book *Lesbian Nuns: Breaking Silence* to the *Penthouse*-owned sex magazine *Forum*. "Grier did not think about what *Forum* represents," says one lesbian, Denise Kulp, office manager for the publication *Off Our Backs*. "I think she was caught up with having a best-seller, a breakthrough book, and she stepped away from being a lesbian publisher and became a 'real' publisher. In the future, I think contributors will be a lot more careful about contracts." Several contributors to the book are outraged that their material has appeared in *Forum* without their consent.

June 11 *The Advocate* reports that the building at 53 Christopher Street in Greenwich Village—once the site of the Stonewall Inn —is now a bagel shop.

June 14 Shortly after leaving the Athens airport, a TWA jetliner, Flight 847, is hijacked by two Lebanese terrorists who force the plane to land in Beirut. It sits on the airport tarmac with forty hostages aboard, for two weeks. Unbeknownst to the world or to the hijackers, two gay lovers—thirty-one-year-old Victor Amburgy and forty-year-old Jack McCarty, of San Francisco—are among the Americans on board. "When they pointed the pistol to your head," McCarty says later, "you had to believe that it was for real. . . . I just looked straight ahead. We were prepared to die. We wanted to do it with as much dignity as possible."

When the hostages finally return safely to the United States (all except twenty-three-year-old Marine Robert Stethem, who has been brutally murdered by the hijackers), Amburgy and McCarty walk together, arm in arm, for their official greeting by the President and Mrs. Reagan. "We wanted to make a statement about ourselves as a team," says McCarty.

June 17 A New Orleans man, Johnny Greene, writes an article for *People* magazine about his personal struggle with AIDS-Related Complex, and is rewarded for his honesty by being immediately dismissed from the Louisiana construction firm that employs him. *People* later hires him as a consulting correspondent.

June 24 More than a year after police raided London's "Gay's the Word" bookstore and confiscated the "obscene" works of Gore Vidal, Paul Verlaine, Tennessee Williams, Oscar Wilde, and others, eight of the store's directors, plus its assistant manager, go on trial for more than seven dozen counts of "conspiring to import indecent literature."
All the charges are eventually dropped.

July 9 "The argument about homosexual teachers making our children homosexual seems to be silly the more you think of it. I myself went to all Catholic schools where the nuns and brothers took the vow of chastity and, I mean, I wasn't even *tempted* to follow that example."
—HENRY MILLER, *New York delegate to the American Bar Association, arguing for passage of a resolution endorsing gay civil rights. The resolution is rejected 161 to 152.*

July 10 "Given a choice between sharing a park with homosexuals or a bunch of white-sheeted, racist, hate-peddling losers, we think we would prefer the homosexuals."
—*Arlington, Texas,* Daily News *editorial denouncing an upcoming anti-gay rally by the Ku Klux Klan in the city's Randol Mill Park*

July 15 A shockingly frail and haggard Rock Hudson makes a public appearance at a press conference to help promote the new cable TV series of his longtime friend Doris Day. Publicists for the actor attribute his cadaverous looks to "the aftereffects of the flu and a couple of sleepless nights."

July 23 A two-year, highly emotional legal battle over the guardianship of a twenty-nine-year-old quadriplegic lesbian, Sharon Kowalski, ends when a Minnesota judge awards custody of the severely disabled woman not to her lover of four years, Karen Thompson, but to Kowalski's father—who immediately puts her in a nursing home and bars visits from Thompson or any other of Kowalski's lesbian friends. "I've never faced such a virulent anger and hatred," says Thompson. "I'm the scapegoat for all the pain, for all the things they can't deal with. . . . As long as I can fight, I will be fighting to get Sharon back; as long as Sharon indicates she wants me to be fighting, I could never leave her."

A publicist for Rock Hudson says the actor is seriously ill with inoperable liver cancer in a Paris hospital.

THE ELUSIVE ROCK HUDSON

"I don't take a stand on anything."
        —Asked in 1977 what he thought of Anita Bryant

"Look, I know lots of gays in Hollywood, and most of them are nice guys. Some have tried it on with me, but I've said, 'Come on, now. You've got the wrong guy.' "

"That's a totally unbelievable role for me."
—Asked if he would consider playing the role of Coach Brown in *The Front Runner*

"I'd like any role that would stretch me, where I was credible. But I'm not about to drag myself up in leather or in chiffon."

"He doesn't have any idea now how he contracted AIDS."
—Hudson's spokeswoman in Paris, initially rejecting press speculation about the actor's sexuality

"I like to keep my secrets to myself, and I guess they will die with me."

August 1 Now available at a magazine stand or checkout counter near you: *Teen Idols* magazine. "PATRICK SWAYZE, Centerfold Guy! BILLY ZABKA, Sexy Giant Beach Poster! JEFF YAGHER & MITCH GAYLORD Live It Up In Puerto Vallarta! GO TO ROB LOWE'S SURPRISE PARTY!!!!! And much, MUCH more." One commentator calls it "*Playgirl* for the bubble gum and video game set."

In the nation's bookstores this month: *Quiet Fire: Memoirs of Older Gay Men* by Keith Vacha, the personal stories of seventeen gay men (most past their fifties) who relate the problems (and, at times, unique pleasures) of being gay in the decades preceding the Stonewall riots.

Actor Bruce Boxleitner—whose fifteen minutes of fame are soon to end with the cancellation of *Scarecrow and Mrs. King*—complains to *Playgirl* magazine that American men are "becoming more and more effeminate" and that "society has deemed *macho* a dirty word."

"What do you call a gay man with no arms and legs? *Roll-aids*."

"Why is everyone in Hollywood terrified of AIDS? *Because they've all had a piece of the Rock*."

"How can you tell whether your prospective trick has Alzheimer's or AIDS? *Just spin him around three times in the room. If he can't find the door, fuck him*."

"Why has Ronald Reagan turned AIDS research over to the Department of Agriculture? *Because AIDS turns fruits into vegetables*." —*Popular AIDS "jokes" making the rounds after revelations that Rock Hudson is being treated for the disease in Paris*

August 8 A publicist for Burt Reynolds denies rumors—reported in the *San Francisco Examiner*—that the actor is in San Francisco receiving treatment for an AIDS-related condition.

August 12 "Something is wrong with the health-care system when a wealthy man and a friend of the President has to go to Europe for treatment."
—RON NAJMAN, *media director for the National Gay Task Force, on Rock Hudson's trips to Paris to receive experimental treatments with HPA-23*

September 3 "We look for actresses who are knowledgeable about sex and not afraid to let the world know. We need camerawomen who are comfortable with sex to experiment with innovative ways of capturing it. . . . To say that porn is violent is sheer ignorance and lunacy. It may be boring and tacky, and that is a consequence of its social unacceptability."
—NAN KINNEY, *producer of Fatale Films, a new line of erotic videos for lesbians*

September 19 A "Commitment to Life" benefit, organized by Elizabeth Taylor and sponsored by the Los Angeles AIDS Project, raises more than $1.3 million for AIDS research and draws such celebrities as Betty Ford, Burt Lancaster, Shirley MacLaine, Sammy Davis, Jr., Linda Evans, and Diahann Carroll. When Burt Reynolds tries to read a "best wishes" telegram from Ronald Reagan, much of the crowd boos.

September 20 Paul Schrader's film *Mishima* opens. The visually striking production—with a trendy score by Philip Glass—goes on for more than two hours with nary a mention of Mishima's homosexuality, a concession Schrader reportedly made to the author's widow in exchange for her assistance with the production.

September 23 *People* magazine runs a cover story, "FEAR & AIDS IN HOLLYWOOD," quoting everyone from Dack Rambo to Joan Collins to Cher on the disease. The article reveals, among other things, that makeup artists on *The Tonight Show* burned their makeup brushes after using them on a gay actor rumored to be sick, and that Joan Rivers now drinks her Perrier straight out of the bottle rather than from a glass. Hollywood porn producer Russ Mitchell also predicts—erroneously, as it turns out—that AIDS "may finally do something to us that the police have been trying to do for the last fifteen years—put us out of business."

September 26   Lily Tomlin and Jane Wagner's *The Search for Signs of Intelligent Life in the Universe* opens to critical acclaim on Broadway.

September 30   Four female impersonators performing at a gay bar in Meridian, Mississippi, are arrested and hauled off by police for violating the city's little-known ordinance against cross-dressing.

A federal court rules that Anthony Sullivan—an Australian who has been living in the United States for more than a decade—must leave the country because he is a homosexual, and gives him thirty days to return to his native country voluntarily—despite the fact that he has a lover of eleven years, Richard Adams, a U.S. citizen who has petitioned the INS to grant Sullivan resident alien status so that the two of them can stay together. Says Adams, "Because of the AIDS scare we have the federal government through the CDC urging people, gay and nongay, to get into relationships, preferably of a monogamous nature. . . . And yet, conversely, we have the government through the INS saying that gay and lesbian relationships are meaningless." One INS official had earlier rejected Sullivan's petition on the grounds that "a bonafide marital relationship [cannot] exist between two faggots."

October 1   "Tony Lama, brn., pointed toes, 14″ tall, heavily polished, smelly, ex. cond., very soft—from hairy-chested gas station attendant with big biceps. $49"

"Massive dk. brn. military lace-up boots, vibram soles, speed lace, heavily polished, old-style, steel toes, great smell—from construction worker who was in the reserves. $49"

"Military combat boots, very good cond., scuffed, cumstained, standard issue, need service/polish, nice stinky smell—from airman at local air base. $15"

"Converse, white hi-tops, All Stars, ex. cond.—from hunky Reno, Nevada wrestler. $19"
—*A few of the hundreds of items for sale this month in a Salt Lake City catalog exclusively for gay shoe and foot fetishists*

"It amazes me that I've been around this long. I always felt I'd wind up tragically—like James Dean. I guess, in a way, I have—though it hasn't ended yet. . . . I'm probably going to die in a matter of months. I'm going into the eighteenth month. I saw a PBS documentary last night—do you know what month they say victims usually die in? The eighteenth."
—*Gay porn star* BEAU MATHEWS, *discussing his struggle against AIDS. Mathews dies nine months later, in the summer of 1986.*

October 2   Rock Hudson dies of AIDS at his home in Los Angeles. He is fifty-nine. Morticians arriving to remove the body have to fight a mob of over one hundred journalists, many of whom are trying to get a coveted "death" shot of the actor for the tabloids. (The tabloids have reportedly offered a huge sum to any photographer who can get a clear shot of Hudson's emaciated corpse.) Only one photographer is finally able to get any kind of snapshot of the dead actor: Hudson in a body bag, on the floor of the funeral home's van.

October 3   With fear over the spread of AIDS nearing fever pitch, New York governor Mario Cuomo announces he is considering closing all gay bathhouses in the state of New York. Meanwhile, the U.S. House of Representatives votes to give Surgeon General C. Everett Koop extra federal funding to close "any bathhouse or massage parlor which in his judgment . . . can be determined to facilitate" the transmission of AIDS.

October 4   West Germany elects its first openly gay member of parliament.

October 7   "The rectum is a sexual organ, and it deserves the respect that a penis gets and a vagina gets. Anal intercourse is a

central sexual activity, and it should be supported. . . . Everybody's too embarrassed to even contemplate this. . . . In fact, it's terribly important because anal intercourse has been the central activity for gay men and for some women for all of history. It's not going to go away."
—*Greenwich Village physician* DR. JOSEPH SONNABEND, *who has gained national attention for his work with people with AIDS*

October 14 I'D SHOOT MY SON IF HE HAD AIDS, SAYS VICAR!
—*British tabloid headline accompanying a photo of the Rev. Robert Simpson holding an all-too-ready rifle to his teenage son's head*

ONWARD CHRISTIAN SOLDIERS

"There will be no satanic churches, no more free distribution of pornography, no more abortion on demand, no more talk of rights for homosexuals. When the Christian majority takes control, pluralism will be seen as evil and the state will not allow anybody the right to practice evil."
—GARY JARMIN, president of Catholics for Christian Political Action

"America is in crying need of the moral vision that you have brought. . . . What swell goals you have!"
—Vice-President GEORGE BUSH, addressing a meeting of Jerry Falwell and his followers

"Nothing is more important to this nation today than this conference . . . not unemployment, not rebuilding our defense capabilities. What *is* important is rebuilding our relationship to God and a right view of the Bible."
—EDWIN MEESE, at a San Diego conference of fundamentalist Christians

---

ONWARD CHRISTIAN SOLDIERS (cont.)

"Even if a husband is beating a wife or kids, divorce isn't the answer. Separation and then a return is okay. You might have to suffer for five years or more, but a woman who is a Christian, who is trying to lead her husband to the Lord, cannot give up on him. The Lord will answer her prayers."
—*Fundamentalist activist* NORMA MERRIN

"The Scriptures are on our side."

—PRESIDENT REAGAN

October 17 The San Antonio City Health Department hand delivers letters to fourteen local people with AIDS, warning them they will be charged with third-degree felony counts (carrying a two- to ten-year prison sentence) if they have sex with anyone other than fellow PWA's.

October 21 Dan White commits suicide by asphyxiating himself in his wife's car, with a hose running from the exhaust pipe to the passenger compartment.

November 1 "My dream was to be a documentary photographer for a travel magazine like *National Geographic*."
—*Currently hot gay photographer* KRISTEN BJORN, *known for his sensuous nude photography of foreign men in exotic locations such as Brazil and South Africa*

November 7 When vice officers in Denver raid a local gay bar and try to close down a live stage show by Divine, many in the audience start to laugh: they think the raid is a joke. It isn't. "She wasn't doing anything objectionable to any of the people present," says one of the bar's owners. "People who come to see Divine know who Divine is. You're not getting grandmothers in there." Patrons got to see about twenty minutes of the show before the police moved in and arrested the bar's owner.

The New York City health department closes down the famous Mineshaft bar. Mayor Koch later praises the undercover health inspectors who infiltrated the club, and says of their final report—which includes graphic descriptions of the sadomasochistic acts, fellatio, and anal sex performed there—"It's tough stuff to read. It must be horrific, horrendous in its actuality to witness."

November 9   Terry Sweeney—the first openly gay performer on network television—joins the cast of *Saturday Night Live*, where he soon gains national attention for his acidly funny drag impersonations of First Lady Nancy Reagan.

November 11   NBC broadcasts *An Early Frost*, the first made-for-TV drama about a gay man with AIDS.

November 13   A forty-four-year-old woman from Manchester, England, Margaret Roff, becomes the first openly lesbian mayor in British history.

December 1   "Physically and mentally, it's destroyed sex for me. I lie in bed and wonder if I'm really gay anymore."
—*Gay Chicago nightclub owner* JIM FLYNT, *on the impact of the AIDS epidemic*

"If ever there was a homosexual plague, this disease is it."
                              —Cosmopolitan *magazine, in an article on AIDS*

December 2   Eight-term congressman and Republican presidential hopeful Jack Kemp denies longtime rumors he is gay. Says Kemp, who is married with children, "I think that any fair-minded person will dismiss something that has nothing to back it up." Kemp calls the rumors—which started in the Sixties, when he worked for a homosexual aide to then-governor Ronald Reagan—a "little tiny piece of poison."

December 19   The telephone company threatens to cut off the phone service of an Atlanta man, forty-six-year-old Edward Johnson, who has programmed his computer to call Jerry Falwell's toll-free "Old Time Gospel Hour" number every thirty seconds for the past eight months. Johnson says he made the calls (which wound up costing Falwell an estimated $500,000) because he was disgusted by the amount of money his mother was giving away every month to the Moral Majority. "She almost gave the family farm away," he tells the press, after finally agreeing to discontinue the calls.

December 31   Heartthrob Ricky Nelson—a favorite of gay men growing up in the Fifties and Sixties—dies in a New Year's Eve plane crash in Texas. He was forty-five.

January 4 Christopher Isherwood dies at the age of eighty-one in Santa Monica, California. He is survived by his lover of thirty-two years, artist Don Bachardy.

January 7 "This isn't *An Early Frost*. This isn't *As Is* or *The Normal Heart*. It's *Dynasty*. It's Alexis and fur and pearls. . . . This ain't a documentary."
—JACK COLEMAN *(who plays* Dynasty's *resident on-again, off-again homosexual, Steven Carrington), on charges that his character is not an accurate reflection of most gay men*

March 13 Jack Kemp once again denies rumors he is gay, this time in an interview on the *Today* show.

March 15 On the video shelf: *Bigger Than Life*, starring first-time gay porn actor Jeff Stryker. Stryker's dark good looks, plus his topman attitude and huge endowment, make him an instant porn

Christopher Isherwood (left) with longtime lover, artist Don Bachardy. GAVIN DILLARD

superstar, and his debut is quickly followed by a string of equally popular hits, including *Stryker Force* and *Strykin' It Deep.*

He later describes himself as being just "another person trapped in a body with a big dick."

March 20 After fourteen years, and despite heated opposition from many of the city's religious leaders, the New York City Council at last passes a gay rights ordinance, 21 to 14. "The sky is not going to fall," Mayor Koch tells reporters. "There isn't going to be any dramatic change in the life of this city."

March 24 William Hurt wins the Oscar for Best Actor for his portrayal of a homosexual window-dresser imprisoned on a morals charge in the film *Kiss of the Spider Woman.*

April 2 An auction of Rock Hudson memorabilia at New York's William Doyle Galleries nets $84,000, including $2,100 for a needlepoint rug made by Hudson and $1,400 for a small wooden stool autographed by Elizabeth Taylor. "He's one of my favorites," says one of the bidders. "Always was. Still is. He was just a nice man. I liked him for his dignity, his class."

April 3   British tenor Peter Pears, lifelong lover of composer Benjamin Britten, dies in Aldeburgh, England, at the age of seventy-five.

April 9   Georgia outlaws gay bathhouses.

April 15   Jean Genet dies in Paris at the age of seventy-five.

May 1   "You have to be a machine. You have to get it up, get it in and get it off on cue. You have to be able to completely divorce yourself from your surroundings and be able to function in any situation. For example, if you're working on location for a film shoot and staying at a motel for seven days, you have to cope with being in unfamiliar surroundings, getting irregular sleep, and living on McDonald's and Kentucky Fried Chicken, and still be able to perform sexually no matter what else is on your mind."
—*Porn producer* WILLIAM MARGOLD, *on what he tells prospective male models*

Lesbian Ann Bancroft becomes the first woman to reach the North Pole by dogsled, after a grueling two-month trip from Ellesmere Island.

May 10   Culture Club's fourth and final album, *From Luxury to Heartache*, enters the nation's Top 40. It climbs no higher than No. 32 and disappears from sight after six weeks.

May 13   Vanessa Redgrave stars as Renee Richards in the CBS made-for-TV movie, *Second Serve*. "Once again," writes television critic John O' Connor, "Miss Redgrave can be found taking chances that few actors could attempt or endure. And once again, she demonstrates why she is one of the most remarkable actresses in the English-speaking world."

May 16 *Top Gun* opens nationwide, and gives Tom Cruise, Val Kilmer, and Anthony Edwards an opportunity to spend a lot of onscreen time with their shirts off or clad in towels, playing volleyball in the sun or having heated arguments in steamy locker rooms. Described by more than one mainstream critic as essentially a gay porn fantasy without the explicit sex, it soon becomes the highest-grossing film of the year, as well as the twenty-fifth-highest-grossing motion picture of all time.

May 27 "It's not important to be gay . . . or important to be white . . . or important to be black. What's important is to be *you*."
—*Venerable novelist* JAMES BALDWIN, *asked what he thinks is the most important issue facing gay people today*

May 30 Fashion designer Perry Ellis dies of AIDS in New York City at the age of forty-six.

June 1 "You know, some people say syphilis came from screwing sheep and pigs, and there are some who say that AIDS may have come from monkeys. So, when the scriptures, not just the Judeo-Christian scriptures, but lots of scriptures say, 'Don't screw animals,' it's not because God doesn't want us screwing animals, he's telling us that if we're going to screw animals, we're going to get things from them. What we've really not dealt with is what if this is not a virus? What if we're manufacturing it? What if by adding endless billions and billions of sperm cells to membranes that are not supposed to handle sperm, you begin to come up with something that is different?"
—*Author* KEN KESEY (One Flew Over the Cuckoo's Nest), *advancing a novel theory, in* Esquire

June 10 Merle Miller, sixty-seven, dies in Danbury, Connecticut.

June 15 A Houston man repeatedly shoots his wife in the face, legs, back, and buttocks after she taunts him with accusations of being "gay, gay, gay" during a fight over what kind of food they should feed their cat. The wife survives; the husband is convicted of attempted murder.

June 17   MADMAN MOAMMAR NOW A DRUGGIE DRAG QUEEN!
—New York Post *headline reflecting recent U.S. intelligence reports that Libyan leader Moammar Qaddafi has taken to dressing in drag and using drugs. According to one source, Qaddafi was dressed as a woman (complete with heavy makeup and stiletto heels) when he recently greeted an entourage of visiting African diplomats in Tripoli.*

June 23   Exclusive Excerpt: THE ROCK HUDSON STORY THE DRAMA OF HIS FINAL DAYS
   The private terror of having AIDS prompted anger—and then denial.
   He threw the *Dynasty* script on the table. "I've got to kiss Linda. What the hell am I going to do?"
   —People *magazine cover teaser this week*

"The AIDS plague has so fed into America's current need to disown the sexual revolution that it has been hard to determine whether the new disease is just a convenient excuse or truly a new Black Plague."

—*Novelist* ERICA JONG

June 30   Despite the optimism of some gay activists, the U.S. Supreme Court once again rules, this time 5 to 4, that states have the constitutional right to outlaw private homosexual acts between consenting adults. The ruling comes in the case of Michael Hardwick, arrested in his Atlanta home in 1982 for having sex with another man.
   "What now?" says *The Washington Post*. "Can we expect an army of police to be assigned to peeping patrol, instructed to barge into bedrooms and arrest anyone who deviates from the most con-

ventional sexual practice. . . . The sodomy laws are an anachronism and an embarrassment, and if the courts won't strike them down, the legislatures must."

July 1   The distinguished science-fiction writer Arthur C. Clarke almost—but not quite—comes out of the closet in an interview in *Playboy* magazine. Asked first about the homosexual themes in his work, especially in his later novels, Clarke answers, "I guess I get more and more daring as I get older." Asked what he means by that, Clarke replies, enigmatically, "I guess I just don't give a damn anymore. Maybe that isn't true, actually. One of my problems now is that I'm not just a private citizen anymore. I have to keep up certain standards, or at least pretend to, so that I don't shock too many people." The interviewer finally asks Clarke outright if he has ever had any "bisexual experiences" himself. "Of course," Clarke tells him. "Who hasn't? Good God!"—but he then quickly demurs, "I don't want to go into detail about my own life, but I just want it to be noted that I have a rather relaxed, sympathetic attitude about it—and that's something I've not really said out loud before. Let's move on."

July 3   Boy George publicly denies persistent rumors he has AIDS. "That is totally ridiculous speculation," he tells the press. "I am not a promiscuous person." Instead, he claims that his recent dramatic weight loss is intentional, part of a new emphasis on physical fitness in his life. A short time later, he is arrested for heroin possession and enters a drug treatment program.

July 4   In the midst of a four-day centennial celebration for the Statue of Liberty, comedian Bob Hope tells a New York audience that the statue, in fact, has AIDS. "But nobody knows," he jokes, "if she got it from the mouth of the Hudson or the Staten Island ferry."

He later issues a public apology for the remark.

July 9   New Zealand repeals its laws prohibiting homosexual acts between consenting adults.

Attorney General Meese's Commission on Pornography releases its final, two-thousand-page report, which recommends, among other things, that the American people and their law enforcement officers launch an all-out war on "smut." Attacked by almost every major newspaper in the country, the commission's members become defensive, especially over charges that they relied almost entirely on anecdotal testimony and evidence from highly prejudiced "authorities" such as leaders of the Moral Majority and other conservative religious organizations. "If we relied on scientific data for every one of our findings," says one of the commission's members in self-defense, "I'm afraid that all of our conclusions, or all of our work, would be inconclusive."

The actual report, meanwhile, goes on to become one of the Government Printing Office's all-time top-sellers, what with its detailed listings and descriptions from various porn films and books (*Pregnant Lesbians No. 1*, *Tranvestite Torment*, *Macho Men in Heels*, et al.) and its occasionally explicit interviews with former porn models.

July 11 Jack Wrangler turns forty.

July 14 The nation's first and only gay savings and loan association, Atlas Savings and Loan of San Francisco, goes into receivership and closes it doors. As with dozens of other savings and loans across the country, Atlas's financial problems had been escalating over the past eighteen months, due to millions of dollars in bad loans.

Roy Cohn tells *People* magazine he is *not* dying of AIDS and he is *not* a homosexual. In fact—he tells the magazine—the one great love of his life is Barbara Walters.

July 15 Citing the recent U.S. Supreme Court decision on sodomy laws, the Missouri Supreme Court votes 5 to 2 to uphold a state law prohibiting gay sex.

> "Just because a literature about gays now exists does *not* mean that people are necessarily persuaded to change their opinions about us. The message they're getting from *La Cage aux Folles* is the same message they've always gotten from the drag shows at Finocchio's. Some sophisticates went to see *Torch Song Trilogy*. But in Dallas, where the show played on subscription, half of the audience left after the first act. So any progress we've made is really minuscule."
>
> —DANIEL CURZON, 1986

July 29 The Chicago City Council, by a vote of 30 to 18, defeats a proposed gay rights ordinance for the city.

August 1 "There are many men in leading positions of power who are homosexuals and yet appear regularly in the media as the leaders of our nation. Gay and closeted, many of them are married and have families. They serve in Congress, the Reagan administration and White House, the judiciary, military, and Washington power circles. . . . In Georgetown, on Capitol Hill, in Foggy Bottom and Alexandria, all-male parties are often graced by some of the big names of our times. The participants include Democrats, Republicans, liberals and conservatives, labor union leaders, and business leaders."
—*Former U.S. congressman* ROBERT BAUMAN, *in his newly published memoir*, The Gentleman from Maryland: The Conscience of a Gay Conservative

August 2 Roy Cohn dies of AIDS in Bethesda, Maryland.

August 8 A petition drive to recall Durham, North Carolina, mayor Wib Gulley falls 1,500 signatures short of the necessary number to force a special election. Fundamentalists in the city have been outraged over Gulley's recent pro-gay remarks and his proclamation of June 22 to 29 as "Anti-Discrimination Week."

Chief Justice William Rehnquist, the high court's most conservative justice. He once offered his opinion that gay campus groups do not, under the First Amendment, have a right to official recognition at universities, and wrote that homosexuality is akin to a communicable disease requiring containment.

August 9   Four years after the first Gay Olympics, Gay Games II opens in San Francisco.

August 12   "Hordes of howling homosexuals are in a foot-stamping snit because the Supreme Court won't okay their bizarre bedtime practices—and they're threatening to prance out of the closet and scratch our eyes out. . . . The squawking boys burned flags, cursed the court and disrupted traffic for hours on end. Between wails, they blew kisses to each other and proclaimed themselves proud as peacocks to be in love with their fellow man."
—Weekly World News *"reporting" on gay outrage over the recent Supreme Court decision, under the headlines "GAYS THREATEN CIVIL WAR! ONWARD SISSY SOLDIERS! PEEVED PANSIES REVOLT!"*

August 15   *Behind the Green Door—The Sequel*, the first hard-core straight porn film to feature the use of condoms, has its world premiere in San Francisco. First-night viewers are charged a $50 "admission" fee, with all proceeds (more than $25,000) going to San Francisco General Hospital's AIDS ward.

August 26 Former professional football player Jerry Smith—who played with the Washington Redskins for thirteen seasons—publicly acknowledges he has AIDS. He dies seven weeks later.

September 15 Former Air Force sergeant Leonard Matlovich is diagnosed with AIDS in San Francisco. A week later, he is admitted to the hospital with pneumocystis and a yeast infection. He has recently lost forty pounds.

September 17 Antonin Scalia—who, as a federal judge, voted to uphold the 1981 expulsion of a gay petty officer from the U.S. Navy—joins the U.S. Supreme Court after the recent departure of Warren Burger. William Rehnquist is promoted to Chief Justice.

September 26 The city of Lynchburg, Virginia, agrees to "forgive" Jerry Falwell $1.4 million in back taxes after Falwell threatens to move his lucrative religious enterprises elsewhere if the city presses too hard for payment.

September 29 AIDS activist Diego Rivera dies of complications from AIDS. "I may eventually die as a result of this disease," he had said on the PBS documentary *AIDS: A Public Inquiry*, "but I would consider my death an act of murder for the lack of government funding. I would consider it murder by my own government."

September 30 On the video shelf: *Bi-Bi Black Boys*. "It's a spicy tale of a shipwrecked Hispanic dreamboat who finds himself rescued by the restless and horny natives."

Also, *Sticky Business*, starring Lee Ryder and Michael Gere.

October 1 "Stuff goes on at the bottom of a pile-up—guys will be giving you one or two. Grabbing your nuts. You get a lot of shit at the bottom of a pile. And spit—a lot of spit."
—*Chicago Bears quarterback* JIM MCMAHON, *asked, "What happens during a game that the fans can't see?"*

October 3 *The Washington Post* reveals that at a recent meeting of the National Security Council, President Reagan suggested that the United States invite Libyan leader Moammar Qaddafi to come live in San Francisco, since "he likes to dress up so much." "Why don't we give him AIDS?" joked George Schultz, to appreciative laughter.

October 4 Stephen Barry, former personal valet to Prince Charles, dies from AIDS.

October 7 The Los Angeles County Board of Supervisors votes to outlaw the sale and use of "poppers."

October 8 Ronald Reagan is named "The Most Interesting Man in America" by a *Ladies' Home Journal* readers' poll.

More than 150 gay protesters march on the steps of the Supreme Court to demonstrate against the recent sodomy law decision. "SODOMY SUCKS, BUT WE CAN LICK THE PROBLEM," reads one demonstrator's sign.

October 22 "The threat of AIDS should be sufficient to permit a sex education curriculum. . . . There is no doubt that we need sex education in schools and that it include information on hetero-sexual and homosexual relationships. . . . The need is critical and the price of neglect is high. The lives of our young people depend on our fulfilling our responsibility."
—*Surgeon General* C. EVERETT KOOP

November 1　This month's *PC World* and *Mac World*—both edited by David Bunell—feature editorials decrying the recent Supreme Court decision on Georgia's sodomy laws. The "personal computer world," writes Bunell, "should think twice about supporting high-tech development in states that lack a decent social climate for high-tech to operate in." The editorial draws more than a thousand letters from readers—80 percent of them in disagreement with Bunell—and the magazine subsequently loses nearly $32,000 in monthly revenues from outraged companies that pull their ads. "I'm shocked," says Bunell, "and I'm concerned about the fundamentalist right-wing Christians who think they founded the country and that America is a Christian country."

"The fiction in *Mandate* is presented for your entertainment. It is in no way meant to encourage unsafe forms of sexual behavior. We urge you to familiarize yourself with the guidelines for safe sex and practice them with your partner. If you have any questions about safe sex, contact your local gay men's health group or your physician."
—*Disclaimer now appearing on the table of contents page of* Mandate *magazine. Similar disclaimers (meant largely to circumvent claims that the magazines are encouraging unwise sexual behavior) have also begun to turn up in other gay "slicks."*

November 2　Flying through the air on stage wires to make a dramatic entrance, Liberace begins the final performance of a lucrative seventeen-day run at New York's Radio City Music Hall. His appearance—gaunt, haggard, the face looking more and more mummified—leads to considerable speculation about his health. It is his last concert.

November 15　In the nation's bookstores this month: the 1987 *I Love a Man in Uniform* calendar, the 1987 Chippendales calendar, the 1987 *Malibu Men* calendar, the 1987 *University Men* calendar, the 1987 *Blues Boys* calendar, the 1987 *Black Gold* (devoted to black men) calendar, the 1987 *California Latin Male* calendar, the 1987 *Firefighters* calendar, the 1987 *Hot Bods* calendar, and at least half a dozen other "beefcake" calendars, few of them explicit, most of them showing wind-swept, rugged "dreamdates" posed in settings (on beaches at sunset, by the pool, astride white horses, etc.) that often seem like scenes from bad romance novels.

November 23 *Parade* magazine runs a query from an anxious reader in Prescott, Arizona, who writes, "I saw on TV the Smothers Brothers describing Ronald Reagan as a 'known heterosexual.' How can they get away with such stuff? Isn't there some way the network can be fined for spreading such a dirty lie?"

The magazine replies: "It is not a lie. Reagan *is* a 'known heterosexual.' Obviously you are confusing heterosexual with homosexual. A heterosexual is one whose sexual attraction is toward a member of the opposite sex. A homosexual is one characterized by a sexual interest in a person of the same sex."

November 24 The mother of *Designing Women* creator Linda Bloodworth-Thomason dies of AIDS, which she contracted through a blood transfusion.

December 1 A Georgia gay man is given a $1,000 fine, sentenced to ten years' probation, and ordered to perform two hundred hours of public service after being convicted under the state's recently upheld sodomy laws. But of course everyone knows the sodomy laws are rarely enforced legal deadwood . . .

Phil Barone is named *Playgirl*'s "Man of the Year." He later complains he has had to change his phone number due to the large number of calls and propositions he's received from male readers of the magazine.

December 2 Ontario, Canada, passes a province-wide gay rights ordinance.

December 4 The city council of New Orleans rejects, 5 to 2, a municipal gay rights ordinance.

December 5   Asserting that the activity constitutes a defacement of federal property, the U.S. Justice Department sends a threatening letter to gay businessman Frank Kellas demanding that he immediately "cease and desist" his practice of stamping dollar bills in the Chicago area with the insignia "GAY $." Kellas began stamping the bills as a way of demonstrating gay economic clout, after the Chicago city council failed to pass a gay rights ordinance in July. According to some estimates, about $17 million in currency has so far been marked with the message. Says *The Chicago Sun-Times*, condemning the Justice Department's pursuit of the matter, "We question whether the limited practice of stamping the legend *GAY $* on dollar bills qualifies as an assault on the U.S. Treasury of a magnitude warranting an investment of time and talent by federal prosecutors and Secret Service agents."

Meanwhile, *The Advocate* suggests that gays take up the practice nationwide: "There would probably soon not be an unstamped piece of U.S. money anywhere."

Gay porn idol J.W. King dies of AIDS at the age of thirty-one in Los Angeles.

The Nevada Supreme Court—meeting twenty miles from the nearest legalized brothel and across the street from the nearest casino—refuses to strike down the state's sodomy laws.

December 8   "I don't got no fucking AIDS."
—*Comedian* RICHARD PRYOR, *joining the ranks of Burt Reynolds, Boy George, and other celebrities recently forced to refute widespread public rumors about their health*

December 9   The current national gay hardcover best-sellers, according to *The Advocate*:

1. *The Lost Language of Cranes* by David Leavitt
2. *Gay Priest* by Malcolm Boyd
3. *The Gentleman from Maryland* by Robert Bauman
4. *Star Woman* by Lynn V. Andrews
5. *Blackbird* by Larry Duplechan

ABOVE: *Gay porn idol J. W. King. "He was a real sweetheart," said one photographer who worked with him.* STEVE JOHNSON, CLOSE-UP PRODUCTIONS **BELOW:** *Malcolm Boyd (left) with his lover,* Advocate *features editor Mark Thompson.* CRAWFORD BARTON

December 11   Austin, Texas, passes an ordinance prohibiting discrimination against people with AIDS in employment, housing, business, medical care, and public services.

December 15   Russian dancer Serge Lifar—the last of Serge Diaghilev's lovers—dies in Paris at the age of eighty-one. In 1925, Lifar had replaced dancer Leonide Massine as both Diaghilev's bedmate and as the *premier danseur* of Diaghilev's Ballets Russes. After Diaghilev's death in 1929, Lifar became ballet master of the Paris Opera Ballet, where he soon prompted controversy with his practice of giving male dancers increasingly prominent roles in ballet productions.

December 20   A new book—*The 'Sissy Boy Syndrome' and the Development of Homosexuality*, by UCLA psychiatrist Richard Green —tries to answer the question whether effeminate boys invariably grow up to be gay. Green found that out of forty-four young boys who exhibited distinctly feminine characteristics in childhood, including a desire to dress up in girls' clothing and a stated wish that they had been girls, about 75 percent of them grew up to be either gay or bisexual.

December 23   On the video shelf: *Big Guns*—or as one critic describes it, "*Top Gun* with the towels off"—starring Mike Henson, Jeff Quinn, John Rocklin, and Rocky Armano.

December 28   New Right activist and outspoken "family values" advocate Terry Dolan dies of AIDS at the age of thirty-six in Washington, D.C. It turns out he was gay.

1987

January 20 *The Advocate* announces that shooting of the long-awaited film version of *The Front Runner* will finally begin next month, with actor Grant Show (costar of the daytime soap opera *Ryan's Hope*) slated to play Billy Sive.

February 1 Citing financial and personnel problems, Canada's *The Body Politic* announces it is ceasing publication.

February 4 Two weeks after publicists denied a *Las Vegas Sun* story claiming he had AIDS, Liberace, sixty-two, dies from the disease, in Palm Springs, California. Spokesmen for the entertainer had earlier insisted that his recent weight loss (more than twenty-five pounds) and shocking pallor were the result of a misguided new health regime, consisting almost exclusively of eating watermelon.

Four days later, the pianist is buried in Forest Lawn Cemetery, in a six-foot white marble sarcophagus embellished with his name in brass on the lid. The grave itself is flanked by two candelabra-shaped trees.

THE ELUSIVE LIBERACE

"He had this idea that no one in America knew he was homosexual, which was preposterous."

—*Journalist* MICHAEL SEGELL

"He thought his personal life was nobody's business. . . . He once told me the happiest he ever was was when he was onstage."

—*Former lover* SCOTT THORSON

"He doesn't much care for the real world, you know."

—*Liberace's sister,* ANGELINA

A Brooklyn teenager, nineteen-year-old Andre Nichols, is acquitted of murder after claiming that he shot and killed his victim—a forty-nine-year-old Catholic priest—in self-defense after the priest allegedly made sexual advances to him. "The basic message of this verdict," says one angry observer, "is that it's OK to kill a priest if you can make people believe he was a fag."

February 14 National Condom Week begins.

February 21 Andy Warhol dies at the age of fifty-eight.

March 6 Vermont becomes the first state to hand out condoms to prison inmates on request.

March 17 The White House reveals that President Reagan has recently undergone testing for AIDS, out of fear he may have contracted the disease during blood transfusions after the 1981 attempt on his life by John Hinckley, Jr. The tests, says an aide, have come back negative.

March 18   "A kind of 1950s conservatism is beginning to emerge." —*Movie producer* DANIEL MELNICK, *on how the AIDS epidemic is affecting new film scripts. Six months later, Hollywood gives the nation* Fatal Attraction, *the* Reefer Madness *of sexual infidelity.*

March 24   In its first major political action since being formed barely two weeks ago, a new group called ACT UP (AIDS Coalition to Unleash Power) stages a boisterous protest in the heart of New York City to demand that the federal government stop dragging its feet on the approval of new drugs that might benefit people with AIDS. Seventeen protesters are arrested for obstructing traffic when they sit down in the middle of the intersection of Broadway and Wall Street.

March 27   A *Newsweek* review of the newly published second edition of the unabridged *Oxford English Dictionary* complains that homosexuals have plundered the word *gay* and irretrievably "damaged" it for future generations. "A delightful and necessary word is now virtually lost to us," laments the reviewer. The complaint —surely as tiresome by now to many heterosexuals as it has been for years to gay men and lesbians—remains, as always, a thinly veiled pretext for homophobia, since most people can still speak of "*hard* candy" without thinking of an erection, of "tennis *balls*" without giggling uncontrollably over testicles, and of "a *black* dress" without recoiling in horror at the thought of African-Americans.

April 1   Actress Rae Dawn Chong tells *Playboy* magazine that the one fashion trend of the 1980s she would most like to see disappear is "men liking other men!"

April 6   "It is unlikely that any major Hollywood romantic symbol will use a condom in the next five years in a movie unless it is a

made-for-TV docudrama. The image is not one they would care
to be associated with."
—*Film critic* ROGER EBERT, *on the film industry's inability to respond
responsibly, rather than hysterically, to the AIDS epidemic*

April 13   A seven-page, much-publicized cover story on teen sex
and AIDS in this week's *People* magazine never once mentions the
subject of homosexuality or addresses the critical issues of gay
teenagers and the disease.

April 24   Television evangelist Jim Bakker—already in trouble for
having paid $265,000 in hush money to church secretary Jessica
Hahn, with whom he had sex in 1981—is now accused of having
also made homosexual advances to some of his colleagues. Says one
PTL aide, whom Bakker allegedly tried to lure into bed, "I know
now the awful feeling a woman must experience when she's being
seduced by a man. It was terrible."

April 27   "In Wilmette, it's now trendy to have an AIDS child at
your birthday party. We're having trouble keeping up with all the
invitations—which is a lot nicer than having bricks crash through
our windows."
                              —*An Illinois mother of a child with AIDS*

May 1   In the nation's bookstores this month: *The Orton Diaries*,
the brilliant, at times scathingly funny diary of gay playwright Joe
Orton, who chronicled the last eight months of his life—when he
was at the height of his fame and notoriety in London—before
being bludgeoned to death by his lover on August 9, 1967.

The exiled former ruler of Cambodia, Prince Norodom Sihanouk
—a devout believer in reincarnation—tells *Playboy* magazine that
his one fervent wish is that he not be reborn as a homosexual in
his next life. "I don't understand homosexuals," he tells the magazine. "I don't criticize them. I respect their way of life. But I bless
heaven for allowing me to be very normal, very normal."

"On the first day of shooting, Rupert and I had this agonizingly long kiss. Luckily we got on very well. When it was over I felt on a complete high with relief."
—*Actor* JAMES WILBY, *on his love scenes with Rupert Graves for the forthcoming film of E. M. Forster's* Maurice, *in which Wilby plays the title character*

May 4 "I've done it all. I've been a gay, a killer, a lunatic, an adulterer, a seducer. A good time was had by all."
—*Actor* MICHAEL CAINE, *in an interview in this week's* People *magazine, which also includes a story on* Saturday Night Live's *"Church Lady" Dana Carvey ("I'm not a cross-dresser, and I've never done anything in drag before"), a story on gay porn star Jack Wrangler and his romance with singer Margaret Whiting, an article on singer Michael Feinstein, and a glowing review of the new film* Prick Up Your Ears

May 5 San Francisco's last gay bathhouse, the 21st Street Baths, closes its doors.

May 6 A British tabloid offers free one-way tickets to Norway for any homosexual who will take one, as a way of helping rid the country of gay men. "FLY AWAY GAYS—AND WE WILL PAY!" reads the offer.

May 7 Stewart McKinney, a Republican from Connecticut, becomes the first U.S. congressman to die of AIDS. He is fifty-six. His widow subsequently establishes a foundation in his name and eventually sets up a medical scholarship for college students interested in working with people with AIDS.

May 9 *Opera News* editor Robert Jacobson, forty-six, dies of AIDS.

May 11 "AIDS has spread so much that I don't want to kiss anyone new on the show. Let's face it, I don't know who he's been with or who his girlfriend or boyfriend has been with."
—Dallas *star* DONNA MILLS

May 22   Anthony Dolan—one of President Reagan's chief speech-writers, and brother to the late Terry Dolan—takes out a two-page ad in *The Washington Times* to condemn recent press reports about his brother's homosexuality and death from AIDS. In particular, he blasts *The Washington Post* (which has been running most of the stories) as a hotbed of "homosexual intrigue."

May 27   With wife Tammy Faye weeping at his side, beleaguered televangelist Jim Bakker goes on ABC's *Nightline* to publicly refute charges of his sexual indiscretions, as well as accusations that he mismanaged funds from his once-thriving television ministry. "I've been married to this man for twenty-six years," Tammy Faye tells host Ted Koppel at one point, "and I can tell you one thing: he's not homosexual, or is he bisexual. He's a wonderful, loving husband." The broadcast—which features long stretches of Tammy Faye alternately giggling and sobbing, and both of the Bakkers professing love for God, Ted Koppel, Jerry Falwell, and everyone watching—is the highest-rated in *Nightline*'s eight-year history.

The *Lambda Rising Book Report*—the first literary journal devoted entirely to reviews of gay and lesbian-themed books, as well as to issues confronting gay authors and readers—publishes its premiere issue.

May 28   Charles Ludlam, forty-four, dies from AIDS.

May 29   U.S. Representative Barney Frank (D-Massachusetts) becomes the second U.S. congressman to openly acknowledge his homosexuality (after Gerry Studds in 1983) when he tells an interviewer from *The Boston Globe* that he is gay. "I don't think my sex life is relevant to my job," adds Frank, "but on the other hand I don't want to leave the impression that I'm embarrassed about my life."

Seventeen months later, he is reelected to Congress by a margin of 70 percent to 30 percent.

May 31   President Reagan gives his first speech devoted exclusively to AIDS. He calls for more HIV testing.

June 1   Pink flamingo lawn ornaments are reported to be making a comeback, with more than three hundred thousand of them expected to be sold this year alone.

June 2   Michael Bennett, creator of *A Chorus Line*, dies of AIDS at the age of forty-four in Tucson, Arizona.

June 8   In what is described as just the first stage of the Reagan administration's new strategy to combat the AIDS epidemic, Attorney General Edwin Meese announces that all federal prisoners will henceforth be tested for HIV, and says that the results of those tests may influence whether some prisoners are ever granted parole. Explains Meese, "One of the factors on when people leave prison certainly has to do with whether they are a danger to the community." Meese also unveils a new plan under which any tourists, immigrants, or refugees who are known to be HIV-positive will be denied entry into the United States.

June 15   George Michael's newly released single "I Want Your Sex" is banned from airplay by several British radio stations because it allegedly promotes promiscuity. In the U.S., MTV reedits the video three times before airing it.

   "I keep reading that there are half a million people in New York infected with AIDS," says one New York DJ who also refuses to play the song. "Though the record doesn't promote casual sex, I think that on the first listen it might strike the average person that way." Radio stations in Cincinnati, Denver, New Orleans, Minneapolis, and Pittsburgh also eventually ban airplay of the single.

June 19   A citizens' task force in Spokane, Washington, recommends getting rid of the city's prostitutes by posting huge billboards downtown that read "DO YOU KNOW IF THAT WOMAN YOU JUST PICKED UP HAS AIDS OR IS AN AIDS CAR-

RIER?" The local *Spokesman-Review* endorses the idea as "fair, humane, and realistic."

June 26 "We have a president who is tough enough to send Marines to Lebanon, tough enough to send bombers to Libya, and tough enough to send battleships to the Persian Gulf, but who can't say the word 'condom' in public."
—*Democratic presidential candidate and former Arizona governor* BRUCE BABBITT

THE PRESIDENTIAL CANDIDATES TALK ABOUT AIDS

"AIDS is spreading and killing in every corner of the world. . . . It is an equal-opportunity merchant of death. . . . Ultimately, we must protect those who do not have the disease."
—GEORGE BUSH

"History will deal harshly with the Reagan administration for its failure to face up to the unprecedented threat of the AIDS pandemic. Not since Hoover has a president done less when he should have known better."
—ALBERT GORE

"While AIDS is a public-health issue, it includes . . . moral problems which cannot be ignored. . . . Whether the problem is teenage promiscuity or drugs or homosexuality, we have learned by experience that noncommittal 'values clarification' does not equip young people to make responsible choices. . . . As President Reagan pointed out, 'When it comes to preventing AIDS, don't medicine and morality teach the same thing?' . . . Yes, they do."
—JACK KEMP

THE PRESIDENTIAL CANDIDATES TALK ABOUT AIDS

"Why is President Reagan so generous with money to take lives in Central America—and yet so stingy with money to save lives here in the United States of America? Why is the President so reluctant to be guided by morality in his dealings with the immoral racist government of South Africa, yet wants only to preach morality in his response to this deadly disease, which is morally neutral?"

—JESSE JACKSON

"It is clear to me that there are some ways in which we should not talk about AIDS. I am referring specifically to the rhetoric of those who have seized upon the AIDS problem in the homosexual population to promote invidiousness, discriminatory and moralistic dogma. . . . Fearmongering and near hysteria only serve to promote division among people. . . . This country wasn't founded by declarations of fear and loathing. It was founded by men and women who went to great ends to build a tolerant and enlightened society. As an American, I cannot in good conscience let the ideal of what it means to be an American get crushed under the heel of hatred and discrimination."

—RICHARD GEPHARDT

July 1 President Reagan names conservative judge Robert Bork —whose homophobia on the bench is well documented—to fill the Supreme Court vacancy left by departing justice Lewis Powell. Bork—who has repeatedly endorsed the idea that there is no constitutional right to privacy, for either homosexuals *or* heterosexuals—is immediately attacked by a wide variety of civil rights groups, women's organizations, and First Amendment advocates, who take the unprecedented step of buying network television commercials to help defeat his nomination.

Four months later, Bork is rejected by the U.S. Senate, 58 to

42. Says an unrepentant Ronald Reagan, "I'll try to find [a new nominee] that they'll object to just as much as they did to this one."

"Moral relativism is the AIDS virus of a democracy: it suppresses society's normal immune response, so that a culture succumbs by stages to the infections of self-destructive behavior."
—*Presidential candidate* JACK KEMP, *reiterating a favorite conservative theme (and now spicing it up by metaphorically linking it to the great boogeyman of modern diseases)*

Gay porn star Bob Shane, thirty-six, dies of AIDS at his home in New York City.

"I love gay people. I believe I was the founder of gay. I'm the one who started to be so bold, tellin' the world! You got to remember my dad put me out of the house because of that. . . . I was wearing makeup and eyelashes when no men were wearing that."
—LITTLE RICHARD, *attempting to appease critics after his previous remarks that homosexuals are sick child molesters*

July 7 Arizona gay activist Ed Buck begins a recall effort to have Arizona governor Evan Mecham—known for his fiercely antigay rhetoric, his advocacy of creationism, and his coziness with local John Birchers—ousted from office. Although Mecham publicly attacks the campaign as the work of the "homosexual lobby," it turns out, in fact, to have huge support among Arizona's voters, who are disgruntled by, among other things, his heavy-handed, dictatorial style, his complaints that the United States has become "too much" of a democracy, and growing evidence of financial mismanagement within his administration.

July 13 Presidential son Ron Reagan tells *People* magazine that while he has personally lost at least a dozen friends to AIDS, and while the federal government has been admittedly slow in its response to the epidemic, his father is probably not to blame. The President, he tells the magazine, is simply getting bad advice from "people who just think about image and votes."

Madonna performs a sold-out, $100-a-seat concert at Madison Square Garden to benefit AIDS research.

July 14 WILLIAMSON POOL CLOSED AFTER SWIM BY AIDS VICTIM
—*Front-page banner headline in the Williamson, West Virginia, Daily News, following the closure and cleaning of a local public swimming pool after city authorities learned that a man with AIDS had swum in it. City officials also ordered a complete scrubdown of the pool's diving board, lounge chairs, and locker room, and park managers dumped sixteen times the normal amount of chlorine into the water after refilling the pool.*

July 15 *The New York Times* lifts its long-standing ban on the word "gay" and advises its editorial staff that the word may now be used in the paper's pages, but only as an adjective, not as a noun.

July 24 A New York man, thirty-two-year-old Edward Becker, is arrested for "promoting prostitution" after he sends a letter to members of the Buffalo Bills football team offering them his sexual services in exchange for season tickets.

July 27 *Sports Illustrated* publishes a five-page obituary and tribute to Gay Games organizer and former Olympic decathlete Tom Waddell, who has recently died of AIDS at the age of forty-nine.

DR. TOM WADDELL

First gay man (along with lover Charles Deaton) to be featured in the "Couples" section of *People* magazine

Paratrooper in the U.S. Army

DR. TOM WADDELL (*cont.*)

U.S. Olympic team decathlete, 1968 Olympic Games in Mexico City

Gymnastics champion, Springfield College, Massachusetts

Specialist in infectious diseases

Personal physician to the brother of the King of Saudi Arabia

Founder of the Gay Games

July 28   Gay filmmaker Arthur Bressan, forty-four, dies of AIDS.

August 2   Sylvester Stallone's ex-wife, actress Brigitte Nielsen—already blasted in the tabloids for her alleged bedhopping and cheating on Stallone—publicly denies stories that she is also a lesbian and has been having an affair with her personal secretary, Kelly Sahnger. "There is not a scrap of truth that I am having an affair with my secretary," says Nielsen, who reportedly, by the way, paid for Sahnger's recent breast and nose job. "If I were a homosexual, these are not the times to hide it. I would say 'yes.' "

August 7   More than a hundred gay men and lesbians, in London for an international gay youth conference, stage a massive "kiss-in" at Piccadilly Circus to protest a twenty-year-old British law that forbids homosexuals from holding hands or making other displays of affection in public. Says one participant, "I cannot even begin to express my outrage at these antigay laws in a supposedly civilized country."

Addressing the National Association of Police Organizations, Ed Meese suggests that while training and education are of course needed to combat what he calls the "fear and misinformation" surrounding AIDS, officers should still wear rubber gloves when dealing with members of any high-risk groups.

The opening of a gay bar, Whispers, in a blue-collar neighborhood
of Saginaw, Michigan, provokes protest demonstrations and violence from the bar's new neighbors. Within days of opening, rocks
and concrete blocks are regularly heaved through the bar's windows, while vandals paint slogans of "FAGS GET OUT!" and
"CLOSE UP!" on the outside walls. Bomb and death threats become an everyday fact of life, and customers trying to enter the
bar are subjected to obscenities from picketers carrying signs,
"SAVE OUR CHILDREN!" and "LEAVE TOWN!" "We want
them faggots out of our neighborhood," one antigay protester tells
the local paper. As the weeks pass, the number of homophobic
incidents aimed at the bar continues to mount: customers' cars are
trashed, the front door is smashed in, there are rampant stories
(investigated by the police and found to be untrue) that a small boy
has been sexually molested in the parking lot. Although owner
Loretta Phelan eventually succeeds in getting a court injunction
against the demonstrators, she is finally forced to close the bar
because of the violence.

August 10   Gay sex symbol and cultural icon Casey Donovan dies
of AIDS in Florida. He was forty-three.

August 15   "You will stop making noise. I can't hear on the
phone and I'm talking to Berlin. Yes, yes, Herr Kruger—they
don't make whips the way they used to . . . You will shoot
your cum into the mouth of my dog . . . Achtung! Achtung!
. . . Joe, I'm scared. I'm really scared. What will they do if they
catch us? . . . First we stick this up your ass, way deep up inside, and then we turn the water on very gently at first so that
you feel the water flowing inside you, and you enjoy the feeling of
your shit flowing out of your ass . . . I'm sending for the troops.
Heil Hitler! . . . The truth is painful, but not as painful as the
whip . . ."
—*"Dialogue" highlights from the recently released gay porn film* Golden
Boys of the S.S., *starring Billy Bud, Dick Dicky, and Bill Bruse, and
directed by Karl Furer*

August 20 The New York *Daily News* reports that singer Olivia Newton-John has personally prohibited any involvement by her husband, Matt Lattanzi, in the perennially on-again, off-again film version of *The Front Runner*. "It's not good for his image," Newton-John tells the paper—leading some show business observers to wonder, *What* image?

The New York State Consumer Protection Board reveals that a significant number of the state's pharmacies are reaping exorbitant profits in the sale of AZT to people with AIDS, with stores quoting anywhere from $900 to over $3,000 for a one-month supply of the drug. The equivalent wholesale price for a one-month supply is $752.

August 21 The country's first drive-through condom store—Personal Products Inc.—opens in a former Fotomat in Hollywood, Florida. It goes out of business a month later.

September 1 "What disturbs me is how gay men all over this country can sit around with their friends dying, their lovers dying, their lives threatened, and not get off their asses and be activists again. Do they have a death wish? What's the matter with them?"

—VITO RUSSO

Calvin Klein advertises "Obsession For Men"—a line of men's toiletries featuring the famous Calvin Klein scent—with provocative ads (which some publications refuse to run) showing four statuesque nude men posed alluringly in the sunlight, and—just to make sure it doesn't look *too* faggy—two inconsequentially placed naked women.

September 15 *The Advocate* celebrates its twentieth anniversary.

"I risk being crushed by the millions of dollars the militant liberals and the homosexual lobby plan to spend against me. . . . If they

destroy me it will be a sad day for conservatives everywhere and most of all for America. In a day and age when militant gay leaders are feeding the nation a steady diet of their 'alternative life-styles' and they stand before the nightly news cameras demanding that the taxpayers pay for their AIDS treatments, I feel it is important for conservatives to stand up for traditional American values."
—*An increasingly desperate* EVAN MECHAM, *seeking to raise more than $1 million to fight the recall campaign against him. Says one Arizona woman, a longtime resident of Scottsdale, after reading the remarks, "It's sick. . . . If I had not found a recall petition and signed one a long time ago, I sure would have gone out and done so today."*

September 17 Barely a week after publicly suggesting that AIDS might indeed be God's punishment of homosexuals—and almost a year after proclaiming that "those who behave in a homosexual fashion . . . shall not enter the kingdom of God"—Pope John Paul II arrives for a visit in San Francisco, where he is greeted by more than three thousand angry demonstrators waving signs that read "POPE GO HOME!" "CURB YOUR DOGMA!" and "I'VE GOT A RING THE POPE CAN KISS!" Says Leonard Matlovich, addressing the largely gay crowd, "It's a pretty sad state of affairs when Ronald Reagan has a better record on AIDS than the Pope has." The Pope later pays a visit to the city's Mission Dolores, where he addresses a gathering of sixty-two people with AIDS. "God loves you all, without distinction, without limit," he tells them. "He loves those of you who are sick, those who are suffering from AIDS and AIDS-Related Complex."

"If he's so damn sure of God's love for people with AIDS," says one unconvinced observer, "why doesn't he sell a couple of his rings and give the money to AIDS research?"

September 18 "We're not squeamish people; we face death every day. But I would rather have an enraged gunman shoot me down than die from AIDS."
—*New York City policeman* PHIL CARUSO

Singer Dionne Warwick. AIDS struck down several of her closest friends.

Maurice and *Fatal Attraction* open on the same day in New York City. Three months later, *The Advocate* reports that while *Maurice* is playing nationwide in fifteen theaters and has grossed $966,000, *Fatal Attraction* is playing in fourteen hundred theaters and has grossed just over $114 million.

September 21 Singer Dionne Warwick is honored by the Department of Health and Human Services for her "exceptional service" in the fight against AIDS, including her donation to AIDS research of more than $1 million from the royalties of her recent hit single "That's What Friends Are For," recorded with Elton John, Gladys Knight, and Stevie Wonder.

October 1 *Playgirl*'s editor-in-chief, Nancie Martin, once again refutes the "myth" that most of the magazine's readers are gay (she puts the figure at about 10 percent) and furthermore claims that the magazine's models "are mostly straight." "But I don't have any figures on that," she adds, "because it's not something you ask. I *do* know that most of the guys we photograph have girlfriends."

Televangelist Pat Robertson announces his candidacy for the 1988 Republican presidential nomination. He later berates the national media for continually referring to him as a "televangelist," saying it's "religious bigotry" and prejudicial to his campaign. "I'm a *businessman*," he testily explains to Dan Rather during an interview on CBS. "I'm a *religious broadcaster*," he tells Tom Brokaw during an interview on NBC. Amazingly, the networks concede the point and begin referring to him as "Christian leader Pat Robertson" or "businessman Pat Robertson."

"Just because it suits Mr. Robertson's present purposes to reinvent his past," notes *The New York Times*, "is no reason for others to practice what he preaches."

Meanwhile, one disgusted voter tells the *Times*, "He says he's running for the family. Does that mean everybody else is running *against* the family? I can't believe he can smile when he says that."

October 7 A federal report commissioned by the Justice Department concludes that "homosexuals are probably the most frequent victims" of bias crimes and hate-related violence in the United States.

October 10 Two thousand gay and lesbian couples exchange vows in a mass wedding held on the steps of the Internal Revenue Service building in Washington, D.C. The mass ceremony is part of a week of gay-related activities and political demonstrations slated for the nation's capital.

October 11 An estimated five hundred thousand lesbians and gay men march on Washington, D.C., in the largest gay rights demonstration ever held. "This is indeed our day," says participant Harvey Fierstein. "We have marched out of the closets." Notes another demonstrator, lesbian activist Nicole Ramirez-Murray, "This is the biggest damn family reunion I've ever been to!" Marching with the demonstrators are several prominent national figures, including Jesse Jackson, Whoopi Goldberg, and Eleanor Smeal. "We are together today to say we insist on legal protection under the law for every American," proclaims Jackson, in a formal address to the protesters. "For workers' rights, for civil rights, for women's rights, for the rights of religious freedom, for the rights of individual privacy, for the rights of sexual preference. We come together for rights for all of the American people."

In a speech criticizing the current administration's response to the AIDS epidemic, Whoopi Goldberg refers to Ronald Reagan as "the fucking President."

The NAMES Project AIDS Memorial Quilt is displayed for the first time, in front of the U.S. Capitol in Washington, D.C. It is the size of two football fields. Within a few years, it will be several times that size.

VOICES FROM THE QUILT

"To 12 Men I Expected to Grow Old With. Nine Who Have Passed On And Three Who Will Join Them Soon."

"I miss you, Roger. Love, Cindy."

"Jac Wall is great in bed. Jac Wall is intelligent. I love Jac Wall. Jac Wall turns me on. I miss Jac Wall."

"The Memory of Each of You Lives in Our Hearts. With Love, From the Nurses Who Served You."

VOICES FROM THE QUILT

"Next Year in Jerusalem"

"The Best Daddy in the World Died of AIDS on March 2, 1987. I Love You Forever Daddy."

"I have decorated this banner to honor my brother. Our parents did not want his name used publicly. The omission of his represents the fear of oppression that AIDS victims and their families feel."

"My Big Brother
He was a grown man when I was born. He made time for me allways. He bought me every warm winter coat I can remember. He taugt me the value of light opra and other music. He allways made a little girl feel real special."

October 13 More than six hundred demonstrators are arrested at the U.S. Supreme Court during a mass protest of Court decisions consistently upholding the constitutionality of state sodomy laws. As police don conspicuous yellow rubber gloves to drag the protesters to waiting police vans, the crowd begins chanting, "Your gloves don't match your shoes!"

October 16 ABC News anchorman Peter Jennings picks gay activist and AIDS Quilt organizer Cleve Jones as his "Person of the Week."

October 19 Morton Downey, Jr.—a former lounge singer turned political television commentator—debuts his gladiator-arena style of TV talk show on superstation WWOR in Secaucus, New Jersey. With his mob-like, equally conservative audience to cheer him on each night, he quickly establishes himself as one of the nation's most prominent and bellicose opponents to gay rights. "The anus," he is fond of telling his audience, to enthusiastic cheers, "is an exit, not an entrance." He also coins a catchy new term, "Pablum pukers," to describe liberals, intellectuals, and anyone else who disagrees with him.

October 22   A New York City prison inmate with AIDS is forced to sue the Department of Corrections for the right to take AZT while incarcerated.

October 29   The Soviet Union claims that, to date, it has had only 165 cases of AIDS—and all but 23 of those in resident foreigners.

November 13   *The Wall Street Journal* runs a front-page article detailing the ongoing national epidemic of fear and prejudice in response to the AIDS crisis. Among the more grisly episodes cited: a Texas man who shot his nephew to death in the belief that the boy had AIDS; a man with AIDS who was regularly pelted by his neighbors with rocks (his nose was eventually broken by three men who attacked him one night); a public housing official in Rochester, New York, who tried to have a woman evicted from her apartment after she let a friend with AIDS stay there; a Dallas post office that ordered certain mail carriers to be disinfected every day after they delivered mail to a local AIDS hospice.

November 14   Aerosmith's "Dude (Looks Like a Lady)" begins a ten-week run in the nation's Top 40. There are reports the band angrily rejected lead singer Steve Tyler's suggestion that they all dress in drag for the song's video.

November 15   Randy Shilts's *And the Band Played On*—a 600-page chronicle of the AIDS epidemic, spanning eleven years from 1976 to 1987—debuts at No. 12 on *The New York Times* best-seller list. "Its importance cannot be overstated," says *Publishers Weekly*.

November 21   Having raided and cleared out a popular gay Levi/
leather bar, the Detour, the night before, the Los Angeles police
department now focuses its resources—including ten police cars,
one fire truck, and assorted other city and county vehicles—to raid
and close down another gay bar, the One Way, ostensibly on
charges that it is violating the city's fire ordinance. Says one outraged L.A. city councilman, "On Saturday night, while the police
were sitting outside the One Way bar, how many other crimes were
being committed around the city? How many people died? How
many homes were burglarized?"

November 30   Author James Baldwin, sixty-three, dies in
France.

December 1   "Sometimes I'm really sorry that I had a part in it,
that I was there. . . . I was helping to make it seem fun."
—BETTE MIDLER, *feeling guilty about AIDS and her days singing at the
Continental Baths in the early 1970s, as quoted in* Vanity Fair

December 10   A Washington, D.C., gay bar, Remington's, garners international attention after it announces a Raisa Gorbachev
look-alike contest in honor of the Soviet First Lady's visit to Washington as part of the third U.S.-Soviet superpower summit. "I'm
not even sure all of them know this is a gay bar and the people
entering the contest will be drag queens," says the bar's manager.
Later, asked what he thinks of transvestites imitating the Soviet
First Lady, a Soviet spokesman replies, "Well, it's a matter of
personal taste, really."

December 17   Marguerite Yourcenar dies at the age of eighty-
four.

———————

Morton Downey, Jr., is arraigned on charges of assault after allegedly slugging a gay guest during the taping of a recent episode of
his talk show.

December 18 Bert Parks, recently dropped as master of ceremonies of the Miss America Pageant, hosts the U.S. Man of the
Year Pageant in Atlantic City. Says Parks matter-of-factly, of the
differences between the two pageants' contestants, "The bathing
suits will be a little different."

December 31 The Department of Defense reveals that in the
last year it purchased thirteen million condoms for U.S. soldiers.

1988

January 5 Raleigh, North Carolina—Jesse Helms's hometown—passes a gay rights ordinance.

February 1 The U.S. Justice Department reveals that it currently employs ninety-three "obscenity specialists."

February 5 The Arizona House of Representatives votes to impeach Governor Evan Mecham, who has become an increasing embarrassment to the state. Mecham, true to form to the bitter end, vows to tear his political enemies "to bits."

February 8 Presidential candidate Pat Robertson—who has recently reasserted in a newspaper interview that AIDS is spread by casual contact, in fact by just breathing the same air as a person with AIDS—finishes second in the Iowa Republican caucuses, behind Robert Dole but ahead of George Bush. His unexpectedly strong showing horrifies party regulars, not to mention gay people and civil libertarians across the country.

"I don't think homosexuality is normal behavior and I oppose the codification of gay rights. But I wouldn't harass them and I wish they could know that. Actually, I wish the whole issue could be toned down. I wish it could go away, but, of course, I know it can't."
—*Presidential candidate* GEORGE BUSH *on gay rights, 1980*

"I believe all Americans have fundamental rights guaranteed in our Constitution—rights such as freedom of religion, freedom of speech, and the right to a trial by jury. No one group should have special privileges granted by government."
—*Candidate* BUSH *on gay rights, 1988*

In its own bid to cash in on the seemingly never-ending national fascination with "beefcake," the normally conservative *Forbes* magazine features a cover photo of a handsome young accountant lounging naked at his desk with his feet up on his computer terminal. The photo is for a cover story on selling stocks short. Quips one observer, "Imagine what it would have looked like for an article on 'long shot' investments."

February 14   Three lesbian guests on *The Oprah Winfrey Show* are introduced as "women who hate men."

February 21   "I was taught to be like everybody else, raised to be normal. I'm still nervous around shopping malls. They're filled with people who think they're normal."
—*Film director* JOHN WATERS

Televangelist Jimmy Swaggart—who for years has ranted against homosexuality, masturbation, Jews, condoms, psychiatry, rock

The aptly named Divine in his last role, in John Waters's breakthrough hit Hairspray. *One critic called it "irresistible," another "gleeful . . . wonderfully tacky."* © 1988 NEW LINE CINEMA CORP. ALL RIGHTS RESERVED.

music, and pornography—steps down as head of his lucrative TV ministry after it is publicly revealed he has been regularly visiting a Louisiana prostitute, who would strip and then assume various lewd poses while the Reverend Swaggart watched and masturbated.

February 29 "Why waste his talents on the presidency? Let's make him a weather satellite."
—*Comedian* WILL DURST, *on Pat Robertson's campaign claims that once, through a personal appeal to God, he diverted a hurricane from the coast of Virginia, where his corporate headquarters are located*

March 7 The incomparable Divine—reaping the career rewards of his first solid mainstream success in the just-released hit *Hairspray* —dies of heart disease in Los Angeles at the age of forty-two.

March 10 *OUT/LOOK*—a new national lesbian and gay quarterly of opinion, politics, and culture—debuts on the nation's magazine racks.

March 13 Porn star John Holmes—who liked to boast of having had more than fourteen thousand sex partners—dies of AIDS at the age of forty-three.

March 20 "I've lost over twenty friends [to AIDS]. I've seen a world vanish—a culture that has been oppressed in one generation, liberated in the next, and wiped out in the next."

—EDMUND WHITE

March 23 Israel legalizes homosexual acts between consenting adults.

March 25 Robert Joffrey, founder and artistic director of the Joffrey Ballet, dies in New York City at the age of fifty-seven, of what is reported to have been "liver, renal, and respiratory failure"—although it is widely assumed he had AIDS. There are stories that the real cause of his death is being obscured out of fear it might somehow tarnish the ballet company's image.

March 29 Georgetown University, the nation's oldest Roman Catholic university, loses an eight-year legal battle to keep from having to provide facilities and financial support to the campus's gay student groups.

March 31 In the course of a *Nightline* discussion on "mercy killing" and voluntary euthanasia for terminally ill people, thirty-four-year-old Marty James of Los Angeles acknowledges having assisted in the suicide of at least one friend with an AIDS-related illness.

April 11 *Newsweek* reports on the growing popularity of a new dance craze, "Da Butt," in which partners rub and bump rear ends or bend over and stick their asses in each other's faces. The "craze" disappears before most people know it was even here.

May 11 His campaign momentum having evaporated almost immediately after Iowa, Pat Robertson—with only forty-five delegates toward the Republican presidential nomination—abruptly announces he will withdraw from the race.

May 12   A study by the New York State Department of Corrections finds that the mean survival time for prison inmates with AIDS is only 128 days, compared with 8 months longer for PWA's on the outside. The department attributes the lower survival period to inadequate (or, more often, completely inept and hostile) medical care for people with AIDS within the prison system.

May 15   Having tied up, tortured, and robbed one gay man the night before, two Hartford, Connecticut, teenagers from a local conservative Catholic high school go out drinking and looking for someone else gay "to beat up." They find their victim when they meet thirty-three-year-old systems analyst Richard Reihl at a downtown gay bar. After talking with Reihl for a few minutes, they all agree to go back to his apartment—where, having accepted a couple of soft drinks from him, the two teenagers knock Reihl in the head with a fireplace log, bind him up with duct tape, and then, despite his begging and pleading, bludgeon him to death with one vicious blow after another to the head and chest.

   Despite attempts by the defense to portray the two teenaged assailants as star athletes and "all-American boys" who deserve leniency and compassion, a judge sentences them to thirty-five and forty years in prison, respectively, for the killing.

May 20   The first-ever Conference on Homophobia Education convenes in Washington, D.C. Sponsored by the Campaign to End Homophobia and cosponsored by a number of church groups and national gay rights organizations, the symposium is held to work out strategies for reducing the widening national epidemic of homophobia and gay-bashing.

May 23   Four lesbians try to take over a broadcast of the BBC's evening news to protest the impending implementation of Britain's notorious Clause 28, which prohibits local governments and public schools from in any way "promoting" homosexuality, or from treating homosexuality as an acceptable alternative lifestyle. "We have rather been invaded by some people who we hope to be removed very shortly," says anchorwoman Sue Lawley, who then goes on to read the news while the studio's staff tries to get the situation under control. One lesbian has handcuffed herself to a camera, causing the television picture to shift and vibrate. Another has handcuffed herself to the news desk. Meanwhile, Lawley's co-anchor, Nicholas Witchell, has managed to wrestle one of the lesbians to the ground and is trying to sit on top of her. "She won't fucking sit still," he complains on the air. The entire episode lasts barely four minutes, and Clause 28—which threatens funding for dozens of the nation's gay rights groups, help hotlines, and community centers—takes effect, as anticipated, the next day.

May 30 "I've learned that God doesn't punish people. I've learned that God doesn't dislike homosexuals, like a lot of Christians think. AIDS isn't their fault, just like it isn't my fault. God loves homosexuals as much as He loves everybody else."
—*Sixteen-year-old PWA* RYAN WHITE, *asked at a public forum, "How does your Christian faith help you with your disease?"*

June 5 *M. Butterfly*—a hit Broadway show starring John Lithgow as a French diplomat who falls in love with a Chinese opera diva, only to learn that "she" is actually a man, and a spy—wins the Tony Award for Best Play.

"If a woman-in-a-man's-body goes after a man, is she attracted to the same or the opposite sex? If a man-in-a-woman's-body wants a woman, is he a lesbian or straight? Prejudice is only cowardice in the face of complexity."
—*U.S. anthropologist* JAY LEMKE, *on transsexuals, 1988*

June 13   One gay man is stabbed and another beaten by a roaming group of teenagers shouting antigay slogans in Central Park.

June 16   Delegates to the Southern Baptist Convention in San Antonio overwhelmingly vote to pass a resolution blaming homosexuals for the AIDS epidemic and condemning homosexuality as "an abomination," "a perversion," and the "manifestation of a depraved nature." However, the resolution notes, God "loves the homosexual."

The Chicago Bomb and Arson Squad is summoned to O'Hare International Airport after luggage handlers anxiously report hearing unusual ticking sounds from a suitcase they were about to load on an aircraft. Upon examination, the suitcase is discovered to be harboring a battery-operated vibrator stuck in the "On" position.

> "Every man should own at least one dress—and so should lesbians."
>
> —Lesbian activist JANE ADAMS SPAHR, 1988

June 20   Gay-bashing talk-show host Morton Downey, Jr., stuns his normally conservative studio audience by introducing a surprise guest: his homosexual brother, Tony, who has AIDS. During the show, Tony claims he was "taught" to be homosexual by an older male relative who allegedly raped him several times when he was a boy. Mort, apparently more interested in how his brother contracted AIDS, demands to know whether Tony has ever had anal sex.

"If my show is canceled three days after Tony's segment airs," Mort tells one national magazine defensively, "they can all go fuck themselves." Downey's now widely syndicated show, however, is in no immediate danger of cancellation: it continues for more than a year before viewers finally tire of his shout-and-shock style of television journalism.

June 22   Leonard Matlovich dies from AIDS at the age of forty-four.

June 26   Art Agnos becomes the first San Francisco mayor ever to ride in one of the city's Gay Pride parades.

July 3   A group of recent studies confirms that hate crimes against gay men and lesbians are increasing across the country, with growing resentment and anxiety over AIDS a major factor in many reported incidents.

July 18   After testifying as character witnesses for another woman being court-martialed for lesbianism, two female Marines are relieved of their duties and harassed by their superiors, for what the military calls an unacceptably "lenient attitude" toward homosexuality. "The word is out," says a lawyer in the case. "You don't testify for women accused of being a homosexual." A spokesman for the Marines acknowledges that the two women were disciplined as a direct result of their testimony.

July 21   Massachusetts governor Michael Dukakis—a "card-carrying member of the ACLU," though he has previously demonstrated some reservations about gay rights—officially becomes the Democratic candidate for president, at the party's convention in San Francisco. In his acceptance speech, he calls AIDS "the greatest public health emergency of our lifetime, and a disease that must be conquered."

July 28   A major, 175-picture retrospective of Robert Mapplethorpe's photographs—"Robert Mapplethorpe: The Perfect Moment"—opens at the Whitney Museum of American Art in New York City.

August 1   In a feature interview in *Playboy*, playwright Harvey Fierstein:

■ reveals that his mother gave him a subscription to *Playboy* when he was growing up, but that the only features he liked were the "Sex in Cinema" articles, because those were the only ones with pictures of naked men.

■ contends that what threatens so many heterosexual men about homosexuality is the fear "that they might enjoy it."

■ rejects the idea that the sexual revolution is over: "*This* is the sexual revolution. What we did in the late Sixties and early Seventies was a bunch of bullshit—child's play, kids let loose in a toy store. . . . The real discovery is that you have to take responsibility for your actions, responsibility both for yourself and for your partner."

■ ardently supports the adoption of children by gay people: "Give us the retarded children, just the retarded kids. *We'll* take care of them. . . . If straight people weren't so fucking uptight, convinced that those children would be sexually abused—*for which there's no proof whatever*—we could close every orphanage in the world. . . . When the fuck did heterosexuals get the patent on home and love and hearth and family?"

August 5   Hollywood screenwriter Colin Higgins—who wrote the original screenplay for *Harold and Maude* and later wrote and directed the films *Foul Play* and *Nine to Five*—dies of AIDS at the age of forty-seven.

August 15   The National Center for Health Statistics reports that AIDS was the fifteenth leading cause of death among Americans in 1987.

"Slogans that teach young people to 'Say No' to drugs or sex have a nice ring to them. But . . . they are as effective in prevention of adolescent pregnancy and drug abuse as saying 'Have a nice day' is in preventing clinical depression."
—DR. MICHAEL CARRERA, *on the issue of sex education and AIDS, 1988*

Despite candidate George Bush's publicly expressed support for legislation barring discrimination against people with AIDS, the Republican Party convention opens in New Orleans with a party platform that gives scant attention to the epidemic. Instead, the platform notes only:

- "Abstinence from drug use and sexual activity outside of marriage is the safest way to avoid infection with the AIDS virus."
- "It is extremely important that testing . . . be carried out."
- "Those who suffer from AIDS . . . deserve our compassion."
- "The Reagan/Bush administration launched the nation's fight against AIDS . . ."—as if that were more an achievement than an unfortunate coincidence of history.

"I'm not happy," says Connecticut senator Lowell Weicker, who has fought unsuccessfully for more liberal party planks not only on the issue of AIDS but on abortion and gay rights as well. He tells *The Advocate*, "I think you've got a bunch of people out here who are intent on preaching to everybody rather than helping and curing everybody."

Three days later, accepting his party's nomination, Bush never once mentions the subject of AIDS in his acceptance speech.

August 16   George Bush announces his choice for a running mate: Indiana senator Dan Quayle, a forty-one-year-old far-right conservative who has most frequently distinguished himself on the Senate floor as a reliable (if somewhat inarticulate) political ally of Jesse Helms and other conservative demagogues, having recently voted, among other things, to allow insurance companies in the District of Columbia to discriminate against people who are HIV-positive, to withhold federal funds for AZT for indigent people with AIDS, to withhold federal funds for AIDS prevention materials that in any way "promote or encourage . . . homosexual activity."

August 18   The Centers for Disease Control announces that while the rate of syphilis and hepatitis B among gay men has dropped

Iconoclastic author Pat Califia: "It's a much more honorable act to rim a total stranger than it is to deny a poor woman an abortion, and it's more righteous to help an underage lesbian sneak into the bar than it is to force her to pray in school." JOHN KENNY

dramatically in the past six years, the incidence of both diseases has been steadily increasing among heterosexuals.

August 22 Two gay men are beaten with baseball bats and then brutally stabbed by a gang of teenagers on Manhattan's Upper West Side.

August 24 Actor Leonard Frey—perhaps best known for his role as Harold in the stage and screen versions of *The Boys in the Band* —dies of AIDS at the age of forty-nine.

August 28 French philosopher Guy Hocquenghem, forty-two, dies of AIDS in Paris.

August 31 Speaking at a Republican fund-raiser, U.S. senator Orrin Hatch (R-Utah) blasts the Democrats as "the party of homosexuals." He later tries to publicly deny having said any such thing—until confronted with an audiotape of the remark.

September 1   In the nation's bookstores this month: *Macho Sluts*, a collection of lesbian erotic fiction by *Advocate* advice columnist Pat Califia. The book—a trailblazing and unabashed exploration of lesbian S&M and raunchy female-to-female sexuality—becomes an instant lesbian bestseller. One appreciative critic dubs it "a bad girl's wet dream."

> "Lesbians own sex toys, have young lovers, do threesomes with their friends, visit the baths, explore bondage, dress up in frilly fetish underwear and spike heels, buy sexually explicit material, go to movies that have lesbian sex in them, shave each other, use poppers, go to the bar for the specific purpose of getting laid, and buy more Crisco than they need for frying chicken. . . . It is right and good for women to reclaim their bodies, dust off their libidos, and follow their clits into some sexual recreation."
>
> —PAT CALIFIA

A recent survey at a major university shows that only 13 percent of the male students routinely use condoms, while 66 percent have never used them at all.

September 6   Pop star Elton John holds a four-day auction (described by one observer as a "high-class garage sale") of memorabilia, collectibles, and unwanted hand-me-downs at Sotheby's in London. During the course of the bidding, one pair of the singer's sunglasses sells for $16,830, while a pair of old license plates from one of his cars fetches $4,481. By the end of the sale, the star has grossed more than $8 million from his discarded belongings.

September 18   "Shut up, fag!"
—SALLIE DORNAN, *wife of conservative, homophobic lawmaker Robert Dornan, responding to a heckler at one of her husband's speeches*

September 27 With public interest in this year's summer Olympics notably more subdued than it was in 1984 (what with the Americans actually having to compete this time against the Russians and all), attention focuses on the one truly bright star on the U.S. team, diver Greg Louganis, who not only refuses to withdraw after injuring his skull in a diving accident, but goes on to win two gold medals. Louganis—widely regarded as the best diver in the history of the sport—is also named the recipient of the U.S. Olympic Committee's "Olympic Spirit Award."

Says the diver, flashing his medals to an appreciative audience back in Los Angeles, "I picked up some *fabulous* jewelry over there."

October 1 Morton Downey, Jr., acknowledges in an interview that he participated in circle jerks with other teenage boys in military school, and that he has sometimes tried, unsuccessfully, to imagine whether there's any man he'd like to kiss or have sex with. When asked by the magazine, however, if he's ever actually touched another guy's penis, Downey testily insists, "No, never. Not even interested. Never touched a dick."

October 11 Born-again Christian evangelist Mario Ivan Levya pleads guilty to charges of having sexually molested several young boys, one of them only eight years old.

———————

Gay entertainer Wayland Flowers—who adamantly refused to publicly acknowledge his homosexuality ("If I can do a good thing for everybody, make everybody laugh and be happy, why fucking kill it?")—dies of cancer at the age of forty-two on National Coming Out Day.

———————

More than 150 demonstrators are arrested at the Food and Drug Administration in Washington, D.C., when they and hundreds of others stage a sometimes violent demonstration against the Reagan administration's policies toward AIDS and the bureaucratic slowness of the FDA's drug approval policy.

October 15   Alexandria, Virginia, passes a gay rights ordinance.

"Dan Quayle was asked the other day if he supports sending military aid to the Straits of Hormuz. 'Well, it's all right to send it to the straights,' Quayle replied, 'but the gays are on their own.' "
—JOHNNY CARSON, *mining the seemingly inexhaustible doltishness of the Republican's vice-presidential candidate*

October 24   *The Advocate* reports that playwright Terrence McNally has completed the first draft of a musical version of *Kiss of the Spider Woman*.

November 1   A University of Minnesota study reveals that there's a one-in-three chance that a homosexual teenage boy living in the United States will attempt suicide. Officials at the Department of Health and Human Services estimate that gay young people may account for as much as 40 percent of all teen suicides in the U.S.

"All we had to do was say 'We love you, Bobby, and we accept you,' and I know Bobby would be here today. Part of me wanted to reach out to Bobby and tell him, 'I love you, you're fine just the way you are.' To me, that was my mother love, that was my conscience. But I couldn't ignore what the Bible was saying. You know, when you don't have the freedom to listen to your own conscience, as I look back on it now, that's wrong . . . terribly, terribly wrong."

—*California mother whose gay son committed suicide after her fundamentalist church unsuccessfully tried to "cure" him*

November 8   Composer Warren Casey—who cowrote the hit musical *Grease*—dies of AIDS at the age of fifty-three.

George Bush is elected President of the United States by a margin of 54 percent to 46 percent over his Democratic challenger, Michael Dukakis.

Harvey Fierstein as Arnold Beckoff in the 1988 film version of Torch Song Trilogy. *"Sex isn't the enemy," he said, defending some of the film's scenes. "That's what I wish people would understand. The disease is the enemy."* © 1988 NEW LINE CINEMA CORP. ALL RIGHTS RESERVED.

In Oregon, voters repeal a year-old executive order by Governor Neil Goldschmidt that prohibited employment discrimination against gay men and lesbians in state government.

November 30 Umpire Dave Pallone is thrown out of the National League by league president Bart Giamatti because of his homosexuality.

December 1 The first World AIDS Day—organized by the World Health Organization—is held.

December 2 The national gay hardcover best-sellers this month, according to the *Lambda Book Report*:

1. *And the Band Played On* by Randy Shilts
2. *Gay Spirit* by Mark Thompson
3. *Early Graves* by Joseph Hansen

4. *Nantucket Diaries* by Ned Rorem
5. *Western Lands* by William S. Burroughs

The national lesbian hardcover best-sellers:

1. *All Good Women* by Valerie Miner
2. *Queen of Swords* by Judy Grahn
3. *Detour: A Hollywood Story* by Cheryl Crane
4. *Unusual Company* by Margaret Erhart
5. *Manwoman's Underclothes* by Germaine Greer

Some gay bookstores report that, even a year after its release, *And the Band Played On* is outselling any other book by almost 3 to 1.

December 9 The Robert Mapplethorpe exhibit opens at the Institute of Contemporary Art in Philadelphia, where it comes and goes without controversy or protest. "It couldn't have been more sedate if it had been an exhibit of Sir Joshua Reynolds," says one patron.

The exhibit is scheduled to go on to Chicago, Washington, D.C., Hartford, Berkeley, and Cincinnati.

December 14 *Torch Song Trilogy*, the film, opens in New York City. Heavily trimmed from the original play (which ran almost four hours, compared to slightly less than two for the movie), it draws mixed reviews from critics, many of whom accuse it of social irresponsibility for its brief but noncensorious scenes of a period in gay life when backroom bars and anonymous sex were the norm for many gay men. Dismissing suggestions that the AIDS epidemic has rendered his comedy-drama anachronistic—or even worse, dangerous—Harvey Fierstein tells *Newsweek*, "Sex isn't the enemy. That's what I wish people would understand. The disease is the enemy. . . . When people say now is not the right time for *Torch Song*, I say now is exactly the right time. Now is exactly when we need to see ourselves as loving human beings, as people in search of ourselves, as people in relationships."

"Homosexuality is God's way of insuring that the truly gifted aren't burdened with children."

—Composer and lyricist SAM AUSTIN, 1988

December 16 Gay recording star Sylvester, forty-two, dies of AIDS.

December 20 Newsman Max Robinson, the first black network news anchorman, dies of AIDS. He was forty-nine.

December 28 A district court judge orders that quadriplegic Sharon Kowalski be moved from the nursing home where her father has placed her (and where she is, according to evaluations, not receiving the rehabilitative therapy she needs) and that she be allowed to receive visits from her lover, Karen Thompson (who has not seen her in more than three years), as well as other lesbian friends. The ruling does not, however, countermand her father's guardianship.

December 31 Performing at a New Year's Eve concert at the Long Beach Arena in California, guitarist Zakk Wylde, of the Ozzy Osbourne band, urges audience members to go out and beat up some "faggots" and "queers." "If you see them," says Wylde, to cheers from the audience, "bash their fucking heads in the ground."

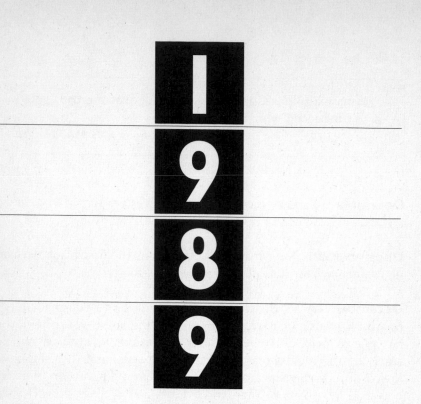

1989

January 23 On the eve of his execution for murder, promising law student turned serial killer Ted Bundy grants an exclusive interview to religious broadcaster James Dobson, and blames pornography for having caused him to strangle and mutilate more than thirty young women during a killing spree that eventually spanned the country. "As good a Christian home as we had," says Bundy, "and we had a wonderful Christian home—there is no protection against the kind of influences that are loose in society. . . . Pornography can reach out and snatch a kid out of any house today." The public, eager for any explanation as to how a handsome, articulate, urbane young man could become one of the most savage and unpredictable killers in U.S. history, eagerly embraces the explanation—which seems peculiar, considering no one has previously believed anything else Bundy said.

January 30 In the nation's bookstores this month: Susan Sontag's *AIDS and Its Metaphors*, a ninety-five-page essay that sets out to shatter all the moral and metaphysical implications ("It's a disease that comes from not loving yourself enough," "It's all mind over matter," "It's God's punishment of promiscuity," et al.) that people—straight *and* gay—have been trying to heap on the illness.

January 31 "Who are you going to imitate today—Molly Ringwald?"
—CHARLES PIERCE, *on the dearth of snappy role models for female impersonators these days*

Twenty-nine AIDS activists are arrested when, during an early-morning protest demonstration, they bring rush-hour traffic on San Francisco's Golden Gate Bridge to a halt.

February 2 Sharon Kowalski and Karen Thompson are reunited for a visit, for the first time in almost four years. According to Thompson, Kowalski "got tears in her eyes. . . . She spelled right out on her alphabet board, 'I love you.' "

February 6 Having debated and rejected similar resolutions for more than a decade, the American Bar Association's House of Delegates finally votes, 251 to 121, in favor of supporting federal legislation to prohibit discrimination against gay men and lesbians.

February 13 "Our security people are concerned about this. These things can be turned into slingshots. They can be filled up with a variety of items and turned into bombs."
—*Texas Department of Corrections official* JAMES RILEY, *on why he opposes the distribution of condoms in state prisons*

February 15 A Los Angeles jury awards Rock Hudson's ex-lover Marc Christian $21.75 million in damages for the emotional distress he claims to have suffered upon learning that Hudson had AIDS. In his suit, Christian (who has consistently tested negative for exposure to the disease) contended that several of the actor's associates purposely kept him in the dark about Hudson's illness and therefore knowingly exposed him to danger. "I learned about his condition on the six o'clock news like everyone else," Christian told the court.

Christian's attorney, Marvin Mitchelson—who stands to receive a good chunk of the jury award—mournfully tells the press that this "is the most unpleasant lawsuit I've ever been involved with."

Says *Chicago Tribune* columnist Stephen Chapman: "Say a car zips by at 100 miles per hour, missing me by inches. Under normal conditions, I'd be frightened and angry, but only for a few minutes. Suppose, though, you inform me I could get $14.5 million if I were to suffer permanent emotional trauma from the event. I might suddenly feel traumatized. Very traumatized. Permanently, severely traumatized."

A judge later reduces the award to $5.5 million.

February 17   Chicago's new gay rights ordinance—which mandates fines up to $500 for discrimination on the basis of sexual orientation—takes effect.

February 27   The Soviet Union reports the case of twenty-nine infants and six mothers, all of whom contracted AIDS in the same hospital through a single unsterile syringe that was used over and over again.

March 1   *Consumer Reports* rates condoms for their reliability. Least likely to fail during intercourse: Gold Circle Coin. Most likely to fail: Lifestyles Nuda Plus.

March 9   Robert Mapplethorpe dies of AIDS at the age of forty-two in a hospital in Boston.

March 13   Greg Louganis fires his longtime manager, R. James Babbitt. Two weeks later, Louganis files for a restraining order to have Babbitt evicted from the Malibu house the two men have shared for the last four years, claiming that Babbitt had threatened, among other things, to expose certain delicate details of their lives together.

March 15 On the eve of his reelection campaign, New York mayor Koch once again reaffirms to the press that, yes, he is a heterosexual. "To me what's amazing," says Koch, "is that this should be the object of discussion."

March 17 Actor Merritt Butrick, best known for his portrayal of Captain Kirk's son in the films *Star Trek II: The Wrath of Khan* and *Star Trek III: The Search for Spock*, dies of AIDS in Los Angeles at the age of twenty-nine.

March 23 A twenty-year-old New Orleans man is found guilty of first-degree murder in the 1987 killing of a Roman Catholic priest. According to testimony, Bernard Joseph and his half-brother, Marcus, tortured, stabbed, and choked the priest for more than an hour in December 1987. During the trial, the defendants claimed they had only been trying to rebuke the priest's homosexual advances.

March 26 "It really was my childhood dream to produce the Oscars. I'm a child of the movies."
—ALLAN *"Can't Stop the Music"* CARR, *chosen to produce the Academy Awards ceremony on March 29. The show—an unqualified critical disaster that begins with Rob Lowe and a squeaky-voiced Snow White warbling a duet against a background of Carmen Miranda impersonators—prompts* New York Times *critic Janet Maslin to write, "This was the first year that the Oscar show was broadcast in the Soviet Union, but it was best not to think about that."*

March 28 Malibu Sales of California markets a supposedly life-size latex dildo cast from the penis of gay porn star Jeff Stryker. Price: $49.95. Stryker later complains, "They added an inch in length. It insults me that they did that."

March 30 The FBI reveals that thirty-three pages of its seventy-one-page file on Andy Warhol cannot be released to the public for "security reasons."

April 1   Lance Loud, now in his mid-thirties, becomes an occasional contributor to *American Film* magazine and is reportedly working as an extra on the movie *Scenes from the Class Struggle in Beverly Hills*.

April 19   In one of the Navy's worst peacetime tragedies, a gunturret explosion aboard the U.S. battleship *Iowa* kills forty-seven sailors while the ship is on training maneuvers in the Caribbean. Ignoring more obvious (and, potentially, more embarrassing) factors—such as a history of safety-related problems aboard the ship and the use of undertrained personnel in conducting maneuvers that day—the Navy quickly moves to blame the tragedy on a lone sailor, Gunner's Mate Clayton Hartwig, who, it is suggested, was despondent and suicidal over the end of a homosexual affair with another *Iowa* sailor.

April 30   Nearly thirty thousand Texans march in Austin demanding an end to the state's sodomy laws, as well as increased funding for the state's AIDS programs. The next day, members of ACT UP wrap the state capitol in red tape to symbolize their frustration with the state's bureaucratic machinery, which, according to one activist, "is often harder on people with AIDS than the disease itself."

May 1   On the video shelf: *Skin Torpedoes*, starring Matt Powers, Lou Kruze, and Jimmy Pike. Also, *Larger Than Life*, with Geoffrey Spears and Sparky O'Toole.

May 3   Pioneering transsexual Christine Jorgensen dies of lung and bladder cancer at the age of sixty-two.

May 9   Gay porn star and filmmaker Fred Halsted—best known for his roles in such films as *Sex Tool* and *El Paso Wrecking Corp.*—commits suicide with an overdose of sleeping pills at the age of forty-nine.

May 12 Forty-four-year-old computer programmer Randy Kraft is found guilty in Los Angeles on sixteen counts of murder in connection with a twelve-year killing spree in which he may have slain as many as thirty-seven young men in three states. According to testimony, Kraft enjoyed picking up hitchhikers (especially military types) and taking them back to his home, where he either drugged them or got them drunk and then raped, tortured, mutilated, and strangled them. In some cases, the torture and mutilation went on for hours, and involved snipping parts of the body (including the nipples and genitals) off with scissors or pouring flammable liquids into the anus or on the penis and testicles and then setting them aflame—all while the victims were still alive. Kraft was finally apprehended when the highway patrol pulled him over for a moving violation and found a dead young Marine propped up in the passenger seat.

He is later sentenced to die in the gas chamber.

May 11 With millions of TV viewers apparently interested now in a "kinder, gentler" America, and the Reagan doctrine of unbridled greed and materialism in ever greater disrepute (what with an anticipated half-a-*trillion*-dollar bailout for the nation's savings and loans), *Dynasty* makes its last appearance on prime-time television, and all the Carringtons, Colbys, Blaisdels, and Fallmonts disappear—at least temporarily—from the nation's airwaves. Ratings for the show have been so poor, hardly anyone even notices the show is gone.

A *Dynasty* mini-series, to tie up whatever loose plot threads were left over from the show, makes its appearance in the fall of 1991.

May 18 U.S. senator Alfonse D'Amato (R-NY) takes to the floor of the Senate to express his outrage over "obscene" and "blasphemous" artwork funded by the National Endowment for the Arts. D'Amato singles out the work of NEA-funded photographer Andres Serrano, whose recent photograph of a crucifix immersed in urine has provoked criticism among religious leaders and political conservatives. "This is not a First Amendment issue," asserts a member of D'Amato's staff defensively.

"You get a hard-on when you look at it."
—*Knoxville Museum of Art director* RICHARD MUHLBERGER, *on how he distinguishes pornography from art*

May 19   First Lady Barbara Bush ignores the reportedly vociferous objections of Chief of Staff John Sununu and prominently displays ten lit candles in the windows of the White House to show her solidarity with the Seventh International AIDS Candlelight Memorial in Washington, D.C. Organizers of the march had asked people in the capital to burn candles in their windows to commemorate friends and loved ones they have lost to the disease.

May 24   Performing at a "Save the Rain Forests" benefit in Brooklyn, Sandra Bernhard and Madonna sing a duet of *I Got You Babe* while bumping each other's rear ends. This, plus a recent joint appearance on *Late Night with David Letterman* during which they suggested they were sleeping together, leads to considerable press speculation about the true nature of their friendship.

June 1   "I've always been in love with men, always. I don't know when I first recognized it as something different, but I've always known that I fit that category. I've always been gay, and for most of my life I prayed not to be that way. I asked God to change me so that I would be like other people. However, the harder I prayed the queerer I got. That must have been God's response."
—LEONARD MATLOVICH, *quoted in the posthumously published biography,* Matlovich: The Good Soldier, *by journalist Mike Hippler*

June 2   The first annual Lambda Literary Awards, for excellence in gay and lesbian writing, are handed out during the American Booksellers Association convention in Washington, D.C. Among the winners: Dorothy Allison's *Trash*, Michael Nava's *Goldenboy*, Paul Monette's *Borrowed Time*, and *Why Can't Sharon Kowalski Come Home?* by Karen Thompson and Julie Andrzejewski.

June 5 Flush from having recently forced the resignation of Democratic House Speaker Jim Wright on ethics violations, the Republicans begin circulating a memo suggesting that his successor, Thomas Foley of Washington, is a homosexual. Although the Republican National Committee eventually apologizes for the memo, insiders report that the Republicans backed off only after Barney Frank (who was in a position to know) threatened to start publicly naming all the closeted homosexuals in the Republican Party. "There is nothing in public life more unprincipled than the politics of innuendo," says one disgusted Republican congressman, James Leach of Iowa. "A kinder, gentler agenda demands an end to the poisoning of standards that assassinates, rather than holds accountable, character."

June 11 Claiming to have accomplished everything he set out to, Jerry Falwell announces that he will officially dissolve the Moral Majority on August 31. He neglects to mention that his equally odious Liberty Foundation, founded in 1986, will continue the crusade against homosexuality, abortion, and pornography.

June 13 Caving in to pressure from political conservatives, the Corcoran Gallery in Washington, D.C., cancels an upcoming exhibit of photographs by the late Robert Mapplethorpe. "It was a close call," says the gallery's chairman, defending the decision. "If you went ahead, I suppose you could say you were upholding freedom of artistic expression against possible political pressure."

June 14 In the nation's bookstores this month: *The Andy Warhol Diaries*, 807 substanceless pages of name-dropping ("Mike Nichols' hair looks so great, so really great"), shallow insights ("You know, I've come to realize lately that Diana Vreeland is just a person"), and the price of cab fares back and forth across New York City ("We cabbed up to the Iranian Embassy—$2.50"). One critic calls it "monumentally tedious."

June 20   Bob Damron—creator of the twenty-five-year-old *Bob Damron's Address Book*, the most popular gay guide of its kind—dies of AIDS at the age of sixty-one.

June 23   An op-ed piece by Samuel Lipman in *The New York Times* praises the Corcoran Gallery's decision to cancel the Robert Mapplethorpe exhibit, and claims that "the lives of our children" are being undermined by "morally unacceptable" art. He dismisses Mapplethorpe's work as "a few raunchy photographs."

June 25   The U.S. Postal Service issues a special "Lesbian & Gay Pride" postmark to commemorate the twentieth anniversary of the 1969 Stonewall riots.

————————

Two hundred people march in Birmingham, Alabama, in the state's first-ever Gay Pride parade.

June 30   On the night the Robert Mapplethorpe exhibit was to have opened at the Corcoran Gallery, laser artist Rockne Krebs projects the entire show, picture by picture, on the exterior of the now-notorious museum.

Meanwhile, the Washington Project for the Arts has announced it will open the exhibit at its Seventh Street gallery.

July 1   Professional bodybuilder Bob Paris acknowledges his homosexuality in an interview in *Ironman* magazine. He later marries fellow bodybuilder Rod Jackson in a highly publicized formal ceremony.

————————

The Centers for Disease Control announces that the number of confirmed AIDS cases in the United States has now topped the one hundred thousand mark.

July 3   *Doonesbury's* Andy Lippincott is admitted to the hospital with AIDS.

July 4 "I never said 'If you are gay, God hates you.' Come on. Be real. I don't understand that. Anybody who really knows me *knows* I wouldn't say that."
—DONNA SUMMER *(who currently has her first hit single, "This Time I Know It's For Real," in years), deflecting reports that she is antigay or has said that AIDS is God's punishment of homosexuals*

July 6 A New York court rules that for the purpose of defining rent-control regulations a gay couple may be considered a "family," and that William Rubenstein may remain in the Manhattan apartment he and his late lover shared for ten years.

July 25 Studio 54 creator Steve Rubell dies at forty-five. The official cause of death is variously reported as hepatitis, a severe peptic ulcer, kidney failure, and a heart attack—although there is widespread speculation that it was AIDS. A lavish funeral several days later draws such luminaries as Donald Trump, Carl Bernstein, Bianca Jagger, and Calvin Klein. One of Rubell's friends calls the service "a good show."

Gay porn actor Johnny Dawes (real name: Brian Lee)—whose films included *Butt Darts*, *Dude Ranch*, and *Bad Bad Boys*—dies of AIDS at the age of thirty-four.

Composer Diamanda Galas's *Masque of the Red Death*—a seventy-minute electronic oratorio about society's inadequate response to the AIDS epidemic—has its American premiere at Alice Tully Hall in New York. Galas was inspired to write the work in part because her brother was diagnosed with the disease.

July 26 Jesse Helms leads a fight in the U.S. Senate to curtail NEA funding for "obscene or indecent art," including artworks that depict "sadomasochism, homoeroticism, the exploitation of children, or individuals engaged in sex acts." The measure is overwhelmingly adopted by a voice vote. Anne Murphy, executive director of the American Arts Alliance, notes that under the new restrictions, "We certainly couldn't produce most of Shakespeare. Certainly not *Richard III*." The Senate measure also specifically bars federal grants for the next five years to two art groups that helped fund the Robert Mapplethorpe exhibit.

"If America persists in the way it's going," says Helms, "and the Lord doesn't strike us down, He ought to apologize to Sodom and Gomorrah."

August 1 "So what if gay people do or don't make up 10 percent of the population? . . . What if only 1 percent of Americans are gay, as the fundamentalists assert? Or for that matter, what if the true figure is 20 percent? An obsession with numbers can divert our attention from the central issues: that women and men in our society are systematically harassed, persecuted, and bashed because they are perceived to be gay and that antigay prejudice is unacceptable whether it's directed against a handful of people or against millions."
—*Essayist* GREGORY HEREK, *on the seemingly never-ending (and ultimately pointless) controversy over exactly how many gay men and lesbians there really are*

Quentin Crisp begins writing for *House & Garden* magazine.

A *Glamour* magazine readers' poll finds that 50 percent believe lesbians should be prohibited from receiving artificial insemination. "If God wanted two women to parent a child," asserts one of the respondents, "man's sperm wouldn't be needed to make baby." Fifty-three percent also said they believe that children of lesbian mothers would be prone to more psychological problems than other children.

August 7 New York's *OutWeek* magazine publishes a list of sixty-six allegedly closeted homosexuals under the headline "Peek-A-Boo," thus igniting a national controversy over "outing."

THE OUTING CONTROVERSY

"Why is it OK to bring out Roseanne Barr as a woman who had an abortion in her youth and OK to bring out Gary Hart as an adulterer and not OK to bring out gays? Why is there a double standard?"

—OutWeek *editor* GABRIEL ROTELLO

"It's philosophical rape. If we don't want policemen coming into our bedrooms, we have to safeguard other people's privacy, too."

—STUART KELLOGG, *former* Advocate *editor*

"I don't believe in the age-old code that one doesn't bring another person out of the closet without their consent. Career and money are no longer sufficient arguments when thousands of people are dying from neglect and hatred and outright abuse. The bottom line is: homosexuality is either OK or it's not."

—ARMISTEAD MAUPIN

"I am disgusted by these AIDS terrorists. I may be a gossip columnist, but I do respect the right of people not to tell me everything."

—LIZ SMITH

"One of the most common charges against outing (and ACT UP) is that both 'go too far,' that they cross some accepted social and political boundary. But the gay movement—and any political movement—has always had to continually 'go too far' in order to get ahead. Certainly the queens, drags, dykes and street queers on Christopher Street went too far when they declared open war on the police at the Stonewall Inn."

—MICHAEL BRONSKI

THE OUTING CONTROVERSY (cont.)

"It's nothing less than psychological rape. . . . All I think the gay men and lesbians of the world want is just a choice, and the choice is to live their life the way they want. Well, when you out someone, you're not giving them a choice, so I don't believe in it at all."

—Gay former umpire DAVE PALLONE

August 16 Amanda Blake, best known for her role as Miss Kitty on the long-running TV series *Gunsmoke*, dies in Sacramento, California, of what is initially reported as lung cancer. Three months later, it is revealed that she in fact had AIDS. The tabloids begin a period of wild speculation over how she contracted it.

August 21 A report from the National Association of State Boards of Education reveals that only twenty-four states require some form of AIDS education in public schools, and of those, eighteen mandate that abstinence be stressed as the best way to avoid contracting the disease. Only three states require that teachers discuss the use of condoms in their AIDS education programs.

August 26 Pat Robertson's Christian Broadcasting Network changes its name to the more benign-sounding "Family Channel."

September 8 In a belated effort to repair its now seriously damaged reputation, the Corcoran Gallery in Washington, D.C., announces plans to present an exhibition on the history of censorship.

AIDS activists disrupt the opening night of *Falstaff* at the San Francisco Opera.

September 10 *The Miami Herald* quotes several Key West businessmen who complain that too many gay men with AIDS are coming to the resort to die. "If this is a great place to die," grumbles one resident, "then it's not a great place to have your winter vacation." According to recent statistics, Key West has a higher per capita AIDS rate than San Francisco.

September 11   *OutWeek* publishes a further list of thirty-one allegedly closeted homosexuals under the headline "Peek-A-Boo II."

The Navy unveils its final, eleven-hundred-page report on what caused the gun turret explosion aboard the U.S.S. *Iowa* last April. The report concludes that an act of suicidal sabotage by Gunner's Mate Clayton Hartwig was the "most likely" cause of the deadly explosion.

September 12   "My dad is where it comes from—he has a huge dick. He makes me look like a baby. It's like an old tree trunk hanging down. . . . When I was a little kid, it used to scare me: 'Whoa, Dad, put that thing away!' "
—JEFF STRYKER, *crediting his now internationally famous endowment to good genes*

September 14   Five members of ACT UP disrupt trading on the New York Stock Exchange to protest the unconscionably high price of AZT as well as the outrageously high profits Burroughs-Wellcome is reaping from it.

September 15   Maud's—described as "the world's oldest lesbian bar"—closes in San Francisco after twenty-three years.

September 18   Still trying to reestablish its credibility after the recent fracas over censorship and national funding for the arts, the Corcoran Gallery issues a public apology for having canceled the Robert Mapplethorpe exhibit back in June. "I feel good about the statement," says the museum's executive director. "I think it is a major step forward."

   Meanwhile, director Christina Orr-Cahall, who canceled the Mapplethorpe exhibit to begin with, has resigned.

September 25 Aging actress turned cop-slapper Zsa Zsa Gabor tells reporters she is terrified of being sent to jail because "they are all lesbians in jail, and I'm so scared of lesbians. Can you imagine being in jail with all those women?" Jokes Joan Rivers, "Zsa Zsa is so stupid. There are no lesbians in prison—they're all in professional tennis."

Gabor later tries to apologize for her homophobic remarks—including an insinuation that the cop who arrested her was a homosexual and therefore jealous of her beauty ("Don't you know, a gay man would not like a woman like Zsa Zsa Gabor. Why would he? I marry all the men he would like")—by telling the press, "I have nothing against gays or lesbians. I have lots of gay boys working for me."

Eventually convicted of all the charges against her—including driving without a valid license and having an open container of alcohol in her vehicle—Gabor complains, "Russia can't be worse than this."

September 28 The FDA approves the use of the drug ddi (dideoxyinosine) in the treatment of AIDS.

September 30 In an interview in *TV Guide*, talk-show host Arsenio Hall denies widespread rumors that he and heavyweight boxing champ Mike Tyson are lovers.

Gay American composer Virgil Thomson—who, among other things, collaborated with Gertrude Stein on the opera *The Mother of Us All*—dies at the age of ninety-two in New York City.

October 1 Denmark legalizes same-sex marriages.

Carter Wallace Inc. begins marketing an extra-large condom, the Magnum, which is 20 percent bigger than regular condoms. The move is seen as a stroke of marketing genius. "After all," asks *Newsweek*, "who in his right mind will ask for the smaller styles?"

"We represent a very, very elegant store. I am not going to have two thousand condoms hanging in my window. I don't care what it represents."
—*Spokeswoman for Tiffany's in Houston, rejecting plans for a condom-filled window display to promote AIDS education and research, 1989*

In an article this month on the hazards of bisexual husbands and lovers, *Cosmopolitan* publishes a checklist of telltale symptoms for nervous women who worry that their boyfriends are secretly swinging both ways. Among the damning clues:

- "Be suspicious if he seems intensely interested in how other men dress."
- "If a man's eyes follow other men, be very cautious."
- "If he looks into another man's eyes for even a microsecond longer than it takes to make socially acceptable eye contact, beware. Heterosexual men do not do it."
- "The boy-boy signals are the same as boy-girl signals: lingering glances, the second look, moving closer to one another, increased animation in each other's presence."
- "Sometimes bisexuals exhibit an intense aversion toward homosexuals, an indication that they are insecure about their own sexual orientation."

Furthermore, the article warns women to be suspicious of men attracted to certain professions, including (but, presumably, not limited to): the theater, fashion, the beauty industry, art and design, fitness, medicine, nursing, social work, counseling, the travel industry, law, import-export work, consulting, and hotel and restaurant work.

October 4 Openly gay Monty Python member Graham Chapman dies of throat cancer at the age of forty-eight. "Somehow," says friend John Cleese, "I think heaven has become a slightly sillier place."

Sign of the times: A feeling of devastation and hope, as an even larger quilt returns to Washington, D.C., October 1989. PHOTO: MARY GOTTWALD, COURTESY THE NAMES PROJECT FOUNDATION

October 5 Former televangelist Jim Bakker is convicted on fraud and conspiracy charges in a federal court in North Carolina. Meanwhile, wife Tammy Faye complains that he is being strip-searched in prison after each of her visits. "They made him bend over in front of all those men!" she sobs to reporters.

October 6 Bette Davis dies at the age of eighty-one.

The NAMES Project AIDS Memorial Quilt returns to Washington, D.C. It has grown from the initial 1,920 panels in 1987 to 10,848.

October 25 Former George Bush media adviser Roger Ailes—mastermind of the controversial, frequently vitriolic television campaign against Michael Dukakis in 1988—is charged with assault after allegedly forcibly evicting an AIDS activist from a Republican fund-raising dinner in New York City. According to one eyewitness, Ailes angrily grabbed the protester by the neck and tried to choke him, before finally beating him in the head and throwing him out.

October 26   A planned college production of Larry Kramer's *The Normal Heart* provokes an explosion of rage and, finally, outright violence in the small community of Springfield, Missouri. After a local state representative demands that college officials cancel the production (on the grounds that it "promotes" homosexuality), a group calling itself "Citizens Demanding Standards" takes out full-page ads in the local paper asking "DO YOU WANT YOUR TAX DOLLARS USED TO PROMOTE HOMOSEXUAL, ANTI-FAMILY LIFESTYLES?" By the time tickets for the play actually go on sale, the newspaper has been filled with angry letters to the editor, including one from a woman who indignantly asserts, "Springfield doesn't need to see two men kissing onstage!" Nonetheless, all eight performances are sold out in less than four hours.

Opening night brings bomb threats to the theater. That same night, arsonists destroy the home of Brad Evans, a college student who has gained widespread attention for his highly vocal support of the production. (The state representative who started the controversy reacts by denouncing Evans as "a Satan worshipper," and implies that Evans burned his own house down.)

"This is a place," notes one college student wearily, "where a favorite pastime of teenagers is to beat up gays they find cruising in the local park."

October 27   In the wake of the historic social changes under way in Eastern Europe, activists from Warsaw, Gdansk, and Wroclaw form a new gay rights group, Lambda, in Poland.

———

Nearly a hundred young people, aged fifteen to twenty-two, attend a city-sponsored Halloween dance for gay youths in Seattle.

November 1   In the nation's bookstores this month: *My Turn*, a memoir of Nancy Reagan's eight-year reign as First Lady. Although the book includes detailed descriptions of her luncheons with Raisa Gorbachev—"blinis with caviar, cabbage rolls, blueberry pie, cookies, chocolates"—and an in-depth discussion of how desperately shabby the china and tablecloths were in the White House when she first moved in, the word "AIDS" is mentioned only once in the entire 384 pages, and that in connection with a brief discussion of Rock Hudson. ("He had been to a White House dinner and had been at my table. I remember sitting across from him and thinking, Gee he's thin. I asked if he had been dieting.")

November 5   Ann Landers endorses bondage as a way for Americans to spice up their love lives. "The final word from here," she tells readers, "is that whatever turns you on is OK so long as there is mutual consent and no inflicting of pain." She also notes, in response to the large amount of mail she's received on the subject, "I had no idea so many people in the United States and Canada were tying each other up."

The newly published *1990 Sports Almanac* reveals that the women's professional bowling circuit has recently been plagued by transvestite bowlers.

November 7   After an episode of the yuppie drama *thirtysomething* opens with two gay men lying in bed together and sharing a few intimate postcoital thoughts, switchboards at ABC affiliates across the country light up with angry and sometimes threatening calls from disgusted viewers. Says producer Marshall Herskovitz of the astonishingly hostile reaction, "I felt like we were in Hollywood in 1958, having a black man kiss a white woman."

Meanwhile, one of the show's regular cast members, Peter Horton ("Gary"), joins the chorus of public indignation. "I actually had a problem morally with that show," Horton tells *Playboy*. "Two guys met and spent the night together. Afterwards, they talked about AIDS—about all their friends who were dying of it. You wanted to say, 'Wait a minute, guys, why do you think that's happening?' "

The controversial episode is later deleted from the series' reruns.

Voters in Concord, California (in the east San Francisco Bay Area), repeal a city ordinance banning discrimination against people with AIDS, 56 percent to 44 percent.

November 9 *Variety* reverses an earlier policy and begins listing the surviving same-sex lovers—noted as "longtime companions"— in its obituaries of gay entertainment personalities.

November 10 Conservative Washington lobbyist Craig Spence —recently implicated in the operation of a male prostitution ring in Washington, D.C.—is found dead, an apparent suicide, in a Boston hotel room. Known as "The Raging Queen" in Washington circles, Spence had considerable influence in the Reagan administration, and reportedly once took two male hustlers on a late-night tour of the White House after allegedly bribing one of the guards.

November 15 Massachusetts becomes the second state in the nation to pass a statewide gay rights law.

November 21 *The Advocate* reports that gay porn star Al Parker has recently spent $5,000 to undergo foreskin restoration surgery. The previously circumcised Parker tells the news magazine, "It's like having a new dick after thirty-six years." The uncircumcised penis will, according to Parker, make its debut in a forthcoming video, *Al Parker: The Uncut Version*.

November 27 "Some things you do because you're not a faggot but because you're a man."
—*Black activist* AL SHARPTON, *crusading for equal rights for all minorities*

November 28 A Texas judge, Jack Hampton, is censured by the state judicial review board for having given a lighter-than-expected sentence to a teenage killer whose two victims were homosexuals. "I put prostitutes and gays at about the same level," Hampton acknowledged in a newspaper interview soon after the trial. "And I'd be hard put to give somebody life for killing a prostitute."

Hampton described the victims as "queers" in explaining why he gave eighteen-year-old Richard Bednarski, who shot the men to death in a Dallas park, only a thirty-year sentence instead of the seemingly requisite life imprisonment.

December 10   More than five thousand activists show up in front of New York's St. Patrick's Cathedral to protest the Catholic Church's policies on homosexuality and AIDS. When several of the protesters enter the cathedral—where John Cardinal O'Connor is conducting mass—and begin chaining themselves to pews and shouting anti-Catholic slogans, police move in and begin making arrests.

"We will not be silent!" cries one demonstrator as the police haul him off. "We will fight O'Connor's bigotry!" Meanwhile, protesters outside continue carrying signs, "CARDINAL O'CON-NOR: PUBLIC HEALTH MENACE," while chanting "You say 'Don't fuck,' we say 'Fuck you!' " More than a hundred demonstrators—including forty-three inside the cathedral—are eventually arrested.

Says rabidly right-wing radio talk-show host Rush Limbaugh, launching into an antigay tirade on his nationally syndicated radio program the next day, "I feel like doing this whole program with just one word: faggie, faggie, faggie. . . . I know that I speak for the decent and normal citizens of this country when I say to those of you of the leftist, militant, homosexual crowd, take it somewhere else. Get out of our schools. Get out of our churches. Take your deadly, sickly behavior and keep it to yourselves. Keep your hands to yourselves, keep your tongues to yourselves. . . . If you can't deal with the guilt of your own existence, then it's time you sought comfort in the Church, rather than looking at it as the enemy."

Both *The New York Times* and Mayor David Dinkins also condemn the protest.

December 15   On the video shelf: *Butthole Banquet II* from Bijou Video. Also, *Batdude and Throbbin: The Sex Crusaders*.

January 1 *Gentlemen's Quarterly*—having gone out of its way for several years to shed its unwanted image as a fashion bible for gay men—publishes a list of twenty-three male celebrities, all of whom share the distinction of being, reputedly, very well-hung. Asks one gay magazine, "Why, oh, why, would your big, brawny, heterosexual audience want to know such queer matters, boys?"

Among the list's honorees: Warren Beatty, James Woods, Matt Dillon, Marlon Brando, Arnold Schwarzenegger, Robert Redford, John Derek, and Milton Berle.

January 6 Ian Charleson, the Scottish-born actor who portrayed Eric Liddell in the 1981 film *Chariots of Fire* and the Rev. Charlie Andrews in *Gandhi* a year later, dies of AIDS at the age of forty in a London hospital.

January 8 The television new year gets off to an inauspicious start with the airing of ABC's tawdry two-hour biopic *Rock Hudson*, based

Former Sunday school teacher and perennial gay rights foe Jesse Helms. Exalted by several major corporations, even before his death.

in part on a book by Hudson's ex-wife, Phillis Gates, and starring Thomas Ian Griffith in the title role. The film is full of unfortunate double entendres, such as in a scene where Hudson, distressed over his closeted gay life in Hollywood, blurts out, "It's like there's this hole inside of me that I can't fill up."

Marc Christian is listed in the credits as a technical adviser.

January 12 Officials at the Polk County Jail in Florida announce they are discontinuing the controversial practice of forcing gay inmates to wear "off-pink" bracelets to distinguish them from the rest of the prison population. The practice—which officials justified as necessary to prevent the spread of AIDS—came under fire from numerous legislators and the American Civil Liberties Union.

January 13 *The New York Times* reveals that several major corporations, including the Philip Morris Tobacco Company, have been quietly donating millions of dollars toward the building of a Jesse Helms museum and library—the innocuously named "Jesse

Helms Citizenship Center"—to be erected near Monroe, North Carolina, beginning in 1992. Says one of Helms's aides, defending the museum (which will house all the senator's papers, tapes of his radio commentaries, and a full-scale replica of his Capitol Hill office), "Helms wants schoolkids to have full access to everything there, with some way of teaching them pretty much our side of the spectrum."

Meanwhile, another congressional aide, Peter Rutledge, tells the newspaper he can think of no other sitting member of Congress with his own museum and library. "You normally require them to die first," says Rutledge.

January 15 In the wake of the U.S. invasion of Panama, press speculation turns to Manuel Noriega's private life, including his alleged bisexuality and his predilection for surrounding himself with gay advisers. One U.S. military officer goes on television to point out—not once, but twice—that Noriega was actually fond of *wearing red underwear*. Other recent revelations include:

- Noriega enjoyed wearing perfume, as well as yellow jumpsuits with matching yellow shoes.
- He supposedly once had a torrid affair with a prominent black male ballet dancer.
- His brother was homosexual, prompting *Newsweek* to speculate that Noriega's "sexual confusion" was due to "his gay brother, Luis . . . the only person Noriega ever trusted completely."
- Noriega repeatedly told his political cronies in Panama that "the queers and the women are the only courageous ones" in Panamanian society.

The lurid press reports, with their implicit connection between homosexuality and despotism, leave many gay men (not to mention bisexuals and men who like red underwear) wondering whether the U.S. has achieved any maturity on sexual issues in the last twenty years.

January 21   Forty-four-year-old beachcomber James Zappalorti, a former Vietnam vet living on Staten Island and described by neighbors as "intelligent . . . very innocent . . . a harmless person," is repeatedly stabbed in the chest and has his throat slashed by two men who taunt him with cries of "Faggot!" and "Queer!" just before murdering him. The two assailants—who were, according to locals, obsessed with the idea that Zappalorti was a homosexual—were previously sent to prison for three years in 1986 for having kidnapped and tortured a gay man.

Says Mayor Dinkins of the recent surge in his city's hate crimes, "When one law-abiding citizen cannot walk down the street, regardless of his or her sexual preference or religion or skin color, all law-abiding citizens suffer. Yesterday it was a gay man; tomorrow will it be an Asian-American? Yesterday it was a Jew; tomorrow will it be a Latino? Yesterday it was an African-American; tomorrow will it be a Catholic priest?"

One of the killers' lawyers later dismisses the gay-baiting aspects of the case as "much ado about nothing."

January 29   Doctors in China report using electroshock and other forms of aversion therapy to "cure" their country's homosexuals. "Some of these homosexuals were ready to commit suicide," says Chinese sexologist Gao Caiqin. "After being cured they are very, very grateful, and they are in tears as they hug us in gratitude."

The story, initially run in *The New York Times*, prompts one supermarket tabloid to print the front-page headline "DOCTORS CURE GAYS WITH ELECTRIC CATTLE PRODS!"

February 1   AGEING TOPS—AGEING BOTTOMS
HIGH-TECH SLAVE TRAINING
HOT WAX SCENES: PREPARING YOUR BOTTOM FOR
    WINTER
SUSPENDING THE HUMAN BODY SAFELY AND SIM-
    PLY
—*From this month's* DungeonMaster, *a magazine devoted to the logistics and more technical aspects of gay S&M*

"I have nothing against homosexuals. I think an orgasm is your thing, and you should fuck whoever the fuck you feel like fucking. Whoever makes you come the hardest, that's who you should be with. And all those people who say you shouldn't do that, fuck them, because it ain't their fucking business."
—*A kinder, gentler* EDDIE MURPHY, *in this month's* Playboy

February 8 A debate in the U.S. Senate over a bill that would mandate the federal compilation of hate-crime statistics (including national statistics on "gay-bashings") finds the otherwise rarely opposed Jesse Helms and Orrin Hatch sniping angrily at one another on the Senate floor.

"We may disagree with that lifestyle," says Hatch, who supports the bill, "but they are human beings and should not be brutalized." He calls violence against homosexuals "wrong and against everything we as Americans stand for."

For his part, Helms denounces the bill as part of a conspiracy by "the radical elements of the homosexual movement," and reiterates his oft-voiced belief that homosexuality "threatens the strength and the survival of the American family as the basic unit of society."

Hatch, a lay Mormon minister who has recently confounded his traditional allies with his growing support for certain key "liberal" causes, says later, "I feel very deeply about people's heartaches and problems, and I don't care what their sexual preferences are. That's their business and I'm not going to judge them by my standards or what I think is right."

The bill passes 92 to 4.

February 10 Director Bill Sherwood—whose only feature film was the critically acclaimed 1986 movie *Parting Glances*—dies of AIDS at the age of thirty-seven.

February 12 Three months after the December revolution that overthrew Romanian President Nicolae Ceausescu, physicians in Bucharest reveal that their country is in the grips of a pediatric

AIDS epidemic, with hundreds of sick children crowding the nation's orphanages and hospitals. Health officials blame the epidemic on Ceausescu's policies, which forbade birth control or the use of condoms in Romania, and which mandated that doctors reuse syringes in hospitals to save money. For years, Ceausescu had denied the existence of the disease in Romania, insisting that it was a problem of "decadent" nations.

February 13 Thirteen airmen are expelled from the U.S. Air Force after a four-month investigation into homosexual activity at Carswell Air Force Base in Texas.

February 16 Pop artist Keith Haring, thirty-one, dies from AIDS. "The hardest thing is just knowing that there's so much more stuff to do," Haring said, six months before his death. "I'm so scared that one day I'll wake up and I won't be able to do it."

February 27 Addressing a group of students in Poughkeepsie, New York, Martin Luther King 3d—son of the slain black civil rights leader—offers the opinion that "something may be wrong" with gay men and lesbians, and elaborates, "Any man that has a desire to be with another man has a problem, in my opinion. And that applies to any woman who has a desire to be with another woman."

He later issues an apology for the remarks.

March 1 "I know politicians who love women who don't even want to be known for that—because they might lose the gay vote. OK? If this is the kind of extreme we're heading toward, we're really in trouble."
—DONALD TRUMP, *giving just one of the reasons why he'd one day like to be known as Senator Trump or even President Trump*

March 2 Conservative activist Paul Weyrich suggests that Orrin Hatch's growing political moderation is motivated by the Utah senator's "burning desire" to be on the Supreme Court. Weyrich cites a 1979 memo in which political consultants told Hatch he could never be seriously considered as a court nominee unless he worked hard to change his image as an uncompromising right-winger.

March 4 Andy Rooney—suspended for three months from *60 Minutes* in the wake of recent homophobic and racist remarks (including an assertion that he wouldn't want to spend time in a small room with a homosexual, and that "homosexual unions . . . lead quite often to premature death")—returns to work two months earlier than anticipated. The show's ratings had dropped precipitously during his absence.

March 15 The second issue of *Tema*, a publication of the recently formed Moscow Union of Lesbians and Gay Men, is published. The group's primary objective is the abolition of Article 121 of the Soviet criminal code, which makes it a crime (punishable by up to five years in prison) simply to *be* homosexual. Although the group has received publicity—some of it surprisingly sympathetic—in the Moscow media, the country's social atmosphere is still repressive enough that the paper has to be secretly printed in Lithuania and brought back to Moscow by train.

A new biography, *The Boy-Man* by Tim Jeal, concludes that the founder of the Boy Scouts, Lord Baden-Powell, was a repressed and often tormented homosexual who subjugated his secret sexual longings to the dictates of Victorian and Edwardian society. Baden-Powell—a former British army officer who often worked as a military spy for his country, most frequently employing the disguise of a delirious, international butterfly enthusiast—got the idea for the Scouts in 1907 after taking two dozen boys on a camping trip to Brownsea Island off the southern coast of England. Before his death in 1941, he also conceived the idea for the Girl Scouts and the Wolf Cubs.

March 18 Malcolm Forbes is posthumously "outed" in *OutWeek* magazine, leading to a rash of "Poor, aging, leatherboy Malcolm" stories in the mainstream media. Two weeks later, the supermarket tabloid *Globe* favors its readers with the front-page headline "HOL-LYWOOD'S SECRET SHOCKER—ROCK HUDSON AND MALCOLM FORBES WERE GAY LOVERS! AND LIZ LOVED BOTH!"

March 22   "WE SHARED GLANCES AT the Evanston North-western Station waiting for the 4pm train on 3/13/90. You wore a light-blue shirt, tan pants, black hair, mustache, glasses. Wanted to talk to you, but you got off train before I could. Our parting glances told me I should try to find you. Call me, please!"

—*Personals ad in* Gay Chicago

Johnny Greene, fired from his Louisiana job in 1985 after he wrote an article about AIDS for *People* magazine, dies from complications of the disease at the age of forty-three.

March 26   *Common Threads: Stories from the Quilt* wins the Academy Award for Best Feature-Length Documentary. It is the second Oscar for gay filmmaker Rob Epstein, who received the first one six years ago, for *The Times of Harvey Milk*.

Fashion designer Roy Halston Frowick, better known to the world simply as "Halston," dies of AIDS in a San Francisco hospital at the age of fifty-seven.

March 28   With the opening of the Robert Mapplethorpe exhibit less than two weeks away, law enforcement officials in Cincinnati, Ohio, warn the local Contemporary Arts Center to cancel the ex-hibit or risk prosecution under the city's stringent antiobscenity laws. "These photographs are just not welcome in this community," says the local chief of police. "The people of this community do not cater to what others depict as art."

Meanwhile, antipornography groups begin picketing the cen-ter. Included in the crowds are several small children holding signs that read "PLEASE PROTECT ME" and "OBSCENITY DESTROYS."

After the exhibit finally opens, a Cincinnati grand jury indicts the center's director, Dennis Barrie, on charges of obscenity and pandering.

"CHILDREN PLAYING GAMES"

British archaeologists excavating the old Lambeth Palace (once home to the Archbishop of Canterbury) in downtown London in 1990 are prepared to find almost anything in the seventeenth-century ruins. Still, they are obviously shocked when, digging carefully through the rubble, they find a beautiful ten-inch-square glazed tile that depicts four exquisitely innocent cherubs sodomizing one another in a kind of heavenly daisy chain. The tile—made in Portugal, and dating back at least to 1660—shows one cherub fellating another while at the same time being sodomized by a third; a fourth cherub is also sodomizing the sodomizer.

Although authorities at the London Museum informally christen the tile "The Bonking Cherubs," an official archaeological catalog more decorously describes it as "Children Playing Games." Its original owner, and how it found its way into Lambeth Palace, remain a mystery.

More than a thousand demonstrators march on the steps of the New York state capitol in Albany to demand increased funding for the state's AIDS programs.

March 29   Delivering his first speech on AIDS since he took office fourteen months ago, President Bush is heckled by National Gay and Lesbian Task Force director Urvashi Vaid, who hollers, "We need your leadership! We need more than one speech every fourteen months!" Vaid, holding a sign reading "TALK IS CHEAP, AIDS FUNDING IS NOT," is quickly "escorted" from the auditorium by police.

April 1   Madonna tells *Vanity Fair* that she is not a lesbian and that Sandra Bernhard is not her lover.

In the nation's bookstores this month: Jack Fritscher's *Some Dance to Remember*, a nostalgic novel about life in the Castro district before the devastation of AIDS. The book is the latest in a spate of safe-sex-era remembrances romanticizing the gay politics, culture, and freewheeling sexuality of the Seventies.

April 2   A *Newsweek* cover story, "The Future of Gay America," draws an unusually heavy amount of reader mail, with about 60 percent of it antigay.

"Homosexuality is a perversion and is unnatural to man's common sense," complains one disgusted reader.

"Do you think showing our children a picture of two male perverts holding hands on the cover of your magazine is going to give them [positive values]?" says another.

"Surely, people commit other hideous sins, but they do not take to the streets to brag about it or expect to be patted on the back or given special privileges because of it," writes a third.

"Your March 12 cover offends me and every adult I have talked to who has seen it," says a fourth.

April 3   Psychic Jeane Dixon predicts that in 1990, "Historical evidence that AIDS is an ancient disease, and not a recent plague, will force a new approach to dealing with the epidemic."

TABLOID FEVER

NEW GAY SEX SCANDAL ROCKS TENNIS! LESBIAN STARS STALK YOUNG PLAYERS IN SHOWERS! TEENS LURED TO ALL-GIRL HOT-TUB PARTIES!

—*National Enquirer*

TABLOID FEVER

SAMMY DAVIS JR'S SECRET GAY LIFE REVEALED!
> —*The Sun*

"I WAS JOHN TRAVOLTA'S GAY LOVER!"
> —*National Enquirer*

HOLLYWOOD DESIGNER'S SHOCKING CLAIMS:
"MY STORMY GAY AFFAIR WITH WILD ELTON JOHN!"
> —*The Globe*

JET PASSENGERS PUNCH OUT PANSIES!
> —*World Weekly News*

LIZ: HER TOP AIDE KILLS HIMSELF! SHOCKING UNTOLD
STORY OF HER GAY SECRETARY'S SUICIDE!
> —*National Enquirer*

April 7 The influential Soviet weekly *Ogonyok* condemns the continuing persecution of homosexuals as an unmitigated violation of human rights and suggests that further victimization of gay men in the Soviet Union will only fuel the spread of alcoholism, prostitution, and the AIDS epidemic.

April 8 After a five-year, highly publicized battle with AIDS, Ryan White, eighteen, dies of the disease in a hospital in Indianapolis.

Former President Reagan eulogizes him in an op-ed piece for *The Washington Post*. "We owe it to Ryan," says Reagan, whose Justice Department once endorsed discrimination against people with AIDS, "to make sure that the fear and ignorance that chased him from his home and school will be eliminated. We owe it to Ryan to open our hearts and minds to those with AIDS. We owe it to Ryan to be compassionate, caring and tolerant toward those with AIDS, their families and friends."

"Here you've got somebody," says Randy Shilts, "who did nothing to help [Ryan White] when he was President now suddenly rallying in talk about 'compassion.' I think it's absolutely egregious hypocrisy and Ronald Reagan should be ashamed of himself."

Ryan's funeral draws a fleet of international celebrities (including First Lady Barbara Bush, Jesse Jackson, and Elton John), and his headstone—engraved with the messages "FRIENDS FOR-EVER, MICHAEL JACKSON" and "LOVE, ELTON JOHN" —quickly establishes itself as a shrine for anonymous pilgrims who come from all over the country and leave flowers, candles, pennies, and handwritten notes. It also becomes the object of vandals, who twice steal a small statue of Ryan's dog from the grave and rip out two trees Mrs. White has planted close by.

Says one local father, summing up Ryan's impact on the community, "I think he made people appreciate their own children more. I know he has mine."

April 15 A twenty-seven-year-old gay man from Burlington, Vermont, suffers a fractured skull, partial blindness, and possible brain damage after being attacked and beaten by a thirty-two-year-old "fag-basher" outside a local gay bar.

Screen legend Greta Garbo, eighty-four, dies in New York City. Several obituaries, including a *People* magazine cover story two weeks later, allude to persistent rumors about the reclusive star's alleged sexual affairs with Mercedes d'Acosta and various other women.

April 16 *The New York Times* reveals that despite Cincinnati's much-vaunted reputation as a bastion of traditional family values and as the "smut-free" capital of America, huge numbers of the city's residents cross the state line every day to partake of the massage parlors, strip joints, prostitutes, and X-rated bookstores in nearby Newport, Kentucky. One Newport merchant reports that business is especially brisk when there's a ball game at Cincinnati's Riverfront Stadium. "I guess they tell their wives the game went into extra innings," he tells the newspaper.

Publicists for Elizabeth Taylor deny rumors, prompted by her recent admission to a Santa Monica hospital, that she is dying of AIDS.

April 21 Nearly two hundred students hold an antihomosexual "Straight Pride" rally at the University of Massachusetts. A short time later, ten of the demonstrators raid and disrupt an anthropology class watching *The Times of Harvey Milk*.

April 27 A blood center in Denver recalls 10,500 pints of blood after discovering there are "glitches" in the center's new automated HIV-testing system. Unfortunately, most of the blood has already been used.

"You don't get AIDS from holding babies, loving them or having them spit on you. Aren't they adorable?"
—First Lady BARBARA BUSH, *snuggling a baby with AIDS at a hospital in Florida, spring 1990*

April 28 "I resent like hell that I was maybe eighteen before I ever heard the 'L' word. It would have made all the difference for me had I grown up knowing that the reason I didn't fit in was because they hadn't told me there were more categories to fit into."
—*Lesbian singer and songwriter* MICHELLE SHOCKED

In its first major public action, about five hundred members of the newly formed group Queer Nation march in Greenwich Village to protest a pipe-bomb attack, which left three people injured, on a local gay bar the night before. Demonstrators wear buttons that read "Stop Enforced Heterosexuality," and chant slogans of "No more violence!" and "Hey hey, ho ho—homophobia has got to go!"

Meanwhile, the group's use of the highly pejorative term "queer" to defiantly identify itself soon catches on in the gay media (with headlines like "Queer Thoughts" and "A Call to Queer Action" popping up regularly), but still rankles some older gays, to the extent that when *The Advocate* runs a cover story describing 1990 as "The Year of the Queer," a significant number of readers take umbrage and threaten to cancel their subscriptions.

Fifteen gay activists are invited to the White House to attend President Bush's signing of the Hate Crimes Statistics Act. The act requires law-enforcement officials to start compiling statistics on crimes resulting from an individual's race, religion, ethnic background, or sexual orientation. "The faster we can find out about these hideous crimes," says Bush, "the faster we can track down the bigots who commit them." Despite the glowing remarks, Bush's own Justice Department refuses at first to keep track of violence against gay men and lesbians on its new Hate Crimes Hotline.

April 30 Cincinnati's Contemporary Arts Center reports that the Robert Mapplethorpe exhibit is drawing approximately twenty-five hundred visitors a day, compared to between two hundred and five hundred visitors a day for previous exhibits.

May 1 "Look, I think the movie is about *guys*, guys who are real fucked up . . . the guys—what guys do . . . this 'guy' energy. I mean, it's a very homoerotic movie . . . this guys stuff . . . guys, guys, guys, guys . . ."
—RICHARD GERE, *discussing all the "guy" interaction in his new film* Internal Affairs

May 7 Closeted gay conservative Carl "Spitz" Channell—a political protégé of Terry Dolan, and convicted last year on tax fraud for his part in the Iran-*contra* scandal—dies of complications from injuries he recently received in an automobile accident. Despite his own homosexuality, Channell was also active in fund-raising for various right-wing, antigay groups. Says a spokesman, "He was the kind of fellow who held true to the small-town values."

Barbara Bush once again draws the ire of White House conservatives when she sends a supportive personal letter to Paulette Goodman, president of the Federation of Parents and Friends of Lesbians and Gays. "I firmly believe," writes Mrs. Bush, "that we cannot tolerate discrimination against any individuals or groups in our country. . . . I appreciate so much your encouraging me to help change attitudes." Randy Shilts dubs Mrs. Bush "every homosexual's favorite First Lady."

May 8 Fitness trainer and former Colt model Paul Barresi "outs" actor John Travolta in an interview in the *National Enquirer*, claiming that Travolta first propositioned him in the showers of a health club and that over the next two years they "had sex dozens of times while [Travolta] was dating girl stars." Barresi later apologizes for the story (while never retracting its essential veracity), claiming that he sold the interview to the tabloid because he needed the money.

May II The film *Longtime Companion* opens in New York City. *Rolling Stone*'s Peter Travers calls it "the best American movie this year . . . funny, touching and vital." The first major studio release about AIDS focuses on a group of upscale New Yorkers dealing with the emotional devastation of the disease throughout the 1980s, and features Bruce Davison as a wealthy Manhattanite whose lover dies from the disease. "I knew I had to do it," says Davison of the role, which earns him a Best Supporting Actor nomination, "because of the importance of it—and because of the friends that I've lost. . . . My agent, my manager, and my commercial agent all died within a year. . . . I think it's probably one of my greatest parts, the kind that comes around once in a lifetime."

Amid the otherwise laudatory reviews, there are two notable dissents: Vincent Canby, who calls the film "self-absorbed" and "insipid," and *People* magazine, which blasts what it calls the movie's "sexual ethnocentrism," complaining that the script places too much emphasis on the impact of AIDS in the gay community—an ironic but predictable criticism from a publication whose articles on the disease have disproportionately focused on babies, straight women, hemophiliacs, and other "innocent victims."

May 12   *Star Trek: The Next Generation* goes where no show has gone in years and presents a bizarrely homophobic episode (bizarre since the program's characters are frequently congratulating themselves on their tolerance and diversity) in which an effete intergalactic art collector kidnaps Lieutenant Commander Data to add to his art collection. "Personally, I'd be delighted to see you go around *naked*," leers the twitchy collector, who also murders a female accomplice in a particularly gruesome manner. The show, along with other recent entertainment anachronisms, signals a return by Hollywood to the comfortably self-congratulatory days of "The Deranged Homo Did It."

Meanwhile, asked why there are no positive portrayals of gay men or lesbians on the show, a publicist for Paramount Studios remarks, "What would you have us do, put pink triangles on them? Have them sashay down the corridors?"

Producers later announce the show will soon begin featuring some positive gay and lesbian characters.

Having recently performed two sold-out concerts at Madison Square Garden, Andrew Dice Clay—self-described as "the most vulgar, vicious comic ever to walk the face of the earth"—is tapped to cohost this week's *Saturday Night Live*. The selection of the homophobic, misogynistic comedian so outrages series regular Nora Dunn that she refuses to appear on the show with him. Guest singer Sinead O'Connor also cancels her appearance in protest.

The show turns out to be the highest-rated in *SNL* history, and Dunn's contract is not renewed the following season.

May 22   Thirty-two male students at Ohio State University are transferred from their dormitory following a seven-month period in which they repeatedly harassed and made death threats against two gay students living there. Says one of the transferred boys, "*I'm* a victim. It was just little things going on, and they're just blowing them out of proportion." Among the "little things": constant threats of physical violence, endless harassing phone calls, and signs saying "DIE FAGS" taped to the gay students' doors.

May 28 "What can you say about a country that tolerates homosexuals but not smokers? I never gave anyone AIDS."
—*Chain-smoking author* TOM CLANCY *bemoaning the country's current wave of antismoking sentiment*

May 30 Amid growing speculation that it tried to whitewash the real cause of the U.S.S. *Iowa* explosion from the beginning, the Navy announces it will reopen its official investigation of the *Iowa* tragedy, and produces evidence indicating that the explosion may have been an accident after all—a conclusion many experts had reached months ago. "The rush to blame Clayton Hartwig was flat wrong," observes Ohio senator John Glenn.

June 1 San Francisco 49ers running back Roger Craig begins appearing in a series of San Francisco newspaper ads for Calvin Klein underwear. The ads, which show him stripped down to a pair of very, *very* tight briefs, prompts one publication to note, a bit disingenuously, "Adoring women are posting the page on refrigerators across the city."

In an interview with journalist Rich Flowers, Quentin Crisp dismisses AIDS as "a fashionable disaster" and remarks, "People have always been dying and some of them die young. I don't believe in AIDS. When I first arrived here there was something called amoebic dysentery, it was all the rage. Then, there was hepatitis. Now, nobody mentions it. And now, AIDS is fashionable."

In the same interview, Crisp advocates government-sponsored extermination of all people over sixty as a way of controlling global overpopulation: "Everyone would be outraged at first but after that they would come to expect it."

June 3 Robert Morse wins a Tony Award for his performance as Truman Capote in the acclaimed one-man Broadway show *Tru*.

Capote's longtime friend Joanna Carson has reportedly been to see the show a dozen times.

June 5   A San Francisco firm, Mayer Laboratories, announces plans to build a condom factory in the Soviet Union to help alleviate that country's desperate condom shortage. The new plant is expected to produce about two hundred twenty-five million condoms annually.

June 9   John Brownell, deputy managing editor of *The Los Angeles Times*, dies of AIDS at the age of thirty-three.

A former French government health minister, Michele Barzach, calls for legalizing brothels in France (and thus medically supervising the country's prostitutes) as one way of helping to curb the AIDS epidemic. A poll shows that 80 percent of the French people agree with her.

June 16   Over a thousand activists from the group Queer Nation march through downtown Manhattan to protest gay-related hate crimes.

June 17   Twelve Marines shouting "Kill the fags!" attack and beat three gay men outside a Washington, D.C., gay bar, leaving two of the men unconscious on the sidewalk. Two of the soldiers are later "disciplined" with fines of $400 each and a thirty-day restriction to barracks.

"I wouldn't want any of those pictures on my walls around here. And I wouldn't go up to any of the pictures at the Whitney Museum and say, 'Hey, that's my son's picture.'"
—HARRY MAPPLETHORPE, *father of Robert Mapplethorpe, on his son's controversial photography. In the same interview, Mr. Mapplethorpe asserts he would have been much happier had Robert "married and raised a family and had a nine-to-five job."*

June 20 The Sixth International Conference on AIDS opens today in San Francisco. President Bush—who has declined an invitation to attend—is instead in North Carolina, sponsoring a campaign fund-raiser for Jesse Helms.

June 22 The Empire State Building is lit up in lavender lights for three days in honor of Gay Pride Week.

June 24 This year's Gay Pride parade in New York City draws a record two hundred thousand marchers. Unfortunately, as usual, it also draws several hundred antigay protesters, some of whom shout slogans of "Perverts on parade, someday you'll get AIDS!"

Chanting "We want action. Where is George?" several hundred members of ACT UP drown out a fifteen-minute closing address by U.S. Secretary of Health and Human Services Louis Sullivan at the Sixth International AIDS Conference. "Today's scheduled speech . . . by Sullivan is not a scientific presentation," says the organization, in a press release. "After ten years of Bush/Reagan rhetoric on AIDS, we will no longer tolerate words without actions."

> "Totally counterproductive . . . offensive to mainstream Catholics, Protestants, and Jews and anybody else . . . outrageous. . . . It is an excess of free speech to resort to some of the tactics these people use."
>
> —PRESIDENT BUSH, *denouncing ACT UP*

June 27 In a nationally syndicated editorial, "Place Blame for AIDS Where It Belongs," conservative columnist Mona Charen blames the epidemic on "the indifference of promiscuous homosexuals" and calls for a halt to the "zillions" already spent on AIDS education. ("Everyone in the world already knows that anal sex transmits AIDS, and studies show that knowledge has little impact on decisions about sexual behavior.") Charen also derides the NAMES Project Quilt because it inspires "guilt." "I don't know about you, but I'm tired of being blamed for the AIDS epidemic."

July 1 "The man I'd most like to meet, of all the gorgeous hunks you've ever featured in *Torso*, is 'Body Beautiful.' His muscles are so powerful he could probably crush me with no effort at all."

"The model whom you refer to as 'Long 'n' Thick' simply takes my breath away. As a connoisseur of well-endowed men, I'm very discriminating when it comes to the size of a man's dick."

"There is something very special, not to mention erotic, about a man who looks as mean and nasty as 'Rough Stuff.' A few bruises are a small price to pay for the privilege of fucking with a guy who holds nothing back. When I get fucked, I don't want to be tickled. I like to feel like I've really been fucked over."

" 'Perfect' is the right word all right! I've never seen a sexier man in my entire life! And believe me, I've been a man-watcher since I can remember. 'Perfect' is the only apt description for this stunning hunk of maleness."

—*From this month's "Letters to the Editor" in* Torso *magazine*

July 6 Bay Area television reporter Paul Wynne dies of AIDS in San Francisco at the age of forty-seven. Wynne had chronicled the development of his disease and his feelings as he neared death in an often wrenching, often wryly funny weekly video diary that aired for nearly seven months on KGO, the local ABC affiliate.

"This is the face of AIDS," he told viewers, in an unsparing close-up of his emaciated face during the diary's premiere on January 11. He then contrasted his current appearance with photographs of how he looked—muscular and robust—before his 1987 diagnosis. In other segments, he gave viewers a "guided tour" of his overflowing medicine cabinet, discussed the financial devastation of the disease, and explored the prejudice and discrimination experienced by gay men as a result of the epidemic (including the instance of a dinner hostess who demanded that two gay guests eat off paper plates while her other guests ate from Limoges). Despite initial fears that he would be subjected to hostility and death threats

as a result of the series, viewer response was overwhelmingly supportive, even at times from unexpected sources. After blasting religious fundamentalists in one segment, he received a letter from a viewer who told him, "The ones you hate are not true Christians and only succeed in making the rest of us look ugly and bigoted."

In the series' last segment, aired shortly before his death, Wynne took his final leave of viewers and told them, "It's been a joy knowing all of you."

July 7 New tests on the tissue samples of a twenty-five-year-old British sailor who died of a mysterious ailment in 1959 reveal that he in fact had AIDS. The tests (involving a form of genetic analysis called DNA amplification) conclusively show the presence of HIV in his system. At the time of his death, the man was suffering from night sweats, weight loss, severe fatigue, and fever, and had been diagnosed with both cytomegalovirus and pneumocystis. Medical records show that his wife and youngest daughter also died from similarly described illnesses. The cases predate the first previously known AIDS case in Britain by twenty-three years.

Meanwhile, a sample of blood from Zaire, also from 1959, tests positive for antibodies against HIV as well.

July 11 The U.S. Senate bans the sale of bottled "poppers" such as "Lockerroom," "Bolt," and "Hardware," effective February 25, 1991.

———————

Hong Kong repeals its sodomy laws.

July 12 With the release of his first film—*The Adventures of Ford Fairlane*—barely one week away and his ambitions for superstardom well documented in recent interviews, Andrew Dice Clay goes on a national media blitz to convince the nation he's neither a homophobe nor a misogynist but rather a performer who's been trying all along to *make fun of* misogyny and homophobia. With tears in his eyes, he tells viewers of *The Arsenio Hall Show* that he's just a hardworking Brooklyn boy trying to make something of himself. Two days later, he tells interviewer Diane Sawyer that he's "misunderstood," and that his stand-up comedy routines as "the Dice Man" don't reflect his real feelings about women or gays at all. For many viewers, the only question in all of this is: why are all the networks according this hypocrite so much free air time?

Ford Fairlane bombs at the box office, and 20th Century-Fox later gives Clay a cash settlement rather than release his next movie.

July 13   *20/20* does a "Whatever Happened to . . . ?" segment on the once-hot disco group the Village People. According to the report, the group is now doing "disco nostalgia" concerts at small clubs in Europe and Australia.

Two Dutch virologists announce they will begin testing tissue samples from the ancient mummified remains of both humans and monkeys to ascertain whether the AIDS virus was present in the environment five thousand years ago. Their work is based on a hypothesis that HIV existed for thousands of years in African monkeys before it mutated into a form that triggered the modern epidemic in humans.

July 15   Dave Pallone's *Behind the Mask: My Double Life in Baseball*—a memoir of his years as a closeted gay umpire in the National League—debuts at No. 15 on *The New York Times* bestseller list. "In this world, it's hard enough to live one life, never mind two," says Pallone, who was dismissed from the National League in 1988 for being gay. "It's difficult to come to the realization that you're gay and to accept it for yourself. . . . I think that the young people of today need a role model. They're finding out about their sexuality so early in life now, and it's time for them to have a role model, and I want to be that role model."

July 16   Philip Morris becomes the object of a nationwide gay boycott in response to the corporation's contributions to Jesse Helms's reelection campaign. Although gay bars across the country begin pulling two of the company's most popular products—Marlboro cigarettes and Miller Beer—the boycott has no discernible effect on Helms's reelection in November. However, gays eventually claim success when, nine months later, Miller Beer announces that its profits in the fourth quarter were down by 54 percent.

July 18   Two congregations of the Lutheran Church—both in San Francisco—are suspended for having ordained gay and lesbian pastors.

July 19   The House Ethics Committee votes unanimously to recommend an official reprimand for Representative Barney Frank for his acknowledged involvement with a male prostitute, Steven Gobie, between 1985 and 1987. The involvement first became public when *The Washington Times* ran an article in 1989 alleging that Frank had paid Gobie for sex and then hired him as a chauffeur and houseboy.

Despite a move by Representatives William Dannemeyer and Newt Gingrich to have Frank censured or even expelled from Congress altogether, the full House votes to accept the Ethics Committee recommendations, and Frank is reprimanded.

July 21   Soviet authorities announce that film director Sergei Paradzhanov, sixty-six, has died. No details are given.

July 24   President Bush nominates New Hampshire judge David Souter to fill the Supreme Court vacancy left by retiring justice William Brennan. Initial press coverage tends to focus on Souter's character and personal background: his erudition, his devotion to his mother, his allegedly puckish sense of humor. "He has a wicked sense of humor that can skewer the most stuffed shirt," one friend is quoted as telling the press. "He has a twinkle in his eye," says another. "He displays the most fantastic, dry sense of humor that you can imagine," says a third. "A Judge with a Sense of Humor," reads one newspaper headline announcing Souter's nomination. Although it begins to sound as if Bush has nominated Howie Mandel instead of another Oliver Wendell Holmes, it isn't clear whether some of Souter's previous court opinions—including one forbidding gay people from becoming foster parents or from adopting children—are regarded as part of the general laugh-fest.

July 26   Three gay men are attacked—one of them slashed in the face with a razor—by a gang of seven youths shouting antigay epithets on New York's Christopher Street. The slashing victim—seventeen-year-old dance instructor Gerarud Stewart—requires more than sixty stitches to his cheeks, chin, neck, and arms.

Other recent homophobic attacks in the city: a gay man battered to death with a claw hammer in Queens, and two lesbians kicked to the ground and beaten by a gang of youths in the West Village. Says one gay New Yorker, "It used to be that when gay men got together, they talked about all their friends dying of AIDS. Now, in addition to that, they talk about who's been beaten up."

July 27   Two men in Adrian, Michigan, are sentenced to prison —one for five years—for having had sex in a public park. "I'm not a guy who believes homosexuality is an acceptable alternative lifestyle," says the presiding judge. "I think it is a serious sickness. It is definitely not a lifestyle I can tolerate." The same judge had previously given a convicted "fag-basher" a relatively lenient sentence, telling him, "I do understand how revolting it is to anyone who is not a homosexual to have homosexual advances made on you."

July 30   "It's reassuring to see *Newsweek* include gay youths in the special teen issue. Just the simple act of acknowledging gay teens and their personal challenges in a nonjudgmental light represents a giant step toward arresting homophobia. Having grown up gay, I know the importance such articles can play in one's life. I'm now thirty-five, and I remember reading *Newsweek*'s coverage of the Stonewall riots in 1969, widely considered the beginning of the gay-rights movement. Your articles were the first objective pieces about gays that I found and a far cry from the typical dusty library book full of misconceptions and condemnation."

—*Reader's letter praising* Newsweek *magazine*

July 31   Warner Bros. announces that director Oliver Stone will soon begin work on a film biography of Harvey Milk. "There wasn't a studio that would touch it," says one of the film's coproducers. "But as soon as Oliver came along, every major studio in Hollywood wanted it." Given the simplistic bombast and adolescent moralizing of Stone's previous films—*Wall Street, Platoon, Talk Radio*—some gay observers are less than thrilled by the announcement.

August 1   Archaeologists in Greece reveal that they've unearthed what they believe to be the earliest known "locker room" in existence, dating to the sixth century B.C. The recently excavated area was most likely used by ancient athletes to undress, do warm-up exercises, oil their bodies, and store athletic equipment.

The Robert Mapplethorpe exhibit opens, without incident, in Boston.

Actor Alan Rachins, best known for his role as Douglas Brackman on *L.A. Law*, takes over the role of Albin in a Florida production of *La Cage aux Folles*.

August 2   In the wake of growing rumors that Supreme Court designate David Souter—a lifelong bachelor—might be gay, the White House begins trotting out a list of women Souter has dated in the past, including a female student he dated in law school and, more recently, a Boston woman who works at a television station.

August 4   Gay Games III, with more than seven thousand gay and lesbian athletes from around the world participating, opens in Vancouver, British Columbia.

August 10   *Gay Pravda* makes its debut in Moscow.

August 15   Three recent surveys and studies:

■ A study of gay men in Albuquerque, New Mexico, finds that 39 percent reported having had anal sex without a condom in the last thirty days.

■ A twenty-five-year study concludes that between 10 and 13 percent of America's Catholic clergy is *actively* homosexual.

■ A poll by *The Moscow News* finds that 27 percent of Soviet citizens support the death penalty for homosexuals.

August 28 "I don't know if you can write an overtly gay song, unless you say something like 'Oh, fuck me real deep in my ass!' . . . I have been accused of not being gay enough—of not writing gay enough—but I wonder if that isn't a bit like accusing a straight man of not being macho enough."
—*Openly gay pop star* ANDY BELL, *of the British group Erasure, whose dance single "Chains of Love" has made it into the U.S. Top 40*

September 4 Voters in Broward County, Florida (including Ft. Lauderdale and Coral Springs), veto a proposed gay rights ordinance, 59 percent to 41 percent.

September 6 Posing as a female transfer student from Greece, a twenty-six-year-old Colorado Springs man, Charles Dougherty, enrolls at the local Coronado High School as "Cheyen Weatherly" and soon distinguishes himself by making the all-girl cheerleading squad. The impersonation escapes detection until school officials ascertain that "Cheyen" does not exist: all "her" background records are fictitious. After being arrested on charges of criminal impersonation, Dougherty is diagnosed as having multiple personalities, and—despite the demands of outraged parents, some of whom suggest he should be given the death penalty—he is sentenced to two years' probation, with the qualification that he receive psychiatric counseling.

September 10 Sandra Bernhard tells *People* that she is not a lesbian and that Madonna is not her lover. "If Madonna and I were really having an affair, I don't think we would be talking about it in public," says the comedian. "I'm not a lesbian and I'm sick of being called one. . . . I want to set the record straight."

"HIGHWAY REST STOPS—Closet Encounters"
—*Informative segment ("Our story is about something quite shocking that's going on in our nation's rest stops. Some of our husbands and boyfriends are spending time there for something we would never suspect.") on this week's* Face to Face *with Connie Chung, on CBS*

September 11   A Wisconsin man, Joseph Wills, is charged with murder and committing a hate crime in the shooting death of a gay man who he claims made sexual advances to him. "I know this sounds odd," says Wills, "but if I had it to do over again, I would do the same thing."

September 14   A gay man with AIDS is brutally beaten while walking his dog in a Denver park at one o'clock in the morning. Doctors later reveal that virtually every bone in the man's body was broken and that his rectum was mutilated by tree limbs and other instruments. His dog was also severely beaten.
There are no leads in the case.

September 15   In the nation's bookstores this month: *It's Still My Turn*, a satire of Nancy Reagan's memoirs by former *Saturday Night Live* performer and openly gay Nancy Reagan impersonator Terry Sweeney. The book coincides with a one-man Off Broadway show in which Sweeney parodies the former First Lady and the entire Reagan era. "I feel my show and book are kind of like group therapy," says Sweeney. "I'm helping a nation of people get over the Reagans. We're still, you know, in Reagan fallout."

September 17   General Motors apologizes for having used the phrase "little faggot trucks" to describe foreign-made pickups in a recent promotional videotape.

SEXUAL ILLITERACY IN AMERICA

In the fall of 1989, the Kinsey Institute undertook a widespread national survey to determine how much Americans actually know about sex. Distinct from a poll gauging opinions or attitudes, the survey presented people with a wide variety of factual questions concerning physiology and sexual functioning. The results—published in 1990 in *The Kinsey Institute New Report on Sex: What You Must Know to Be Sexually Literate*—were appalling.

Half believed that AIDS is transmitted by anal intercourse even when neither partner is infected with the virus. Half also did not know that oil-based lubricants (such as Vaseline) can cause condoms to disintegrate during sex. Only 18 percent believed that American women ever masturbate. And 50 percent did not know that a woman can become pregnant during menstruation. Forty percent could not say what the length of the average penis is.

"No wonder we have the highest teenage-pregnancy rate in the Western industrialized world," said the survey's designer, June Reinisch. "No wonder the rate of sexually transmitted diseases continues to grow. And no wonder the AIDS crisis has not abated."

September 23 The Liberace Museum in Las Vegas is reported to be the third-largest tourist attraction in Nevada (after casino gambling and Hoover Dam), drawing an estimated two hundred thousand visitors a year. Among the museum's most popular displays: the world's largest rhinestone (115,000 carats), a $750,000 floor-length mink cape, and a pair of red-white-and-blue sequined hot pants Liberace wore for the nation's Bicentennial celebration.

Supreme Court Justice David Souter. Once he was seated on the high court, his decisions generally fell right in line with the conservative majority.

September 27   The European Court of Human Rights at Strausbourg votes 10 to 8 that transsexuals have no right to change the sex listed on their birth certificates, and 14 to 4 that they have no right to marry. The ruling comes as a result of a legal appeal by British model Tula, who was seeking an end to British laws that persecute and discriminate against transsexuals.

October 1   "Are we the gay wing of the women's movement, or the women's wing of the gay movement?"
—*Lesbian activist* TORIE OSBORN, *neatly summarizing the dilemma faced by lesbians, who often feel disenfranchised by both*

October 2   David Souter is confirmed as the 105th justice of the U.S. Supreme Court.

October 5   Cincinnati Contemporary Arts Center director Dennis Barrie is acquitted on charges of obscenity and pandering, in relation to last spring's Robert Mapplethorpe exhibit. "The war on smut didn't start here," says one disgruntled anti-Mapplethorpe crusader, "and it won't end here."

October 9   Number of ads for phone jack-off services in the current *Advocate*: eighty-six. Number of similar ads in an issue in 1983: eighteen. In 1978: zero.

Meanwhile, the publication has changed its tag line from "The National Gay Newsmagazine" to "The National Gay and Lesbian Newsmagazine."

October 14   Legendary conductor and composer Leonard Bernstein, seventy-two, dies following a heart attack in New York City.

October 15   "If you should see grown men walking hand in hand, ignore it. They are not 'queer.' "
—*Advice from a U.S. government pamphlet on the Middle East, distributed to U.S. soldiers stationed in Saudi Arabia as part of Operation Desert Shield*

When the local St. Louis chapter of Parents and Friends of Lesbians and Gays tries to participate in the county's "Adopt-A-Roadway" project, highway commissioners panic and threaten to abolish the entire program rather than allow the group to participate. Objections center on the fact that, under the program, the organization's name would have to be printed on a prominently displayed highway sign marking the stretch of road it had "adopted." "What's next?" asks one indignant citizen. "Parents and Friends of Satanic Children?" Although commissioners debate the issue for weeks—and the PFLAG chapter itself is publicly compared to Nazis, the Ku Klux Klan, pornographers, dope pushers, and prostitutes—the St. Louis County Board of Highways and Traffic finally votes to allow the group's participation in the antilitter project.

October 17   In the midst of a heated—and protracted—congressional debate over the federal budget, Rep. Henry Hyde (R-Illinois) publicly insults Barney Frank for being a homosexual and suggests

that Frank has been too busy performing quickie sex acts in the
congressional gymnasium to fully understand what's going on in
Congress. Hyde later apologizes for the remark.

October 18   Having laughingly boasted that their bombs would
work like "a meat grinder making fag-burgers," three white supre-
macists are convicted in Boise, Idaho, of conspiring to blow up a
gay disco in Seattle.

Former Supreme Court justice Lewis Powell offers the unexpected
opinion that, looking back on it now, he "probably made a mistake"
when he cast the deciding vote in 1986 upholding the constitutionality of Georgia's sodomy laws. "When I had the opportunity to
reread the opinion a few months later," says Powell, "I thought
the dissent had the better of the argument."

"The justice's changing his mind after he leaves the court,"
notes one gay activist, "just doesn't do lesbians and gay men a hell
of a lot of good."

October 23   "We've all been very influenced by the gay scene. I
learned everything that I know about show biz from drag queens."
—KIRBY KIER, *lead singer of the group Dee-Lite ("What Is Love?")*

"I know how it feels to be a woman because I *am* a woman.
And I won't be classified as just a man."
—Rock legend PETE TOWNSHEND, *publicly acknowledging his bisexuality
for the first time in the fall of 1990*

October 24   The Smithsonian Institution accepts a small donation
of gay and lesbian artifacts for inclusion in its National Museum
of History collection. Among the items: posters, buttons, leaflets,
and bumper stickers from various gay rights campaigns. "I'm tickled," says Supervising Curator Keith Melder. "This way we have

a permanent piece of this movement's history." The collection will, however, be stored in a nonpublic area for the time being.

———————

Performance artist John Sex, thirty-four, dies of AIDS in New York City.

October 26   A gay Colorado Springs Army colonel is dismissed from the service and sentenced to nine months in Leavenworth Prison for having hugged and kissed another man in public and for having appeared in drag for an AIDS benefit at a local gay bar.

October 27   After thirty-eight years on the books, a federal law prohibiting gay and lesbian foreigners from entering the United States (on the grounds that "sexual deviation" is a mental illness) is repealed by Congress.

October 28   Placido Domingo, Itzhak Perlman, André Watts, and Jean-Pierre Rampal perform a benefit concert that raises $1.5 million dollars for the Gay Men's Health Crisis in New York.

October 30   Female impersonator Craig Russell dies of AIDS in Toronto at the age of forty-two.

November 1   In the nation's bookstores this month: *An American Life*, Ronald Reagan's 748-page political autobiography, most of it devoted to his eight-year term as President. Unlike his wife's memoir, the book does not mention the subject of AIDS even once.

———————

"Look, boys and girls, here come two guys named Charles and Martin and they're holding hands. Isn't it unusual to see two grown men holding hands, boys and girls? That's because Charles and Martin are homosexual men. . . . Can you say 'disgusting faggots'? Sure you can. Homosexuals are grown-ups who go into the bedroom and do things to each other. Things that would make a dog vomit. Have you ever seen a dog vomit, boys and girls? Wasn't it yukky? Well, the things homosexuals do to each other are even

more yukky than that. Can you say 'loathsome perversion'? Sure you can. . . . Pretty soon we'll go and visit Charlie and Martin in the AIDS hospice, and we can watch them rot. That'll be almost as yukky as that dog vomiting, won't it, boys and girls? And after they finish rotting, Charlie and Martin will croak. Ribbit, ribbit. Say goodbye Charlie, say goodbye Martin."
—*Recorded telephone message for schoolchildren, from the Ku Klux Klan in Kansas City, Missouri. Klansmen passed the phone number around local schoolyards and playgrounds and encouraged kids to call it for a "fun time." Another message at the same number targeted "nigger dope pushers."*

Popular rapper Chuck D. of the group Public Enemy denounces homosexuality as abnormal and morally wrong and defends the group's viciously antigay lyrics on the grounds that "love between men shouldn't involve sex." He also asserts that homosexuality is an anomaly in the black community, forced on blacks by bigoted whites eager to weaken and eradicate them.

November 6 Despite preelection polls that have showed him fighting for his political life against black Democratic challenger Harvey Gantt, Jesse Helms handily wins reelection to another six-year term in the U.S. Senate. Helms describes his victory as "God's will."

Meanwhile, in other elections:

■ Texas judge Jack "I don't care much for queers" Hampton is reelected to the Dallas judiciary.
■ Voters in San Francisco approve a "domestic partners" referendum (which goes into effect Valentine's Day 1991), while at the same time electing two openly lesbian women to the Board of Supervisors.
■ Barney Frank is returned to Congress with a 65 percent majority of the vote.
■ Boston University president John Silber—who once claimed that including gay rights protections in the university's charter "would permit all forms of perversion and sex with animals and children

and anything else"—is defeated in his bid to become governor of Massachusetts by moderate Republican William Weld.

■ San Francisco mayor Dianne Feinstein loses her bid to become California's first woman governor. Her victorious opponent is Republican Pete Wilson, who (many people note) seems to have spent an inordinate amount of time studying Ronald Reagan's head tics and voice intonations.

■ Deborah Glick is elected the first openly lesbian member of the New York State Legislature. She takes her oath of office two months later, with her left hand on a copy of *Sisterhood Is Powerful* instead of a Bible.

November 7   Gay activist and film commentator Vito Russo— accurately described by one friend as "one of the most beloved figures in the gay community"—dies of AIDS at the age of forty-four.

November 8   Mary Robinson—having run on a hitherto unimaginable platform that included support for both abortion and gay rights—is elected President of Ireland, the first woman head of state in Irish history. At the beginning of the campaign, oddsmakers gave Robinson a thousand-to-one chance of being elected.

November 12   "I've collected no less than seven ads that show a shirtless father holding a nude baby up to his chest or over his shoulder. It's become a visual cliché."
—*Madison Avenue ad man* TED LITTLEFORD *on the recent "daddy" boom in American advertising*

November 20   A London judge rules that sadomasochistic sex is a crime, even when the participants are consenting adults, and convicts fourteen gay men of having committed "criminal assaults on themselves" for participating in various masochistic activities— including spanking and mild genital torture—at one of the men's homes. The fourteen are later sentenced to prison.

November 26   *Newsweek* reports a staggering increase in silicon body enhancement—once almost exclusively the province of women—among men who feel humiliated by the size and shape of their pectorals. Other recent notable advancements in plastic surgery for men: liposuction for love handles ($4,000), buttock implants to perk up a flat rear end ($6,500), calf implants to beef up the legs ($5,500), and liposuction on the upper neck to obtain that "firm-jawed" look ($2,500).

December 1   "If you go out and say 'Women are bitches' and 'Let's kill gay people,' you're considered controversial, on the edge. I don't hear those comics really being on the edge about anything. All they're doing is saying something to a group of people who agree with them. It's just baiting a crowd."
—JAY LENO, *on the comedy styles of Eddie Murphy and Andrew Dice Clay*

December 5   MTV, whose popularity during the last decade has rested almost entirely on its ability to give adolescents an endless stream of "soft-core" rock videos featuring female models in black lace underwear and shirtless muscle boys in tight jeans, bans Madonna's latest video, *Justify My Love*, on the grounds that it contains scenes of simulated masturbation, S&M, voyeurism, and bisexuality—all the things MTV viewers have thought they've been getting from the network for years. Complains Madonna, "Why is it that people are willing to go to a movie and watch someone get blown to bits for no reason and nobody wants to see two girls kissing or two men snuggling?" It turns out that *lots* of people want to see the banned five-minute video clip when it goes on sale just in time for Christmas, at $9.99, in music stores across the country.

"I wouldn't have turned out the way I was if I didn't have all those old-fashioned values to rebel against."

—MADONNA

December 7 The opening of a rural AIDS clinic in Oxford, Alabama (population nine thousand), results in threats of violence against the staff and clients. "I have no compassion for homosexuals," says the town's mayor, who is leading a campaign to have the clinic moved somewhere else. One neighbor tells the press he doesn't want his children to "see sick people, AIDS patients, up and down the street here." Another man, who lives across the street from the clinic, says that he and his wife plan to sit on their front porch all day staring at the people going in and out, just to show how much they can't stand them.

     Although some recent estimates show rural cases of the disease increasing at about 37 percent a year, the clinic is one of only five of its kind in rural America.

December 8 Hollywood producer Jerry Wheeler—who struggled for years unsuccessfully to get *The Front Runner* made into a motion picture—dies of AIDS. He was forty-four.

December 14 Arsenio Hall gets into a shouting match with two gay hecklers during a taping of *The Arsenio Hall Show* in Los Angeles. After the two criticize him for not having more gay guests on the show, Hall yells back, "There are a lot of gay guests on this show, but it's none of your damn business that they are gay!" Hall—who has himself been the object of several recent "outings"—becomes even more defensive when he's criticized for regularly making homophobic jokes during his opening monologue. "I do black jokes. I do gay jokes," he responds testily. "I'm a *comedian*."

December 15 Several newspapers report on the growing popularity of a new fashion accessory: "Safe Ears," clip-on earrings made of gold-foil-wrapped condoms. "It's difficult and ironic," notes one columnist, "that we are celebrating a new kicky accessory whose height of popularity is almost solely due to a fatal plague."

———

On the video shelf: *How the West Was Hung*—"Bobby Robinson, Eldon Singer and Jon are just a few of the cow pokes who drop

their drawers and shoot their pistols in this double barreled western!"

December 18   Dr. Stanley Biber, internationally renowned for performing 60 percent of the world's sex-change operations at his hospital in Trinidad, Colorado, handily wins election to Trinidad's city council despite virtiolic opposition from evangelical Christians and others who labeled him "immoral," "tainted," and "a monster" for his surgical practice.

December 19   Pat Robertson calls homosexuality "an unbelievable abomination . . . the worst sin of the Bible," and predicts that "it may even soon be against the law to publicly criticize it."

December 21   According to a recently released MTV poll, 92 percent of the country's album-buying teenagers say it would make no difference to them if they found out their favorite rock star was gay or lesbian.

December 24   Openly lesbian actress Pat Bond, sixty-five, dies of lung cancer. Bond was best known for her memorable appearance in the 1978 documentary *Word Is Out* and for her various one-woman shows, including the critically acclaimed *Conversations with Pat Bond* and *Gerty Gerty Stein Is Back Back Back*.

December 30   *Entertainment Tonight* announces that the much-ballyhooed hairless-chest look for men has fizzled out and isn't going to be much of a fad this year after all.

December 31   John Travolta proposes to starlet Kelly Preston while the two are vacationing at the Palace Hotel in Gstaad, Switzerland. According to *People* magazine, Preston "screamed" when Travolta first "popped the question." Although she reportedly accepted, no wedding date is initially set. The two finally marry in the fall of 1991.

British actor and gay activist Ian McKellen is knighted by Queen Elizabeth II.

People magazine reports that its April 23 cover story on the death of Ryan White drew the most reader mail—more than one thousand letters—of any story all year.

In the same issue, AIDS researcher Dr. Anthony Fauci is chosen as one of the "25 Most Intriguing People of 1990."

The growing impact of AIDS on the American heartland is evidenced when the normally conservative *Farm Journal*—an agricultural magazine that usually restricts itself to articles on quackgrass control and fertilizer efficacy—does a sympathetic and informative cover story, "AIDS Invades Rural America." The article notes that, along with the growing number of cases diagnosed in small towns across the country, many people with AIDS (including some gay men) are abandoning the big cities and returning to family farms in rural areas for emotional support and comfort.

The Centers for Disease Control reports that the U.S. death toll from AIDS has just topped the 100,000 mark, with 100,777 deaths from the disease as of late December. There are now approximately 1,100 AIDS deaths in the United States per week.

INDEX

Abzug, Bella, 19, 28, 67
Academy Awards, 18, 38, 44, 137, 187, 238, 254, 311, 336; streaking of ceremony, 65
Accu-Jac masturbation devices, 80
ACT UP (AIDS Coalition to Unleash Power), 271, 312, 321, 347
Ads, gay personal, 36, 74–75, 336
Advertising, male imagery in, 11, 154, 235, 345, 362
Advocate, The, 7, 8, 18, 25, 26, 68, 75, 81, 85, 91, 94, 96, 98, 100, 109, 110, 114, 133, 144, 154, 159, 169, 179, 189, 202, 208, 214, 217, 223, 230, 242, 266, 269, 283, 300, 304, 327, 342, 358
Advocate Men, 221
Aerosmith, 288
Aesthetic Realism, 34
AFL-CIO, 214
After Dark (magazine), 11, 32, 49, 52, 63, 77, 81, 193
Age of Consent (album), 236
Agnos, Art, 298
AIDS, 183, 190, 195, 203, 205, 206, 207, 208–10, 213–14, 218, 219, 221, 230, 237 passim; deaths from, 211,

213–14, 231, 239, 248, 256, 260, 262, 263, 265–66, 267, 269, 273–74, 275, 276, 278, 279, 280, 281, 294, 297–98, 301, 304, 307, 310, 311, 316, 317, 320, 329, 333, 334, 336, 339–40, 346, 348–49, 360, 362, 364; demonstrations, 271, 303, 309, 312, 314, 320, 328, 337, 347; early reports of, 173, 176; education, 210, 221, 263, 280–81, 299–300, 320, 323; and film industry, 246, 251, 271, 272, 343–44; jokes, 214, 245, 258; and news media, 193, 195, 200, 207, 208, 288; prejudice surrounding, 230, 242–43, 247, 273, 278, 288, 297–98, 327, 345, 355, 364; presidential candidates on, 276–77, 291–92, 299–300; and prison system, 270, 275, 288, 295, 309; in Soviet Union, 288, 310, 339; virus discovered, 221
AIDS and Its Metaphors (Sontag), 308
AIDS: A Public Inquiry (TV documentary), 262
Ailes, Roger, 324
Air Force, U.S., 82, 157, 334
Air Music (musical composition), 93

Alabama, 316, 364
Alabama, University of, 64
Alexander: The Other Side of Dawn (TV movie), 106
Alexandra, Princess of England, 240
All Good Women (Miner), 306
Alliance for Gay Artists, 187
All in the Family (TV series), 82
Allison, Dorothy, 314
Allred, Gloria, 202
Almendros, Nestor, 222, 227
Alpine County, Calif., 13
Alyson, Sasha, 152
Alyson Publications, 152, 198
Amburgy, Victor, 242
American Association for the Advancement of Science, 75
American Bar Association, 22, 58, 212, 243, 309
American Civil Liberties Union (ACLU), 108, 176, 298, 330
American Family, An (TV series), 53
American Gigolo (film), 147
American Journal of Psychiatry, The, 129, 161
American Life, An (Reagan), 360
American Medical Association, 81
American Medical Foundation for AIDS Research (AMFAR), 205
American Psychiatric Association, 61
American Sociological Association, 7
Amyl nitrite ("poppers"), 118, 129, 186, 263, 349
Anal Pleasure and Health (Morin), 186
Anchorage, AK., 89
Anderson, John, 151
And Puppy Dog Tails (play), 14
Andrews, Julie, 187
Andrzejewski, Julie, 314
And the Band Played On (Shilts), 288, 305, 306
Andy Warhol Diaries, The, 315
Anita Bryant's Spectacular (TV special), 150
Ann Arbor, Mich., 47
Annie Hall (film), 104
Ansen, David, 155
Answered Prayers (Capote), 228
Appledorf, Howard, 195
Apuzzo, Virginia, 197, 231
Are You Running With Me, Jesus? (Boyd), 97
Arizona, 73, 78, 278, 283, 291

Arkansas, 102
Army, U.S., 127, 360
Arsenio Hall Show, The (TV show), 349, 364
Arzner, Dorothy, 143
Ashley, Elizabeth, 147
As Is (play), 237
Askew, Reubin, 105, 108
Aspen, Colo., 116
Asses (Houston), 124
Association for the Advancement of Behavioral Therapy, 51
Atascadero State Hospital, 37
Atlas Savings and Loan Co., 155, 259
Auden, W. H., 6, 59
Austen, Roger, 105, 225
Austin, Sam, 307
Austin, TX, 184, 267, 312
Australia, 127
Austria, 38
Avedon, Barbara, 188
Aversion therapy, 37, 51
Axthelm, Pete, 168
AZT, 282, 288, 300, 321

Babbitt, Bruce, 276
Babbitt, R. James, 310
Bachardy, Don, 253
Baden-Powell, Lord, 335
Bader, Bill, 211
"Bad Girls" (song), 137
Baez, Joan, 51, 67
Bakker, Rev. Jim, 152, 272, 274, 324
Bakker, Tammy Faye, 274, 324
Baldwin, James, 256, 289
Baldwin, Roger, 176, 220
Ball, Lucille, 148
Bancroft, Ann, 255
Bannon, Ann, 203
Barber, Samuel, 164
Barnes, Djuna, 192
Barnet, Mary Angela, 18
Barnett, Marilyn, 59, 167, 198
Barney, Natalie Clifford, 29, 43, 129, 192
Barone, Phil, 265
Barresi, Paul, 343
Barrett, Ellen Marie, 100
Barrie, Dennis, 337, 354
Barry, Stephen, 263
Bars, gay, 26, 40, 66, 101, 157, 250–51, 281, 321; raids on, 1–2, 16, 196, 289
Bassey, Shirley, 38

Bathhouses, 8, 91, 93, 117, 178, 209–10, 220, 248, 273. *See also* Continental baths, Everard baths
Bauman, Robert, 158, 211, 260, 266
Beaton, Cecil, 147
Beatty, Warren, 329
Beauty Queen, The (Warren), 65
Beauvoir, Simone de, 119
Beaux Arts Ball, 151
Beefcake, national interest in, 49, 50, 55, 60, 90, 123, 134, 160, 192, 197, 205, 210, 213, 214, 221, 230, 235, 245, 256, 264–65, 282, 290, 292, 362–63, 365
Behind the Green Door—The Sequel (film), 261
Behind the Mask (Pallone), 350
Belew, Judith, 20
Bell, Alan, 186
Bell, Andy, 354
Bell, Arthur, 19, 67, 122, 141, 222
Bennett, Michael, 80, 92, 275
Bent (play), 144
Berenson, Marisa, 44, 58
Berger, Helmut, 12
Berkeley, Bud, 94
Berkeley, CA, 232
Berle, Milton, 155, 329
Bernhard, Sandra, 314, 338, 354–55
Bernstein, Leonard, 358
Bette: The Life of Bette Davis (Higham), 180
Beyond the Valley of the Dolls (film), 24
Biber, Dr. Stanley, 365
Billings, Robert, 164
"Bisexual Chic," 67
Bjorn, Kristen, 250
Black and White Men Together, 199
Blackbird (Duplechan), 266
Black Panthers, 23
Blacks, discrimination against by other gays, 101, 189, 199
Blackwell, Earl, 88
Blake, Amanda, 320
Bloodworth-Thomason, Linda, 265
Blueboy Forum (TV show), 102
Blueboy magazine, 81, 94, 96, 103, 105, 121, 177
Bodybuilding craze, 71–72, 171
Body Politic, The (newspaper), 117, 191, 269
Bond, Pat, 365
"Boogie Woogie Bugle Boy" (song), 56

Bookstores, gay, 68, 237, 243
Boozer, Mel, 156
Bork, Robert, 227, 277
Born in the USA (album), 222
Born to Raise Hell (film), 92
Borrowed Time (Monette), 314
Bosom Buddies (TV series), 161
Boswell, John, 156, 170
Bowie, David, 32, 50, 57, 76, 206
Boxleitner, Bruce, 245
Boyd, Rev. Malcolm, 97, 123, 266
Boy George, 219, 220, 228, 258, 266
Boy-Man, The (Jeal), 335
Boy Scouts, 335
Boys in the Band, The (film), 3–4, 16, 32, 122, 301
Boys in the Band, The (play), 3, 14, 24, 32, 90, 122, 151, 301
Boys in the Sand (film), 43, 52
Boys of San Francisco, The (film), 192
Boy's Own Story, A (White), 196
Bradley, Tom, 91
Brando, Marlon, 89, 329
Bremen, Barry, 145
Bremer, Arthur H., 51
Brennan, William, 351
Bressan, Arthur, 239, 280
Bridges, Jeff, 105, 230
Briggs, John, 120, 126, 128
Briggs Initiative, 120, 124
Britt, Harry, 133, 210
Britten, Benjamin, 70, 94, 99, 255
Bronski, Michael, 232, 319
Bronski Beat, 236
Brooks, Mel, 216
Brooks, Romaine, 29
Broshears, Rev. Ray, 58
Brothers (TV series), 224
Brothers Should Do It (film), 202
Brown, Helen Gurley, 184
Brown, Dr. Howard J., 60
Brown, Jerry, 142, 176, 182
Brown, Rita Mae, 66, 92, 195
Brownell, John, 346
Brownmiller, Susan, 29
Bryant, Anita, 15, 65, 82, 100, 101, 103, 108, 109, 110, 111, 114, 117, 119, 125, 126, 150, 153, 161, 169, 211, 244
Buchanan, Patrick, 235
Buck, Ed, 278
Buckley, William F., Jr., 6
Bundy, Ted, 308

Bunell, David, 264
Burger, Warren, 219, 238, 262
Burke, Glenn, 197
Burke, Paul, 25
Burnett, Carol, 92, 172
Burroughs, William S., 306
Burton, Richard, 5
Bush, Barbara, 314, 340, 342, 343
Bush, George, 199, 249, 276, 292, 300, 304, 324, 337, 341, 347, 351
Butch Cassidy and the Sundance Kid (film), 90
Butrick, Merritt, 311

Cabaret (film), 44
Cadmus, Paul, 187
Cagney & Lacey (TV series), 188
Caine, Michael, 137, 273
Califia, Pat, 223, 302
California, 78, 96, 98, 119, 153, 219, 231, 327; Department of Motor Vehicles, 45; Proposition 6, 124, 126, 128, 129
California Suite, 137
Callas, Maria, 112
Cameron, Paul, 190–91
Camille (play), 56
Canada, 122, 125
Canby, Vincent, 343
Can't Stop the Music (film), 144, 154, 155
Capote, Truman, 14, 104, 228, 345
Carr, Allan, 144, 311
Carrera, Dr. Michael, 299
Carroll, Diahann, 246
Carson, Joanna, 228, 304, 346
Carson, Johnny, 12
Carswell, G. Harold, 94
Carter, Jimmy, 89, 90, 94, 98, 101, 103, 119, 120, 125, 147, 149, 156, 159, 164, 169, 219
Carter, Lillian, 125, 236
Carvey, Dana, 273
Casey, Warren, 304
Castro, Fidel, 223, 227
Catholic church, 4, 22, 88, 91, 120, 283, 328, 354
Caulfield, Maxwell, 191
Ceausescu, Nicolae, 333
Celluloid Closet, The (Russo), 175
Census Bureau, 180
"Chains of Love" (song), 354
Chambers, Jane, 203

Changing Homosexuality in the Male (Hatterer), 32
Channell, Carl "Spitz," 342
Chanticleer's Carol, The (musical composition), 181
Chapman, Graham, 323
Charen, Mona, 347
Charles, Prince of Wales, 263
Charleson, Ian, 329
Chataway, Mark, 210
Cheever, John, 107, 226
Cheever, Susan, 226
Cher, 218
Chicago: Board of Education, 73; City Council, 260, 265, 310
Child custody, gay-related cases, 86, 98, 130, 140, 172, 196
Children: adoption, 107, 108, 140, 299, 351; of lesbians, 95
China, 332
Chong, Rae Dawn, 271
Chorus Line, A (musical), 80, 92, 93, 152, 275
Christian, Marc, 215, 309–10, 330
Christian Broadcasting Network, 152, 320
Christianity, Social Tolerance, and Homosexuality (Boswell), 156
Christine Jorgensen Story, The (film), 112
Christopher Street (magazine), 92, 140, 153, 157, 161, 180, 186, 198
Chrome (Nader), 123
Chuck D., 361
Chung, Connie, 355
CIA, 100
Cincinnati, 337, 340, 342, 357
Civil Rights Act (1964), 67
Civil rights protections for gay men and lesbians, 58, 66, 69, 77, 88, 116, 117. *See also* Legislation
Claiborne, Craig, 195
Clancy, Tom, 345
Clark, Karen, 232
Clarke, Arthur C., 121, 258
Clay, Andrew Dice, 344, 350, 363
Cleaver, Eldridge, 23
Cleopatra Jones (film), 57
Cline, Philip Bruce, 165
Coalition for Better Television, 171
Cockettes, The, 14, 158
Cohen, Alexander, 59
Cohn, Roy, 66, 104, 134, 166, 259
Coleman, Jack, 253

Colombia, 24
Colorado, 47, 78
Color Purple, The (Walker), 208
Combs, Frederick, 32
Coming out, 31, 43, 60, 82, 85, 97, 129, 192, 207–08
Common Threads (film), 336
Concentration camps, memorial to gay victims of, 240
Condoms, 310, 322, 346
Conference on Homophobia Education, 295
Connecticut, 38
Consenting Adult (Hobson), 82
Consenting Adult (TV movie), 235
Constanza, Midge, 101
Contemporary Arts Center, Cincinnati, 336, 342, 357
Continental Baths, 12, 29, 45, 64, 289
Coors, Joseph, 109
Coors Beer Company, 109
Copland, Aaron, 229
Corcoran Gallery, 315–16, 320
Corday, Barbara, 188
Corey, Al, 163
Corona, Juan, 35
Cosmetics, for men, 66
Cosmopolitan, 55, 148, 184, 234, 323
Court, Margaret, 174
Coward, Noël, 55
Craig, Roger, 345
Crane, Daniel, 193
Cranston, Alan, 91
Crawford, Joan, 177, 180
Crisp, Quentin, 113, 235, 318, 345
Cronkite, Walter, 61
Crowley, Mart, 3, 151
Cruise, Tom, 212, 225, 256
Cruising (film), 141, 142, 148, 150
Cruising (Walker), 54
Cruse, Howard, 202
Crystal, Billy, 112
Cuba
  gay refugees from, 151
  repression of gays in, 223, 227
Cukor, George, 202
Culture Clash (Bronski), 232
Culture Club, 203, 255
Cuomo, Mario, 248
Curry, Tim, 70
Curzon, Daniel, 260
Cycle Sluts, 70

"Da Butt" (dance), 294
"Daddy" craze, 161, 362
Dade County gay rights ordinance, 108, 119, 122, 124
Dallas Cowboy Cheerleaders, 145
Dallesandra, Joe, 27, 55
Daly, James, 126
Daly, Tyne, 189
D'Amato, Alfonse, 313
Damned, The (film), 12
Damron, Bob, 316
Dancer From the Dance (Holleran), 128
Dancing in the Dark (video), 222
Daniels, Luke, 192
Dannemeyer, William E., 129, 191, 351
Darling, Candy, 65
Daughters of Bilitis, 28, 205
Dave Kopay Story, The (Kopay), 85
David Susskind Show, The, 34
Davis, Bette, 324
Davis, Brad, 205
Davis, Ed, 80, 238
Davis, Sammy, Jr., 246
Davison, Bruce, 343
Dawes, Johnny (Brian Lee), 239, 317
Ddi (dideoxyinosine), 322
Dear Abby, 22
Death in Venice (film), 35
Death in Venice (opera), 70
Decker, Bruce, 230
"Declaration on Certain Questions Concerning Sexual Ethics" (Vatican), 87
Dee-Lite, 359
Defense Department, 4, 290
Delaware, 47
Democratic National Convention: of 1972, 45; of 1976, 156; of 1984, 205
Democratic Party, 154
Denmark, 322
Dennis, Patrick, 98
De Palma, Brian, 222
Derek, John, 329
Der Ring Gott Farblonjet (play), 56
Destro, Robert, 207
Detour (Crane), 306
Deukmejian, George, 219
Deveau, Jack, 199
Diaghilev, Serge, 267
Diamond, David, 225
Dick Cavett Show, The (TV series), 29
Different Story, A (film), 126
Dignity, 216
Dillon, Matt, 213, 229

Dinkins, David, 328, 332
Disco, 66, 72, 81, 84, 98, 101, 104, 112,
    117, 123, 127, 128, 130, 131, 133,
    134, 137, 141, 148, 157, 350
Disco (Goldman), 131
"Disco Duck" (song), 98
Diseases, gastrointestinal, 96
Diseases, venereal, 69, 96, 256, 300–01
Disneyland "Gay Night," 123
Diversions and Delights (one-man show),
    110
Divine, 176, 207, 293
Dixon, Jeane, 338
Dog Day Afternoon (film), 48
Dolan, Anthony, 274
Dolan, Terry, 267, 274, 342
Dole, Robert, 292
Dollar bills, stamping of, 266
Domestic partners law, 200, 232, 361
Domingo, Placido, 360
Donahue, Phil, 115, 122, 197, 236
Donaldson, Herb, 182
Donovan, Casey, 43, 52, 189, 281
"Don't Leave Me This Way" (song), 101
Doonesbury (comic strip), 88, 316
Dornan, Robert K., 98, 302
Dornan, Sallie, 302
Dorsen, Norman, 108
Downey, Morton, Jr., 287, 289, 297, 303
Downey, Tony, 297
"Do You Really Want to Hurt Me?"
    (song), 203
Drag, 24, 28, 34–36, 56, 57, 64, 155,
    172–74, 189, 200, 207, 218, 238,
    247, 251, 309, 326, 354, 360
Driesell, Lefty, 85
Drummer (magazine), 89, 96, 105, 137,
    161
Dublin, Ireland, 204
"Dude (Looks Like a Lady)" (song), 288
Dukakis, Michael, 298, 304, 324
Dukes, David, 144
Dunaway, Faye, 177
DungeonMaster (magazine), 332
Dunn, Nora, 344
Duplechan, Larry, 266
Durst, Will, 293
Dynasty (TV series), 163, 183, 219, 253,
    257, 313

Eagleton, Thomas, 159
Earl, Roger, 92
Early Frost, An (TV movie), 251

Early Graves (Hansen), 305
Earrings, for men, 211
Ebert, Roger, 24, 272
Ebony (magazine), 167
Edwards, Blake, 187
Eld, "Big" Bill, 236
Elfin, Mel, 199
Elizabeth II, Queen of England, 94, 194,
    366
Ellis, Perry, 256
El Paso Wrecking Co. (film), 312
Embinder, Donald, 81, 94, 177
Enemy Mine (film), 226
Episcopal Church, 100
Epstein, Joseph, 24
Epstein, Robert, 233, 336
Equal Rights Amendment, 46, 184, 193
Errol Flynn: The Untold Story (Higham),
    158
Eugene, OR, 123
Eurythmics, 210, 223
Evans, Linda, 246
Evening with Quentin Crisp, An (one-man
    show), 113
Everard Baths, 106
Evert Lloyd, Chris, 173
*Everything You Always Wanted to Know
    About Sex, But Were Afraid to Ask*
    (Reuben), 11
Executive Suite (TV show), 97, 101
Exon, James, 106

Faggots (Kramer), 129
Fain, Nathan, 136
Falconer (Cheever), 107
Falwell, Jerry, 107, 140, 146, 152, 173,
    179, 186, 190, 197, 198, 208, 215,
    220, 224, 227, 228, 232, 237–38,
    249, 252, 262, 315
Family Circle (magazine), 12
Family Protection Act, 171
Family Research Institute, 190
Fancy Dancer, The (Warren), 65
Farm Journal, 366
Fashion trends, among gay men, 17, 22,
    70, 82, 137, 156, 170, 194, 206
Fassbinder, Rainer Werner, 142, 191,
    205
Fatal Attraction (film), 271, 284
Fauci, Dr. Anthony, 366
FDA, 236, 303, 322
Feast for Laughter, A (Claiborne), 195
Fe-Be's bar, 26

Federal Bureau of Investigation (FBI), 46, 94, 205, 311
Feinstein, Dianne, 133, 200, 362
Feinstein, Michael, 273
Female Trouble (film), 77
Feminism, 28, 30, 58, 85, 180, 357
Ferraro, Geraldine, 224
Fierstein, Harvey, 34, 207, 222, 286, 298–99, 306
Finch, Peter, 38
Finland, 169
Fire Island, 48, 154
Fisk, Dick, 215
Flamingos, pink, 275
Flanner, Janet, 129
"Fleet's In, The" (painting), 187
Fleming, Art, 116
Flesh (film), 57
Florida, 60, 98, 173, 354
Florida, University of, 169
Flowers, Wayland, 303
Flynn, Errol, 158, 180
Flynn, Ray, 224
Flynt, Larry, 215, 232
"Fly, Robin, Fly" (song), 84
Foley, Thomas, 315
Football, 30, 85, 176, 262
Forbes, Malcolm, 335
Forbes (magazine), 292
Ford, Betty, 246
Ford, Gerald, 89, 97, 98
Foreskin (Berkeley), 94
Forster, E. M., 20, 28, 39, 273
Forth Into Light (Merrick), 19
Fortune and Men's Eyes (play), 14
Foster, Dr. Jeanette Howard, 174
Foster, Meg, 189
Fox and His Friends (film), 142
France, 33
Frank, Barney, 159, 274, 315, 351, 358, 361
Frankie Goes to Hollywood, 232
Freedoms Foundation, 15
Frenn, George, 21
Frey, Leonard, 301
Fricke, Aaron, 153
Friedan, Betty, 55
Friedkin, William, 16, 141, 142, 148, 149
Friedman-Kien, Dr. Alvin, 173
Fritscher, Jack, 338
From Luxury to Heartache (album), 255
Front Runner, The (film), 231, 269, 282, 364

Front Runner, The (Warren), 65, 78
Funeral Games (Renault), 186

Gaard, David, 14
Gabor, Zsa Zsa, 6, 322
Gacy, John Wayne, 131, 149, 197
Galas, Diamanda, 317
Games and novelties, gay-oriented, 98, 105, 111, 128
Gantt, Harvey, 361
Garbo, Greta, 340
Garland, Judy, 1, 2
Gates, Phyllis, 330
Gay Activists Alliance, 19, 24, 138; "Firehouse," 34, 70
Gay American Arts Festival, 153
Gay American History (Katz), 111
Gay Atheists League of America, 198
"Gay Bob" (doll), 128
Gay Deceivers, The (film), 5
Gay Erotic Film Awards, 239
Gay Games, 21, 195, 261, 280, 353
Gay Insider USA, The (Hunter), 50
Gay Liberation Front, 9–10, 205
Gay liberation movement, 23, 29, 48, 58, 60
"Gay Liberation" (sculpture), 219
Gaylord, Mitch, 226
Gay Men's Health Crisis, Inc., 183, 206, 360
Gay News, 48, 109, 205
Gaynor, Gloria, 72, 133
Gay Power, Gay Politics (TV documentary), 151
Gay Power (newspaper), 7
Gay Pravda, 353
Gay Priest (Boyd), 97, 266
Gay Spirit (Thompson), 305
Gaysweek (magazine), 126
Gearhart, Sally, 180
"Gender-fuck" look, 14, 70
General Motors, 355
Genet, Jean, 205, 255
Gentleman from Maryland, The (Bauman), 260, 266
Gentlemen's Quarterly, 329
Georgetown University, 294
Georgia, 241, 255, 264, 265, 359
Gephardt, Richard, 277
Gerber, David, 170
Gere, Richard, 144, 147, 342
Gernreich, Rudi, 239
Giamatti, A. Bartlett, 198–99

Gielgud, Sir John, 119
Gilliatt, Penelope, 38
Gingrich, Newt, 211, 351
Ginsberg, Allen, 3
Giteck, Lenny, 171
Glamour (magazine), 318
Gleason, Jackie, 16
Glenn, John, 215, 345
Gless, Sharon, 189
Glick, Deborah, 362
Gobie, Steven, 351
Gold, Ronald, 60
Goldberg, Whoopi, 286
Goldenboy (Nava), 314
Golden Boys of the S.S. (film), 282
Goldman, Albert, 131
Goldschmidt, Neil, 114, 305
Goldstein, 64, 68
Goldwater, Barry, 173
Good Housekeeping, 119
Goodman, Paul, 92
Goodman, Paulette, 343
Gorbachev, Raisa, 289, 325
Gore, Albert, 276
Graham, Billy, 26, 81
Graham, Bob, 173
Grahn, Judy, 306
Grammy awards, 218
Gravedigger (Hansen), 186
Graves, Rupert, 273
Grease 2 (film), 191
Great Britain, 8, 21, 57; Clause 28, 296
Greece, 353
Green, Bob, 108, 153
Green, Richard, 267
Green, William, 194
Greene, Johnny, 243, 336
Greer, Germaine, 42, 306
Grier, Barbara, 242
Guccione, Bob, 213
Gulley, Wib, 260
Gurganus, Allan, 71

Haake, James, 216
Haber, Jack, 231
Hahn, Jessica, 272
Hairspray, 293
Hairstylists, 22
Hall, Arsenio, 322, 364
Hall, Richard, 173
Halsted, Fred, 78, 312
Halston, 104, 336
Hamilton, George, 174

Hamlin, Harry, 185, 186
Hampton, Jack, 327, 361
Hanks, Tom, 161
Hansen, Joseph, 186, 305
Harden, Johnny, 156
Hardwick, Michael, 194, 257
Hargis, Billy James, 88
Haring, Keith, 334
Harper's magazine sit-in, 24
Harris, Bertha, 118
Harris, George ("Hibiscus"), 158
Harrison, Rex, 5
Hart, Sam, 185
Hart to Hart (TV series), 151
Hartwig, Clayton, 312, 321, 345
Harvey Milk School, 239
Hatch, Orrin, 301, 333, 334
Hate Crimes Statistics Act (1990), 333
Hatterer, Lawrence, 33
Hauser, Rita, 22
Hawaii, 47
Hawn, Goldie, 172
Hearst, Patty, 83
Heckler, Margaret, 221, 239
Heckman, Neva Joy, 20
Helms, Jesse, 52, 159, 173, 291, 300,
      317, 330–31, 347, 350, 361
Hepatitis B, 300
Herberg, Will, 8
Herek, Gregory, 318
Herskovitz, Marshall, 326
Hexum, Jon-Erik, 205
Hickok, Lorena, 143, 144
Higgins, Colin, 299
Higgins, William, 192
Higham, Charles, 158, 180
Hijackings, 114
Hill, Benny, 189
Hinson, Jon, 165
Hintnaus, Tom, 197
"Hippies", 10, 40
Hippler, Mike, 314
HIV test, 236, 275, 341
Hobson, Laura, 82, 235
Hocquenghem, Guy, 301
Hoffman, Abbie, 10
Hoffman, Dustin, 199
Hoffman, William, 237
Holleran, Andrew, 64, 128, 198
Holmes, John, 294
Home Before Dark (Cheever), 226
Homosexual Handbook (d'Arcangelo), 40
Homosexuality: as addiction, 218;

blamed on automobile accident, 88; blamed on pornography, 33; causes, 33, 42, 142, 187, 215, 218, 267; "cures," 33, 34, 36–37, 51, 139, 161; as disease, 22, 61; Landers on, 215; as psychiatric disorder, 61
Homosexuality in Perspective (Masters and Johnson), 138
Homosexual Matrix, The (Tripp), 83
Homosexual "types," 8–9
Hong Kong, 349
Hooker, Dr. Evelyn, 8
Hoover, J. Edgar, 46–47
Hope, Bob, 258
Horton, Edward Everett, 25
Horton, Peter, 326
Hot l Baltimore (TV series), 74
"Hot Stuff" (song), 137
Houston, Thelma, 101
Houston, TX, 235
Hudson, Rock, 215, 221, 243, 244, 245, 248, 254, 257, 309, 326, 329–30
Hughes, Howard, 158
Humphrey, Hubert, 88
Hunter, John Francis, 50
Hunter, Tab, 176
Hurt, John, 113, 190
Hurt, William, 230, 254
"Hustle, The" (song), 66
Hustler (magazine), 161, 215, 232
Hyde, Henry, 358
Hyde, H. Montgomery, 21

"I Am What I Am" (song), 219
Ianucci, Robert, 154
"I Feel Love" (song), 112
Illinois, 38
"I'll Tumble 4 Ya" (song), 203
Immigration, gay problems with, 33, 97, 168, 174, 193, 247, 360
Improper Conduct (film), 223, 227
Internal Affairs (film), 342
Internal Revenue Service, 73, 285
International Football Federation, 176
International Times, 36
"In the Navy" (song), 136
In Touch (magazine), 60, 229, 240
Iowa, U.S.S., 312, 321, 345
Iran, 136
Ireland, 362
Isherwood, Christopher, 6, 44, 253
Israel, 294
Italy, 113

It's Still My Turn (Sweeney), 355
"I Want Your Sex" (song), 275
"I Will Survive" (song), 133

Jackson, Henry "Scoop," 61, 90
Jackson, Jesse, 214, 277, 286, 340
Jackson, Michael, 23, 218, 228, 232
Jackson, Rod, 316
Jacobs, Paul, 213
Jacobson, Robert, 273
Jagger, Bianca, 317
Jagger, Mick, 10, 67, 211
James, Marty, 294
Jarmin, Gary, 249
Jeal, Tim, 335
Jennings, Peter, 287
Jepsen, Roger, 171–72
Jockstrap ads, 70
Joffrey, Robert, 294
John, Elton, 23, 51, 64, 66, 76, 84, 88, 98, 218, 284, 302, 340
John Paul II, Pope, 283
Johnston, Jill, 85
Jones, Bob, 149
Jones, Cleve, 287
Jones, Grace, 161
Jones, Randy, 144
Jong, Erica, 235, 257
Joplin, Janis, 27
Jordan, Barbara, 91
Jorgensen, Christine, 112, 312
Journal of Homosexuality, 57
"Journal of the Plague Year" (Holleran), 198
Joy of Gay Sex, The (Silverstein and White), 117, 125
Joy of Lesbian Sex, The (Sisley and Harris), 117
Judges, gay, 152, 176, 182
Justice Department, 10, 266, 285, 291, 339, 342
"Justify My Love" (song), 363

Kael, Pauline, 13, 187
Kathleen and Frank: The Autobiography of A Family (Isherwood), 43
Katz, Jonathan, 111
K. C. & The Sunshine Band, 84
Keating, Charles, 26
Kellogg, Stuart, 319
Kemp, Jack, 251, 253, 276, 278
Kesey, Ken, 256
Key West, FL, 134, 320

KGB, 31, 155
Khomeini, Ayatollah, 136
Kier, Kirby, 359
"Killing of Georgie, The" (song), 110
Killing of Sister George, The (film), 24
Kimball, Spencer W., 110
King, Billie Jean, 36, 59, 141, 167, 168, 170, 173, 199
King, Coretta Scott, 213
King, Jon, 202
King, J.W., 163, 202, 214, 266
King, Larry, 167
King, Martin Luther, 3d, 334
King, Perry, 126
Kinks, The, 25
Kinney, Nan, 246
Kinsey Institute New Report on Sex, 356
Kirk, Paul, Jr., 239
Kirkup, James, 109
Kirkwood, James, 189
Kissinger, Henry, 54
Kissing To Be Clever (album), 203
Kiss of the Spider Woman (film), 254
Kiss of the Spider Woman (musical), 304
Klein, Calvin, 154, 197, 282, 317, 345
Kloss, David, 139
Knight, Gladys, 284
Koch, Edward, 67, 116, 120, 196, 251, 254, 311
Koop, C. Everett, 248, 263
Kopay, Dave, 85
Kowalski, Sharon, 243–44, 307, 309
Kraft, Randy, 313
Kramer, Larry, 129, 183, 237, 325
Kramer, Tim, 214
Krebs, Rockne, 316
Kronemeyer, Robert, 159
Kronenberg, Anne, 115
Ku Klux Klan, 120, 235, 243, 361

La Cage aux Folles (film), 162, 190
La Cage aux Folles (musical), 212, 219, 222, 260, 353
Lachs, Stephen M., 142
Ladies Almanack, The (Barnes), 191
Ladies' Home Journal, 126, 161, 263
LaLanne, Jack, 150
Lambda Literary Awards, 314
Lambda Passages (bookstore), 237
Lambda Rising Book Report, 274, 305
Lambda Rising (bookstore), 68
Lambeth Palace cherubs, 337
Lancaster, Burt, 116, 246

Landers, Ann, 215, 326
Landis, John, 209
La Tourneaux, Robert, 122
Lattanzi, Matt, 282
"Lavender Panthers," 58
Lavender World's Fair, 92
Laws: antidiscrimination, 21, 45, 46, 67, 89, 94, 120, 123, 181, 219, 235; discriminatory, 33, 40, 46, 67, 239; forbidding sale of sexual materials, 26; and same-sex marriage, 22, 73, 78. *See also* Sodomy laws.
Leal, Orlando Jimenez, 223
Lear, Norman, 74, 172
Leather subculture, 79–81, 91, 139, 150, 192, 332, 362
Leavitt, David, 191, 266
Le Duc Tho, 54
Legal Services Corporation (LSC), 172
Legislation, gay rights, 35, 43, 60, 66, 77, 82, 89, 100, 102, 105, 107–08, 116, 121, 122–23, 129, 154, 190–91, 194, 199, 204, 214, 224, 228, 231, 238, 254, 259, 265, 291, 303, 310, 354; federal, 67, 81, 90, 94, 101, 111, 151, 185, 216, 222
Lemke, Jay, 296
Lemon, Denis, 110
Lennox, Annie, 210, 219, 223
Leno, Jay, 363
Leopold, Nathan, 38
Lesbian and Gay Associated Engineers and Scientists, 190
Lesbian Nuns (book), 242
Levine, Richard M., 219
Levya, Mario Ivan, 303
Lewis, Carl, 226
Lianna (film), 206
Liberace, 16, 79, 198, 264, 269, 356
Liberty Foundation, 315
License plates, personalized, 45, 54
Lifar, Serge, 267
Limbaugh, Rush, 328
Lincoln, NE, 190–91
Lindsay, John, 18–19, 35, 60
Linkletter, Art, 150
Lipman, Samuel, 316
Lisbon Traviata, The (play), 112
Little Richard, 278
Lobotomy, 37
Loeb, William, 58, 67
Logan, Joshua, 66
"Lola" (song), 24

Lonesome Cowboys (film), 4, 57
Longtime Companion (film), 343
Look (magazine), 12, 23, 32
Lord Won't Mind, The (Merrick), 19
Los Angeles AIDS Project, 246
Los Angeles Board of Supervisors, 263;
    City Council, 69; Police Depart-
    ment, 79, 91, 95, 289
Los Angeles Times, 128, 202, 228, 238, 346
Lost Language of Cranes, The (Leavitt), 266
Loud, Lance, 53, 312
Louganis, Greg, 226, 303, 310
Love, Sidney (TV series), 179
Love That Dared Not Speak Its Name, The
    (Hyde), 21
"Love That Dares To Speak Its Name,
    The" (poem by Kirkup), 109
"Love to Love You, Baby" (song), 112,
    131
Ludlam, Charles, 56, 274
Lutheran Church, 21
Lynde, Paul, 50, 183

Maccubbin, Deacon, 69
McCarthy, Eugene, 45
McCarty, Jack, 242
MacDonald, Boyd, 171
McDonald, Larry, 172, 213
McDonald Amendment, 172
McDonald's Corporation, 104
McGovern, George, 45, 160
"Macho Man" (song), 127
Macho Sluts (Califia), 302
McKellen, Ian, 366
MacKenzie, Philip Charles, 224
McKinney, Stewart, 273
MacLaine, Shirley, 246
McMahon, Jim, 263
McNally, Terrence, 74, 112, 304
Madison, WI, 77
Madonna, 278, 314, 338, 354, 363
Madsen, Scott, 235
Magazines, gay, 57, 60, 77, 80, 81, 92,
    94, 96, 103, 121, 125, 137, 157, 161,
    170, 177, 178, 179, 180–81, 189,
    192, 193, 198, 216, 220, 221, 230,
    240, 264, 273, 293, 348
Making Love (film), 185
Manchester Union Leader, The, 58, 67, 81
Mandate (magazine), 77, 122, 216, 220,
    264
Manhattan Review of Unnatural Acts, The,
    170

Manilow, Barry, 29, 230
Mann, Erica, 6
Mansell, Dr. Peter, 203
Manwoman's Underclothes (Greer), 306
Mapplethorpe, Robert, 136, 140, 204,
    216, 298, 306, 310, 315, 318, 321,
    336, 342, 346, 353, 357
Marches, gay rights, 3, 9–10, 33, 56, 67,
    108, 127, 143, 169, 173, 204, 263,
    280, 285–86, 312, 341, 346
Marcus Welby, M.D. (TV series), 69
Margold, William, 255
Mariel boat lift, 151
Marotta, Toby, 186
Marriage, same-sex, 20, 22, 73, 78, 108,
    223, 285, 317, 321
Marshner, Connie, 184
Martin, Val, 92, 239
Maryland, 171
M*A*S*H (TV series), 50
Masque of the Red Death (oratorio), 317
Massachusetts, 241, 327
Massachusetts, University of, 341
Massine, Leonide, 267
Masters and Johnson, 138–39
Mathews, Beau, 214, 248
Mathis, Johnny, 192
Matlovich, Sgt. Leonard, 82, 157, 262,
    283, 298, 314
Matlovich: The Good Soldier (Hippler), 314
Mattachine Society, 205, 240
Maud's bar, 321
Maupin, Armistead, 94, 319
Maurice (film), 273, 284
Maurice (Forster), 28, 39, 273
Mayor of Castro Street, The (Shilts), 186
M. Butterfly (play), 296
Mead, Margaret, 130, 220
Meat (anthology), 170
Mecham, Evan, 278, 283, 291
Medical Center (TV series), 25
Meese, Edwin, 164, 236, 241, 249, 259,
    275, 280
Meese Commission on Pornography, 259
Meggyesy, Dave, 30
Melnick, Daniel, 271
Memoirs (Williams), 84
Menotti, Gian Carlo, 164
Mercouri, Melina, 81
Merrick, Gordon, 19
Merrin, Norma, 250
Metropolitan Community Church, 7, 224
Meyer, Russ, 24, 64

Miami, FL, 100, 103, 105, 107, 108, 237
Michael, George, 275
Middle Mist, The (Renault), 56
Midler, Bette, 45, 56, 66, 111, 116, 289
Midnight Cowboy (film), 18, 34
Milk, Harvey, 115, 126, 130, 131, 139,
    217, 238, 352
Miller, Merle, 31–32, 181, 256
Millett, Kate, 28
Mills, Donna, 273
Mineo, Sal, 14, 88
Mineshaft bar, 251
Ministers, 81, 100, 221
Minnesota, 46, 55, 122, 231
Minnesota, University of, 304
"Minor Heroism" (Gurganus), 71
Mishima, Yukio, 29
Mishima (film), 246
Miss America pageant, 58–59, 213, 290
Missouri Supreme Court, 46, 259
Mr. Adonis Contest, 49
"Mr. Benson" (serial), 137
Mr. International Leather, 140
Mitchelson, Marvin, 310
Mitchum, Robert, 202
Moment by Moment (film), 132
"Momism" 40
Mommie Dearest (film), 177
Mondale, Walter, 108, 156, 197, 217,
    224, 231
Mondo Trasho, 176
Monette, Paul, 314
Montale, Eugenio, 114
Morali, Jacques, 127
Moral Majority, 140, 158, 164, 166, 172,
    198, 229, 252, 315
Moravia, Alberto, 114
Moreno, Rita, 74
Morgan, Mary, 176
Mormon Church, 110, 333
Morrison, Jim, 15
Morse, Robert, 345
Moscone, George, 85, 130, 139, 217
Moscow Union of Lesbians and Gay
    Men, 335
Moving! (film), 74
MTV, 175, 232, 275, 363, 365
Muhlberger, Richard, 314
Murders, 35, 131, 149, 270, 311, 313,
    332; of gay men, 88, 95, 130–31,
    136, 160, 165–66, 167, 176–77,
    195, 226, 295, 327, 352, 355
Murdoch, Rupert, 149

Murphy, Eddie, 201, 209, 214, 234, 240,
    333, 363
Muskie, Edmund, 61
My Brother, My Slave (novella), 80
Myra Breckinridge (film), 20
Mystery of Irma Vep, The (play), 56
My Turn (Reagan), 325

Nader, George, 123
Naiad Press, 203, 242
Najman, Ron, 246
Naked Civil Servant, The (Crisp), 113
NAMES Project AIDS Memorial Quilt,
    286–87, 324, 348
Nancy Walker Show, The (TV series), 97
Nantucket Diaries (Rorem), 76, 306
National Commission on Reform of Fed-
    eral Criminal Laws, 31
National Conference on Lesbian and Gay
    Aging, 179
National Endowment for the Arts
    (NEA), 313, 317
National Enquirer, 338, 343
National Football League (NFL), 30, 85
National Gay Rodeo, 111, 212
National Gay Task Force, 60, 101, 121,
    122, 141, 147, 152, 184, 197, 205,
    215, 228
National Lampoon, 105
National News Council, 152
National Organization for Women, 54
National Pro-Family Coalition, 184
National Review, 8, 13
Nava, Michael, 153, 314
Navratilova, Martina, 141, 174
Navy, U.S., 40, 111, 136, 227, 321
Near, Holly, 174
Nebraska, 106
Nelson, Ricky, 252
Nevada, 104; Supreme Court, 266
"Never Can Say Goodbye" (song), 72
New Hampshire, 80
New Jersey, 57, 127
Newman, Paul, 78, 90
New Mexico, 77
New Milford, CT, 72
Newport Naval Station scandal, 226
Newsweek, 22, 39, 67, 98, 107, 136, 168,
    199, 222, 271, 294, 306, 322, 338,
    352, 363
Newton, Huey, 23
Newton-John, Olivia, 282
New York City: Council, 35, 43, 62, 67,

82, 180, 204, 254; Department of Consumer Affairs, 40; Executive Order 70, 120; Police, 12, 16, 58, 125
New York City Gay Men's Chorus, 181
New York *Daily News*, 3, 46, 174, 282
New Yorker, 13, 21, 39, 71, 129, 192
New York Native, 161
New York State: Consumer Protection Board, 282; Court of Appeals, 162; Department of Corrections, 295; Department of Motor Vehicles, 54
New York Times, 2, 3, 19, 23, 28, 33, 47, 54, 56, 59, 74, 102, 109, 123, 127, 136, 142, 144, 150, 154, 166, 173, 178, 184, 199, 204, 208, 219, 240, 279, 285, 288, 316, 328, 330, 340, 350
New Zealand, 258
Nickles, Don, 159
Nielsen, Brigitte, 280
Nightwood (Barnes), 192
Nin, Anaïs, 235
Nixon, Richard M., 13, 20, 26, 31, 40, 59, 61, 94
Nobel Prize for Literature, 61
Noble, Elaine, 70, 92
Noll, Kip, 191, 202
Noriega, Manuel, 331
Normal Heart, The (play), 237, 325
Northern Ireland, 198
Nude sunbathing, 69
Nugent, Ted, 91
Numbers (magazine), 121
Nureyev, Rudolph, 20

Oates, Joyce Carol, 235
Obie Awards, 56
O'Connor, John Cardinal, 328
O'Connor, Sandra Day, 177, 238
O'Connor, Sinead, 344
Odd Girl Out (Bannon), 203
O'Hair, Madlyn Murray, 198
Oh! Calcutta! (musical), 14
Ohio State University, 344
Oklahoma, 120; Supreme Court, 196
Olfson, Ken, 97
Olympia Press, 40
Olympics, 226, 303
Once Is Not Enough (film), 81
One for the Gods (Merrick), 19
Ono, Yoko, 235
Ontario, Can., 265
Opel, Robert, 65, 120

Opera News, 49, 273
Oprah Winfrey Show, The, 292
Oregon, 47
Ortleb, Charles, 92, 161
Orton, Joe, 19, 272
Orton Diaries, The (Orton), 272
Osborn, Torie, 357
Osborne, John, 7, 229
Ostrow, Steve, 64
Outing, 22, 174, 318, 319, 343, 365
OUT/LOOK (magazine), 293
Out of Their League (Meggyesy), 30
Outweek (magazine), 318, 319, 335
Overcoming Homosexuality (Kronemeyer), 159
Oxford English Dictionary, 271

Palimony suits, 126, 167, 198, 199
Pallone, Dave, 320, 350
Palmer, Jim, 154
Parades, gay pride, 22, 47, 69, 108, 126, 173, 316, 347
Paradzhanov, Sergei, 67, 351
Parents and Friends of Lesbians and Gays, 175, 358
Paris, Bob, 316
Parker, Al, 327
Parks, Bert, 290
Parting Glances (film), 333
Partners (film), 190
Pasolini, Pier Paolo, 84, 113
Pat Collins Show, The (TV show), 64
Patrick, Robert, 231
Patriot for Me, A (Osborne play), 7, 229
Paul IV, Pope, 91
Paul Lynde Show, The (TV series), 50
PC World (magazine), 212
Pears, Peter, 70, 94, 255
People (magazine), 117, 148, 174, 179, 218, 220, 227, 230, 235, 243, 246, 272, 278, 279, 336, 340, 343, 365, 366
People for the American Way, 172, 236
Perlman, Itzhak, 360
Perry, Frank, 78
Perry, Rev. Troy, 7, 20
Persian Boy, The (Renault), 55, 98
Personal Best (film), 184
Petersen, Wolfgang, 226
Peyrefitte, Roger, 91
Philip Morris Tobacco Company, 330, 350
Phone sex, 161, 234, 358

Pierce, Charles, 36, 116, 309
Pink Flamingos (film), 76
Playgirl, 55, 60, 67, 102, 156, 163, 245, 265, 285
Playing the Game (Austen), 105
Pleasure Beach (film), 239
Podesta, Anthony, 236
Poland, 325
Police, 1–4, 12, 58, 91–92, 93, 117, 125, 139, 165–67, 181, 191; attitudes toward gays, 79, 95, 111; gay and lesbian officers, 79, 95, 111, 144
Police Woman (TV series), 170
Polk Street Fair, San Francisco, 69
Polyester, 176
Poole, Wakefield, 43, 74
Pornography, 26, 33, 43, 57, 59, 78, 79, 92, 102, 109, 180, 200, 241, 246, 253–54, 256, 309
Portland, Ore., "Gay Pride Day," 114
Portugal, 66
Powell, Jody, 103
Powell, Lewis, 238, 277, 359
Power, Tyrone, 158
Presidential Commission on Pornography (1970), 26
Presidential Medal of Freedom, 219
Preston, John, 137, 180
Preston, Robert, 187
Price, Vincent, 110
Prick Up Your Ears (film), 273
Prince, 178, 224, 227
Princeton University gay dance, 56
Procter and Gamble, 171
Pro-Family Christian Coalition, 212
Pryor, David, 103
Pryor, Richard, 113, 266
Public Enemy, 246
Public schools, 107, 120; teachers, 73, 121, 128, 204, 239
Publishers Weekly, 31, 111, 123, 288
Pumping Iron (Butler and Gaines), 71
Purple Rain (album), 224

Qaddaffi, Moammar, 257, 263
Quaaludes, 56
Quayle, Dan, 300, 304
Quebec, 117, 200
Queen of Swords (Grahn), 306
Queer Nation, 341, 346
Querelle (film), 205
Question of Love, A (TV movie), 130
Quiet Fire (Vacha), 245

Rachins, Alan, 353
Rampal, Jean-Pierre, 360
Ramrod bar shootings, 160
Randall, Tony, 49, 179
Rattigan, Terence, 116
Reagan, Maureen, 152
Reagan, Nancy, 66, 164, 166, 169, 242, 251, 325, 355
Reagan, Ronald, 78, 128, 152, 160, 164, 166, 169, 185, 205, 206, 208, 219, 222–23, 227, 230, 231, 235, 239, 240, 242, 245, 250, 251, 263, 265, 274, 276, 277, 278, 283, 286, 313, 327, 339, 360
Reagan, Ron, Jr., 160
Reddy, Helen, 235
Redford, Robert, 78, 90, 329
Redgrave, Vanessa, 255
Reed, Lou, 55
Reed, Rex, 190
Rehnquist, William H., 40, 238, 262
Reinisch, June, 356
"Relax" (song), 232
Renault, Mary, 55, 98, 186, 216
Republican Party National Convention: of 1984, 227, 228; of 1988, 300
Reuben, Dr. David, 11, 69, 149
Reynolds, Burt, 55, 123, 245, 266
Richards, Renee (*formerly* Dr. Richard Raskind), 96, 104, 255
Ridiculous Theatrical Company, 56
Riggs, Bobby, 59
Ripploh, Frank, 178
Rise and Fall of Ziggy Stardust and the Spiders from Mars, The (album), 50
Risky Business (film), 212
Ritz, The (play), 74
Rivera, Diego, 262
Rivers, Joan, 219, 246, 322
Rizzo, Frank, 44
Robbins, Alan, 120
Robertson, Rev. Pat, 152, 191, 285, 291, 293, 294, 320, 365
Robinson, Mary, 362
Robinson, Max, 307
Rock Hudson (TV movie), 329
Rocky Horror Picture Show, The (film), 70, 142
Rocky Horror Picture Show, The (musical), 57
Roff, Margaret, 251
"Roger" (model), 105
Rolling Stone magazine, 98, 111, 237, 343

Rolling Stones, 10, 34, 178
Roman Catholic Archdiocese of New York, 120
Romania, 334
Rooney, Andy, 335
Roosevelt, Eleanor, 35, 143, 144
Rorem, Ned, 75, 93, 205, 306
Rotello, Gabriel, 319
Royko, Mike, 111
Rubell, Steve, 105, 147, 317
Rubyfruit Jungle (Brown), 66
Russell, Craig, 360
Russell, Ken, 76, 129
Russian River area, Calif., 159
Russo, Vito, 175, 190, 227, 282, 362

"Safe sex," 221, 264
Safire, William, 66
SAGE (Senior Action in a Gay Environment), 114
St. Denis, Ruth, 43
Saint disco, 157
St. Patrick's Cathedral, 4, 67, 328
Salo, 120 Days of Sodom (film), 113
San Francisco, 177; Board of Supervisors, 115, 121, 130, 133, 152, 361; Police Department, 144; School Board, 107
San Francisco Giants, 203
Santa Cruz County, 81
Sarandon, Susan, 70, 143
Sarne, Michael, 4, 21
Sarris, Andrew, 104
Sartre, Jean-Paul, 33, 119
Saturday Night Fever (film), 117
Saturday Night Live (TV series), 251, 344
Sayles, John, 206
Scalia, Antonin, 227, 262
Schell, Maximilian, 7
Schlafly, Phyllis, 152, 227
Schlesinger, John, 18, 38
Schmeichen, Richard, 238
Schmidt, John, 155
Schneider, Maria, 54, 67
Schools for gay youths, 208, 239
Schoonmaker, Craig, 22
Schrader, Paul, 147, 246
Schultz, George, 263
Schwarzenegger, Arnold, 71, 72, 230, 329
Science News, 190
Scientific American, 190
Scott, Norman, 93

Scott, Paul, 121
Seagren, Bob, 112
Search for Alexander the Great (TV program), 169
Search for Signs of Intelligent Life in the Universe, The (play), 247
Seattle, WA, 129
Second Serve (TV movie), 255
Segal, George, 219
Segel, Mark Allan, 61
Segell, Michael, 270
Segretti, Donald, 61
Selleck, Tom, 205
Separate Tables (play), 116
Seventh International AIDS candlelight Memorial, 314
Sex, John, 360
Sexton, Jimmy, 102
Sextool (film), 78, 372
Sexual Politics (Millett), 28
Sex-Variant Women in Literature (Foster), 174
Shack, Ruth, 228
"Shame, Shame, Shame" (song), 81
Shane, Bob, 278
Sharpton, Al, 327
Shawn, Ted, 42
Sheen, Martin, 235
Sherman, Martin, 144
Sherwood, Bill, 333
Shilts, Randy, 90, 186, 288, 305, 340, 343
Shirley and Company, 81
Shocked, Michelle, 341
Siegel, Eli, 34
Sihanouk, Prince Norodom, 272
Silber, John, 361
Silkwood (film), 218
Silver Convention, 84
Silverstein, Dr. Charles, 117
Simmons, Richard, 179
Sisley, Dr. Emily, 117
'Sissy Boy Syndrome' and the Development of Homosexuality, The (Green), 267
Sisters of Perpetual Indulgence, 146
Sixth International Conference on AIDS, 347
60 Minutes (TV series), 106, 335
"Smalltown Boy" (song), 236
Smeal, Eleanor, 286
Smith, Alexis, 81
Smith, Bessie, 27
Smith, Jerry, 262

Smith, Liz, 319
Smith, Maggie, 137
Smithsonian Institution, 359
Soap (TV series), 112
Society for Individual Rights, 205
Sodomy laws, 8, 10, 21, 31, 58, 60, 67, 90, 96, 99, 104, 171, 176, 194, 241, 257, 259, 265, 266, 312; decriminalization in foreign countries, 6, 24, 38, 198, 258, 294, 349; decriminalization in U.S. states, 33, 38, 47, 55, 78, 81, 94, 103, 106, 107, 127, 162, 206
Some Dance to Remember (Fritscher), 338
Some Kind of Hero (film), 189
Sonnabend, Dr. Joseph, 249
Sons of Harvard (Marotta), 186
Sontag, Susan, 308
Soul On Ice (Cleaver), 23
Souter, David, 351, 353, 357
Southern Baptist Convention, 297
Soviet Union, 31, 67, 155, 288, 310, 339, 351, 353; Article 121, 335
Spahr, Jane Adams, 297
Spain, 86
Spann, William Carter, 90
Spence, Craig, 327
Spielberg, Steven, 208
Spitz, Mark, 50
Spock, Dr. Benjamin, 47
Spofford Juvenile Detention Center, 29
Spokane, WA, 275
Sports Illustrated, 70, 168, 279
Springfield, MO, 325
Springsteen, Bruce, 221
Stallion (magazine), 189
Stallone, Sylvester, 210, 280
Starr, Adele, 175
Starsky and Hutch (TV series), 116
Star Trek: The Next Generation (TV series), 344
Star Woman (Andrews), 266
Staying Alive (film), 210
Stéber, Eléanor, 45
Stein, Gertrude, 129, 322
Steinem, Gloria, 29
Stevens, Marc, 97
Steward, Samuel ("Phil Andros"), 112, 198
Stewart, Rod, 110
Sticky Fingers (album), 34
Stone, Oliver, 352
Stonewall Inn raid, 1–2, 126, 243

Stonewall riots, 2, 21, 316
"Straight Pride" rally, 341
Streaking, 65
Stryker, Jeff, 19, 253, 311, 321
$TUD (Steward), 198
Studds, Gerry, 193, 209, 211, 213, 274
Studio 54, 105, 134, 147
Studio One (Hollywood club), 66
Suicide, 244
Sullivan, Louis, 347
Summer, Donna, 112, 123, 131, 136, 137, 148, 166, 218, 317
Sunday, Bloody Sunday (film), 38
Sununu, John, 314
Susa, Conrad, 181
Susan B. Anthony dollar, 141
Swaggart, Jimmy, 227, 292
Swann, Glenn, 19
Sweeney, Terry, 251, 355
Sweet Dreams (Are Made of This) (album), 210
Sylvester, 134, 307

Take Off the Masks (Boyd), 123
"Tales of the City" (daily serial), 94
Taxi Zum Klo (film), 178, 197
Talese, Gay, 150
Taylor, Elizabeth, 246, 341
Tchaikovsky, Peter Ilyich, 164
Teen Idols magazine, 245
Television boycotts, 171
Television, gays portrayed on, 25, 29, 34, 50, 51, 53, 64, 69, 74, 82, 97, 101–02, 106, 112, 113, 116, 130, 151–52, 163–64, 169, 170, 179, 183, 188–89, 198, 219, 224, 236, 251, 253, 292, 297, 313, 326, 329, 344
"Territory" (Leavitt), 191
Texas, 173, 184, 194, 250, 267, 312
Thank God It's Friday (film), 123
That Certain Summer (TV movie), 51
Thatcher, Margaret, 194
"That's the Way (I Like It)" (song), 84
Thirtysomething (TV series), 326
Thomas, Richard, 78
Thompson, Karen, 244, 307, 309, 314
Thompson, Mark, 305
Thomson, Virgil, 322
Thorpe, Jeremy, 93
Thorson, Scott, 198, 270
Three's Company (TV series), 102
Through the Past, Darkly (album), 10

Thy Neighbor's Wife (Talese), 150
Time (magazine), 8, 13, 28, 39, 58, 67, 82, 88, 119, 131, 149, 209
Times of Harvey Milk, The (film), 233, 238, 336, 341
Tiny Tim, 12
To Be or Not To Be (film remake), 216
Tolson, Clyde, 47
Tomlin, Lily, 131, 235, 247
Tom of Finland, 120
Tony Awards, 74, 92, 207, 222, 296, 345
Tootsie (film), 199
Top Gun (film), 256
Torch Song Trilogy (film), 306
Torch Song Trilogy (play), 207, 260
Toronto police, 117, 165
Torso (magazine), 192, 199, 348
Towne, Robert, 184
Townshend, Pete, 359
Transsexuals, 65, 75, 96, 104, 112, 180, 255, 312, 357, 365
Trash (Allison), 314
Trash (film), 27
"Trask Amendment," 173
Travel tours, 55
Travolta, John, 117, 131, 210, 343, 365
Trestrail, Comm. Michael, 194
Tripp, C.A., 83
Tru (one-man show), 345
Trudeau, Garry, 88
Trump, Donald, 134, 317, 334
Tula, 179–80, 357
20/20 (TV series), 207, 350
Tyson, Mike, 322

Uncircumcised Society of America (U.S.A.), 94
Unitarian Church, 223
United Church of Christ, 47
United Methodist Church, 221
United Nations Human Rights Commission, 22
U.S. Civil Rights Commission, 185, 207
U.S. Civil Service Commission, 81
U.S. Congress, 46, 67, 171, 193, 211, 274, 360
U.S. House of Representatives, 98, 159, 165, 172, 177, 211, 248; Ethics Committee, 209, 351
U.S. Open tennis championships, 96, 104
U.S. Patent and Trademark Office, 126

U.S. Postal Service, 316
U.S. Senate, 46, 317, 333, 349
U.S. State Department, 101
U.S. Supreme Court, 40, 46, 57, 60, 90, 94, 177, 194, 221, 233, 238, 257, 259, 262, 263, 277, 287, 334, 351, 353, 357
United Way, 242
Unusual Company (Erhart), 306

Vacha, Keith, 245
Vaid, Urvashi, 337
Valeska, Lucia, 184
Vanity Fair (magazine), 204, 289
Variety, 43, 78, 327
Veber, Francis, 190
Vector (magazine), 94
Venice Beach, Calif., 69
Vermont, 270
Victor/Victoria (film), 187
Vidal, Gore, 4, 6, 20, 56, 125, 243
Videos, gay porn, 192–93, 199, 202, 221, 237, 253–54, 262, 267, 312, 327, 328, 364; music, 175, 275, 288, 363
Vietnam, 54; peace marches, 10
Village People, 127, 130, 136, 144, 154, 350
Village Voice, 3, 56, 67, 104, 111, 170, 178
Virginia, 90, 304
Visconti, Luchino, 12, 35, 89
Viva (magazine), 60

Waddell, Tom, 279
Wagner, Jane, 131, 247
Walker, Alice, 208
Walker, Gerald, 54
"Walk on the Wild Side" (song), 55
Wall Street Journal, 85, 218, 288
Warhol, Andy, 4, 27, 34, 55, 57, 104, 270, 311, 315
Warren, Patricia Nell, 65
Warwick, Dionne, 284
Washington, D.C., 177; Human Rights Commission, 101
Washington Post, 164, 216, 257, 263, 274, 339
Waters, John, 76, 125, 176, 193, 293
Watts, André, 360
Wayne, John, 34
Weicker, Lowell, 300
Weiner, Maurice, 83

Weintraub, Jerry, 141
Weiss, Ted, 184
Welch, Louie, 230
Welch, Raquel, 20
Welcome to the Pleasuredome (album), 232
Weld, William, 362
Welk, Lawrence, 150
"Wendel" (comic strip), 202
West, Damon, 90
West, Mae, 4, 20, 83, 160
Western Lands (Burroughs), 306
West Germany, 6, 248
West Hollywood, CA, 231
West Point, 150
West Virginia, 94, 204
Weyrich, Paul, 334
"What It Means to Be a Homosexual"
    (Miller), 31
What the Butler Saw (Orton play), 19
Wheeler, Jerry, 231, 364
White, Byron, 238
White, Dan, 115, 130, 137, 139, 161,
    217, 250
White, Edmund, 92, 117, 183, 196, 294
White, Patrick, 61
White, Ryan, 296, 339, 366
White Night riot, 139
Whiting, Margaret, 273
Whitmire, Kathy, 230
Whittlesey, Faith Ryan, 164
"Who Do You Think You're Foolin' "
    (song), 166
"Why" (song), 236
Why Can't Sharon Kowalski Come Home?
    (Thompson and Andrzejewski), 314
Wichita, KS, 122
Wilby, James, 273
Wilde, Oscar, 110, 243
Wildmon, Rev. Donald, 171, 179

Will, George, 107
Williams, Paul, 108
Williams, Tennessee, 47, 84, 134, 203,
    220, 243
Williams, Vanessa, 213
Willis, Gordon, 147
Wilson, Lanford, 74
Wilson, Pete, 362
Windows (film), 147
Winters, Shelley, 36, 57
Wisconsin, 186, 206
Wojtowicz, John, 48
Wonder, Stevie, 284
Woodlawn, Holly (Harold Danhaki), 28
Woods, James, 329
Woodward, Joanne, 235
Word Is Out (film), 122, 365
World AIDS Day, 305
Wrangler, Jack, 79, 259, 273
Wylde, Zakk, 307
Wylie, Philip, 40
Wynne, Paul, 348
Wyoming, 107

Yale, Joey, 78
Yale University Repertory Theater, 74
"Y.M.C.A." (song), 130, 154
York, Michael, 44
"You Make Me Feel (Mighty Real)"
    (song), 134
Young, Gay and Proud, 152
Yourcenar, Marguerite, 149, 289
Yousling, Jim, 240

Zaire, 349
Zeffirelli, Franco, 208
Ziegler, Ron, 20
Zmed, Adrian, 205
Zorro, The Gay Blade (film), 174

PLUME

PAST . . . PRESENT . . . FUTURE

(0452)

☐ **HIDDEN FROM HISTORY** *Reclaiming the Gay and Lesbian Past* **by Martin Duberman, Martha Vicinus, and George Chauncey, Jr.** "One comes away from reading this collection with not only a broadened and deepened conception of the history of homosexuals but also with fresh, more sensitive conceptions of sexuality itself."—*Washington Post Book World*   (010675—$12.95)

☐ **COMING OUT:** *An Act of Love* **by Rob Eichberg, Ph.D.** An inspiring call to action for gay men, lesbians, and those who care . . . "Presents a keen, compassionate insight into human behavior."—*Lambda Book Report*
(266858—$10.95)

☐ **AFTER THE BALL:** *How America Will Conquer Its Fear and Hatred of Gays in the 90s* **by Marshall Kirk and Hunter Madsen.** "Provocative. Heretical. A warning against fanning the fire of bigotry."—*Time*
(264987—$10.95)

☐ **COMING OUT UNDER FIRE** *The History of Gay Men and Women in World War Two* **by Allan Berube.** This powerful and long-overdue work explores in depth the lives of military men and women who found themselves fighting two wars—one for their country and the other for their survival as targets of military policy that labeled them "undesirables."   (265983—$10.95)

Prices slightly higher in Canada.

Buy them at your local bookstore or use this convenient coupon for ordering.

NEW AMERICAN LIBRARY
P.O. Box 999, Bergenfield, New Jersey 07621

Please send me the books I have checked above.
I am enclosing $_____ (please add $2.00 to cover postage and handling).
Send check or money order (no cash or C.O.D.'s) or charge by Mastercard or VISA (with a $15.00 minimum). Prices and numbers are subject to change without notice.

Card # _____ Exp. Date _____
Signature _____
Name _____
Address _____
City _____ State _____ Zip Code _____

For faster service when ordering by credit card call 1-800-253-6476

Allow a minimum of 4-6 weeks for delivery. This offer is subject to change withuot notice